"Oh, the sneaky wonder of *Chance H*[illegible] Robinson. This book has the heart, intrigue, and secrets of Shakespeare but is written with the sensual prose of our time. If you are looking for a book that surprises all the way through, this is the book for you."

—Ann W. Garvin, author of *The Dog Year*

"*Chance Harbor* is a genuine, moving portrayal of the intricacies of relationships between sisters, mothers, and daughters. Robinson's skillful storytelling, smooth pacing, and vivid characters combine to show us that no matter our secrets, misgivings, and mistakes, compassion is the most precious human virtue. A truly authentic, engrossing story."

—Sonja Yoerg, author of *House Broken* and *The Middle of Somewhere*

Haven Lake

"Robinson . . . handles numerous plot threads deftly, alternating between her characters with finesse . . . The ending provides an enjoyable, but not pat, resolution to many of the issues faced by the characters. Fans of Barbara Delinsky and Diane Chamberlain will enjoy this moving family drama."

—*Booklist*

continued . . .

Written by today's freshest new talents and selected by New American Library, NAL Accent novels touch on subjects close to a woman's heart, from friendship to family to finding our place in the world. The Conversation Guides included in each book are intended to enrich the individual reading experience, as well as encourage us to explore these topics together—because books, and life, are meant for sharing.

Visit us online at penguin.com.

"*Haven Lake* is an emotionally charged novel about love, loss, and the intricacies of modern family. Robinson weaves a plot so poignant you won't be able to put it down." —Emily Liebert, author of *Those Secrets We Keep* and *When We Fall*

"The relationships in this story are multifaceted and deep, and readers are continually engaged as the layers are revealed. This is a poignant novel that leaves readers thinking." —*RT Book Reviews*

"In *Haven Lake*, Holly Robinson expertly depicts the ways in which we hurt the ones we love most, and our propensity for forgiveness. Real and raw, the characters stayed with me long after the last page was turned."
—Lorrie Thomson, author of *What's Left Behind* and *Equilibrium*

Beach Plum Island

"Robinson masterfully paints the portrait of a damaged family in the quake of a tragedy, struggling to put the pieces back together again. Each sister is sensitively drawn, their individual dramas meticulously rendered . . . a thoughtful exploration of the fragility, and the tenacity, of the ties that bind." —T. Greenwood, author of *Bodies of Water*

"Holly Robinson is a natural-born storyteller, and her tale . . . will keep you turning those pages as she quietly but deftly breaks your heart."
—Yona Zeldis McDonough, author of *You Were Meant for Me*

"Robinson tugs at your emotions. . . . *Beach Plum Island* is a triumphant family saga filled with heart and hope. I couldn't put it down!"
—Amy Sue Nathan, author of *The Glass Wives*

"[An] absorbing, bighearted novel."
—Elizabeth Graver, author of *The End of the Point*

"Robinson uses *Beach Plum Island* to explore the conflicts that can surface between brothers and sisters, half sisters and half brothers, and stepsiblings when divorces rip families apart and remarriages attempt to weave them into a new fabric." —*The Daily News of Newburyport* (MA)

"A family novel with plenty of emotional punch."

—*Concord Monitor* (NH)

The Wishing Hill

A *Ladies' Home Journal* Great Summer Read

"Many readers will surely glimpse themselves in this vivid, compassionate novel." —Margot Livesey, author of *The Flight of Gemma Hardy*

"Who and what make us who we really are? In Robinson's luminous novel of buried secrets, she explores how the past can jump-start the future, how motherhood can be more than genetics, and why finding yourself sometimes depends on discovering the truth in others."

—Caroline Leavitt, *New York Times* bestselling author of *Is This Tomorrow*

"A novel that sings: of love for a child, loss and regret for a life, and the quiet triumphs of survival and finding each other again."

—Susan Straight, National Book Award nominee for *Highwire Moon* and author of *Between Heaven and Here*

"A story about love, loss, secrets. . . . I loved this book."

—Maddie Dawson, author of *The Stuff That Never Happened*

"With equal parts compassion and honesty, *The Wishing Hill* explores love, redemption, and forgiveness . . . an easy and engaging read."

—Michelle Xiarhos Curran, *Merrimack Valley Magazine*

"Robinson's first novel sparkles with warmth and wit. . . . compelling."

—*Booklist*

"A good beach read for those who like to reflect on the complexity and messiness of family relationships." —*Kirkus Reviews*

ALSO BY HOLLY ROBINSON

The Wishing Hill

Beach Plum Island

Haven Lake

Chance Harbor

Holly Robinson

NEW AMERICAN LIBRARY
Published by New American Library,
an imprint of Penguin Random House LLC
375 Hudson Street, New York, New York 10014

This book is an original publication of New American Library.

First Printing, October 2015

For more information about Penguin Random House, visit penguinrandomhouse.com.

LIBRARY OF CONGRESS CATALOGING-IN-PUBLICATION DATA:

Robinson, Holly, 1955—
Chance harbor/Holly Robinson.
p. cm.
ISBN 978-0-451-47150-5
1. Domestic fiction. I. Title.
PS3618.O3258C48 2015
813'.6—dc23 2015017405

Printed in the United States of America
1 3 5 7 9 10 8 6 4 2

Set in Adobe Caslon Pro

For my husband, Dan, who keeps my heart, mind, and belly so very happy.
For our children—Drew, Blaise, Taylor, Maya, and Aidan—
who teach me the meaning of the word "adventure" with everything they do.
And for Mom: You are still, and always, my best reader and cheerleader.

Chance Harbor

PROLOGUE

Catherine's cell phone rang at ten o'clock. She fumbled for it on the table beside her and answered despite not recognizing the number. "Hello?"

It was her niece, Willow. Her voice was a whisper, thrumming with fear. She had to repeat herself twice before Catherine understood her.

"Mom told me to call you after her bus left," Willow said. "Can you come get me? Please?"

Willow was at South Station in Boston. Alone.

Catherine yanked a coat on over her pajamas. She'd been downstairs watching television; her husband, Russell, was already in bed. She imagined the furious conversation she'd have with Zoe tomorrow, when her sister decided to return from whatever oh-so-exciting party or man had called her away: *On what planet is it okay to leave your ten-year-old daughter alone in Boston at night? In a bus station? Even you should know better!*

Catherine didn't wake Russell before plunging into the chilly night. She charged down the porch steps and out to the car before realizing she was still wearing slippers. She didn't turn around.

She ran two red lights driving from their house in Cambridge to Boston, making the trip to the bus station in record time despite construction on the BU Bridge.

In South Station, she swept the lobby with her eyes, heart hammering. It was nearly empty. A pair of businessmen waltzed by with briefcases, their shoulders stiff as coat hangers beneath their suits. A woman in a flowered jacket passed, hand in hand with two children, walking so fast that the smallest boy was lifted right off his feet. Homeless people were draped across the benches like forgotten blankets.

Finally, she spotted Willow. Her niece was huddled in one corner of a wooden bench, a backpack at her feet, her pale hair a knotted spiderweb over her black fleece jacket.

Catherine kept her voice calm. "Hey, sweet girl," she said. "What are you doing staying up so late, huh?"

Willow started to cry. "I didn't know what to do, so I called you like Mom said. I'm sorry."

"Nothing to be sorry about. You did the right thing. Don't cry. I'm here. Everything's going to be okay." Catherine bent low over Willow, turning to glare at the vagrant woman camped closest to her niece until the woman slid off the bench and loped off, her hat pulled low.

What might have happened if she hadn't come to get her? What if she'd been on call at the clinic tonight? Or, God forbid, what if she and Russell had taken up Mom's offer to spend the week at Chance Harbor?

"Where's your mom, honey?" She brushed a strand of hair out of Willow's eyes.

"I don't know. She told me to sit here and wait for you. *Without moving*." Willow's lower lip trembled. "I didn't move the whole time. I promise. Can we go now? I'm tired."

"Absolutely." Catherine took Willow's small, cold hand in hers, and thought, *Goddamn you, Zoe. I'm going to kill you when I see you.*

Of course, she didn't know yet that her sister had disappeared.

CHAPTER ONE

Eve had fallen asleep easily, but woke with a start and didn't know where she was. Her pillow was damp. She thrashed about, searching for Andrew.

Then, with a lurching sensation, she remembered: her husband was dead. She was alone at their summer house in Chance Harbor for the first time in her life.

Eve reached for the lamp on her bedside table. Her wrist connected with a drinking glass and sent it flying. Water sprayed the sleeve of her nightgown as the glass tumbled to the floor with a smash.

She used the flashlight app on her cell phone to pick her way around the broken glass to turn on the overhead light. Her face, reflected in the mirror above the oak bureau, looked like a stranger's. Gaunt, the chin too sharp, the cheeks hollow. Her short brown hair had grown out, the curls springing nearly to her chin now.

Eve ignored the broken glass—easier to vacuum it up in the morning—and pulled on her jeans and a sweater. It was only three a.m., but she'd never get back to sleep now. She took her book downstairs and made coffee. When you lived alone, schedules mattered less. That was both good and bad.

Coffee in hand, she grabbed the car keys and jammed her feet into sneakers, then got into the car and drove to East Point, where she parked beneath the lighthouse and walked over to the chain-link fence. She could hear a distant foghorn, a low moan in the dense liquid darkness. The beam from the lighthouse swept across the sea.

Here, the Northumberland Strait met the Gulf of Saint Lawrence. The colliding tides roiled and waves crashed against the cliffs below her. This was the perfect place to watch cormorants and gulls dive and to search for the slick bobbing heads of seals. The first time Andrew had brought her here, the year before they were married, he had wrapped his arms around Eve's waist and said, "We're not just at the easternmost tip of Prince Edward Island, you know. We're standing at the end of the world."

The tall grass along the fence rippled like water around her feet. Eve waded through it to one of the picnic tables on the bluff. She sat on top of it, her feet on the bench, and stared out to sea, trying not to think about her husband, Andrew, and his final betrayal.

She had lost a daughter and now her husband. She was alone. Those were the facts she had to face.

Eve returned home when the sky was pearl gray with dawn. The wind had died down, leaving the sea dead calm and the dull silver of pewter, except for the sparkling path of the new sun. The island seemed to be holding its breath. She had stretched out on top of the picnic table and slept a little; now she felt surprisingly energized.

She had made some progress in the house, going through the closets to separate the things she wanted to keep from those she would give away or leave in the house when she sold it. She would have to make at least one more trip here with a trailer to get some of the bigger family heirlooms, like the green tapestry couch that had been Andrew's mother's.

She also had to find a contractor, a roofer, and a painter willing to come before spring, when the house would officially go on the market. Meanwhile, in addition to fixing up the house, she also had to sort through the small barn at the back of the property.

She walked through the tall dew-sparkled grass to the barn door, took a deep breath, and pushed it open. The door creaked and groaned.

Inside, the barn was lit by small windows. The sunlight streamed through them in dusty ribbons. There was a panicked flutter of barn swallows overhead as Eve's eyes adjusted. The barn was divided into two rooms by a half wall; one room was for the mower and trash cans and bikes, the other for Andrew's workshop. His tools were neatly hung in their usual places, and his tall black rubber boots stood by the door.

So strange, how you could love and hate a person with equal intensity. She and Andrew had first met when Eve was a new college graduate and took a marketing job in one of his companies south of Boston. They were married six months later. Andrew was older by a decade and had a magnetic, commanding personality, even more so because of his slight Scottish brogue—inherited from his father—and because he was beautiful to look at.

Yes, beautiful. Not handsome, the way many women described their lovers and husbands, but beautiful, with that startling thatch of reddish blond hair, his sweet smile, his neat hands.

A musician's hands, Eve had thought at first. Then she'd gotten to know Andrew and realized that his instrument was the computer; the music he played was the software he designed—entire symphonies in code that helped companies compile information and mine data.

They'd gotten married in Newburyport's city hall but had held their real wedding on Prince Edward Island, right here in the garden behind the Chance Harbor house, surrounded by the extended MacLeish family beneath a rose arbor with the blue sea and red cliffs behind them.

Now, as Eve touched one of the hammers, idly feeling the smooth wooden handle between her fingers, she had the strangest sensation that at any moment Andrew might walk in and start telling her about his latest repair project. He'd been putting up new gutters last year. That was why he came to the island: to tinker. "Tinkering is my religion," he said. "With this house, I've got physical therapy for the rest of my life."

But of course Andrew would never work here again. Loneliness coursed through her body like an electric shock, so intense and painful that the floor tipped and Eve had to catch herself on the long workshop table.

After a moment, she went back to the house and grabbed the stack of boxes she'd brought from the garage of their house in Newburyport. Another of Andrew's pack-rat habits was to break down every box that arrived at their house and keep it "just in case." He'd be pleased she was reusing them, Eve thought with a smile. She'd always blamed Andrew's inability to throw things out on his island upbringing: here, nothing was wasted.

She ferried the boxes out to the shed. She could offer the tractor and snowplow and tools to Andrew's cousins. They could pass them on to anyone else who wanted them. She had no need for more tools, and Andrew would be heartbroken if she sold them.

Eve had nearly reached the shed with the boxes when an enormous black animal—at first glance it was easy to imagine it was a bear—appeared out of nowhere and came lumbering up to her. A dog. But whose?

She looked around. Nobody seemed to be walking the dog or calling for it. It must be one of the local farm dogs; she knew the sheep farmer at the end of the road had several.

The animal circled her legs, grinning, tongue lolling. It had the height and heft of a Saint Bernard. This wasn't the sort of dog you typically saw up here on the island, where the farmers kept shepherds or mutts, the Americans brought golden retrievers, and the people from Montreal brought their lapdogs to the beach in sparkly collars. No, this was a dog you'd want with you in an avalanche, where it would lie on your body to keep you from dying of hypothermia or would tow you down the mountain.

"Well, aren't you nosy," Eve said, laughing as the dog stood beside her, gazing up at her face with merry yellow eyes. It was difficult not to feel joyful in the company of a creature so unreservedly glad to see you.

The dog kept her company as she began sorting Andrew's tools and packing them in boxes. She had to be careful not to fill the boxes too full or she wouldn't be able to move them. Once each box was packed, she taped it shut and labeled it carefully with a list of contents. She stacked the boxes on the other side of the shed with the bicycles. They'd have to go, too; no way could she fit four bikes in her car.

By the time Eve was ready for lunch, she'd nicknamed the dog "Bear" and let him come inside, where the animal happily galumphed around the house and then settled into a heap of black fur after devouring half her sandwich.

As she was writing up a list of tasks she hoped to complete in the coming week, Eve heard a truck drive by. Too slow to be an islander. They treated this road, which bisected the island from the south shore to North Lake, like a highway.

Now the car was pulling into the driveway. Probably a neighbor. Nobody called ahead here. They just assumed you'd want company. Andrew's cousin Jane had already stopped by twice, once with biscuits and a second time to ask if Eve wanted help. She did not. Andrew's aunt Maggie had come by as well, bringing snowflake rolls and homemade blueberry jam, saying there was bingo up at the church, and did Eve want to join her, try her luck tonight?

"Might make enough to fix up this old place," Maggie had said, eyeing the roof.

Eve didn't have the stomach for bingo, either.

She sighed now and ran her hands through her hair. She thought she'd seen everyone by now. Had hoped she was done with explanations about why she was selling the family's island house.

The dog heard the truck, too. Bear picked up his head and tipped his ears forward, muzzle raised, whiskers trembling. His entire body had gone rigid with anticipation. There was a sharp whistle from outside, and the dog went to the door, turning to look over his shoulder at Eve to make sure she got the message.

She opened the kitchen door and stepped out onto the deck, shading her eyes against the sun as the dog trotted across the yard, tail waving, to greet a man standing by the truck.

The man rubbed the dog's ears, murmuring something Eve couldn't hear, then raised his head to look at her. "So you're the one who kidnapped my dog. I've been looking for this son of a gun all morning."

"He just appeared. I wondered who he belonged to, since I haven't seen him before."

"He was in my truck and must have jumped out when I stopped at the store down the street. Didn't think this guy had it in him. Sorry for the bother."

"No bother. He was a perfect gentleman."

The man walked toward her, the dog keeping pace. Eve thought she'd never seen anyone like him. He seemed to be assembled from the parts of contrasting men. He was tall and slim, but with a weight lifter's broad shoulders and heavily muscled arms. He wore a pair of expensive rubber boots, the sort she'd seen in catalogs, but his blue flannel shirt was faded at the elbows and his green barn jacket had a torn pocket. His pants were the sort of heavy-duty brown trousers an electrician might wear, but a gold Rolex glittered on his wrist.

The man's hair was gray—silver, really, though she could tell by the few streaks of color left in it that it had once been dark—and a little too long in front. He pushed it off his forehead impatiently, but when he reached the deck and looked down at Eve, his eyes were as calm and deep gray as the sea had been this morning.

Eve's mouth went dry. She had the strangest feeling that she'd met this man before, but couldn't imagine where that might have been. She stuck out her hand. "I'm Eve MacLeish," she said.

"Darcy MacDougall." His big hand engulfed hers, his eyes quiet and still on her face. Then he released her.

Eve laughed. "I should have known you'd be a Mac-something."

"Sure I am. Scots galore out on this part of the island." He glanced beyond her at the house. "This your summer place?"

So he could tell she was from away. Her accent, probably. Eve nodded, not wanting to get into anything about Andrew's family. For all she knew, this man was another relative. "What about you? Where are you staying?" She could tell now that he wasn't an islander, either.

"North Lake. Been here since Landing Day in July. My first time seeing it. Quite a spectacle."

"Yes. I've always loved Landing Day." Eve bit her lip, remembering the early mornings she'd taken the girls to North Lake to watch Landing

Day, the day the lobster fishermen brought in their traps for the season. She'd met Malcolm, Andrew's cousin, there. That meeting had altered her life more than any other, in some ways.

"This is a great spot," Darcy was saying, his gaze traveling beyond her to the house. "I bet you've got a hell of a view from behind your house." He gestured with his chin. "Mind if I have a look?"

Eve was startled. No islander would ever be this forward. "No," she said. "The view's free."

"My favorite price."

She kept pace with Darcy's long strides, the dog between them, trying to see her house as he must: the peaked roof and yellow clapboards, the deep green shutters, the ornate white gingerbread trim. There were some late perennials in the beds behind the house, but the containers and window boxes were a mess of rotting plants. She'd have to clean those out before she closed up the house for winter, too. So much work left to do. That was good: better to be busy than sad.

They stood together in front of the trellis that separated the house from the stairs leading down to the beach. "Anne of Green Gables would have loved it here," Darcy said, surveying the long weathered boardwalk leading to stairs descending the cliff to the sea.

"I'm sure," Eve agreed. "Anne would have called it 'the Sea of Shining Waters.'"

He turned to look at her, cocking an eyebrow. "You know Anne wasn't real, right?"

"Of course."

Her tone caused Darcy to raise both hands in surrender. "Sorry. It's just that, anytime I take someone to visit the Lucy Maud Montgomery museums in Cavendish, I hear tourists asking where Anne lived."

"I'm not a tourist." Eve waited for him to ask how long she'd had the house, or why she—someone whose accent clearly marked her as from away—was staying so late in the season. Those were the usual questions. When Darcy didn't ask them, she felt compelled to say, "Actually, I always felt sorry for Lucy Maud Montgomery."

"Really? Why?"

"I don't know how she could have written *Anne of Green Gables*, spitting out pages and pages of gossipy good cheer and platitudes, when she was so depressed."

"She was depressed? Huh," Darcy said. "I had no idea. The only thing I know about Montgomery is that her books about Anne have inspired busloads of Japanese women to come here and buy those straw hats with red braids attached."

"Oh, yes. Lucy had a tough time," Eve said. "She committed suicide when she was about my age. Pills, I think. They found a note. Something like, 'I have lost my mind by spells and I do not dare think what I might do in those spells.' Then she goes on to ask for God's forgiveness. Her depression probably had a lot to do with caring for her wreck of a husband."

"Or maybe something to do with her mother dying and her father marrying a stepmother who didn't like her," Darcy added.

Eve stared at him, then laughed. "So you *do* know all about Lucy Maud Montgomery."

"Only what my daughter tells me. She read *Anne of Green Gables* when she was a kid and was psyched when I got a job up this way. She's been up here twice already this summer and spent most of her time at the museums."

"My older daughter loved the books, too. What kind of work do you do on the island?"

"Wind energy," Darcy said. "I'm a solar engineer. I'm up here as a consultant, monitoring the turbines at East Point."

"A lot of people around here complain about them," Eve said, thinking of Cousin Jane, who lived across the street from the turbines and was always fearful that one of the blades might shear off and fly into her house.

"Yes, well, tell the complainers that these ten turbines produce enough energy for twelve thousand homes and are displacing seventy thousand tons of greenhouse gases each year."

As Darcy continued talking about the project and a grant he was writing to install a wind farm at another location on the island, Eve wished she'd put on a little makeup. Strange to be standing next to a man so much taller than she was. Eve was five foot ten. She was an inch taller than Andrew and had always thought they fit well together in bed. Malcolm, too, was about her height. What would it be like to be with a man so much taller than she was? Darcy must be well over six feet.

Abruptly, Eve felt self-conscious as she realized Darcy had stopped talking and was watching her curiously. She hoped he hadn't asked a question. Even more, she hoped he hadn't guessed her thoughts. Heat flamed in her cheeks and she turned away. "Where did Bear go?" she asked, scanning the backyard and gardens.

"Who? Oh! You mean Sparrow."

"Sparrow?"

Darcy grinned. "The dog's named after Jack Sparrow the pirate, not the bird. My son named him. I'm just dog-sitting while my son's in California."

"What's he doing there?" Eve asked, thinking with some relief that being married with children probably meant Darcy was a normal, reasonable man and not one of those off-the-grid types you found living here, the escapees from New York or Boston who saw how cheap the houses were on Prince Edward Island and snapped them up. They all thought they'd go native until the first winter hit and the roads disappeared under blowing snow. Then the houses went up for sale again.

"He's getting an MBA at Stanford. Looks like you're doing a fall clear out," Darcy said as they walked back toward his truck and passed the barn. He whistled for the dog.

Eve had left the barn doors open while she had lunch; the boxes were visible to one side. "Yes. It's a good time of year to do it."

"Too bad you missed the seventy-mile yard sale a couple weekends ago."

She made a face. "I've been to that yard sale. I always come away loaded down with more junk than I sell."

Darcy laughed. "You've been up here in the fall before, then."

"I've been on this island in every season. But I'm still 'from away,' as far as everyone here is concerned."

"Me, too, even though my grandparents immigrated here from Scotland before they moved to New York."

"So where do you live now? I mean, when you're not here."

"Vermont. I was at the university there, in the engineering department, for many years. I still teach a class or two when the mood strikes." Darcy whistled again. The dog finally wandered out of the barn, blinking in the sudden sunlight and making them both laugh. "Well, better let you get back to things. Thanks for looking after the dog."

"No problem. It was nice to have company," Eve said.

They shook hands good-bye, and she was struck by another jolt of recognition. What was it about this man that made her feel so comfortable?

You'd think sophomore year of high school would be less about pranks and posers, but so far none of the kids seemed to have gotten that memo. Matt Tracy had already set fire to a trash can during English, making the smoke alarm go off, and the alpha girls were taking selfies of themselves in geometry.

Willow might have to throw herself out a window if she had to stay in geometry one more second. The teacher, Mr. James, was scary clean, using hand sanitizer every twelve seconds.

He had tried teaching them about angles and vectors by having the class make paper airplanes while ranting about "making math fun." This would have been okay if Mr. James weren't so totally OCD. The poor guy folded and refolded the same stupid piece of paper, while the robotics nerds and gamer geeks made airplanes with weights and counterweights out of bent paper clips or whatever. The student planes zoomed around in circles until one of them hit Mr. James right between the eyes. Bitchy Shelly Paradiso practically peed her pants laughing.

Now Mr. James was back at the board and Willow was drawing in her notebook. The only class she liked was art. She'd spend all day in art if she could. Last year, when Mrs. Lagrasso (whom the kids called "Mrs. Fat Asso") taught her freshman art class, Willow had fallen in love.

That's what art felt like to her: love. She got goose bumps of happiness every time Mrs. Lagrasso showed them another series of paintings or sculptures. Willow had been to art museums with Catherine and Russell, of course, but when she saw art through the eyes of Mrs. Lagrasso, it was different. Mrs. Lagrasso understood the power of art to surprise you with feelings you didn't know you had.

"What are you drawing? A monkey?" a voice said over Willow's shoulder.

It was the new kid, Henry Something-or-Other the Third. Pretty much every boy in her school was named after somebody else, or two somebodies. Like it was too much work for their parents to think up original names.

"It's not anything. Just trying not to slit my wrists while we listen to this crap." Willow flipped her notebook shut.

"Man, you got that," Henry said, leaning back again.

They'd been seated alphabetically on the first day of class and had to keep those seats all year—another thing Willow hated about geometry.

Henry's desk was next to hers. He was a ginger giant, with hair the color of paprika, long legs, and eyes like pennies. He said something else, but Willow pretended not to hear him and focused on the board, which Mr. James was filling with formulas, while she thought about her drawing.

It wasn't a monkey, but it wasn't nothing, either: it was actually a sketch of a homeless woman she'd seen this morning as she and Russell crossed Boston Common.

Not even eight o'clock in the morning, and the woman was sitting on a bench by the Frog Pond with her metal cart stuffed with trash bags. She was blind; a white cane was leaning on the bench beside her. The woman was playing a scratched-up old guitar. A handful of coins lay in her open guitar case.

Russell was speeding along ahead of her, but Willow slowed down to look at the woman. She was beautiful, in a strange cartoony way, with giant yellow sunglasses, a bright rainbow tam over shiny black licorice hair, a long black skirt, and a bright red shawl. Like a human-shaped piece of art.

What kind of homeless person got pimped out to play music for a few coins before the benches were even dry? Had the woman slept here?

Willow waited until she was about a dozen feet away, then turned around with her camera. She'd taken a photography class using a manual camera this summer; now she tried to always shoot in black-and-white. In geometry, she'd been sketching the woman because she was thinking about how to hand tint the photographs of her. She wanted to make hand-colored pictures like the ancient ones hanging in Nana's house in Chance Harbor.

Spanish II came after geometry. A brutal class. Senorita Yolanda didn't assign seats, but Henry sat next to Willow anyway, wrapping his long legs around the chair rungs.

Willow was thinking about her photographs when Senorita asked her a question in Spanish. Henry bailed her out by answering it for her. She answered the question after that, though, even using the right preterit tense for *ir*, always tricky: *fui*.

"Thanks," Willow said as she walked to lunch with Henry towering next to her. "I owe you."

He shrugged. "Thirty percent of our grade is participation, right? So, hey. I participated. What do you have next? Lunch, right?"

"Lunch, then art and chemistry. You?"

Henry looked pathetically hopeful. "Lunch. We could sit together. After that, English and European History."

He'd have Russell for history, Willow realized. She was about to say this, to give Henry a heads-up on Russell as a teacher, when there was a commotion in the hall. A group of senior girls was headed their way.

One of them, Nola Simone, was the queen bee: wherever she went, the drones buzzed around her. As Willow watched, Nola shook her shining hair around her shoulders. Her hair was the color of oak leaves in fall, bright gold and yellow. Nola held her phone at arm's length, taking selfies of herself surrounded by her friends as they moved through the hall, oblivious to the fact that everyone else had to paste themselves against the walls to make way.

Not that anyone would have tried to stop them. Watching Nola walk by, with her heart-shaped face and hot bod, her hair like all of the autumn months captured into a single elastic, was like seeing a unicorn: all you could do was stand there with your mouth open and hope she might kick magic fairy dust in your face.

"Hey, Willow," said Trent, one of the juniors in Willow's geometry class, a hockey player and a douche bag. He didn't usually bother her, though; Willow prided herself on her high invisibility factor. She dressed to blend in and kept her mouth shut. Now she cringed as Trent shouted, "Why aren't you walking with Nola and her posse? You should definitely be in that photo. Get in there, dude!"

Willow gave an elaborate shrug. "No, thanks. Why should I?"

"Because you're one big family now," Trent said, elbowing the guy next to him, another hockey kid whose fuzzy beard looked like a wild animal sleeping on his face.

"Me? Right. Like Nola and I are even the same species." Willow started walking again.

Trent was trailing her, still talking. Henry kept up with her. This should have made Willow feel better. Instead, now she had to worry that Trent might start harassing Henry because he was with her.

"Hey," Trent said, still using his fucking hockey-rink voice. "Is it true Nola's been getting some extra-special help in history? A little one-on-one? Some *hands-on* learning from your dad?" He cracked up.

"Whatever," Willow said without slowing down. She'd heard the rumors about Nola and Russell, too, but so what? Every guy in school wanted to hook up with Nola—teachers, students, coaches.

"Wow, you sure shut down Trent," Henry said, letting his breath out in a whoosh after they'd rounded a corner and made sure Trent wasn't trailing them to the cafeteria. "So that girl with the phone is Nola?"

"Right. Nola Simone. Senior," Willow said.

"Mean girl alert?"

"Not really. Don't worry about her. Nola doesn't bother with the small stuff. She probably won't even notice you."

"I am but dirt on her shoe?"

"A speck," Willow corrected. "One speck of dirt on her Jimmy Choo."

Henry laughed as they kept moving with the flow to the cafeteria, where they sat with Willow's only two friends at school, Kendrick and Carly.

Lunch was surprisingly okay. Not because of the food, but because it was different, sitting with a guy instead of being three fringe chicks.

Kendrick was seriously Goth, all in black: eyeliner, T-shirt, hair dye, boots. Willow and Carly went more for grunge, both of them wearing hoodies and high-tops like a uniform. Easy, cheap, and your body was camouflaged. Nobody could say you were too fat or too skinny or had booty or whatever. They just wrote you off as artsy freaks and geeks.

By the end of the day, Willow was feeling like she might survive sophomore year. Mrs. Lagrasso had shown them slides from a MET exhibit of Matisse's paintings and the textiles that had inspired them. Then she'd given them free time and Willow had made progress on her sketches. She booked time in the darkroom for Monday.

She usually rode the subway home with Russell. He stayed after school for office hours or faculty meetings while she worked with the newspaper staff or went to Spanish club, but none of the after-school activities would start until next week. Willow thought about hanging out in the music room, where Kendrick played drums in a way that made Willow's entire spine feel like it would crumble into dust.

No, too nice a day to waste more of it inside. She'd rather go to the Common with her camera and sketch pad, maybe wait for Russell by the Park Street station. Catherine wouldn't be home until dinner, and Willow still got freaked-out in empty houses since that time her mom passed out on the couch and set the apartment on fire with her cigarette. Willow'd had to call the fire department when she was like seven years old.

A better idea: she'd find Russell and see if he wanted to go to the North End for pizza. Catherine could meet them in Boston when she was finished at her clinic.

By now nearly everyone was gone. The deserted hallways suddenly seemed too wide. The light streamed in ribbons through the classroom windows, and the wood floors had turned to gold. A few lockers gaped open. Nobody locked anything at Beacon Hill School. What would be the point? They could all buy ten or fifty of whatever they wanted, here in this prep school that squatted in the shadow of the State House's gilded dome.

The carpet was tongue colored and spongy beneath her feet. In the east wing, where most of the faculty offices were located, the teachers' lounge had an overstuffed sofa and flowered chairs in front of a fireplace. The doors were heavy wood, each with a brass nameplate.

Russell's office was at the very end of the faculty hallway. She never came down here—usually they just texted if they wanted to meet up—but her feet had carried her along while she'd been intent on her pizza plan. She could almost taste the cheese.

Willow was close to Russell's office when she heard a noise from inside it like somebody choking. The hair on the back of her neck rose like needles, prickly under her T-shirt.

"But I can't wait anymore," a girl moaned. "You have to tell her."

The girl's voice sounded deep and sad, Willow decided: not scared. So nobody was being mugged or stabbed.

Willow crept forward, listening hard. The crying was definitely coming from Russell's office. That made sense. Russell had won Best Teacher of the Year two years in a row because he could make history as exciting as *Game of Thrones*. It was like Russell actually knew the people on the pages of your history book personally.

"William Howard Taft?" he'd say. "Now, there was a guy with an eating disorder! He tried to eat himself to death, probably because he couldn't live up to his parents' high expectations or get out from under Roosevelt's shadow, poor bugger."

Plus, from everything Willow had heard other kids say, Russell treated his students like actual people. If you had a problem with an assignment or got into trouble, he'd help you.

Maybe one of his AP students was already suffering a meltdown over college. A lot of seniors here applied early decision to their top choices, which were usually Harvard, Harvard, or Harvard.

The sobs had turned into a low humming, a sound like water flowing over rocks. Willow hesitated outside Russell's partly open door. She couldn't see inside his office. She should text him, maybe, not embarrass the shit out of whoever was in there.

No, that was stupid. She was right here. And Russell might be psyched to have her interrupt him. Then he could ditch the crier and leave. It was Friday, after all.

Willow knocked. No answer. Just that river of voices. She pushed open the door and started to say hey, then stopped. It felt as if she'd swallowed a ball of string.

Russell was holding Nola Simone in his arms. Their faces were pressed close together, foreheads touching. Then, as if it were all happening in slow motion, Russell put his mouth over Nola's.

Willow felt sour ick rise in her throat and slowly backed out of the room. She ran blindly down the hall's carpeted floor so fast that she ran straight into the swinging fire door and banged her forehead on the glass.

Her eyes filled with tears. She kept running until she was out of the building, speeding down the hill and across Beacon Street to the Common, ignoring the stitch in her side.

She plowed right through the clump of people standing at the corner, waiting for the bus. Willow wished she could join them. She wanted to step onto some crowded bus and disappear.

By the time Catherine parked on Newbury Street, it was raining and the streets were dotted with umbrellas, bright spots of light against the slick gray pavement. She'd forgotten her umbrella but didn't mind. It was a light rain, the sort of drizzle that always seemed to be falling in Scotland when they'd visited her father's extended family. Like a damp shawl flung over your head and pinned into place.

She hoped the cool, humid air would clear her head. It had been a brutal day at the clinic. She'd been treating children with ear infections, fevers, stomachaches, sprained ankles—even one possible case of meningitis—since early this morning.

Cell phones rang, blared, and played salsa or Bollywood tunes in the waiting room as anxious parents did the work-family fandango. Although she was one of the senior nurse practitioners in the practice, Catherine never had the heart to tell parents to obey the "Please Turn off Your Cell

Phone" sign by the front desk. She left the office etiquette to Alicia Sanchez, the energetic receptionist who spoke three languages but hardly seemed older than Willow.

The thought of Willow made Catherine smile as she neared the restaurant where she was supposed to meet Russell for dinner. While most parents complained noisily about their teenagers—drinking or drugs, sex or reckless driving—Willow was easy and sweet. A gift.

Of course, whispered a cynical voice in Catherine's head, *Willow's not your real daughter. Maybe that's why she's so easy.*

No. Catherine refused to let herself think that way. Willow was hers now. Had been for the past five years, ever since that night she'd called Catherine to say Zoe had left her at South Station. Alone.

Soon after Zoe's disappearance, Catherine and Russell had filed the paperwork to become Willow's legal guardians. As furious as she still felt whenever she thought about Zoe abandoning her daughter, a part of Catherine was grateful. She'd offered to take Willow before, whenever Zoe's living situation looked sketchy, but her sister had always refused.

"She's my kid and belongs with me," Zoe would say fiercely, even if she was living in a shelter or once again boomeranging back into their parents' house in Newburyport.

Catherine knew her life was more complete with Willow in it. She and Russell hadn't been able to conceive a child of their own despite eight years of IVF treatments that had left her feeling like a bloated pincushion. That agony was over now. She'd given herself permission to quit trying to get pregnant on her thirty-seventh birthday last year.

She felt her phone buzz and pulled it out of her pocket to glance at the text. Russell: he'd arrived at the tapas place and had scored a table. With this rain, they'd have to sit inside now. Too bad.

On the other hand, as Catherine climbed the steps to the restaurant, she remembered how beautiful it was, with its burnished copper tables and red walls, the hand-painted pottery pitchers filled with sunflowers on the tables. They hadn't been here since their wedding anniversary several months ago.

Russell had managed a table by a window on the second floor; from this vantage point, the umbrellas bloomed like lilies floating on a stream of pedestrians.

"Good job on the table. Sorry I'm late," Catherine said.

He stood up to kiss her cheek. "I'm just sorry you had to get wet."

"Doesn't matter. Feels good to cool off after the day I've had."

"That frantic?" Russell had ordered a pitcher of sangria. He poured a glass for her as she sat down.

"Awful. I was hit by a last-minute stampede of parents panicking before the weekend. Like every kid in the city decided to get sick because a full week of school was too much to take." Catherine opened the menu. "How was your day?"

"Oh, fine."

"What about Willow? How is she? I meant to call her when I left work, but the train came right away."

"I don't know. I never saw her all day. I texted her when I left school, but by then she was already home. She seemed fine with the idea of hanging out with your mom tonight, even though it was a last-minute plan."

"Good. Maybe Willow's mood will be better tonight than it was this morning."

Russell shrugged. "Probably. I don't know why you were so worried. Mornings and teenagers just don't mix."

He was right, of course. The teenagers Catherine saw in her office kept zombie schedules. Online all night, hardly able to function the next day.

Catherine always felt lucky that she'd married a man who understood children. That was evident the day they met, when she and Russell were both seniors at the university and working as orientation leaders for incoming students. They'd played all sorts of team-building games, and he was great at jollying even the sulkiest girls and sleepiest potheads into participating. He was handsome and sweet, especially kind to the overwhelmed new freshmen. Together, they'd comforted one girl whose boyfriend had broken up with her that weekend and had talked a couple of drunk boys out of elevator surfing.

After their orientation duties were over, Catherine invited Russell back to her studio apartment. They'd drunk cheap beer and played Scrabble as they talked. He had teased her about having a Canadian accent, imitating the way she said "sorry" and "about." Her father's fault, she told him: she'd spent weeks at a time on Prince Edward Island growing up, was half Canadian. Had a passport to prove it.

"Home of Anne of Green Gables," she'd explained when Russell was confused about where, exactly, PEI was. "The Canadian Maritimes. Just keep driving northeast from Massachusetts past about five million pine trees through Maine and New Brunswick. You used to have to take a ferry from New Brunswick or Nova Scotia to the island, but now there's a bridge."

As Russell stood up to leave that first night, she'd decided: he was the one. She was still a virgin, had guarded herself from involvements while focusing on her studies, but this man was steady and she was about to graduate. His hair was a tangle of brown curls she could imagine grabbing by the handful, and his eyes were like blue chips of ice against his tan. He'd wanted to be a teacher even back then.

Catherine felt certain they were meant for each other. It wasn't difficult to convince Russell to spend the night on her futon. They'd been apart very few nights since then, except for last month, when he'd been so busy with his book that she'd gone up to PEI with Willow to spend part of August while Russell stayed in Cambridge to write.

She had hesitated about the separation, knowing she'd miss him. But her mother had seemed so lost since her father's death in May, and Willow was so heartbroken at the thought of not going up to Canada that Catherine felt like she had no other choice. Besides, as Russell gently pointed out, he'd get more writing done without them around.

They had agreed that Catherine would take Willow to Chance Harbor alone. But, before that, she and Russell had left Willow with friends and gone to New York City by themselves for a spectacular weekend of walking Central Park, getting lost in the MET, seeing a Broadway show. Their usual lovemaking was comfortable, though sometimes so predictable that it might as well have been scripted. That weekend, though, they'd stayed in a hotel with an Asian theme and made the kind of love you can only have in hotels, assuming positions on the floor and in the armchair that they'd never attempted at home.

Catherine left for Chance Harbor after that feeling cherished and oddly powerful, even happy that she and Russell would be apart for a few weeks. It would be sad to be in the Chance Harbor house without her father, she knew, but at least this way her mother wouldn't have to go up there alone the first time. Besides, while they were in Canada, she and Russell would miss each other. Catherine took pleasure in anticipating their passionate reunion. Maybe this was what their marriage needed, the sort of jolt that would make it feel fresh again after so many years of challenges: long work days, infertility, Willow, Russell's father's death and then her own father's, too. All of that had taken a toll on them.

Russell hadn't disappointed her. On the day of their return in August, after Willow went to bed, he had led Catherine into the bedroom, gently removed her clothes, and given her a full-body massage, whispering, "Tell me what to do. I'll follow your every command."

Catherine sipped her sangria and shivered with pleasure. Maybe he'd be in the mood tonight. He'd been too tired to make love all week.

They ordered their usual tapas and the menus were whisked away. Russell poured them each another glass of sangria and she raised her glass to his. "*Salud*," she said. "Here's to the weekend. Thanks for arranging all this with Mom. I thought she might be too tired, since she just made that drive back alone from Chance Harbor. That must have been a brutal trip."

"She seemed happy to do it. Feeling better?"

"Oh yes." She smiled at him over the rim of her glass. Tonight it would be *her* turn to serve *him*, she decided. "What about you? Tell me about your day. You must be glad the first week of school is over."

"Not so bad," he said. "I told you, didn't I, that I have two upper-level history classes? Both are small. Just one section of freshmen. Easy. It was a relief to be back in a routine, actually."

"But you must miss the free time you had to work on your book this summer," she said, surprised.

"Not really. It's still a joy, teaching."

Catherine heard the strain in Russell's voice but couldn't decipher it. Was he worried about something? Tired? That was probably it. She'd found Russell on his laptop in the living room early every morning this week, working on his book long before she and Willow even came downstairs, "before my head gets crowded," he explained. She was proud of his focus and told him that now.

"We're so lucky, aren't we?" she said, gazing into her ruby-colored sangria with its slice of orange in the crystal glass. "We're blessed to have each other and work we love."

"Lucky. We are. Yes."

Russell agreed in such a distracted way that Catherine forgot her drink and looked up at him. He was holding his phone under the table, staring at it like a lost man with a compass. "Who are you texting? Willow?"

"No," he said, tucking the phone back into his pocket.

She would have pressed him, but the waiter arrived and began setting plates on the table. She was starving, Catherine realized.

Russell saw her expression and pushed the plates toward her. "Go for it," he said. "I had a late lunch."

They ate and talked more about the day's events, then moved on to discuss her mother's recent decision to sell the house at Chance Harbor. "I hate the idea," Catherine admitted. "I've always loved fantasizing about summers on the island with Willow and her children. But I don't see how we can take it on."

"No. We can barely keep up with our own house."

"I know. Besides, realistically, even if you have the whole summer off, I can't get away more than three weeks a year. If Mom doesn't want to go to Chance Harbor without Dad, what's the point? The poor house would be one of those sad summer places that's closed up most of the year."

"Well, don't give up yet. Your mom might change her mind." Russell dipped a hunk of bread into the warmed goat cheese. "I think she's being too hasty. Grief is clouding her perspective."

"I know," Catherine said. "But she says it will be too hard for her to be there without Dad. Funny. I never really thought of my parents as being close, especially after the whole thing with Zoe. But Mom really seems to miss him. I guess that's natural after so many years, but he sure wasn't an easy man to love."

"Eccentric and stubborn," Russell agreed. "But those qualities got him off the island and into high tech. I always admired the guy."

"I know. He liked you, too." Catherine was quiet for a minute, her throat tight with grief. Occasionally she saw a small, wiry man who resembled her father and her sorrow fell like a veil, clouding her vision. If the pain of missing him was like that for her, what must it be like for her mother?

She reached for a helping of grilled asparagus. "The thing is, I know Dad would want us all to keep going to PEI," she said. "Chance Harbor was the one place I saw him act completely relaxed." She smiled. "Remember how Dad started behaving like a ten-year-old the minute we arrived, so excited and happy? I don't think I ever heard him laugh as much anywhere else."

When Russell didn't respond, Catherine lifted her head from the asparagus. He was focused on his cell phone again, holding it under the table, his eyes cast down at its screen. Catherine could hear the phone vibrating, an angry sound like a dentist's drill. "You might as well answer it," she said. "You're not listening to me anyway."

Russell looked up sharply. "No, I'm listening." He picked up a shrimp and bit into it so quickly that Catherine heard the crunch from her side of the table; he must have forgotten to pull the shell off the tail. Nonetheless, he kept mindlessly chewing, his gaze still distant.

Catherine felt a slow panic rising and set down her fork. "What's wrong? Are you all right?"

"I'm fine," Russell said, then dropped the shrimp and buried his face in his hands, shoulders quaking.

"Oh my God. What is it, honey?" Catherine reached over to touch his wrist, but Russell flinched away.

After a moment, he put his hands down. His eyes were red-rimmed but dry. "Sorry."

"So," she said slowly, "I'm guessing you surprised me by arranging this date tonight for a reason. What is it? Are you ill?" She swallowed hard around a sudden knot of fear, thinking: cancer. They were at that age when everyone was being diagnosed.

"No. I'm fine."

"Is someone we know ill?"

"Nothing like that."

When Russell fell silent again, Catherine felt a flash of irritation. She'd had a tough day and was too tired to play twenty questions. "Did you lose your job?"

Russell laughed, a sudden unexpected bark. "Not yet. But soon, probably. I'm sorry."

"Shit," she said, doing some quick mental calculations: the mortgage, car payments, utilities. They could make it on her salary, barely. But if Russell were laid off, Willow would lose her tuition waiver. What then? "That's bad news."

"No kidding."

"But why would they let you go?" Her mind was stumbling through a thicket of possibilities. "You've been there longer than almost anyone. Did the school lose its accreditation? Is there a funding issue? I don't get it. Surely they could have warned you before the school year started. . . ."

"It's nothing like that." Russell's voice was brusque now. "It's nothing to do with the school or their money. It's me."

Now Catherine's hands went clammy. Last year a teacher was fired for looking at child pornography on a school computer. Another teacher was suspended for making racist remarks about a Native American student.

She couldn't imagine Russell—her ethical, kind, compassionate, loving, smart husband—doing anything that would harm his students or cost him his teaching job. No, this had to be a mistake. They'd fight it. She had two friends who were lawyers. It would be all right.

"Please," she said. "Don't make me guess anymore. Just tell me."

Russell tried to smile but didn't succeed. His mouth twisted up on one side and down at the other corner, making him look like a stroke victim. "I'm going to be a father," he said.

"*What*?" She stared at him, certain she'd misheard.

"It's true." The smile was working its way into a more familiar shape, the grooves deepening on either side of Russell's handsome mouth into a nearly recognizable expression of happiness. But his eyes were still red and his knee was jumping under the table as he repeated tonelessly, "I'm going to be a father."

"And yet, how funny. I'm not going to be a mother," Catherine said, clutching her drink as if they were in the middle of an earthquake, magnitude 8.8. But it wasn't the glass or the table or the floor trembling. It was her. She had started shaking all over.

Russell winced. She realized that he'd been doing a lot of wincing lately. It was okay when they were talking about newspaper headlines, house chores, or car repairs. But she absolutely did *not* want him wincing at her. Like she was the cause of his distress. "I'm sorry," he said.

"That's all you have to say? *I'm sorry*?" Her voice rose on the last two words, causing a few diners to glance in their direction. Good. Let them be witnesses to this sudden collapse of their marriage.

"I'm . . ." He stopped himself in time. "Words can't express how terrible I feel, Catherine. I never meant to hurt you. Listen, I'm not really very hungry. Have you eaten enough? Maybe we should get out of here." He glanced around.

The restaurant was full—the height of the Friday-night post-work crowd—and now Catherine understood that's what Russell had counted on. When he'd asked her out on this "date," he must have been planning to announce his big news in public to keep her reaction in check. He was going to have a baby!

A baby, something they'd both wanted and hoped for and paid big money for and failed at for years. A decade of wasted energy, foolishly hoping for something that came to nothing. Together they'd mourned and then come to terms with being childless. Then they'd become Willow's guardians. A miracle family. They were happy.

Or so she'd thought.

Catherine was shaking even harder now—from doubt, fear, shock, and, most of all, fury. Russell was still watching her, but he was also fondling the phone in his pocket, perhaps silencing a call. A call from the mother of his child, no doubt, wondering if he'd done the dirty deed, delivered the news and, P.S., done it while having dinner in the same restaurant where Russell had taken her—Catherine, his wife!—to celebrate their last wedding anniversary.

Diamonds: he'd given her a pair of diamond earrings. She'd given him a watch. They'd kissed while walking down Newbury Street that night, and on impulse they'd ridden the swan boats in Boston Public Garden with a group of giggling Japanese tourists who had captured Russell and Catherine in their pink cloud of happiness on videos they would take home to Japan as part of their Boston memories. She and Russell would be kissing in the cloud for eternity, no matter what happened here on earth.

"Why leave?" Catherine said. "Where would we go to finish our conversation? Home to Willow and my *mother*?" She glanced out the window. Still raining. "Who is she?" She suddenly flashed on the hours Russell had spent working on his book in his office, on how he'd stayed home in August instead of coming with them to Chance Harbor.

"Nobody you know," he said.

Her body felt numb with shock, but some part of her mind was still engaged, sorting through data like a computer, examining possibilities. How could getting another woman pregnant cost Russell his job? Then it dawned on her. "She's someone you work with, right?"

Russell had the grace to look surprised. That must be the expression he reserved for clever students who spoke up in class. "Yes. Look, this wasn't anything I ever imagined doing, Catherine. It just kind of happened. It was like being swept down a mountain in an avalanche. All I could do was swim to the surface and hope I ended up in one piece."

"Do. Not. Tell. Me. You. Love. Her." She spit the words out like ice cubes.

The waiter appeared. He was dark and handsome, just what a Spanish restaurant required, though his Indian features suggested he was Mexican or Guatemalan. He was savvy enough to sense disaster and looked anxious. "More tapas, señores?"

"I think we've had enough to eat, thank you." Catherine fixed her eyes on Russell, daring him to make a run for it. "But we'd love another pitcher of sangria."

"Another pitcher?" Russell raised an eyebrow. "Really, do you think that's . . . ?"

The waiter glanced from one to the other and made his decision. "*Sí, señora,* I will bring that for you *pronto*," he said, and dashed off with a flash of shiny black shoes.

"I plan to be here for a while," Catherine said, settling back in her chair, "hearing all about how you're finally going to have that baby you always wanted."

"Believe me, it was an accident." Russell closed his eyes as his phone vibrated again.

"Just answer the damn thing," she said. "We both know who it is."

He shook his head. "She can wait."

"Only for about nine more months." Catherine noted the sudden flush rising from Russell's neck—he always got blotchy when he was upset—and said, "What? Is it less than that? How long before the happy event?"

"I don't know."

"Oh, come on, Russell. I bet you can figure it out. When did she tell you about the baby? This week? A month ago?"

"Mid-August."

Why was he being so cagey? Guilt, she hoped. "All right. That wasn't so hard, answering a simple question, was it? Here's another one: When's the baby due?"

"January fifteenth."

"January?" Catherine did a quick calculation. "*January*? You were busy fucking some woman without protection while we were burying my *father*?"

"It wasn't like that!" Russell's face was on fire now, a patchwork of pink and white.

The waiter arrived with the new pitcher of sangria and, after glancing at them both, set it squarely in front of Catherine and beat another hasty retreat.

"No?" She poured herself a glass. A full glass. "Tell me, then, what it was like."

"Don't do this to yourself, Catherine."

"I'm not doing anything to me. You are. So tell me. Who is she? What does this have to do with you losing your job? Is she another teacher? A parent? A trustee?" Her eyes widened as she pictured the only colleague of Russell's she knew well, the curvy Spanish teacher, a lively brunette in her twenties who was married to the head of school. Second marriage, of course. "Not the head's wife, Yolanda?" That would certainly explain Russell being let go from work.

Russell remained silent as Catherine felt panic rising from the pit of her stomach to clog her throat, a sour physical lump too enormous to swallow. She was having trouble breathing around it.

As Russell's face mirrored her stricken expression, she finally let herself understand what he'd hoped to hide from everyone. "It's a student."

"Yes," Russell said, a soft exhalation of sound. "I'm so sorry."

"I swear to God, Russell, if you apologize to me one more time, I will cut your balls off with this knife." Catherine waved the serrated bread knife around for emphasis, causing the waiter to rush over again.

"More bread?" he suggested.

Catherine smiled at him around teeth that felt like fangs. "No, thank you."

The waiter reached for the knife with a knowing look. He must have been familiar with knife-wielding jilted wives. Catherine obediently handed it to him. Then she passed him the bread basket and her dishes, too, after whisking crumbs into her palm and dumping those on her plate out of habit. She'd been a waitress for too many years to leave a mess. "You can take all this away. We're nearly done here. Thank you."

"As you wish." The waiter bowed and removed the aftermath of their dinner.

"I cannot believe I married a pervert." Catherine clung to her anger, which was all that kept her from dissolving.

"Please, Catherine. Lower your voice."

"You abused a child!"

"She's eighteen," Russell said. "Hardly a child."

"She's hardly older than your own daughter! What will Willow think of you doing this to her?" Catherine folded her arms to stop herself from slapping him.

"I didn't do this to Willow!" Russell said. "And I didn't do it to *you*, either. It just happened, Catherine."

"Stop saying that!" Catherine shouted, causing heads to swivel. Good! Let them look. Let Russell's face stay scarlet and shamed. "Obviously this girl didn't make a baby all by herself. How did this even happen, Russell? I swear to God, I will not leave this table until you tell me who it is. I'm bound to find out anyway. Tell me!" She threw back another gulp of sangria.

He sighed, wincing again. "Her name is Nola Simone. I met her last year. She was in my AP history class and started coming in for extra help. And, well. Those extra help sessions turned into actual conversations about things we're both interested in. Things you don't really care about," he added. "Nola loves hearing me talk about my dad's career in politics and my memoir. She's a Civil War buff, too, just like I am." He spread his hands. "We connected on commonalities."

Catherine rolled her eyes. "Commonalities? Like what? Like you were registering for the draft when she celebrated her first birthday?"

"Make fun of this all you want, Catherine, but it's not a crush or a passing thing. What Nola and I feel for each other is real."

"How did it start being real? As in, physical?" She would probably be sorry later, knowing these details, but she couldn't stop herself from asking. This girl was a child and Russell was an idiot.

Russell hadn't touched the sangria in his glass. She poured it into her own. The second pitcher was empty except for the soggy fruit, as colorful and limp as dead betta fish, lying in the bottom. "Come on. You owe me that much. How did the affair start? In your office?"

The flush, which had begun its retreat back down Russell's neck, returned. "The first time, yes. Nola admitted that she was starting to have feelings for me. Powerful feelings."

"Was this before or after you gave her an A?"

"Don't be nasty, Catherine. It doesn't suit you."

"Maybe I'm trying on a new persona to match the new personality you bought at the Playboy Mansion. How many times did you do it in your office?"

"Jesus, I don't know."

"Was this going on all summer?"

He nodded. "I couldn't leave her, Catherine," he said. "Nola's delicate. That's why I didn't go to Canada with you and Willow. I couldn't. You don't understand what it did to Nola, thinking about me being gone for so many weeks. I was honestly afraid she might harm herself. That's how intensely she loves me."

"Oh my God, Russell. Listen to yourself! Wasn't our marriage even worth you trying to stop seeing this girl? I don't understand. Are you trying to tell me you stayed with her because you felt *sorry* for her? Didn't our relationship count for anything, compared to a few hours with a girl who's barely old enough to *vote*?"

"I know it sounds awful," Russell said. "I can't explain it, except to say Nola's young, but not really that young. She knows a lot more than I do about some things. Traveling, for instance! Nola has been all over Europe and Asia with her family. Places I've always wanted to see."

"I don't care if she's been to Shangri-La. She's a child! She can't even order a beer in a sports bar!"

Russell glanced nervously at the other diners, every one of whom was watching avidly. "Please, Catherine. Keep it down. I'd hoped you'd be more reasonable than this."

"Well, sometimes our hopes amount to nothing, don't they?" she said, and dumped the pitcher of bloody dead fruit over Russell's head before walking out of the restaurant and into the rain-drenched street.

CHAPTER TWO

On Sunday morning, Willow made up a story about meeting a friend for coffee in Harvard Square—as if she even liked coffee, which tasted like dirt—and headed out the door with her sketch pad. She needn't have bothered lying. Her grandmother seemed as happy to see her leave as Willow was to get out of there.

They'd had fun together Friday night, eating at Willow's favorite burrito place in Harvard Square and then sitting with cups of frozen yogurt on one of the curved walls near Out of Town News, where they'd watched some guy do wicked cool paintings with a spray can.

Later that night, they were watching a movie when Catherine called to ask if it was okay if she didn't come home until Sunday. As Willow listened to her grandmother's end of the conversation—"Of course. You know I'm always happy to spend time with her; just enjoy yourself"—she pictured Catherine and Russell going to a hotel, fighting about Nola maybe, if he told her about the kiss, then making up.

She didn't like picturing kissing or anything like that. Not after the last boyfriend her mom had. Unfortunately, thinking about Russell and Nola made Willow remember him, something she tried never to do. She had to sleep with her light on. Otherwise she'd picture Tom, the guy who

Mom called the Real Deal even after Willow said she didn't like him, sneaking into her room.

"But why don't you like Tom?" her mom had asked, frowning as they sat at the kitchen table waiting for Tom to come home to the fried chicken Zoe had bought at the grocery store to eat with a can of beans for dinner. "He's so much better than Doug, don't you think?"

If you'd asked her before Tom moved in with them, Willow would have said anybody would be a step up from Doug the Slug, who'd lived with them for two years and had kept saying his back hurt too much for him to get a job. Doug was the reason her mom went back to doing molly after she'd given it up for, like, a year. Doug was why Mom drank, too, and forgot to pick up Willow from school sometimes.

Finally, after Mom came home early from work one night and found Willow freezing on the porch while Doug did coke with one of the neighbors, she'd screamed at him and dumped the Slug. They'd moved out of the apartment that night, leaving almost everything behind so Doug couldn't find them again.

"But how do you know he won't, Mom?" Willow had demanded. She was seven by then and tired of moving. She had also learned that not everything her mom said was true, even if Mom believed it herself.

"Because he's too freakin' lazy," Mom said, with an eye roll and her laugh that was like a thousand purple cartoon butterflies. You couldn't help laughing when Mom did.

They'd moved in with Nana and Grandpa for a month and then to a new apartment, smaller but cleaner than Doug's, and things were good for a while.

"I'm really getting my shit together now," Mom had said, after she'd found a new job as a waitress. She'd dumped a heap of shiny silver coins onto the kitchen table, then grinned and pulled out a wad of ones and fives. People tipped great in the new place, and Mom didn't even have to pool her tips like she'd done in the club where she'd worked before. Plus, now that Willow was nine and old enough to stay on her own, they didn't have to pay a sitter.

Then the Real Deal came into their lives. Tom acted like Mr. Normal, and even Willow could see he was good-looking for somebody so old. Tom had a few teeth capped in gold, but most were white and straight. He had a nice haircut and long sideburns and he wore boots, like a country-western singer.

Tom even had his own car, a shiny red one that he drove fast with the sunroof open. Once, he'd picked Willow up from school and let her ride home standing on the front seat, her head out the window. He'd whooped and hung on to Willow's leg to keep her from falling out.

But Tom didn't want to touch only Willow's leg. He wanted to touch her in other places. She'd been hearing "stranger danger" stuff in school since kindergarten and knew that wasn't okay. But her mom was so happy and Tom gave her money. They finally had electricity all the time and plenty of food, too. How could Willow make her leave the Real Deal?

She couldn't do it. Willow decided to just stay away from Tom. She got involved in after-school stuff and played soccer on weekends, making sure she wasn't ever alone with him in the apartment. Tom wasn't living with them; whenever her mom was working, Willow said she'd rather stay home by herself than have him come babysit her. "I'm not a baby, Mom," she said. "I'm almost ten. It's insulting."

"You're not scared here at night by yourself?" Her mom had looked doubtful, squinching her pretty blue eyes. She knew Willow was afraid of the dark. Always had been, since the fire.

"I'm fine. You like it when Tom comes to your work and picks you up, right? You could even spend the night at his house. I can get myself to school in the morning."

So mostly that's what happened. For months, things went on like that, Willow tricking herself into thinking things were okay and taking care of herself.

Then, one night, Tom had come to the apartment while Mom was at work, saying he had to use their Wi-Fi because his was down. Tom opened his laptop on the kitchen table and started "working the numbers," he said after kissing Mom good-bye. "We'll have our own place soon, a real house," he'd said to Mom. "We'll be a family. You, me, and Willow."

Willow hadn't said anything, just stayed in the living room doing her homework in front of the TV and planning how to run away if he actually did move in.

She tried to forget Tom was in the kitchen. Then he called her in there. "Willow, honey, can you help me with something on the computer? Just for a sec?"

Willow was good on the computer. Most adults were hopeless. She sighed and went into the kitchen. "What?"

"Here. Look at this," Tom said.

She couldn't tell what she was looking at right off, then realized it was a man and a woman. The man's penis was in the woman's mouth. The woman was skinny and wore bright red lipstick, but she wasn't really a woman. More like a girl her own age. No hair anywhere.

"That's disgusting," Willow said.

"Oh, no, it feels real good, doing that." Tom hooked his arm between Willow's thighs before she could move away. "I could show you how to do it. I'd pay you twenty dollars, too. I know you and your mom could use the money, right?"

After a moment of frozen panic, Willow had felt his fingers moving like worms into her underpants. She kicked his chair so hard he almost tipped over; then she ran out of the apartment and down the street to her friend Morgan's house. Morgan made her tell Mom, and they'd moved out of the apartment the next day to some crap house with, like, eighteen people sleeping everywhere, even on the floor. They'd never seen Mr. Real Deal again.

After that, of course, everything happened the way Willow had thought it would: Mom crying for days, saying she was sorry, then getting high and sleeping a lot.

The one thing Willow had never predicted was Mom giving up. Not just on her, but on life. She had, though, saying, "You're better off without me, sweet pea," when Willow cried at the bus station and begged her not to leave.

Now, as Willow walked down Mass Ave toward Harvard Square, she wondered why it felt so bad, having Catherine and Russell stay out all night. It wasn't like she'd been abandoned in a bus station. Catherine had assured them she'd be home today, that she just needed a little break.

"Work was really getting to me," she'd explained to Willow on the phone after talking to Nana. "You don't mind, do you? I know it's probably good for Nana to have some company, too. She's lonely since Grandpa died."

Catherine would come home, Willow told herself. She wasn't Zoe. Catherine would never run away and leave her. Russell, either.

Would they?

At Cambridge Common, she stopped to watch a bunch of people playing Frisbee. Another group was setting up some kind of tightrope between two trees. Harvard students, probably.

She sank down onto the silky grass and took out her sketch pad and pencils. Really, what would happen to her if Catherine and Russell decided to split up? Would they even want to keep her? Catherine always talked about how Willow made them a family, but what if there was no husband? Would she spend part of the time with Catherine and the rest of the time with Russell, like her friend Kendrick did with her divorced parents?

Willow felt a tear sliding down her cheek and scrubbed at her face with one hand just as someone called her name.

She turned around so fast that she got a cramp in her neck and said, "Ow."

"Well, 'ow' to you, too." It was Henry. He trotted over like a redheaded giraffe and collapsed next to her. "What are you doing here?"

"I live here," Willow said, pointing toward Davis Square. "Down that way."

"That's weird. Me, too. I didn't think anyone from school lived in Cambridge."

"I didn't either. Especially not a rich third!" When he looked confused, Willow added, "You know: named after your grandfather and dad."

"Oh!" Henry reddened and tugged out a blade of grass, flattened it between his thumbs, and blew on it. The grass shrieked like a dying cat. "Being named after your father doesn't exactly make you rich," he said.

"It just means your parents were probably too scared of making their own parents mad to give you an original name. We're poor as dirt."

"Good," she said.

"Thanks a lot."

"Hey. I don't want to be the only pauper at Beacon Hill School. So if you live in Cambridge, why do you go there?"

"Better education, tonier colleges accepting our fine graduates," Henry said. "Or so goes the lingo at home. My parents are both professors and I'm the youngest kid in our family, so they've been thinking about my college choice pretty much since I blew out the candle on my first birthday cake. Why are you there?"

"Because it's free," she said.

"Whoa. Presidential merit scholar?"

"No. My dad teaches there." When she saw Henry frown, Willow added, "Russell Standish, history? He's really my uncle. That's why we have different last names. But he and my aunt have been raising me since my mom took off when I was ten."

"Shit. That must have sucked."

Henry's brown eyes were so sympathetic that Willow turned away. "Yeah, well. Mom couldn't keep things together. She's probably dead now."

"So you're saying you're better off? That's good, I guess."

Willow felt disappointed by his response. But what was he supposed to say? *Gee, you must be resilient and wonderful, going through hell like that?* She'd like to hear somebody say that just once. Though what Henry said was still better than that shrink Catherine made her see for a while, the one who said, *It would be normal for you to have trouble forming attachments, Willow.* Like she was some kind of Lego brick with the wrong number of holes.

"What are you not drawing today?" Henry was looking at her notebook.

"The trees," Willow said. "Did you know that George Washington stood under that elm tree over there when he first took charge of the Continental Army?"

"I did, actually," Henry said. "My dad teaches history at Simmons.

Did you know that one of Washington's favorite dishes was cream of peanut soup? Or that he had all his teeth pulled?"

Willow laughed. "I didn't know about the soup, but I knew about his teeth. Russell says George Washington had a set of ivory teeth made."

"Yeah. Ivory from hippos, set in silver."

They high-fived. "So, where are you going now?" Willow asked.

"Anywhere but home, where my sister's practicing her flute. Talk about 'ow.' Want to hang out?"

Willow nodded and gathered her things. Any distraction was a welcome one. By the time she got home, Catherine and Russell would be there.

The tomatoes had taken over. That was always the way with vegetables in September, Eve thought as she contemplated Catherine's garden: some plants thrived, bullying their way through the August heat and September's chilly nights while others rotted away, leaves tattered into lace by insects.

Why did Catherine even bother growing her own vegetables? So impractical. There were grocery stores and produce stands on practically every corner in Cambridge.

She'd probably put in a garden thinking this would be a good activity for Willow, something healthy and outdoorsy. A mother-daughter bonding activity. Catherine had always treated motherhood like a graduate school project, studying every aspect of parenting. Right now there were four books on her bedside table about teaching your child to be ethical, independent, happy, and unplugged. As if working mothers didn't already feel guilty enough.

Gardening was an admirable impulse, but Eve hated to see food wasted. She got to work picking tomatoes, laying them gently in the basket she'd brought out from the kitchen. At least she could boil them down and freeze the tomato sauce for Catherine to use this winter.

As she picked them, Eve thought about that strange phone call on Friday night. Why had Catherine suddenly needed a weekend away? Was it really because she was exhausted from a tough week at work? Eve didn't buy it, yet it was true that Catherine hadn't sounded at all like her usual brisk, competent self.

"Please, Mommy, can you stay with Willow for the weekend?" she'd begged. Catherine had never called her "Mommy." Only Zoe did that.

When she'd picked the tomatoes, Eve started weeding, uncovering a few squash, eggplants, and even runner beans that were still firm and edible.

Of course, she had no right to be critical of Catherine's garden. Her own had gone wild after Andrew died. Eve knew she should be doing a fall cleanup, but still couldn't face the jobs around the house that had always been Andrew's.

Whenever she went out to the garden, she imagined her husband there in one of his floppy-brimmed hats. This should have made her feel closer to him. Instead, Eve's eyes would sting like someone had thrown sand in them and she'd have to dash back inside to the safety of her kitchen.

Too much time on her hands. That was the problem. All her life Eve had prided herself on being useful. A necessary person. She had always enjoyed being busy, even during those precious years when the girls were young and she was exhausted from juggling motherhood with her job as a public relations director at the hospital.

Then, in a blink of an eye, she was alone, with more empty hours than she cared to count. Directionless. Lost.

She had clung to her job after the girls moved out, missing them so much that she'd had to keep their bedroom doors closed for weeks after each of them left for college. Work had gotten her through that, and then, later, through Zoe's disappearance. She'd been only the assistant director back then, so she could afford to take time off during those first terrifying months they were searching for Zoe.

For a while she'd coped after Zoe disappeared. Convinced her daughter was alive, Eve had thrown herself into looking for her. She'd embraced the early casseroles and candlelight vigils by neighbors, made posters, and put up ads long after Andrew agreed with the cops that Zoe was most likely dead. At the same time, Eve had nightmares for years: Zoe falling off the top of a building. Drowning. Trapped in a fire.

Nothing to do with reality. Odds were better that Zoe had followed another druggie boyfriend to live in yet another tenement building where the windows were always open, sheets tacked across the windows and flapping in the breeze.

Eve had been to many of those apartments through the years. She'd brought Zoe and Willow food and clothes, even money, though Andrew knew nothing about that. The last place she'd visited had red velvet wallpaper, raised and soft to the touch. The floor was carpeted red, too, and stained in places; there was a fish-shaped design by the sink, a bird shape in the bedroom. The door to the apartment was painted black with a silver metal knob as bright as a tooth filling. Pots and pans coated with food were stacked in the sink and on the counter. Yet, when Eve had opened the cabinet doors, she'd found nothing to eat but a few tins of tuna.

For years after Zoe disappeared, she had searched: driving through small towns and showing her daughter's picture to anyone who would look, canvassing bus stations and homeless encampments, calling hospitals and shelters. Occasionally she would read about a body found and worry that it was Zoe's. That maybe one day her daughter had taken too much of something and stumbled in front of a car. No ID, a Jane Doe in a different state.

Or another, more likely scenario: Zoe murdered, maybe by accident, as an afterthought, by warring drug dealers or another addict. Her daughter's broken body tossed into a Dumpster or an empty building, or into the woods like those deer and raccoon carcasses, the roadkill they saw in New Brunswick on the way up to their house on Prince Edward Island every summer.

Yet Eve had kept looking for Zoe through the years. She had even gone on national television to plead for Zoe's return and had made Andrew go with her on air. She'd done local television before, was comfortable in front of cameras, but the studio in New York was still a surprise. So small, crowded with people and equipment.

Eve had let them do her makeup and hair at the studio, sitting in a row with other guests waiting for their three minutes of fame as the crew applied eye concealer, combed and sprayed her hair, brushed lint off her jacket. Meanwhile, she'd been thinking, *Why? What does it matter how I look, when my daughter's missing?*

Then she and Andrew were seated in orange swivel chairs with the cameras on. The news anchor, a woman in a red dress so bright it hurt, wound her spray-tanned legs together as if they were made of rubber and asked Eve questions about Zoe. At the end of the interview, she'd asked, "Is there something you'd like to say to your daughter if she's listening?"

"Don't lose hope, Zoe," Eve had said, staring directly into the camera. "Wherever you are, know that we're using every resource to find you. And we *will* find you, honey. Help is on its way."

Nothing had come of the interview. Years of investigating by the police and two different private detectives they'd hired at great expense turned up very little as well.

Eve was promoted to director of public relations at the hospital shortly after her television appearance. A pity promotion. Two years later, the hospital offered her a golden parachute—a forced retirement, no other way to look at it.

She'd worked at the hospital for twenty-five years. Her career was her identity; she felt lost without it. More important, after Zoe disappeared, her job was the lifeline that had kept Eve tethered to earth. It gave her something to do besides obsessively search for Zoe on her own after Andrew refused to pay for a third private investigator.

"I'm as sorry about this outcome as you are, honey," Andrew had said. "But we give our kids wings so they can fly out of the nest. Zoe followed her own compass. The consequences were tragic, but at least she's at peace now."

"But what about *me*? I'm not at peace!" Eve had shouted at him.

That was the last time they'd dared speak about Zoe. The memory of their daughter had the power to tear them apart, just as her tumultuous existence had nearly destroyed their marriage and their faith in themselves as parents when Zoe lived with them.

Eve wiped sweat from her forehead and continued attacking the weeds in Catherine's garden, wishing she could tear these thoughts out of her head the same way she was ripping plants from the ground. But it was impossible. Even now, five years after Zoe's disappearance, a small, stubborn part of her refused to believe her daughter was dead. If Zoe had truly left them, Eve was certain she would have felt a shift in the cosmos, a tear in the very fabric of the universe.

Eve carried the baskets of tomatoes over to the picnic table. Why go back to that horrible time in her life? It was over. All of it, finished: the worry over Zoe, the fights with Andrew, the disappointments of work and marriage, her husband's final betrayal.

Much of her life was over. Work. Motherhood. Nothing left for her to do but occasionally help Catherine, who had never really seemed to need her at all, even as a child.

Eve was searching the garden shed for a pair of clippers when she heard a car pull into the driveway. It must be Catherine. She wiped her hands on her shorts and walked around the side of the house to greet her.

She reached the driveway and saw that Catherine was still in the parked car. How odd. Her daughter was gazing straight ahead, her hands on the steering wheel as if she were still driving.

Where was Russell? Maybe Catherine dropped him off at school. Russell sometimes went into his office on Sundays to get a head start on the week, or to work on his boring-sounding book, a memoir of life with his father, a second-rate senator from Virginia.

Eve walked toward the car and stood directly in front of it, then waved, feeling foolish. "Hello!"

Catherine continued staring through the windshield, trancelike. The car engine was still running. Eve remained where she was for a few seconds, puzzled, waiting for Catherine to notice her.

Her daughters were both blond; there was no mistaking the fact that they were sisters. But where Zoe was endowed with curves that had drawn male attention too early and had always approached life with a swagger in her walk, Catherine was shy and pretty in a way that was too aloof for men to approach her. She was ethereal-looking and moved like a dancer. Her high cheekbones were sharply defined and her nose was small and pretty. Her skin was flawless; Zoe's face had a light dusting of freckles, as if someone had sprinkled cinnamon on her as an afterthought.

Andrew used to call Catherine "our sweet fairy." For Zoe, he'd come up with the name "Meteor," claiming that their younger daughter "always leaves a flaming trail of destruction in her wake."

Today, if Eve hadn't known this was Catherine in the driveway, she might not have recognized her. This woman looked too pinched and tired. Her eyes were vacant. What on earth could have happened?

Eve circled around to the driver's window and rapped on it with her knuckles. "Catherine? Are you all right?"

Catherine didn't startle, as Eve had expected, but instead swiveled her head slowly and opened the window. "Oh. Hi, Mom."

Eve slowly reached through the window and shut off the ignition. "Hi. Where's Russell, honey?"

Catherine's eyes sparked a brighter blue, but otherwise her expression remained flat. "He had things to do. He'll be here later."

"Oh. Well." At a loss, Eve stepped back. "Did you two have fun?"

"It was fine."

Obviously, things were far from fine, but Eve didn't want to pry. She bit her lip and stood there, watching Catherine do nothing. At last she said, "Why don't you come in and have some coffee?"

"I've had enough coffee," Catherine said. "Buckets of coffee."

"Are you hungry? Have you had lunch?"

"No. And no."

"Fine." Frustrated, Eve opened the rear door of the car. "You look tired. I'll help you carry your things inside and then I'll be on my way. Maybe you can grab a nap before Willow gets back."

Hearing Willow's name seemed to snap Catherine awake. She eased herself out of the car and shut the door cautiously, as if it might fall off its hinges. "Where is she?"

"Meeting a friend in Harvard Square."

"What friend?"

"I don't know. Somebody from school, she said."

"But Willow doesn't have any friends from school who live in Cambridge!"

Puzzled by the sudden sharp edge in Catherine's voice, Eve said, "Well, maybe it's a friend from school who lives in Boston, but wanted to meet in Harvard Square. I could have misheard."

"Did you get a name?" Catherine looked agitated now, shifting her weight from one foot to the other. "You should have checked to see who it was. I'd better text Willow right now."

"Stop." Eve put a hand on Catherine's arm. "Willow is a responsible girl. She'll be fine. There's no sense in doubting a child before she gives you any reason to."

"Yeah, look how well that worked with Zoe."

Eve inhaled sharply at the stinging rebuke. "No mother can watch over her children every minute. And Willow isn't Zoe."

"I know. I'm sorry, Mom. It isn't really Willow I'm worried about. It's the other kids at school. Some of them aren't very nice. They're awful, in fact."

"She'll be fine," Eve repeated, though now she was feeling anxious, too. "Let's go in the house where it's cooler."

There was no overnight bag in the car, of course. She gathered a laptop, Catherine's purse, and a plastic bag with a hotel's name on it off the backseat.

In the kitchen, Catherine texted Willow, and Eve considered texting Russell. He never should have let Catherine drive in this state.

Eve poured some of the strawberry smoothie she'd made for Willow this morning into a glass and handed it to Catherine. "Sit. You really do look exhausted."

"I'm fine," Catherine said, but she obediently dropped into one of the kitchen chairs, took a few sips of the smoothie, then folded her hands on the table after her phone buzzed and she'd looked at it. "Okay. Willow texted back to say she's with Henry from school, whoever that is. She'll be home for dinner. Did she seem okay this weekend?"

"A little quiet, maybe," Eve said. "Probably worn-out from adjusting to school. We ate in Harvard Square and watched a movie Friday night. Yesterday she did some homework and I took her to that art store she loves. We made our own pizza for dinner. The only odd thing was that she still seems to need her light on when she sleeps. Catherine, what's going on?"

A slight tremor ran through her daughter's body. "Russell and I are getting divorced."

"*What?*" Shocked, Eve propped herself against the counter and stared at her daughter's bowed head, trying to imagine what could have brought this on.

Catherine and Russell had a wonderful marriage! Eve didn't think she'd ever heard them argue or exchange those bitingly sarcastic remarks so many couples did. Even the infertility treatments—years of disappointment and expense—hadn't split them apart.

She momentarily flashed through the fights she'd had with Andrew: over money, over their respective infidelities, over Zoe most of all. They had gotten through all of that.

Or at least that's what she'd believed until the very end. Now she would never know if their marriage would have held together after Andrew's final lie.

Catherine wound her hands together. "I know what you're going to say, Mom, so don't."

"How can you possibly know what I'm going to say?"

"Because it's written all over your face."

Catherine's face was still tight, her mouth a thin line. But at least she seemed calmer. Sitting in her own kitchen probably helped. There was nothing like seeing the familiar way the morning light hit your teakettle on the counter to remind you that you were alive and functioning.

"What am I thinking, then?" Eve asked.

"That our marriage can be fixed. You always think everything can be fixed, Mom. And everyone."

Catherine was referring to Zoe, of course, but Eve refused to be derailed. "Well, I do think you might be hasty, suddenly announcing that you're getting divorced. The two of you seemed fine on Friday."

"Fine? Really?" Catherine shook her head. "Just out of curiosity, what did Russell say when he called you on Friday afternoon to ask if you'd stay with Willow?"

Eve frowned, thinking back. "That you and he needed a night out, and would I come down to look after her. I said I was happy to do it and he thanked me. That's it."

"Didn't it seem at all odd that Russell called you and not me?"

Eve shrugged. "I suppose I did wonder, but then I decided he was probably trying to surprise you."

Catherine made a face. "He surprised me, all right."

"Is it you or him?"

"Me or him what?"

"Who wants the divorce."

"Both of us know it's over."

"My God, Catherine. Surely this deserves more thought than just one bad weekend?"

"No. It absolutely does not. It's done. *I'm* done." Catherine rose from the table. "Listen, I think you're right. You should go, Mom. I'm sorry. Thank you for coming, but I need a nap. I didn't sleep well at the hotel."

"Please," Eve said. "Don't rush into this."

A grimace twisted her daughter's pretty features. "Funny. That's exactly what you said to me when I wanted to marry Russell. Guess I should have listened."

"Listen to me now, then! I don't presume to know the inner workings of your marriage, but you and Russell are both good people who love each other. And you both love Willow! Think of what this will do to her."

"Trust me. All I've done this weekend is think about what this will do to Willow," Catherine said, her voice breaking.

Eve felt sick to her stomach. If Catherine set her mind on something, that something was likely to happen. "Are you sure you don't want me to stay tonight?"

"Yes. It's better if you go home," Catherine said, then left the kitchen, head and shoulders bowed as if she were marching to her own execution.

In a minute Eve heard the bedroom door slam. She stood alone in the kitchen, staring at the sweating glass her daughter had left on the table and wondering what in the world would happen now.

CHAPTER THREE

Miraculously, Catherine made it through Sunday dinner after her mother left and Willow came home: beef stew from the freezer, a salad made from the remnants of romaine and tomatoes her mother had brought in from the garden. She'd dodged Willow's questions about Russell, diverting her with questions about her new friend, Henry. It broke Catherine's heart to look at her daughter, laughing and chattering away like any nicer-than-average fifteen-year-old, and thinking about what it would do to Willow when she discovered that Russell and one of her classmates were having a baby.

She sent Willow upstairs to do homework and get ready for bed while she cleaned the kitchen. What the hell was she going to do with so many tomatoes?

Catherine started to dump them into the compost bucket, then stopped herself. She might need these tomatoes. Money would be tight now. The head of school was bound to act swiftly once he caught wind of the situation. Russell would definitely be fired. He might even be charged with some criminal act, for all she knew.

She managed to keep things together as she went upstairs to kiss Willow good night, telling her that Russell would be home later but might have to go into school early.

"I'll see him tomorrow at school, right?" Willow asked, settling against her pillows with a book.

"Right." Catherine heard the note of anxiety in Willow's voice and leaned forward to kiss the girl's forehead. Her hair rose from the static electricity and gave them both a shock, making Willow laugh. "Good night. Don't stay up too late reading."

"I'm glad you went to a spa," Willow said, as Catherine started to close the door. "We should go together sometime."

"Sure," Catherine said. "Maybe for your sixteenth birthday," she added with a smile. "'Night, now."

She went downstairs, glad that Willow had believed her story. The truth: it was a cheap motel on Route 1 by the airport. She'd stopped only because she'd been too shaken and too woozy from the sangria after that horrible dinner with Russell on Friday night to drive home. The motel had pink plastic chairs outside the bright blue doors, as if this were Florida, not Boston. The rugs had smelled like wet socks. There had been several truckers' rigs in the parking lot, and television noise emanated from every wall, as if she were surrounded by speakers.

Catherine didn't care. She'd taken two antihistamines to ensure that she would sleep.

Saturday morning, she had awakened feeling like somebody was pounding spikes into her head. She'd gone for a massage at the spa across the street, where she'd been vaguely horrified by the sight of a dainty Vietnamese woman weaving thread through an older woman's eyebrow hairs and yanking them out.

In one of the back rooms, Catherine had stripped off her clothing and gotten facedown on a table beneath a warmed blanket, applauding herself for seeking a tension reliever that wasn't also a destructive behavior.

Unfortunately, all the massage did was make her cry. It was the warmth of those small hands on her shoulders that had done it. She'd had to ask the masseuse to stop. She'd given her a good tip anyway. Then Catherine had climbed off the table, pulled her clothes back on, and returned to the hotel after stopping at a liquor store to buy a bottle of whiskey. All of her resolutions about healthy behavior had flown out the window: she drank the whiskey straight from the bottle. It made her stomach burn, but at least it helped her sleep.

She had alternated between crying so hard that her eyelids were encrusted with salt and feeling angry. *How dare he*, Catherine thought during those times when fury kept her going. How dare Russell have the life he'd always wanted—a pretty wife and a baby of his own!—while she was stranded with their old life, the tired one built through hard work and determination as they'd gone to grad school, carved out careers, bought a house, and spent every cent they had and some of her father's money, too, on infertility treatments that proved she was barren?

Barren. That word said it all about her, emotionally and physically.

The worst of it? She hadn't seen this coming. In the past year, she had celebrated their wedding anniversary and birthdays, made love to her husband several times a week, shared meals and house chores and her father's death and Willow's art with him, all without having any idea that her husband was being unfaithful. For *months*! How could she have been so clueless?

She and Russell had spoken by phone twice while she was at the hotel. During those conversations, she'd pressed him for details. Russell told her how, the weekend he was supposedly biking with a college friend, he'd actually been with Nola on her father's sailboat. He confessed, too, about the Back Bay hotel Nola had put on her credit card to celebrate Russell's birthday.

"She's a very determined girl," Russell said, sounding awed. "What Nola wants, she gets."

"But I don't understand," Catherine had said, truly mystified. In a way, curled up on the motel bed's slippery floral spread with the phone pressed to her ear had been like talking to Russell before they were married, from her dorm room to his. She could almost imagine they were still getting to know each other: this was like talking to a stranger. "Why does she want to be with you, Russell? Out of all the boys she could choose?"

He had sounded equally bewildered. "I don't know. She says I'm smart and cool and funny." He cleared his throat. "I thought Nola was on the pill, and she thought I'd had a vasectomy since I didn't have any kids of my own. The pregnancy was an accident. But now Nola says she wants my baby and will die without me. I believe her."

A powerful aphrodisiac, that kind of damsel-in-distress need. Catherine wanted to hate this girl. But Nola was a child, she reminded herself, no matter what Russell said about her. Worldly! At eighteen!

Oh, Russell, Catherine thought as she stepped into the shower now. *You've lied to me, but you've lied to yourself more.* And that knowledge made her cry again, her anger evaporating as she felt the pain of losing him.

After the shower, Catherine pulled on her flannel pajamas and robe; she felt so chilled from the shock of it all that her teeth were chattering. She and Russell had agreed they couldn't keep this from Willow for long. The kids at school would be blowing up their phones the minute word was out. Catherine suspected the student rumor mill was already churning. They probably had hours left. Maybe minutes. She wanted to protect Willow from that ugliness.

Russell was due home anytime now. They had agreed yesterday that he could come by the house after Willow was in bed to collect some of his clothing and other things. They would tell her about the divorce tomorrow at dinner, together, as the experts suggested.

They had also agreed that Catherine would stay in their small Cambridge house with Willow. The mortgage was modest and neither of them wanted to uproot her. When Catherine had asked where Russell planned to live, he'd said he had no idea, sounding so forlorn that Catherine had almost felt sorry for him. Then her fury returned when he said, "It doesn't really matter where I go now. Once Nola and I are married, of course, we'll need something big enough for a baby. Luckily, she has a trust fund."

Remembering this made Catherine run into the bathroom and throw up. She retched again and again as she tried to rid her body of anger, grief, and Russell.

She'd just finished brushing her teeth when she heard the key in the front door. She'd have to change the lock, Catherine thought, then scolded herself: Why? Russell was still Russell. Nice, compassionate, honest.

No, scratch that last thing: her husband was far from honest. She scrubbed her face clean with a washcloth, hung it up, and went downstairs to greet him.

Russell hadn't shaved and he wore the same clothes he'd had on Friday night. They were wrinkled and stained. He looked like a chiseled, good-looking actor made-up as a homeless person. She wondered if he'd been sleeping in his office.

"Do you need a suitcase?" she asked. "The black roller is in the front hall closet."

"You sure you won't need it?"

"Go ahead. Take it." *Take everything.*

She sat in the living room, wishing she were the sort of person who knitted or did scrapbooking. She didn't want to turn on the television, for fear of waking Willow, and her stomach couldn't handle any more alcohol. But sitting there with nothing to do was agony.

Finally, she remembered the laundry—she normally did it on Saturdays—and carried the hamper down to the basement to throw the clothes in the washer. She pulled Russell's clothes out of the hamper and stuffed them into a trash bag. He could do his own damn laundry.

By the time she'd returned to the living room, Russell was sitting in one of the wingback chairs by the fireplace. "I just took what I could carry in this." He gestured to the suitcase beside him. "I'll have to get the rest of my stuff later. Look, I wish we could work something out."

"Like what? You and your child bride coming to live here with the baby?" She dropped the trash bag of his dirty clothes on top of the suitcase.

"No. Not that."

"What, then?"

Russell dropped his head into his hands. "Jesus, Catherine. I don't know. I can't think straight."

"Obviously you haven't been thinking straight for a while. You've been following your dick."

He jerked his head up. "There's no need to be nasty."

"And yet somehow I can't seem to stop myself."

"You're hurt. I understand that."

"I'm fucking angry, too. Don't forget that, Russell."

He held up both hands in surrender. "I get it. But bitching at each other isn't going to help the situation. We've got to try to work something out."

"About what?" Catherine demanded. "Custody? I've already said you can see Willow whenever. But she's not going to want to live with you and Nola. That much I know."

"No, not about custody. About a place for me to stay until things are out in the open. I've been thinking that maybe I could stay here at the house until then." At the look on her face, Russell became defensive. "Look, it's my house, too. I even contributed most of the down payment. Why should I be the one forced to leave?"

"Because you're the asshole. This is all your fault."

"This is a no-fault divorce state," he reminded her. "And I'm only talking about staying here for a little while. A few weeks, at most."

"Seriously? Are you insane?"

"Think about it." Russell had adopted his soothing teacher's voice. "It's going to be expensive for me to rent an apartment anywhere in Boston or Cambridge. You know how landlords want first and last months' rent, a deposit. Where will we get that kind of money?"

"Borrow it from your trust-fund baby! That's not my problem!"

"It's our money, Catherine. At least until the divorce is official, everything is a fifty-fifty split. I'm not even certain I'll have to pay child support, realistically, since Willow's not mine and I have my own child on the way."

"Just when I think you can't sink any lower, there you go!"

Russell, trapped in his own delusions, acted as if he hadn't heard her. "Plus, if I'm staying here, I can at least help out by taking Willow to and from school until the administration finds out and does something. I'm hoping Nola and I can keep this quiet until we're married. Maybe even until Christmas."

Nola and I. Married. Catherine stared at him. "Russell, if you think your hottie girlfriend will keep your secret until Christmas, you're a moron. She's a *teenager.* She's going to tell her friends. She'll probably put it on Twitter, for Christ's sake. She'll send Instagrams of her growing belly to all her followers! Some other student will tell her parents, and then the shit will really hit the fan. I hope you've thought about a different career, because you'll probably never be allowed to teach again! And no matter what happens, Nola will definitely not want you to still be living here with your *wife.*"

"What about Willow? Have you thought about her?"

"How can you even *ask* me that, when you couldn't think about your own daughter long enough to keep your dick in your pants instead of screwing one of her classmates?"

"I've told you—Nola's not in Willow's class." Russell's voice was still calm. "She's a senior this year. Eighteen. Almost nineteen."

"That's old for a senior," Catherine said suspiciously. "Have you looked at her driver's license?"

"She took a year off to ski in the Alps with her mother when she was ten."

"Oh. Perfect."

"Anyway," Russell went on, "the age of consent to marry in Massachusetts is sixteen. Nola's old enough to make up her mind about whether to marry me or not. She's an adult."

Catherine picked up the suitcase with both hands and hurled it at him, missing Russell's kneecaps only because he was agile enough to leap to one side. "An adult?" she yelled. "An adult who probably didn't even have boobs or her *period* five years ago! I don't care if you sleep on the street! We can talk to Willow tomorrow like we planned. Then we're *done.* Now go!"

Russell stood up slowly from the couch, eyeing her warily as he moved toward the front door. "I still love you," he muttered. "I wish you weren't being like this, Catherine. It's not like you at all."

Her husband looked so miserable that, just for a second, Catherine remembered how he'd come home two years ago and said his father had died, looking bewildered and lost. She'd cradled his head on her shoulder while he cried.

The problem with life, she thought, was that the past was always with you.

She crossed her arms and backed away from the door, giving Russell and his suitcase plenty of room to leave. "Well, this is the new me," she said. "Get used to it."

Hand tinting photographs was easier than Willow had thought it would be. She'd used colored pencils first—that's what one of the artists she'd found online did—trying them out on a picture of a boy on a skateboard. The kid was mid-flip beneath some low-hanging branches of a tree.

Willow put the picture on the table in front of her and sat back to study it. Outlining the sweatshirt with the red pencil had made it really pop. She was just wondering whether to color the leaves, too, when a couple of senior girls showed up. Art was one of her few classes with seniors, and these girls were always late.

Geneva and Joy: two lumpy, friendly girls. Virtually identical, especially when they were wearing field hockey uniforms and ponytails and those mouth guards that made them look like angry gorillas. One girl had a dad who worked at the State House, but Willow couldn't remember which.

To her surprise, the seniors plopped down at her table instead of taking their usual seats in the back of the room. "So," Geneva said. "Is it true?"

"Is what true?" Willow picked up the yellow pencil, her eyes on the leaves in the photograph. These two girls weren't mean, so she felt no sense of alarm. Just rich kids whose conversations mostly circled around clubbing and college boys, now that they had fake IDs.

"About your dad and Nola!" Joy had leaned forward to whisper, but her whisper was a hiss so loud that everyone in class, including Mrs. Lagrasso, turned to look at them.

"Girls!" she snapped. "Stop bothering Willow and do something productive."

Joy and Geneva pretended not to hear. They pressed closer.

"'Everything we hear is an opinion, not a fact. Everything we see is a perspective, not the truth,'" Willow said, cornered enough to repeat a quote by Marcus Aurelius that Russell had scrawled on their kitchen chalkboard. Thanks to Russell, she knew more than she'd ever need to know about Roman emperors.

"Yeah, well, the opinion around school is that Nola's your dad's—"

"Girls!" Mrs. Lagrasso was standing next to them, her eyes aiming like light sabers at the seniors. "Go to your seats immediately and start working, or I'm docking your midterm grade."

"Yes, ma'am. We apologize for interrupting, ma'am." Joy flashed her whitened teeth at Willow before moving off with Geneva to their usual table, where the two of them pulled out drawing paper and charcoal but did their usual nothing.

"That's a nice effect," Mrs. Lagrasso said to Willow, looking at the photograph. "You might want to let it dry until tomorrow, then go over it again with the pencils to emphasize details."

"Thanks," Willow mumbled, ducking her head. She was trying to hear what Geneva and Joy were saying. Something about a "baby daddy."

Suddenly, it was as if the room went dark and a single thought lit up in her brain: Nola was pregnant.

Willow fixed her eyes on the box of colored pencils, trying to anchor her body in the chair. It was no use. Now she was floating above her body while her mind trotted down a scary black tunnel to the truth: Russell was the father of Nola's baby. That's why Nola had gone to him on Friday afternoon; why Russell didn't come home last night; and why Catherine was acting like a zombie, moving around the house like her soul had been sucked out of her body.

And everybody at school already knew. Except her.

Mrs. Lagrasso called to Willow from the front of the room, her voice like a faint foghorn across the ocean. The other students flowed toward the door and shot curious glances in Willow's direction. "I'd like to speak with you for a moment after class," Mrs. Lagrasso was saying.

Willow ignored the teacher and shouldered through the door. Once she broke free, she escaped down the narrow back stairs that smelled like moldy towels. She had to leave through the secret exit Kendrick had shown her in the music room before anyone else could tell her truths she didn't want to know.

Andrew had died in May, four months ago. Throughout the summer, Eve had seen dogs in the neighborhood sleeping outside on driveways and porches and lawns, lying on their sides, wet tongues loose in their mouths, sides twitching with forbidden dreams, and wanted to join them, taking refuge in sleep.

For weeks after her husband was gone, Eve couldn't even answer the phone. She closed herself in the bathroom and ran the faucet whenever it rang so she wouldn't have to hear it. But her friends had gathered around, steadily pulling her out of the house. Out of herself. And Catherine had somehow managed to persuade her to go up to Chance Harbor and open the house, at least for part of August, saying, "It'll only be worse if you wait, Mom."

Today she was at the mercy of steadfast Melinda, her best friend, hurtling south on Route 1 toward Ipswich. Melinda blew through two yellow lights as if there weren't a canoe attached to the roof of her car with nothing more than twine they'd found in Eve's garage.

Melinda was determined to take her canoeing, despite knowing even less about canoes than Eve, who had found Andrew's canoe two months ago, buried beneath all of the other rubble in the garage. Melinda was also laboring under the illusion that they were going to train for a triathlon; after they went canoeing, she said they would go running. Five miles. God save her.

She and Melinda put the canoe in on the Ipswich River beneath a row of tall hemlocks, where the ground was soft with needles. Eve used to bring the girls here on fall weekends to collect owl pellets, which they'd bring home and dissect; in the summers they'd jump off the rope swing tied to one of the tallest trees leaning over the river.

"I don't think I've ever been here when there weren't kids jumping off that rope swing," Melinda said. "Thank God it's off-season. There's a place that rents canoes upriver, and it's like a traffic jam here some weekends, with all of those know-nothings ramming their boats into one another."

"Ha. Like you and I aren't know-nothings." Eve pulled the canoe into the water and steadied it while Melinda stepped into the prow.

"We aren't know-nothings," Melinda said. "We're risk takers. Movers and shakers."

"Though not in the canoe, I hope," Eve said. "I'm in no mood to swim."

"Relax. The water's so low right now, you'd probably be able to wade to shore."

The September sky was a soft, uncertain blue. The purple loosestrife looked bright against the green cattails and the river was dotted with white lilies. Eve was suddenly content, putting her muscle into paddling with Melinda.

Soon they were moving at a good clip along the river, startling painted turtles lined up on logs into plopping into the water. They admired the metallic-looking green dragonflies and a beaver's dam, lifting their paddles to glide soundlessly by a great blue heron on the bank. As they passed, the bird lifted into flight, its wings and body huge and prehistoric above them.

She thought of Andrew, of him not able to see this glorious autumn, this river, the heron's silvery blue silhouette. Zoe wouldn't see it, either. Impossible to believe they were both gone, while here she sat beneath this tender sky on a river that stretched before her, uncaring and serene, peaceful.

Everything Eve was not.

Afterward, they tied the canoe back onto the car and went running. Even now, after several months of consistent training with Melinda prodding her along, Eve found that it was still hard going. It took her a mile or so before she fell into the right rhythm. Running was all about breathing, no matter how far you ran.

She was drenched in sweat by the time they returned to the parking lot and began stretching. Melinda was a powerfully built woman, short and stocky, half Italian, her black hair streaked with silver. Andrew used to call them "Mutt and Jeff" because Melinda was Eve's physical opposite; Eve was lanky and tall, had cut her curly light brown hair to chin length in her forties and had kept it that way since. Less bother. Occasionally she thought about coloring it, now that she had a few streaks of gray, but honestly, what would be the point?

Andrew had teased her about looking like Amelia Earhart. When Eve was let go from her job at the hospital, he'd given her a brown leather bomber jacket and a plaid scarf to celebrate "your new era of Amelia Earhart exploration."

"You do remember that Earhart's plane took a nosedive, right?" Eve had reminded him. "Is that the kind of ending you have in mind for me?"

After a moment of red-faced embarrassment, Andrew had recovered and said, "At least she was doing what she loved. Now it's your turn."

Melinda brought Eve back to the present, saying, as she always did after a run, "Well, we won't set any world records, but we got off our duffs and broke a sweat. Good job."

"No small feat for old mares like us," Eve agreed. This was her standard line, too. But Melinda heard the off note in her voice.

"You okay?" Melinda asked.

It would be a long time before Eve would be okay again. But at least today she could give a more concrete answer: "I'm worried about Catherine."

"Wow. That's different," Melinda said. "I always think of Catherine as a beacon of sanity in our crazy world. Why?"

"She just told me that she and Russell are getting divorced."

"You're kidding!" Melinda stopped stretching and stared at Eve. "Those two always seemed joined at the hip. What's going on?"

"I don't know. It's all very sudden and mysterious." Eve recounted the weekend's events. "All Catherine said when she asked me to stay with Willow for the rest of the weekend was that she needed time away. A part of me even wondered if Catherine was asking me to hang out with Willow for my sake, not hers. She knows how down I get on weekends, because Andrew and I always used to do something together on Sundays."

Eve had to pause and swallow the lump in her throat, ambushed suddenly by fragmented memories of Sunday brunches and movies. Andrew had been the sort to plan out every day. She had loved that about him. "But then Catherine came home Sunday night and dropped this bomb with no explanation at all."

"Bizarre." Melinda bent over and grabbed her ankles. Her voice was slightly muffled against her knees. "Have you talked to her since?"

"Twice. Monday morning before she went to work and again last night." Eve leaned against the car and did faux push-ups, struggling a little to breathe and talk at the same time. "Both times she said the marriage is over. 'A flatliner,' she told me."

"And you haven't spoken to her again?"

Eve shook her head. "I tried calling several times, but she hasn't picked up my calls. She's not responding to my texts and e-mails either. At this point it feels like I'm harassing her."

"Maybe Catherine's avoiding you because she's afraid you're going to try to change her mind."

"She'd be right," Eve said. "I can't stand the thought of her marriage going up in flames. Catherine and Russell have worked through so much already. I hate what a divorce could do to Willow, too, after what that poor child has been through. Catherine should definitely not be making such a sudden move."

"It could be less sudden than you think," Melinda suggested.

"No. I would have picked up on something."

Melinda frowned. "It could be an untenable situation. Russell could have done something unforgivable."

"I can't see it. Russell has always been rock-solid. Pretty much the most reliable man on the planet."

"On the outside, sure," Melinda said. "But there are always things inside a marriage that we can't possibly know. One of them could be having an affair."

"Maybe. I just don't know." Eve bent down to hide her expression, retying a shoelace that was perfectly tied already. She knew it was possible to feel like you were falling in love even if you were married. She had nearly demolished her own marriage in a few short, turbulent, painful weeks with another man. She'd never told any of her friends about her affair. Or about Andrew's.

"How's Willow handling all this?" Melinda asked. "Have you talked to her since the weekend?"

"No. She's not answering her phone or replying to my texts, either. I'm worried."

"That *is* worrying." They reached for their water bottles and drank. "So what are you going to do?"

"I was considering driving down there tonight," Eve said. "Bad idea, right?"

"Terrible," Melinda agreed. "What time are you leaving?"

"Right after rush hour."

At home, Eve showered and ate a light supper of salad and half a tuna sandwich. By eight o'clock she was on the road to Cambridge and imagining what excuse she could use to explain her sudden appearance on Catherine's doorstep. The most plausible one was that she'd gone to a movie with her friend Bea, who lived in Brookline.

No. Catherine would probably see through any excuse, and why bother to lie?

Eve pulled up in front of Catherine's small white two-story house less than an hour later. Built in the 1850s, it looked like a doll's cottage, sandwiched between a brick prewar apartment building and a massive pink Victorian with a wraparound porch. That was the wonderful thing about Cambridge: there were architectural surprises around every corner.

Catherine's car was parked in the driveway and lights blazed in every room. Eve locked the car and felt her way up the dark front walk. She hesitated on the front porch—should she knock? Ring the bell?—then opened the door the way she always did, calling Catherine's name.

Willow greeted her, running down the stairs with a finger to her lips. For a moment, silhouetted against the hall light, with her new curves and her straight, pale blond hair spread like a shawl across the shoulders of her blue hoodie, Willow looked so much like Zoe that Eve couldn't breathe.

Not that Zoe had ever thrown her arms around Eve's waist the way Willow did right now. Since middle school, Zoe had struggled to be independent, constantly trying to push her parents away. She'd succeeded with Andrew.

"Hey," Eve said, pulling Willow close. "You okay? I've been trying to reach you for two days."

"No. Everything totally sucks. Dad's back."

"Back?" Eve asked, not knowing what to think.

Willow nodded. "He's in the kitchen with Mom. Fighting. All they do is fight. They made me go upstairs." Willow burrowed her face against Eve's leather jacket. "Make them stop."

"Oh, baby girl. I'm sorry, but I'm not sure I can," Eve said, eyeing the hallway to the kitchen. Maybe Russell and Catherine were working things out after all and she'd panicked for nothing. "I should probably go. I can visit another time."

"No! You have to stay with me!" Willow took her arm and led Eve into the living room.

Willow had regressed; she sounded petulant and half her age, Eve thought. Her granddaughter's anxiety—so out of control when Zoe first left, then gradually calmed through years of therapy, even medication for a little while—was clearly kicking back in again. Willow was even sucking on a lock of her hair, a habit she'd worked hard to break in middle school.

Catherine's usually tidy living room looked like the scene of a bar brawl. The painting over the couch—pears and a blue pitcher—hung at a cockeyed angle. Dirty plates and mugs cluttered the coffee table. A heavy white ceramic lamp had toppled over and the braided rug was rucked up on one side. Eve hoped there hadn't been any actual physical altercation between her daughter and Russell.

In the dim light cast by the overturned lamp, she could see that Willow's eyes were red-rimmed and swollen. "What's going on, Willow?" Eve asked. "What are they fighting about?"

"You don't know?"

"No."

"They're getting divorced." Willow dropped onto the couch and tucked her hands beneath her thighs. "Dad wants to marry somebody else."

"*What?*" Eve felt the wind go out of her so fast that she nearly doubled over. She sat down beside Willow and put an arm around her shoulders. "Are you sure?"

"Yeah. You would be, too, if you knew."

"Knew what?" It was wrong to quiz Willow, but Eve was desperate for information.

"About the *baby*!"

Confused, Eve released Willow and swiveled to face her. "What are you talking about? *What* baby?"

"Dad's." Willow pressed her face against Eve's shoulder. Eve smoothed Willow's hair, thinking, Oh, Christ. That bastard hadn't just cheated on her daughter. He'd gotten another woman pregnant! If Russell had listed a thousand different ways to hurt Catherine, this would have been at the top of the list.

Eve clenched her jaw in fury. "I need to talk to them."

She felt her granddaughter's breath on her neck as the two of them walked rapidly down the hallway. When Eve stopped suddenly in the kitchen doorway, her granddaughter ran into her, nearly propelling Eve over the threshold. She clutched the doorframe to halt her momentum.

Catherine and Russell didn't even notice. They were seated on opposite sides of the kitchen table. The table was one Andrew had made for them, a long pine table like the one Catherine had admired in a farmhouse they'd stayed in during a family trip to Provence. Her daughter was leaning across it, shouting: "Well, too bad! You should have thought of that before! You'll be lucky if I don't go after your pension, too!"

Russell's head was bowed, his broad shoulders hunched over. Eve flashed back to a scene similar to this one in her kitchen many years ago, when she and Andrew could have been caught in a similar tableau. Her anger at Russell transformed into something more complicated.

Somehow, she found the courage to speak. "Hello, Catherine. Hello,

Russell." Eve hated the formal, strained sound of her own voice. "I hadn't heard from you two in a while, so I thought I'd drop by."

She hoped she was smiling and not grimacing. Russell looked miserable and exhausted, while her daughter radiated a furious energy that was causing her cheeks to turn pink and her delicate profile to look fierce and sharp.

"*Drop by*?" Catherine swiveled around to face Eve and stood up, rolling her eyes. "Are you insane, Mom? It's almost nine thirty! You didn't just *drop by*. You're here to poke your nose in where it doesn't belong!"

"Nana does so belong, and I want her here," Willow said from behind Eve.

"And I told you to stay upstairs while your father and I talk," Catherine snapped. "Now, go do your homework!"

Eve thought Willow would obey. She'd always been an obedient child. Nothing like her mother in that way. But the rules of the game had clearly changed. Her granddaughter stepped forward and stood next to Eve in a gunfighter's stance, crossing her skinny arms. "What does it matter if I do my homework? It's not like I'm going to school tomorrow," Willow said. "Obviously."

"Goddamn it, Willow. I said go upstairs *now*!" Catherine shouted.

"There's no need to shout at her, Catherine," Russell said. His face was bleached of color and his voice sounded hoarse. "None of this is Willow's fault."

"Oh, I know that. We *all* know whose fault this is," Catherine said, spinning around to face him across the table again.

Catherine had moved so fast that the corner of her sweater caught on the chair. For a moment she was trapped in that twisted position, her lip curled in a snarl.

Eve was too stunned to speak. Catherine had always been the peaceful, sensible one in their family. The tranquil baby who smiled at everyone, even strangers on the street. The child she and Andrew always counted on to be responsible. Reasonable. Thoughtful. Calm. She'd been able to quiet her little sister's tantrums like nobody else, leading Zoe by the chubby hand to look at a butterfly or lie in a sunny corner and read a book. Zoe had always looked up to Catherine, until Catherine had started scolding her like everyone else. Then it was war.

Eve stepped forward to free Catherine's sweater from the chair despite how easy it was to imagine her daughter turning on her with the same rage she was showing Russell. Catherine was too focused on her husband to notice.

"Fine," Catherine said. "I won't shout at her, Russell. You obviously know best. What do you want to do? Have a family meeting? Sure! Let's take this opportunity to explain to Willow why she's going to have to leave school without even having a chance to go back and clean out her goddamn *locker*."

"I don't think we need to explain things to Willow," Russell said evenly. "Not right now. This is between you and me."

"Why? Don't you think Willow deserves to know what's really going on? Are you trying to *protect* her now? Sorry. It's too late for that. So let's give Willow the bare facts." A pulse throbbed in Catherine's temple as she turned to Willow. "Honey, your father has been fired for unprofessional conduct. That's why you can't go back to Beacon Hill School tomorrow. Or ever again."

"I know that already," Willow muttered.

"Why were you fired, Russell?" Eve asked. "I thought you were having an affair. Why would they fire you for that?"

"Go ahead and tell my mom what you've been doing with all your spare time. The spare time when you were supposedly writing your *memoir* about being a senator's son. It's almost ten, and I'm going to bed. One of us has to get up tomorrow morning and be functional. Especially now that we're a one-income family."

Catherine fled the room. Eve felt her knees go soft with shock. "What's all this about, Russell? Why did you lose your job?" Behind her, Willow shifted her weight but didn't move.

"Because I've been seeing a woman at school," he said, then sat down at the table again, cradling his head in his arms and knocking over a glass of water in the process. Water pooled toward the edge of the table and began dripping onto the kitchen floor.

"You're a stupid asshole cheater—that's why," Willow said. "Mom's right. You're a perv," she added, and then she was gone as well, her footsteps thundering up the stairs and shaking the small house.

Eve wondered what the hell she was supposed to do now. Russell was clearly devastated, his breathing coming in sharp gasps as he hid his face and tried to control his weeping.

She busied herself at the kitchen counter, rinsing dishes and putting them in the dishwasher. When the counters were clear and Russell was quiet again, she turned around and leaned against the sink, drying her hands on a dish towel. "I have to say that I'm really surprised, Russell. I never would have expected this from you."

Russell straightened, his face flushing red as if she'd slapped him. His forehead was creased from leaning on his wristwatch. "I don't expect you to understand."

"Try me."

He put a hand over his eyes. "Trust me. This is not something you need to hear, Eve."

"Maybe not. But maybe you need to know that my marriage with Andrew was not always easy, either. I was not always faithful."

"What?" Russell dropped his hand and stared at her in shock. "When?"

"You don't need to know the details." Eve was already regretting having told him even this much.

"But you and Andrew stayed together almost fifty years," Russell said. "You were happy."

"We were often happy," Eve agreed. "But every happy ending is built of sand. For a while I was in love with another man. Early in our marriage."

Russell was leaning forward a little in his chair. "So you do understand how it can happen," he said eagerly. "How things can go from zero to sixty even when you're trying to hit the brakes."

"I do." Eve thought for a moment about telling Russell that her husband had strayed from the marriage before she did, but it felt disloyal to Andrew to reveal that. "I understand how sometimes you feel loneliest in a marriage. You can be sleeping in the same bed with someone else but feel like there's an ocean between you. I get that. But my point is that eventually Andrew and I worked it out. You and Catherine could, too."

Eve stopped, embarrassed. She was lying: she and Andrew hadn't really worked things out. She only thought they had.

Russell seemed calmer now. "I'm sorry you went through all that, Eve. But our situations aren't at all parallel. I don't have any choice in the matter. I have to get divorced and marry this other woman. Like you, I never meant to hurt anyone, but things spiraled out of control. And now, well . . ." He held up both hands, palms up in surrender. "Now there's a baby to consider. I'm going to be a father! What else can I do but marry her?"

"You could share custody with the child's mother and pay child support but stay married to Catherine. People do that."

"I know. But I don't want my child growing up without a dad."

He was already a father, Eve wanted to point out, but of course that wasn't strictly true. Russell was Willow's uncle and legal guardian. That wasn't the same. This baby would be his blood. Could even carry his name. Was Russell in love with the baby's mother? He hadn't once mentioned love. But maybe he wouldn't, not to his mother-in-law.

"The thing is, I never thought I'd get the chance to father my own child," Russell was saying. "It's what I've always wanted. And Catherine, well, she wasn't the same after we went through the miscarriages and fertility treatments. She turned a little cold, you know?"

Eve wrapped her arms around her torso, facing him. "What are you trying to say?"

"Oh, you know what I mean. A man needs to feel truly desired if he's going to stay happily married."

"And this new woman desires you?" Eve asked, feeling her jaw clench. "Is that what you're saying?"

"God, yes. It's partly her age, I know," Russell said, in a misguided attempt to appear modest. "After all, she's young, still a senior . . ." He checked himself, but it was too late.

"Your baby's mother is a senior at the school where you teach?" Eve said.

At her tone, Russell looked wounded. Aggrieved. "She's almost out of high school—eighteen now and soon to be nineteen. We'll get married as soon as I can get a divorce. I'm grateful to Catherine for not throwing up any roadblocks there."

Eve's sudden fury propelled her across the kitchen so fast that it felt like she'd flown across it, her feet not even touching the floor. She grabbed Russell's shirt collar and hauled him to his feet. He raised his arms in protest, then dropped them when he saw her expression.

"Get out," she said, not shouting, but issuing the words in a way that made Russell flinch.

"Hey, I thought we were both being honest here," he said. "You had an affair. So did I. Shit happens, right? You know I never meant to hurt any—"

"Stop making excuses! I said *get the hell out*!" Eve shoved Russell so hard that he nearly lost his balance. He recovered and began walking backward out of the kitchen with his hands high in the air, as if she were pointing a gun at him instead of her finger. "Willow was right when she called you a 'stupid asshole cheater.' You aren't in love with this girl. You saw your chance for an easy lay and took it! That's all this is. Get out now, you pathetic jerk, before I call the police!"

"Hey! What are you doing? You can't throw me out of my own house," Russell said, but continued his retreat.

Eve followed him down the hall, her footsteps speeding up so that his did, too, even though he was still walking backward away from her. "This is no longer your home, Russell," she said. "You need to leave now before I call the police. You are unwanted here. Good-bye."

She locked the door behind him. Upstairs, she checked on Willow, who appeared to be asleep with her headphones still tucked into her ears. She walked past the door and found Catherine in bed, too, lying on her back, a pillow over her face. Eve lay down beside her, breathing hard.

"Go away." Catherine's voice sounded like it was coming from the bottom of a well.

"You should have told me what really happened," Eve said. "I'm so sorry."

Catherine pulled the pillow off her face and threw it across the room. "How could I tell you, Mom?" she demanded. "I can't even stand telling *myself* what really happened!"

"How long have you known?"

"Since Friday. Even then Russell didn't tell me everything. It's been coming out in bits and pieces. Apparently Russell has been screwing this girl—this *student*—since last spring. He couldn't help himself, he says. Now he's lost his job as well as his mind. End of story."

"Not quite the end." Eve turned onto her side and looked at her daughter, whose cheeks were shiny with tears.

She remembered, suddenly, a night when she'd come into Catherine's room long ago, when Catherine was eighteen, a high school senior herself. Zoe would have been a freshman. Catherine had stormed upstairs after a party—that in itself was strange, since Catherine wasn't the sort of child who threw tantrums—and announced that Zoe had been at the same party with one of the senior boys, "putting on a big show and letting everyone know how slutty she is."

Eve had tried to lie on Catherine's bed that night, to talk about it, but Catherine had shut down completely and told her to leave. To Eve's shame, she'd done it. She'd left Catherine, upset and alone, and gone out to hunt for Zoe, whom she'd never found. Zoe had come home at five o'clock in the morning, showered, and gone to school as if nothing had happened. They'd grounded her for a month. She just kept sneaking out.

How often, Eve wondered, had she chosen to focus on the troubled daughter over the one who seemed to have it all together?

"What do you mean, it's not the end of the story?" Catherine was asking. "I hope you're not going to tell me I have to make things work with my husband for Willow's sake."

"No, no. I don't believe that," Eve said. "What I meant was, there's more to come. You need to think about what you really want. You have a role to play in how this all unfolds."

"That's simple. I want Russell to burn in hell."

"That's how you feel at this moment, sure. But given a choice, would you work on this marriage, Catherine? I know Russell wants to be involved in this child's life, but it doesn't sound like he's in love with the mother. Do you still love him?"

"I did until, let's see . . . about eight o'clock on Friday night. Now I don't know." Catherine covered her eyes with one hand. "I thought we had a good marriage, Mom. Russell and I were still having sex, for God's sake! And now he's fathering a child with a child!"

"You could still try to dissuade him," Eve said, "if that's what you really want. You could fight for your marriage and win, maybe. I don't think Russell's thinking very clearly."

"He's thinking with his dick," Catherine said. "But it doesn't matter. I'd divorce him even if he climbed those stairs and came into this bedroom on his knees. How can you even suggest that I think about working on my marriage after something like this?"

"Because I think it's important for you to consider what *you* want, apart from Russell."

Catherine's laughter had a hysterical edge. "But that's the point. I've never been apart from Russell! We raised each other, Mom. I've never even had sex with another man. Is that pathetic or what? I don't know what I want because I don't know who I *am*. I always thought I was going to be a wife and a mother. For a while I was, but now it turns out that everything was a sham."

"No, it wasn't. Everything between you and Russell was a long and complicated marriage, like it is for most of us."

Catherine turned away from her, shoulder and hip protruding from the sheet, her waist dipped and narrow. She was very still. Eve didn't know whether to go or stay. She felt hollowed out by sorrow. Would telling Catherine about her own affair help her get through this?

Probably not. Unlike Eve, Catherine had done absolutely nothing wrong.

Eve stifled a sigh, thinking about meeting Malcolm. It was Landing

Day on Prince Edward Island, the day the lobster boats brought in their last catch of the season. Eve had taken Catherine down to the docks at North Lake. Andrew was spending the summer sorting out a company in California, leaving her alone at the house in Chance Harbor with Catherine, who'd just celebrated her second birthday. It was the summer after she'd discovered, during a weekend getaway in Vermont, that Andrew was still seeing Marta, after he'd promised over and over that it was finished.

Malcolm was one of Andrew's many cousins. He had stepped out of his lobster boat after the last of his traps were in and walked along the dock in his waders and yellow rubber overalls, the bib dangling by one strap, revealing the holes in his black T-shirt and the pale skin beneath it. He kept his eyes locked on Eve's as he traveled the length of the splintery dock to where she'd been standing with Catherine to watch the boats.

When he reached them, he kept his eyes on Eve's face, but bent down to touch one of Catherine's blond curls, wrapping it around his finger like a ribbon.

"You're like a little mermaid, you are," Malcolm said. He was speaking to Catherine, but it was as if he'd laid his hand on Eve's head, his fingers warm on her scalp, claiming her as his.

His blue eyes were kind, and he had the same ruddy coloring as Andrew and most of the others in the MacLeish clan. He was widowed with two young children; it had been an unhappy marriage, Eve suspected, though he'd never really said.

Malcolm started dropping by to help her with things around the house at Chance Harbor and often stayed for a beer or even dinner. He would find Eve with Catherine on the beach, too, and help them build elaborate sand castles decorated with driftwood and shells. Other cousins, aunts, and uncles joined them; it was all innocent, except for Cousin Jane's occasional sharp, knowing glances.

Lobster season was over, so Malcolm had plenty of time on his hands; besides, he was family and she enjoyed the way he traced his words in the air with long fingers when he spoke, painting pictures for her of the sea and its storms; of whales bigger than his boat and rocky shores where some said they'd seen mermaids; of the ghost ship ablaze on certain nights, a burning ship that disappeared whenever sailors tried to reach it in time to save the men jumping overboard.

A few weeks after they'd first met on the docks, Malcolm leaned across her kitchen table at Chance Harbor and said, "I know this is the wrong thing to say, but I'm in love with you, Evie."

Evie. Nobody had ever called her that before. It made her feel like a different person, a woman who was still hopeful about life. A woman who felt cherished and desirable. A woman who wore long skirts and thin blouses with silver jewelry that suggested waves breaking on a beach, instead of her everyday fleeces and jeans.

Another few days went by. They began kissing good night. Sometimes they sat in the car and kissed for hours. They held hands whenever they watched TV at her house or found themselves alone on the beach, or they swung Catherine between them if they couldn't do that.

Finally, she invited Malcolm into her bed. "I want you to stay with me," she whispered. "Just one night, all night long. I want to be close to you. To sleep with you, that's all. Nothing more has to happen."

Andrew had flown from California to a sales conference in Europe by then, and Eve suspected he might be seeing Marta still, but she didn't ask him.

She had thought it would be difficult to undress with a stranger, but Malcolm made it easier by declaring that she was beautiful, lovely, desirable. He'd repeated those words with every article of clothing she dropped to the floor in front of him.

"I'm a lucky, lucky man," he'd said when she was naked, his eyes lingering on Eve's breasts and hips and thighs and face. When she finally lay down beside him, Malcolm's body felt like home, so similar to Andrew's build, yet with a fisherman's muscles and scars. She'd traced them with her fingers, her tongue.

They had kissed and tangled their limbs like teenagers, growing slick with sweat, and of course they didn't just sleep together. They made love several times that night, until both of them were drunk on fatigue and rubbed raw. Malcolm sneaked out of the house carrying his boots, but he came back again and again that summer.

Eve listened to the grandfather clock in the front hall chime the hour. Ten thirty. "Do you want me to leave?" she asked as Catherine turned onto her back again.

"I don't care." Catherine glanced at her mother. In the dim light, her narrow face glowed a milky white. "Just don't try to tell me I can work things out with Russell. I can't do it. I won't do it. I'm going to divorce *him* even if he doesn't divorce me. After that I don't care what he does."

"Don't lie. It doesn't suit you."

"No?" Catherine's face was ugly with rage. "Who does lying suit, then? Everybody else? Zoe was a liar. Russell's certainly doing okay in that department. Who doesn't lie, Mom? You and Dad?"

Eve said nothing, feeling guilty that she'd been more honest with Russell than with her own daughter. She sat up. "You should get some sleep, honey. I'll go to the guest room."

"No." Catherine reached over, circled her fingers around Eve's wrist the way she'd done as a child whenever Eve came into her bedroom to tend her: fevers, bad dreams, a broken heart. "Stay with me, Mom."

Eve lay back down against the pillows, her daughter's delicate fingers anchoring her firmly in place. Eventually Catherine's breathing slowed.

When Eve looked over at her again, Catherine was asleep, her lips parted, her soft blond hair falling over her eyes as it always had when she was a child. Eve brushed the hair off Catherine's forehead and watched her sleep, wishing she could smooth away the hurt, too.

CHAPTER FOUR

As she entered the examining room for her next appointment, Catherine glanced through the slim file. Her patient—a two-week-old baby boy—had been born vaginally without complications, with normal weight and Apgar scores. Why, then, was his head lolling on his neck? And why was he wheezing?

Catherine found the mother's name on the chart and said, "Hello, Kayla. My name is Catherine Standish. I'm one of the nurse practitioners here. What's going on with Jamie?"

"He's sick." The girl was texting; she didn't lift her eyes from the phone.

God help me, Catherine thought, barely restraining herself from grabbing the phone out of the girl's hands and tossing it into the waste bin for needles.

She lay the baby down on the exam table and began undressing him. With infants, one common cause of breathing difficulties was RSV, a respiratory virus. But there was more going on here. Most babies made eye contact during exams or screamed bloody murder, depending on temperament. This one did neither. He was dull-eyed and listless. Floppy.

"Tell me more," she urged the mother. "How long has Jamie been sick?"

"Two days? Maybe three."

Catherine glanced at the girl as she took the baby's temperature. The mother couldn't be much older than Willow. Or Nola. Why did so many ill-equipped teenagers pop babies out like PEZ dispensers, while women like her, with careers, cars, retirement plans, and—until last week—a husband, couldn't bear children, even with armies of fertility specialists?

No. She wasn't going to dwell on that, or on Russell and his baby. *Get through the day,* Catherine told herself. *Then you can fall apart.*

Kayla had blue-black hair and a butterfly tattoo on her wrist. Her cargo pants were too tight, the loose skin of her post-pregnancy belly gathered above the waistband, mushroom white beneath the hem of her black T-shirt.

"What are his symptoms?" Catherine asked. "Has Jamie been vomiting? Running a fever? Crying more than usual?"

"All that stuff, yeah."

"I see." Catherine glanced at the thermometer. No fever now. She measured the baby's head and length, then moved Jamie's frail limbs between her hands to test his reflexes. They were off, but maybe he was dehydrated. "How much did he vomit?"

"A shitload," the girl said. "He makes himself puke when he cries. I had to shake him to shut him up." Kayla continued to glare at her phone, texting with rapid, furious jabs of her thumbs.

"You *shook* him?" Catherine took a deep breath to control her temper. Shaking a baby, especially as young as this one, would pitch the brain back and forth inside the skull, potentially causing brain damage.

The girl rolled her eyes without looking up from her phone. "It's not like I shook him *hard*," she said. "I just needed him to pay attention. I swear to God he's ADHD. Jamie's always crying to get me to pick him up. But I don't want to spoil him, you know?"

"There's no such thing as spoiling a baby." Catherine knew her anger was starting to seep through. "Babies only cry when they need something. It's your job as a parent to figure out what it is. Tell you what. I'm going to sign you up with a nurse who teaches free parenting classes at the hospital, okay? She can help you. I know the first few months of motherhood can be rough. And it's hard to raise a baby on your own."

"I'm *not* alone!" Kayla said. "And my boyfriend's old enough to know what to do with a baby. He's already got two."

Catherine focused on keeping her expression neutral as she palpated the infant's abdomen. She didn't like what she saw. The baby's rib cage was bruised and there was an inch-long, plum-colored bruise on his hip. She held the stethoscope to the infant's chest, then gently diapered and dressed him.

She picked him up and held him close to her shoulder, cupping his hot head with her palm. His bones felt hollow. As always with cases of neglected and abused kids in her care, there was a tug in her lower belly. She longed to walk right out the door with this baby and take him home.

"How old are you, honey?" she asked.

"Sixteen. Everybody says I look older, though." Kayla slid her phone into the back pocket of her pants. A second later, the phone buzzed and she whipped it out again. "Crap," she said, staring at the screen. "Is this going to take much longer? I really gotta be someplace."

"Just a few more minutes. Wait here. I'll be right back." Catherine carried the baby out to the main office, where she asked Alicia to call an ambulance. Then she called the Department of Children and Families to file a report.

A hectic hour later, everything was sorted. She'd filed the 51A form, and the emergency team from DCF had arrived at the office to accompany Kayla and her child to the hospital in the ambulance. Afterward, Catherine locked herself in her office, allowing herself to cry as she wrote up her notes and waited for the call from the social worker.

Finally it came. "The pediatric neurologist agrees with you," the social worker reported. "Definitely shaken baby syndrome. Kayla will be charged with abuse."

Catherine closed her eyes. "Is that really necessary? Kayla's just a kid herself. She needs help, not a criminal record. And what if the father did it?"

"We know that's a possibility, of course," the social worker said. "This wasn't my choice, either. I promise we'll do a solid investigation."

Alicia knocked on her door a few minutes later, telling Catherine her next appointment had canceled. When she saw Catherine's expression, she said, "Go home. We can handle your appointments."

"No, you can't," Catherine said. "We're already overbooked. And I'm better off working here instead of going home and stewing about that poor baby. I'll go out to eat my sandwich and get some air, but I'll be back in an hour."

Catherine took a brisk walk down to the Charles River, where she escaped most days to eat lunch in solitude. The river was nearly empty of boats now that it was September. She choked down half of her food without tasting it, then called Bethany.

She and Bethany had been friends since nursing school; they'd been bridesmaids for each other the same year and had planned their pregnancies for the next, imagining their children growing up as close as cousins. They'd succeeded in getting pregnant the same month and had happily swapped tales of morning sickness and thickening waists. Catherine, however, lost her baby at four months, and lost every baby after that, though one pregnancy had lasted six months. Four miscarriages in all.

Bethany had her baby, and, two years later, twin boys. Her oldest, a daughter, was in high school now. Catherine hadn't thought she could be around Bethany and her family. Had been afraid she'd resent Bethany for her easy fecundity and jolly disorganization as a mother. Instead, the opposite had happened: Bethany's children had become part of Catherine's family as well.

She adored Bethany's kids, who were all as noisy and plump as her friend. They often spent weekends and vacations together. Willow had benefited from this as well: Bethany always knew what to do in a crisis, whether that involved finding a gluten-free, nut-free recipe for a school bake sale or where to go for the perfect trendy sneakers at the start of school.

They always shared schedules on a Google calendar, so Catherine knew Bethany would be home now. "Hey," Bethany said. "Thank God you called. I was just waging a war on dirt, and dirt was kicking my butt. What's up?"

Catherine spilled it all: Russell and Nola, the shaken baby, and how she'd nearly fallen apart today at work. Bethany made all of the right sympathetic noises, including, several times, "that rat bastard" when Russell's name was mentioned, then said, "We definitely need a pub date! Friday okay?"

"Friday's perfect," Catherine said, and smiled for the first time all day.

Still, she went through her afternoon appointments like an automaton, depressing tongues and listening to heartbeats, issuing prescriptions and counseling worried parents about fevers and teething, eyesight and speech, vaccinations and autism. She probably shouldn't be here at all. Willow was at home alone. Catherine hadn't had the heart to enroll her at the public school right away. She'd hated to go to work and leave her; she'd done so only after extracting a promise from Willow that she'd stay in the house and text her every two hours, which Willow had done. This was just the beginning of her life as a single parent, and Catherine was already worn-out.

She furiously wrote out an antibiotic prescription for a mother whose toddler had an ear infection. "Your daughter may need tubes, since this is her third infection in the past six months," she said, trying to smile at the child—a little girl all in pink, right down to sparkling ballet shoes—and feeling the edges of her face crack.

"Tubes?" the mother said in alarm. "What do you mean?"

"It's no big deal. A minor surgical procedure to prevent recurring ear infections and possible subsequent deafness."

"My God." The mother had paled.

"We'll talk about that next time," Catherine said, thinking, *You think that's bad? Ha! Let me tell you about my husband. Please.* To the little girl, she said, "Okay, my nurse, Julia, is going to give you a shot."

"But I don't want a shot!" the little girl screamed.

"Too bad," Catherine said. "Everybody gets shots here."

She ignored Julia's horrified glance and racewalked out of the room. Anger, she was discovering, was a useful emotion. It let you do and say all of the things you would normally filter out.

In the next exam room were a father and son. The boy was four years old, according to his chart, but he looked younger. He was sitting on the table and working so hard to breathe that he was sucking his abdomen in beneath his rib cage. His hair was a startling orange and his hazel eyes were enormous and frightened.

Catherine introduced herself and asked their names to double-check them with the chart, as she always did. "This is my son, Brady," the father said, after introducing himself as Seth Cunningham.

She talked to Brady about the animal posters hanging on the wall as she examined him. His heartbeat was abnormally fast. A clatter of racehorse hooves in her ear. He was really struggling to take in oxygen.

"Does Brady have a history of asthma?" she asked.

The father, Seth, shook his head. "I don't know."

She gave him a look before moving the stethoscope to Brady's skinny back. Seth's hair was a rich chestnut color that had probably started out as red as his son's; despite his height, Seth had the biceps and barrel chest of a man who worked in construction or some other trade that required lifting heavy objects. She wondered what he did for a living. Maybe he was a highway worker or a mechanic?

No, the hands and nails were too neat. Probably Seth was unemployed—that would explain why he was here with his son in the middle of the day—and spent his free time working out.

"Has Brady been sick long?" she asked.

"I'm not sure."

"He isn't running a fever. Was he before?"

"I don't know. I just picked him up this morning."

"Does he have a history of allergies? Or has he suddenly come into contact with some new substance or a pet? This looks like an asthma attack provoked by an allergic reaction."

Seth raised his hands. "No idea. You tell me."

Anger blurred her vision for a moment. Some fathers shouldn't answer to any name but "Loser." How could this man not even know if his own kid had allergies? Brady was four years old!

Divorced dad and absentee father, probably. The sort who got his kid once a week and thought he was doing his fair share.

She warmed the stethoscope and listened to Brady's chest. Kids suffering from pneumonia typically had rales, which sounded like a crackling noise and indicated sputum in the airways. Those experiencing asthma attacks had dry coughs and wheezed when they exhaled, like Brady.

She'd better act fast. Brady was starting to panic, the anxiety amplifying his symptoms. His lips were starting to take on a blue tint.

Catherine asked Julia to bring an inhaler. "This is what I call my special rescue medicine," she told Brady. She demonstrated how he should put it in his mouth and watched while he took a puff. To the father, she explained that she was using a pressurized, metered-dose inhaler.

"What's in it?" Seth asked.

"Albuterol, a corticosteroid that acts as a bronchodilator," she said. "You wouldn't want to rely on it for long-term or regular treatments, but it's a good emergency measure when he suffers a flare-up like this. We'll have to run tests, of course, but I'd say Brady has chronic asthma and this is a flare-up." She smiled at Brady, pleased to see color seep back into his cheeks. "You sit there for a few minutes with Nurse Julia and rest, okay? Your dad and I are going to my office to set up your next appointment."

Catherine led Seth across the hall and seated herself behind the desk. "Why don't you know anything about your son's medical history?" she demanded. "He could have died! You should have brought him to the ER, not waited for an appointment here. What's *wrong* with you?"

Seth had remained standing. Now he narrowed his eyes at her. "What the hell's wrong with *you*, scolding me like a kid in the principal's office? Not very professional, sweetheart. Did you get up on the wrong side of the bed or something?"

"Did you actually call me *sweetheart*?" Catherine folded her arms, trying to contain the rage building beneath her diaphragm. "You'd never do that if I were an MD instead of a nurse practitioner."

"I thought you *were* a doctor!" Seth sank into the chair across the desk from her and rubbed his face. "Look, I apologize. We got off on the wrong foot. I came here because I live close by and I needed to know how to help my son."

"Know his medical history, for starters!" Catherine shouted. "Is that really so difficult?"

Seth glared back at her. "You don't know one thing about me or my situation! Look, thanks for seeing us. I appreciate what you did for Brady. Now, just give me what we need and we'll be on our way."

"He needs an asthma specialist."

"You're right, *Ms. Standish*." Seth made a big show of reading her name tag. "I'm sure Brady needs more than just a *nurse practitioner*."

"Yeah, like a father who's more than half-awake," Catherine said under her breath. She wrote a prescription and handed him a business card with the name and number of a pediatric respiratory specialist. "Go see this guy. He'll help you put Brady on regular medications, as well as providing a prescription for emergencies like these."

"Thank you." Seth stood up. "I would tell your supervisor exactly how helpful and compassionate you've been, but I don't have the energy to deal with that right now. I'll hope your mood improves and you won't terrorize any more parents."

After he'd gone, Catherine dropped her head into her hands. Three more hours until she could go home.

A sharp rap on the door brought her head snapping upward. "Yes?"

"It's me. Julia."

"I'll be out in a minute."

"I'm sorry, but we need to see you right now."

We? "All right. Whatever."

The door opened and Julia entered the office. She stood with her back straight and her chest out, like an opera singer. "Your next patient is here, but I've given her to Dr. Wentworth," she said. She spoke slowly, forming every syllable, as if Catherine were deaf and lip-reading.

"Why?" Catherine said. "I'm fine."

"No, you're not. You've made two patients cry, and the doctors and I all heard you shouting at that last patient's dad. Everyone heard you, actually," she added, glancing over her shoulder in the direction of the crowded waiting room. "We think you need to go home."

"I can't do that," Catherine said. At home, everything reminded her of Russell.

Last night, she'd crammed his clothing into trash bags and taken apart his bike so he could carry it on the subway. She was damned if she'd give him their car. She'd put the bulging trash bags, along with the bike, outside the bulkhead to the basement. It was going to rain today and she was glad, imagining the soggy cartons disintegrating in Russell's hands. She'd even poured his beloved Chinese tea into the compost. Then she'd had a sudden fit of fury and dumped the compost into the kitchen disposal. Grinding it up was another rare moment of satisfaction.

"Well, you can't stay in the office," Julia was explaining patiently. "You're not doing anybody any good here."

Now Dr. Patel, the pediatric director, crowded into the room behind Julia, frowning behind her square black eyeglasses. "No, indeed not," she said kindly. "You are scaring the patients, Catherine. We have had several complaints. You must take the rest of today off and possibly the week as well, while you hopefully resolve whatever matter is obviously troubling you. I believe we owe you vacation time."

"I'm sorry," she said, and burst into tears.

Awkwardly, Dr. Patel leaned her round body across the desk and patted Catherine's shoulder, enveloping her in a cloud of cinnamon and coffee. "I am sure things will look better to you in the morning."

"I seriously doubt that," Catherine said.

She gathered her things and left the office, ignoring the stares of everyone in the waiting room even when the metal water bottle dropped out of her backpack and clanged onto the tiled floor. Catherine froze as the water bottle rolled across the room, everyone's eyes on it as if the bottle were a grenade, then picked it up and fled the building.

It was raining hard by the time she emerged from the T station closest to home. She'd forgotten her umbrella and kept her head down as she hurried along Mass Ave to the subway stop. The rain stung like tiny bees against her face and arms, her skin too chilled from the office air-conditioning. Several of the physicians and nurses seemed to require air-conditioning year-round now for their menopause-induced hot flashes. Last month one of them had bought battery-operated "crone fans" to put on all of their desks. Everyone had laughed about it. Oh, the hilarity of women past their prime! Sisters applauding their own invisibility and inevitable decline!

Sisters like her, almost. She was nearly forty. About to enter a new stage of life.

Catherine stopped to catch her breath, leaning against a building as she thought about how Russell was about to enter a new stage as well. But his would be crammed with the adventure and excitement of new beginnings, of parenthood. Everyone would perceive Russell as vibrant and lucky, with his young wife and baby. She would be a crone, while Russell would be like one of those aging male movie stars who always gets paired with dewy, twenty-year-old starlets.

There was a sharp tapping on the window next to her. Catherine flinched and raised her head, blinking against the rain. Water streamed down the collar of her blouse, and her hair was a misery of wet strands clinging to her head.

She wiped her eyes. To her horror, the person on the other side of the glass was the father she'd shouted at in her office: Seth. She blinked harder and saw that she'd been leaning against the window of a small corner store. Now she noticed people emerging from its red door with sacks of groceries. Seth was similarly burdened by bags. His son, Brady, was nowhere in sight.

Probably left him alone in the car, Catherine thought furiously. Like a dog.

Now Seth was outside and standing next to her, so quickly that it seemed like he must have walked straight through the glass. He awkwardly held a red-and-white-striped umbrella over both of them, his bags of groceries—cloth bags, she noted, so Cambridge, so PC, so fucking environmentally correct that she wanted to puke—slung over one arm.

"Are you all right?" he asked, shouting a little to make himself heard over the steady rain and whoosh of passing traffic.

"I'm fine," she snapped back. "What about Brady? Where is he?" She made a point of looking around.

"I left him with my neighbor so I could get his prescription filled and grab a few groceries. I thought maybe ginger ale and ice cream would appeal to him."

"Oh." Catherine felt the anger drain out of her like the water rushing down the gutter in the street.

"He's breathing much better now," Seth volunteered. "And I made an appointment for tomorrow with the asthma specialist."

Want a medal? Catherine nearly asked, but she bit her bottom lip to trap the words inside. She was too exhausted to be combative. Besides, she ought to save her strength for later.

For Russell.

She felt her face do odd things, as if the rain had softened her skin and bones. She imagined her entire body folding in on itself like cardboard. "Good you made that appointment," she said. "See you."

She walked away. Her arms and legs still weren't working properly, as if she were a puppet with tangled strings, but she forced herself to put one foot in front of the other.

"Are you really okay?" Seth called from behind her.

"I'm fine!" she shouted, but her willpower wasn't enough to drive her body forward. She lurched to a stop, causing a woman passing to stare at her in alarm.

Catherine didn't want to imagine what she must look like. She closed her eyes the way she remembered Willow doing when she was small and playing hide-and-seek, as if shutting her eyes and blocking out the world could render her invisible.

"Right. You are definitely *not* fine." Seth had come up behind her. "You'd better come with me."

"My house isn't far," Catherine protested.

"Wherever your house is, it's too far. Mine is closer." Somehow, despite the umbrella and the groceries, Seth managed to take her arm. He began steering her forward.

They'd walked only half a block when Seth turned into the front entrance of a brick building, nodding at a uniformed doorman as they entered a foyer with a marbled floor. Glass doors opened into a pale blue hallway, where it took all of Catherine's strength to remain standing while they waited for the elevator. When it came, she leaned her forehead against one wall of it the minute the doors slid shut.

"Are you sick?" Seth was sounding more and more alarmed. "Should I call your office?"

"No. Not sick." Her voice echoed in the hollow space and she felt her stomach lurch as the elevator began its ascent.

When the elevator doors opened again, Catherine didn't even bother to look at what floor they were on. If Seth were a serial killer, fine. This was as good a day to die as any other. Meek and dripping, she followed him down another blue hallway to a black door with a silver knocker shaped like a lion's head. He unlocked the door and stood back for her to enter first.

They were higher than she'd thought: an entire vista of Cambridge spread before them. The tall windows were streaked with rain. She sat down on a sofa covered in gold fabric and let her head fall back against it, then worried her wet hair might leave a mark and sat up straight again.

Seth read her thoughts. "It's fine. You can't hurt that thing. It's a beast. Sit back. I'll go get Brady from across the hall."

She felt more rainwater snake down her neck and shoulders as she studied the apartment. It was obviously expensive—condo? rental?—and well kept. The parquet wooden floors gleamed between scattered bright Orientals and the artwork was mostly landscapes in greens and blues. Around a corner, she could see into the kitchen, painted a soft plum, copper pans hanging from a ceiling rack. No sign of a child living here.

Now she remembered what Seth had told her in the office: he had just picked up Brady. From where? From whom? An ex-wife, presumably.

Oh, who cared? There were so many miserable marriages in the world. What was one more?

She sternly commanded her muscles to lift her body off the sofa. They disobeyed her and remained limp. How was she going to get home? She needed to shut herself in her bedroom, maybe have a drink or three, figure out what to say to Russell. Decide how they would handle Willow.

What was that awful word? How they would *coparent*?

Whatever happened, she was determined to keep things on an even keel for Willow. She closed her eyes.

The door opened. Footsteps approached. "Is she awake?" Brady whispered. It was the kind of whisper some children used that made them sound like they were trumpeting through a megaphone.

"I don't know," Seth whispered back. "Should we make her a snack just in case?"

"Milk and cookies!" Brady said.

He sounded so gleeful that Catherine felt her mouth twitch, despite her mood. She kept her eyes closed. The boy would want to surprise her. At least somebody should be happy today.

She opened her eyes when she heard a tray being set on the coffee table in front of her. On it were chocolate chip cookies, a glass of milk for Brady, and a pot of tea with two mugs. She made the appropriate noises and found that pretending to be happy actually helped a little.

Brady served her cookies on a red plastic plate while Seth poured the tea. They talked about Brady's breathing, which he described as "sort of weird, like I was whistling, only I can't do that yet!"

After their snack, Brady went off to watch television in another room while she and Seth had second cups of tea.

"I'm so sorry," she said. "I was rude in the office. Then I had the nerve to land on your doorstep."

He gave her a quizzical look. "It's fine. You were upset."

"I would have made it home. But thank you." She had eaten half a cookie to please Brady, but Catherine felt it sticking in her throat now, the crumbs like shards in her throat. She took another sip of tea.

"Want to talk about it?"

She supposed she owed him some kind of explanation. "My husband has left me for someone else. I just found out."

He nodded. "Been there. Done that. It's rough." He jerked his head in the direction of the TV noise, the frenetic music of a cartoon. "Didn't have any access to my child until this morning. Brady's mother broke our shared custody agreement and took him to Amsterdam when he was six months old. She's Dutch. I was fighting to make her bring him home, but got snarled in red tape forever. Then, this morning, she suddenly showed up, said Brady was sick and she was done. The only time he's not clinging to my leg is when he's watching TV, poor guy."

Catherine frowned. "Your ex said she was done with what? With Brady?"

"Apparently. For now, anyway." Seth sighed. "I lost everything, fighting that custody battle: my savings, my house, my job. Pretty ironic."

"Why?"

He made a face. "I'm a divorce lawyer, but I've only seen Brady three times since he was born. That's why I didn't know he had asthma. Now Vivian says it's my turn to raise him."

"And how do you feel about that?" Catherine twisted her hair, still damp, into a knot at the base of her neck.

He looked startled. "I'm delighted. How should I feel? He's my son."

"Oh." She picked up her teacup, steadied her shaking hand against her chest. "That's good, then."

"You have children?"

"A daughter. She's fifteen."

"This news is hard on her, I expect."

"I imagine so. It's tough to tell right now. She acts like everything's fine."

"I'm sure it's not."

"Gee. Thanks."

He held up his hands. "I apologize! It's just that, in my work, I see lots of kids who seem to cope fine until, one day, they don't. Keep an eye on her is my advice. What about you? Will you be all right tonight? Do you have someone who can stay with you for a bit?"

"No. But I'll be fine."

"It might help, not to be alone," he said. "You're never more alone than when someone has rejected you."

"That's a funny way of putting it, but you're right. That's just how it feels: like I've been rejected for not being good enough. Did Brady's mother leave you for someone else?"

Seth ran a hand through his hair, pushing it back off his forehead. She had assumed, when she'd first seen him in the office, that he was a young father, but now she could see from the deep lines across his forehead that he must be as old as she was, at least. "Brady's mother left me for many reasons," he said. "Most are too boring to talk about. Can I get you something more substantial to eat? A sandwich, maybe?"

She shook her head. "I should be going. I'll be all right now."

Seth studied her for a minute, then said, "It could help, you know, to talk to somebody impartial. Someone who's been through this."

"I doubt very much that most people have been through this particular thing," Catherine said, and stood up. "But thanks." She reached out to shake his hand as they reached the front door together.

"Say good-bye to Brady for me."

Seth held her hand and gave her such a searching look that she imagined he could see into the darkest, most terrified corners of her mind. "Call someone to stay with you tonight," he said. "Promise me."

"I promise," she lied, just so he would let her go.

On Thursday morning, Willow was surprised to see the blind beggar in the rainbow hat sitting beneath a tree on Cambridge Common. You hardly ever saw homeless people here. Plus, how would a blind beggar get from Boston to Cambridge?

Maybe she'd taken the subway. Or been picked up and brought to a shelter. That was probably it: Cambridge had, like, five homeless shelters.

Or maybe the woman had come to Cambridge because the Boston cops trotted around on their horses like sheriffs and yelled at people, even at the skaters trying to land ollies on their boards. Like yelling at skaters would help make the world a better place. If every guy had a skateboard, the world would have a lot less war. They should just give out skateboards to terrorists in Afghanistan or wherever.

Willow had been hanging out on Cambridge Common all week, even though Catherine had told her to stay in the house. "Spend this week thinking about where you might want to go to school," Catherine had suggested.

As if she had a choice.

Willow had overheard Catherine talking to her friend Bethany about money, worrying that maybe they'd have to sell the house, or at least the car, if Russell didn't get another job.

She knew, too, that Nana had tried to give Catherine money, but Catherine had refused it. "I'm not Zoe," she had said, whispering so she thought Willow wouldn't hear her.

On the Common, Willow usually sat on a bench near the playground because she'd be invisible here, blending in with the foreign nannies. Most didn't look much older than she was and a lot of them were just as blond.

Catherine had told Willow to stay away from social media, too. She'd taken away Willow's computer "for your own good," forgetting that Willow knew the password for the home computer and could Google stuff on her phone. Russell being fired "for inappropriate conduct with a student" didn't make any of the big news sites, but the story was all over social media. Willow wanted to puke every time she Googled and got another hit. She kept looking for stuff anyway.

The tweets and Facebook posts had slowed down, but every now and then someone made another comment. Half the people posting called Russell a perv who should be locked up and castrated. The other half—kids at her school, mostly—said Nola was a nympho slut who couldn't keep her knees together even around the teachers. *Old bald dude beats out entire Beacon Hill Div. I football team to win Nola trophy,* Trent had tweeted.

Willow kept an eye on the homeless woman, who was strumming her beat-up guitar. The tin can was at her feet, but what was the point? Nobody but students used Cambridge Common during the day, and Harvard students were so rich that they acted poor all the time, wearing ratty polo shirts and crap sweatpants. That woman should come here later, when the professors and businesspeople were walking home from work.

Maybe she was going to stay all day. What else did a homeless person have to do? In a way, that wasn't much different from what Willow was doing now: waiting for nothing.

She shifted her weight on the bench, alternating her attention between the homeless woman and a nanny trying to calm down a little kid who was howling. His cheeks were red and his hair stood up in a mini black Mohawk. The nanny finally picked up the kid and carried him back to his stroller, the little boy's feet thumping against her skinny legs.

Just then, the homeless woman bent over and took something furry out of the bag by her feet. An animal? She set it down on the ground, but it didn't move. Was it even alive?

Willow squinted at it. After a minute she decided it was a dog. It was brown and had a squashed face like one of those stupid Ewoks in the old Star Wars movie that Russell made her watch with him, saying, "This is a classic."

"A classic geek movie," Willow had teased, feeling good that Russell wanted to share a movie with her. She'd even made popcorn.

Stupid asshole cheater.

It was a dog, definitely, running back and forth next to the bench like some dumb windup toy.

Willow had always been scared of dogs, after a bad experience with a pit bull in one apartment she'd shared with her mom, but this one was so small, she wanted to touch it.

She stood up and gathered her things. The nanny in the platform shoes had given the little boy a bottle and he was quiet now, his eyes almost closed as the nanny rocked his carriage with one foot and texted, her dark frizzy hair like a cloud over her round brown face. She glanced up and smiled as Willow walked by, her eyes a surprising turquoise.

Willow wanted to photograph her, but she was afraid to ask. The woman might be illegal, like a lot of the nannies who worked for the parents of kids she knew at school. She didn't want to get anybody into trouble.

The homeless woman was still playing with the dog, making it dance around on its little hind legs. How did she feed it? Did she sleep on the street with it, or take it to her shelter?

Willow kept edging closer, thinking she could sneak up on them, but the dog sensed her presence and whirled around, wagging its stub of a tail and barking. Shit, shit, shit.

"Hello?" Willow said, trying to put a smile in her voice so she wouldn't scare the woman.

She raised her head in Willow's direction, sort of, then turned her head to the side, as if she were listening closely with one ear.

Probably not deaf, Willow thought. More likely just traumatized or nuts. What had happened, that this woman had ended up blind and playing guitar for money? Was she really homeless? She didn't actually look that dirty.

Willow dropped down on the grass next to the puppy and started playing with it. "Cool dog. Is it yours?"

The woman continued strumming the guitar without answering. So either she was deaf or just didn't like talking. That was cool. Willow didn't need anyone else talking to her, telling her shit she didn't want to hear.

"Is it okay if I take a picture of your dog?" Willow asked, glancing up.

To her surprise, the woman nodded. Okay. So she could hear. Unless she was just randomly moving her head.

Willow took out her camera. The dog's head was oversized for its body and it had funny ears that stood up in little triangles. Its muzzle was smashed nearly flat, as if it had been pressed against a wall. Overall, this puppy looked like it had been put together out of spare parts. Willow smiled every time she looked at it.

The woman moved to the far side of the bench and pulled her shawl up to hide half her face. "It's okay," Willow reassured her. "I'm not taking your picture. Just the dog. Your dog made me smile. That's, like, the first time I've smiled in a week. Since my parents decided to get divorced."

The woman turned her head sharply in Willow's direction. Willow pretended not to notice, but she was dying to photograph the woman's clothes up close, to get those contrasts in texture between her rainbow tam and shawl, between awesomely bright fabrics and that black hair in shiny knotted ribbons. The hair was so black, it looked fake.

She kept talking. The guy who took their school pictures did that to relax you. "Yeah, now I'll be like most kids, I guess, shuttling between two houses. I mean, if my dad even gets a house, now that he's having a baby with this girl from my school."

Willow glanced up when she heard a sharp intake of breath. What the hell? The woman was clutching the guitar like it was a joystick and the world was a video game. Was she having a seizure?

No cops around. Never when you needed them. But the nannies in the playground probably knew first aid, right? Willow bet you had to do all kinds of training to get a crap job like changing the diapers on somebody else's kid.

"You okay?" she asked, sitting down beside the woman.

The woman had the shawl pulled up over her nose and turned away, but nodded.

"So you really can hear me!"

The woman nodded again.

"Okay, that's good. I was starting to think maybe you were deaf." Willow settled back against the bench, pleased. Maybe if they got to know each other the woman would let her do a portrait. Or she could do a documentary series of pictures following a homeless person around Boston! Mrs. Lagrasso would love that!

Then she remembered: no more art classes with Mrs. Lagrasso. Her eyes burned. She didn't want to start her whole life over. Not again.

Willow felt the puppy scrambling up her leg. "Do you mind if I hold your dog?"

When the woman shrugged, Willow bent down and scooped the puppy into her arms. Its belly was round and hard and warm. His ears were going crazy, twitching back and forth as he stood on his back legs and tried to lick her face. Willow laughed and said no, like, ten times before the dog curled into a ball on her lap and settled down.

The woman was silent, staring straight ahead now. Willow followed her gaze. They were sitting directly in line with the bench where Willow had been hanging out every afternoon by the playground. She wondered if the homeless woman had been here in the park all along and she just hadn't noticed her.

Willow felt comforted by the dog on her lap. The wagging had stopped, and the dog felt heavy as a brick. Sound asleep, even snoring a little through that mashed nose. So cute.

"I probably won't have any friends for, like, two years after all the shit that's happened," she said. "I know these are first-world problems, but my life pretty much sucks right now."

The woman stood up suddenly and gathered her things. Shit, Willow thought. She'd offended her. Here she was, whining about friends, when this woman probably didn't even know where she was going to sleep.

Willow noticed the woman's boots as she bent to put her guitar in the case and snapped it shut. The boots were better than they should have been, like the kind they sold in that shoe store in Harvard Square with the weird displays. Maybe she'd stolen them. Or it could be that the shelter gave them to her. Anyway, the woman was walking away in those boots, using her cane to guide her, the guitar in her other hand, the big cloth bag slung over one shoulder.

"Hey!" Willow hurried after her, carrying the puppy. "You forgot your dog!"

The woman held up a hand, waving Willow away. She kept walking, shoulders hunched beneath the red shawl, and mumbled something.

"What did you say?" Willow kept pace.

"Friend," the woman said, her voice a surprise, a low growl, as if it took everything she had to say it.

Did she have sore vocal cords? A tracheotomy, like in that horrible TV ad with the ex-smoker talking through a tube in his throat?

Finally, Willow's mind pieced together what she meant: the woman wanted Willow to keep the dog. She felt sorry for Willow and thought she needed a friend.

Crap. Life was really in the toilet if a homeless blind woman felt sorry for you.

"No, no," Willow said. "This is your dog. You need to take it with you. I don't think my mom even likes dogs."

The woman kept walking. She was surprisingly fast for an old blind person with a cane. They'd nearly reached Mass Ave, and the traffic noise made conversation impossible, even if the woman had been willing to talk.

"Really," Willow called, despairing now as the woman continued her head-down journey. "I can't take this dog."

"Friend," the woman said again. Then she pulled the shawl up higher, wrapping it completely around her face except for the glasses, and dashed straight into the oncoming traffic.

Willow screamed and closed her eyes as a car horn blared. When she opened them again, the woman was gone, leaving Willow with the puppy in her arms.

CHAPTER FIVE

On Friday afternoon, Catherine met Bethany after work at the Fiddler's Son, an Irish pub near Porter Square. The place was dark and empty except for three stocky men hunched on barstools, their bodies a trio of commas. The dim light and sticky floor matched Catherine's mood.

She had gone into the office despite everything, and was proud of having held things together even under the scrutiny of Alicia, fish-eyed Julia, and the other medical staff. Now she was relieved to escape.

As they shared a shepherd's pie and a plate of fries, Catherine went into another rant about Russell and Nola and her worries about Willow and money. Afterward, she didn't feel more relaxed or happier, though. She felt woozy and stupid, like a bloated cow in her itchy brown mohair sweater. The kind of cow with the shaggy coat and huge horns. What were they called?

Scottish Highland cattle. Dad had taken them to Scotland once to meet the branch of the MacLeish family that had sensibly opted to stay put instead of immigrating to Prince Edward Island and chancing death by fever or shipwrecks. One of Dad's uncles had raised Scottish Highland cattle. They'd walked through a field of them, and the shaggy prehistoric beasts had terrified Catherine.

Zoe, of course, had gone right up to one and kissed it on the nose.

Her sister had always been the brave one. Or the crazy one, depending on your point of view. Catherine knew her parents had always counted on her to be solid and dependable and that Zoe had resented her as a tattletale and a scold. But what nobody knew was how much Catherine had yearned to be more like her younger sister. She'd always cared too much about failing to take any real risks. She colored inside the lines. Followed maps instead of her nose. And where had that gotten her?

Here, a blowsy, soon-to-be divorcée and single mom, drinking beer in a sticky pub at four in the afternoon.

"Earth to Catherine?" Bethany asked. "Want another beer?"

"God, no." Catherine tugged the collar of the sweater away from her neck. "Another drink and I'll be under the table. I need to keep my wits. Russell's bringing Willow back after dinner. Then I have to help her pack for PEI. She and Mom are leaving Sunday."

"I still think you should go with them."

"I need to work. Who knows what will happen with Russell's job situation? The headmaster asked him to resign. He promised to keep things on the down low with the media, but the story may come spilling out anyway. Russell will probably never teach again."

"Oh, I don't know," Bethany said. "Nola's eighteen, right? In the scheme of things, is that even a worthy headline? Russell's not like that pervy teacher they just caught in Boston."

"What teacher?"

"You know, the guy shooting secret videos of middle school girls in the locker room and posting them online. And Russell's definitely a notch of sleaze above that swim coach who was having an affair with the girl he was training for the Olympics. She was only fourteen."

"I know. But Russell was this girl's teacher. It was still an abuse of power and a violation of school policy. Russell also said her dad might press charges even if the school doesn't. I think that's why he's marrying her."

"Well, duh. Russell adores you. He'd never leave you if he hadn't gotten her pregnant." Bethany ordered them each another beer.

Catherine wondered if Bethany was right. Should she be fighting for their marriage, as her mother had suggested? She didn't see the point. No matter how much she'd loved Russell, he clearly hadn't been happy with her, or he never would have done this.

Bethany was the only friend Catherine had confided in about Russell. Since then, she'd been showing up to watch movies after dinner, hanging out with Willow some afternoons while Catherine worked, and dropping off food that Catherine forced herself to eat. She had a voice like a foghorn and wore layered clothing in bright colors that always made her look like a bouquet of flowers. Red lipstick was her trademark, along with earrings made out of found objects: sea glass, small forks, feathers. Today Bethany's earrings were shiny and green and noisy, some sort of giant insect's shellacked wings. They shouldn't have been beautiful, but they were.

Catherine picked up her beer and sipped it. *Too dumb to live*: That's what she and Bethany used to say about the girls in those horror movies they'd loved to watch on weekends after marathon study sessions in nursing school, the girls who descended into dark basements by themselves even after their friends were hacked to pieces by some masked guy with a chain saw.

"Too dumb to live, that's how I feel," she told Bethany now.

Bethany grinned, understanding the reference at once. "No, you're not."

"Yes, I am. I should have seen this coming."

"That's ridiculous! How could you have?" Bethany demanded. "Russell has always been so attentive and loving. The ideal husband."

"There must have been clues, though. How could I have missed the fact that Russell was sleeping with someone else? Especially a student? Russell and I have been through hell and back together. He wasn't just my husband. He was my best *friend*." Catherine felt her voice scrape raw on the last word. She clamped her lips shut.

"Poor girl. You're a mess, and I don't blame you," Bethany said, putting her arm around Catherine's shoulders. "That's why you should go to PEI with your mom and Willow. You need to get away."

"I can't. They're swamped at work."

"So? I'm guessing you have sick time and vacation days piled up. You need a mental-health vacation."

Catherine shook her head. "That's not what it would be, though. I'd go crazy up there, with nothing to do but go through my dad's stuff and watch Mom cry. It was so bad when we went up in August that I vowed never again. Now Mom's determined to clear out the house and put it on the market, so it'll be even worse. We won't just be saying good-bye to the house but to Dad all over again, and I hate wallowing. You know that about me."

Bethany rapped her knuckles on the table hard enough to make Catherine jump. "Oh, come on! Your mom is grieving and needs your help. You're feeling stuck. Just go! You'll have a better perspective on everything if you do. Besides, this may be your last opportunity to see Chance Harbor."

"Don't remind me." Catherine felt her stomach twist. "I still can't believe Mom's selling the house. Dad would have a fit."

"Maybe not. Your dad was a stand-up guy who loved your mom. He'd want her to do whatever made her life easier."

Bethany was right, of course. Catherine's guilt over her own reluctance to go to Chance Harbor deepened as she said, "Mom has always been better at coping than I am. Clearing out the house could do me in. Sometimes I see Dad on the street, you know? It hasn't fully sunk in yet that he's gone for good."

Bethany put her hand over Catherine's. "I know. You two were so close."

"We were, yeah. Dad always said I was the son he never had. He taught me everything: fishing, sailing, driving a stick. Even how to hunt and dress a deer."

"Zoe, too?"

Catherine felt the smile slide off her face. "No. They were always butting heads. Dad got frustrated with Zoe. Even I thought he was too hard on her."

"Sad."

"I know. But don't feel too sorry for Zoe. She always did exactly what she wanted. Nobody could stop her. I tried. So did my parents. She had plenty of chances to turn her life around, but she never took them." Catherine swallowed another sip of beer, though she didn't really want it anymore. "I don't know. Today, maybe there would be a medication for whatever she had wrong with her. I'm guessing these days she'd be diagnosed with something like oppositional defiant disorder."

"Is that even a real thing? It sounds made-up."

"I know. But it pretty much describes what was wrong with Zoe." Catherine was surprised to look down and see that her knuckles were white on the beer bottle. As much as she missed her sister, she was still furious at Zoe for making life harder for their entire family.

Now Zoe was some horrible statistic and Catherine was left feeling awash with conflicting emotions anytime she thought of her: sorrow at her absence, guilt at the relief she felt about Zoe being gone, resentment at having to clean up after Zoe's emotional wreckage, and rage at what Zoe had done to hurt Willow.

"Was she always wild? Even as a little kid?"

Catherine nodded. "Zoe never stopped moving. She had one bad idea after another. If there was a high point on a walk—a stone wall, a tree—Zoe would be at the top of it before you knew she was gone. The first time she was suspended, she was in fourth grade. The teacher caught her running a casino in her desk and taking money from the other kids."

Bethany laughed. "She sounds interesting, anyway."

"Oh, she was. Nobody was more fun than my sister. Or more beautiful. That was part of her problem, too."

"You're beautiful," said Bethany, always loyal. "Did you look a lot alike? I can't remember. She was blond like you, right?"

"Blonder." Catherine tugged at a lock of her straight hair. "Zoe had that kind of curly blond hair you see on princesses in Disney movies. And she always kept it long. Drove guys crazy, that hair."

"So Willow looks a lot like her mom."

Catherine nodded. "Yes. Zoe had a body to die for, too. Like Willow's going to have. Willow tries to hide hers, but Zoe loved showing it off. Made Dad nuts, the way the boys were always coming around, even when Zoe was in middle school."

"I bet."

"It didn't help that Dad thought Zoe was wasting her potential to do something with her life. She was so smart—quicker than I am, in a lot of ways—but she never paid attention in school. She was too caught up with her friends and boyfriends. Partying hard. It's amazing she ever got into college. Nobody was surprised when she got pregnant and dropped out at the end of her freshman year. Even when my parents said they'd take care of Willow if she wanted to go back to school, Zoe still couldn't get her act together."

Catherine forced herself to take another sip of beer. Why dredge through all of that again? Zoe was gone.

"Nobody knows who Willow's dad is, right?"

"Zoe wouldn't say."

Bethany gave her a sympathetic look. "And I'm guessing you wouldn't try finding him even if you had a name."

"Right. I know that's awful and selfish. The thing is, if the guy wanted to claim Willow, he would have done it by now, right? Zoe was always easy to find. I mean, until she disappeared completely. That's why I want to kill Russell—he didn't just cheat on me; he's abandoning Willow."

"You don't know that," Bethany pointed out. "Some dads become more involved after divorce."

"Maybe. But he'll be busy with his new family, don't forget."

"Go to Canada," Bethany said. "You're tense and exhausted because you're adjusting to life as a single working mom."

Catherine frowned. "That's part of it. But I think it's also because I have to see all of these young moms with their kids and have it constantly thrown in my face that I can't have what they do. I thought I was over not having children of my own, but lately I've been feeling ticked off at every idiot high school girl with a baby. It sucks that Nola's got this cute little baby bump and my husband while I'm stuck with midlife muffin and our mortgage."

Bethany was trying hard not to laugh but failing; she ended up snorting beer out her nose. "Oh my God," she said, mopping her face with a napkin. "Catherine, you are about the last woman on earth with a midlife muffin. You're the size of a minnow! And, okay. Russell will have a baby. But that doesn't guarantee he'll be happy. Wait until Nola's nagging him to change diapers while she does Pilates or whatever."

"What I don't get is why she wanted my husband in the first place."

"Probably some kind of daddy complex," Bethany said, "and Russell is smart and handsome. She's young and thinks she's in love—until she's not. Then Russell's in for a fall."

"You're probably right," Catherine said, "but somehow that still doesn't make me feel better. And you know what the worst thing is?"

"Uh-oh. What?"

"Sometimes I fantasize about Nola realizing she doesn't want the baby, so Russell takes the child and comes back to me. How sick is that?"

Bethany grinned. "Are you kidding? It's the perfect solution. You'd have a surrogate without having to shell out a gazillion dollars."

They started laughing. Then, suddenly, Catherine felt exhausted. Her brain was on overdrive. "I'd better get going," she said.

They linked arms as they stepped outside. It was already getting dark. Another sign that autumn was here. A narrow band of gold light dimpled the underside of purple clouds going black at the edges like rotting fruit.

They parted at the Porter Square T station, where Bethany took the subway back to Boston but Catherine opted to walk home.

She and Russell had agreed that he'd take Willow every other weekend and have dinner with her once a week, on Wednesdays. A traditional custody arrangement, though they'd also agreed to be flexible. So grown-up and civilized. Like co-owners of a business franchise.

Tonight they'd arranged for Russell to take Willow to dinner even though it was technically Catherine's Friday, because Willow would be in Canada next week. Many of Catherine's divorced friends had admitted they'd quickly learned to love having a few nights a month to themselves, with no children to feed or prod through odious homework. "Even if you just take a long soak in the tub with a glass of wine, it's like a vacation," one friend claimed.

But Catherine found the prospect of facing an empty house depressing. She'd have to sign up for classes and start working toward her doctorate or something. Maybe an MBA.

As she opened the front door and heard his voice, she realized Russell must have already brought Willow home. Damn it. It wasn't even six o'clock! She wasn't prepared to see him yet. She reeked of beer and the house was still a mess.

A shiver crawled up her spine. This scene felt too familiar and too strange at the same time. Russell's shoes were paired in the corner by the hatstand. His black wool coat was draped over the hall chair, the same place he always dropped it no matter how much she hounded him to hang it up. At least she wouldn't have to put up with *that* anymore.

"Hello? Willow? Russell? I'm home!"

"We're in the kitchen," Russell yelled back.

Catherine rounded the corner into the kitchen and saw the dog first. A puppy, small enough to hold in two hands. It had a whorled brown and white coat, a curly piggish tail, and a crumpled face like a troll's. The puppy was lying in the middle of the kitchen floor and chewing on one of Willow's old sneakers. At the sight of Catherine, it lifted its ugly squashed face, eyeing her while still teething on a shoelace. It had the nerve to wag its tail.

"Whose puppy?" Catherine said.

"Mine," Willow answered.

Her daughter was perched on one of the stools by the counter. She looked terrible, like one of those strung-out skaters around Harvard Square. Willow's hair was unwashed and stringy, and she wore the same blue hoodie and jeans she'd worn all week.

"What do you mean, it's yours?" Catherine asked.

"Just what I said." Willow lifted her chin, and suddenly it was as if Zoe were sitting in the kitchen with them. Zoe, high on something, telling their parents *no way* was she staying home at night and missing that rave or whatever. All Willow needed was black eyeliner. "It's my dog," Willow said. "I found it in the park."

"Come on, Willow. We can't possibly keep it," Catherine said.

"Why not?" Willow's voice had an unfamiliar edge.

"Well, for one thing, that animal probably belongs to someone else," Catherine said.

"Yes, I told Willow that she has to make signs and hang them around," Russell said. "She should report the dog to the SPCA and the police, too."

Catherine spun around and folded her arms, glaring at him. "Hello? Did anybody ask your opinion? No. This isn't your house anymore. You don't get a vote."

She spoke more sharply than she'd intended, to cover the fact that her knees had gone wobbly the minute she'd seen Russell's face, his familiar broad shoulders encased in his favorite tweed jacket. Russell had never smoked a pipe, but that jacket had always made Catherine imagine she smelled cherry tobacco.

She wanted to do what she had always done when greeting her husband every day for the past fifteen years: to walk over to him and tuck her head in the hollow beneath his chin.

Catherine forced herself to take a deep breath. She didn't want to give Russell the satisfaction of knowing how hard her heart was pounding as she stood there, or of how much she was hoping—foolishly, she knew—that maybe he had arrived early at the house to see her. To tell her that he'd made a horrible mistake.

She would forgive him if he did that, Catherine decided. They'd put this nightmare behind them.

Just then the toilet flushed in the bathroom off the kitchen and the door swung open. "Hey. Just so you guys know? You're out of toilet paper in there."

Nola. In her kitchen! Catherine had seen pictures of her, of course—had scoured through Willow's yearbook to find them, had even Googled and Facebooked and checked out Twitter and Tumblr, searching for images. She'd found plenty. Because of that detective work, she had known before seeing her that Nola would be beautiful. But nothing could have prepared her for the sight of this extraordinary creature.

The girl didn't even look human. More like some digitally generated girl in a video game, the sort who would wear a leather bikini and tall boots while wielding a saber. She was incandescent, too, as if she'd been permanently posted beneath a spotlight. The kitchen dimmed around her.

Nola was several inches taller than Catherine, maybe even taller than Russell. Her flawless skin gleamed across high Nordic cheekbones, and her blue eyes were framed in thick black lashes that looked false but probably weren't. She had the kind of hair meant to be spun into gold or let down from a tower for a prince. Hair that would keep growing as Nola slept and waited, with her rosebud mouth, for a prince to arrive on a white horse and wake her with a kiss.

Too bad the prince had to be Russell. Russell, who surely didn't have any idea what he'd gotten himself into with this girl. Catherine could tell at a glance that Nola was used to being in charge, child or not. Or maybe *because* she was a child, the child of a wealthy family.

As if this really were a fairy tale, Catherine felt her own skin instantly dry and crack. She was aging five years for every second she stood in front of Nola. Her knees and back, always slightly achy after hours of tending patients, were burning with pain, and her hair fell in frayed ribbons across her shoulders.

"Sorry." Russell had the grace not to look at Nola. "We meant to leave before you got here. We just finished dinner and were dropping Willow off when she asked us to come in and see the puppy. Nola, this is my . . ." And here he stopped, reddened, and tucked his hands into his pants pockets, no doubt rendered mute by having his two worlds clash.

Nola stepped forward, well schooled, her hand outstretched to shake Catherine's. "Hello. I'm Nola," she said. "Nola Simone. And you must be Catherine, Willow's mom. It's very nice to meet you."

Dear Miss Manners, What's the proper way to greet your husband's pregnant child-mistress? Catherine ignored the outstretched hand, other than noting the French manicure, and wondered how this child had enough wits about her to openly acknowledge that Catherine was Willow's mom while managing to verbally sidestep the whole "wife" booby trap.

"I wish the pleasure were mutual, but it isn't." Catherine's mind was fumbling through a haze of fury and pain toward the obvious facts now available to her: Nola must have a car. She and Russell had taken Willow out to dinner together and brought her home.

Where were this girl's parents? Why hadn't they put a stop to things? Or had they only found out about Nola and Russell when everyone else had, when it was too late?

Catherine met Nola's blue eyes and held them. The girl finally dropped her gaze, saying, "I know this is, like, awkward or whatever."

There. *Now* Nola sounded her age, Catherine thought, cutting her eyes at Russell before saying, "Why? What could possibly be awkward about meeting your lover's wife?"

"Mom!" Willow gasped and put a hand to her mouth.

Whether Willow was shocked, delighted, or both, Catherine couldn't tell and was too tired to care. She turned her back on Nola and noticed for the first time that her black-and-white linoleum floor was spotted with puddles of puppy pee.

Good. She hoped Nola stepped in one. She'd had time to notice Nola's expensive shoes, too, without letting herself look anywhere at the girl's body between her knees and shoulders.

"Thank you for bringing Willow home," Catherine said, proud of her voice, steady and cool. "That was a big help. Now, if you'll excuse us, Willow and I need to discuss this dog."

"There's nothing to talk about. I'm keeping it," Willow said.

Impossible, Catherine thought: she couldn't deal with life as a single mother and cope with a dog, too. "I don't see how. You're leaving for Canada early Sunday morning and I have to work. You'll be in school when you come back. Who do you suppose will take care of the dog while we're both out of the house? Puppies are like babies," she said before she could stop herself. "They need a lot of attention. You and I do need to talk about this, young lady." God, she sounded like a school principal.

"Fine. Whatever," Willow mumbled. "Bye, Dad. See you next week, I guess. After I figure out the whole stupid school thing."

"Bye, pumpkin. You'll do great no matter what school you end up choosing." Russell stood up and kissed Willow on the cheek. Willow remained frozen to the spot, her face a mask of nonchalance.

"Bye, Willow," Nola said, shifting an enormous teal suede purse onto one shoulder.

Willow didn't answer.

Catherine followed them down the hall. After they'd exited the house, it took all of her strength not to slam the door. She made sure to latch the chain and throw the dead bolt home before she doubled over, willing herself not to cry. Once she started, she might not stop.

A few seconds later, someone knocked. Catherine opened the door as far as the chain would allow. Russell stood there, shivering in the damp breeze.

"What now?" she said.

"I forgot my coat and shoes."

Catherine glanced over her shoulder and saw that Russell's shoes were still in the hall. So was his black overcoat. He must have been in a hurry to exit. Or in a fog. She debated. Russell definitely deserved to go home cold and barefoot. But then he'd just turn up again tomorrow.

She sighed and opened the door, standing aside while he retrieved his things. Russell didn't put the coat or the shoes on; he stood in front of her, the overcoat slung over his arm and the shoes dangling from one hand, and said, "It kills me to see you hurting like this."

"Yeah, well. You must be a dead man, then."

"I'm so sorry, Catherine." His voice broke. "I've ruined everything."

"Don't give yourself so much credit. Willow and I will survive." Catherine kept her eyes averted, feigning interest in the painting that had hung in the hallway for so long that she'd stopped seeing it until now: a Scottish castle. A pallid watercolor done by one of her father's cousins. She should take it down. She had hung it up only to make Dad happy.

Russell said, "I know you don't want to hear what I think about Willow and the dog—"

"You're right. I don't."

"All right. Then I won't tell you to let Willow keep the puppy. She needs something right now to make her smile."

"Thank you for not saying that. Now get out."

"I'm going," Russell said. "But listen. I'd be glad to take care of the dog during the day while Willow's at school and you're at work, if that would help."

Catherine considered this. "You mean you'd come by the house and let the dog out in the yard, then bring it back inside?"

"Yes. If that's all right with you, of course."

"What about weekends when you have Willow? Would you take the dog then, too?"

"Of course." He spread his hands and attempted a smile. "It's not like I'm working. My time is my own until I find another job. And I know it would mean the world to her. Willow has always wanted a dog. We should have said yes before this. Think about it."

"I will. But only if you promise to never bring that girl here again."

Russell frowned. "Look, let's not be one of those divorced couples who has to meet in a neutral place during custody exchanges. We can do better than that."

"Oh, we'll be civil. For Willow's sake, I am not shouting at you, swearing, or setting your hair on fire. We will mediate our divorce and split things down the middle. But that girl must never come to my house again. Ever." Catherine crossed her arms.

"Of course. Like I said, Nola and I meant to get out of here before—"

"No," she interrupted again. "You misunderstand. I'm saying that you can't bring Nola with you, even in the car, when you drop off Willow. I don't want her anywhere near me. Or our house."

"Oh, come on, Catherine. Don't you think that's being a little unreasonable?"

She glared at him and felt a surprising zing of pleasure as Russell backed up so fast he nearly fell off the front step. As if being bitchy gave her some kind of superpower.

"All right," he said. "I'll make sure I'm alone whenever I come here."

"Fine. I'll think about letting Willow keep the dog."

"Thank you. I'll be going now. Good night," Russell said, but he continued to stand there, shoes in one hand, his eyes searching her face.

Searching for what? She had no answers for him. Willow would have a pet to distract her from sorrow and pain. Russell would have his new wife and baby. What would she have? Work. Sticky pub dates with Bethany. Wednesday night baths after her footsteps echoed through empty rooms.

Catherine shoved Russell a little on the chest. "Go on. Your girlfriend's waiting." She shut the door behind her husband and pressed her forehead to the cold wood.

When the girls were small, the drive from Massachusetts to Prince Edward Island seemed to take forever. That was partly because they made the trip many times before the eight-mile-long Confederation Bridge was built to replace the ferry. Andrew had been so excited about the bridge going up that he'd always made them stop to take pictures of it under construction.

"This is one of Canada's top engineering achievements," he'd eagerly told the girls, who could hardly be bothered to look out the window. "A marriage of art and engineering. Think of it! We're driving over the world's longest bridge across ice-covered waters!"

Eve didn't share his excitement about the bridge. In her view, it was sturdy rather than beautiful, a ponderous structure. They'd made the railings so high you could scarcely see the water from the car. Besides, she missed taking the ferry from New Brunswick to PEI. She had loved the excitement of driving onto the boat in a line of cars, the breakfasts of eggs and potatoes in the cafeteria as they waited for the island's red cliffs and lighthouses to slowly slide into view.

When the kids were small, they used to split the trip into two days of travel. They counted themselves lucky on the first day if they made it as far as Saint John, an industrial city with historic brownstones, Gothic stone churches, and a harbor full of ships and cranes. More often they didn't make it past Bangor, Maine. There, Andrew always insisted on staying in one of the cheap chain hotels near the airport and eating take-out Chinese because he hated that city.

Any way they did it, though, Maine was always the leg of the journey that Eve dreaded. MAINE, THE WAY LIFE SHOULD BE, or MAINE, THE VACATION STATE, read the highway signs and bumper stickers, but she and Andrew had a different slogan to describe that endless hypnotic tunnel of pine trees and toll booths: "Maine, the Infinite State."

"Well, what's it going to be?" Eve asked Catherine and Willow as they set out from Newburyport on Sunday morning. "Twelve hours straight on the road, or do we want to spend the night in Saint John?"

"Do hotels allow dogs?" Willow asked.

"Some do." Eve glanced in the rearview mirror at her granddaughter and smiled. "We'll find one, if that's what you want."

"I'd rather drive straight through, since I can only realistically take a few days off from work," Catherine said. "But do you feel up to that, Mom?"

Eve shrugged. "Sure. I'm an old hand at this. And I'll have plenty of time to rest after you leave me up there. I'm just grateful that you were willing to make the trip."

"All right, then," Catherine said. "I vote that we drive straight through. What about you, honey? You okay with that?" She turned around to look at Willow.

Eve glanced in the mirror again and saw that Willow had taken the puppy out of its box and was cradling it on her lap now. The dog nodded with its eyes half-closed, like one of those bobblehead animals people put in the rear windows of their cars. "I don't care. As long as we stop and give Mike a pee break." *Mike?* Eve mouthed at Catherine.

Catherine shrugged.

They stopped every few hours to walk Mike and stretch their legs. They'd hit that September sweet spot between beach traffic and leaf peepers. The road yawned empty. Even the Maine rest stops, with their moose statues and fast-food counters, were virtually tourist free except for a few adventurous seniors in campers.

Eve felt a familiar prickling of grief as she watched one elderly couple emerge from a Winnebago. One had a cane, the other a walker. She and Andrew had joked about selling their house in Massachusetts one day and touring the country in one of those things, making up names for their camper that would drive the girls crazy: "The Wayfarers," "The Vagabonds," "The Gypsy Wanderers."

As they got back on the road, Eve tried to clear her mind of everything but the driving. Otherwise her brain might seize with worry over the breakup of Catherine's marriage, or shut down with grief because this familiar highway was conveying her back to Chance Harbor, where it was impossible to escape her memories of Andrew and their life together.

She and Andrew used to agree that every person carries a landscape inside them. Andrew's was Prince Edward Island, with its secret pink coves and tidy Victorian farmhouses, its flowering white potato fields and bright lupine, the dark red cliffs and sparkling water views.

"Your landscape is so much more complicated than mine," Andrew had told Eve once while they were lying in bed at the Chance Harbor house after making love. He'd traced his fingers lightly down her throat; between her breasts and to her navel; then slowly, agonizingly, between her legs, making her draw a sharp breath of pleasure. "You, my darling wife, are nothing at all like an island. You're like the Merrimack River where it opens into the ocean: all dark water and unpredictable tides and hidden marshy inlets, sweet in some places and salty in others."

"You make me sound awful," Eve had complained.

"Ah, you misunderstand me." Andrew took her into his arms, pulled her close. "What I mean is that you're as mysterious and mighty and useful as a river wide enough to transport goods and people. I will never get tired of exploring you."

"That's fine," she'd said. "Just one thing. Don't ever call me 'wide' again."

He'd laughed.

Eve had been dreading this return trip to the island. Even with Catherine and Willow to help her, she didn't know where she'd find the strength to finish clearing out the Chance Harbor house, much less actually make that phone call to a Realtor to put it on the market. Selling the house felt like selling part of herself.

This was selfish of her, perhaps, asking for Catherine's help at a time like this. But maybe having these immediate, physical tasks could help both of them grieve the multiple losses of the past few years.

Catherine was leaning her head against the window with her eyes closed, but Eve didn't think her daughter was asleep. She was probably pretending in order to avoid conversation. That was fine. What would she say to her daughter anyway?

They arrived in Brewer by noon and ate at the Eagles Nest, another of their traditions. Lobster rolls for her and Catherine, a grilled cheese for Willow. The dining room jutted out over the Penobscot River. The sky was a brilliant blue. Below it, the water frothed in gleaming black-and-white pools around rocks with so much light gray lichen that they looked covered in lace.

Willow finished eating first and went out to walk the dog while Catherine and Eve split a slice of apple pie and drank their coffee. "It's so strange, being here without Dad," Catherine said, her eyes on the river, tracking a bald eagle circling over the spiny fir trees lining the opposite bank.

"I know. He's the one who brought me to this restaurant the first time," Eve said. "Feels like a hundred years ago. I didn't think I could ever set foot in this place without him. But it feels surprisingly normal because you and Willow are with me. Thank you, honey."

"Quit thanking me, Mom! I know I'm miserable company." Catherine put her fork down and sighed. "I met her, you know. That's what finally convinced me to make this trip."

"Who?" Eve asked, then realized. "Oh! And?"

"Nola is everything a man could want: young, sexy, and rich."

"She won't be sexy for long," Eve felt compelled to remind her. "That girl will be an overwhelmed teen mother soon, poor thing."

"Don't you dare feel sorry for her!" Catherine hissed.

"I know this is difficult for you. But that girl is just a confused child. I do feel sorry for her. And for Russell. On some level, he must know he's making a terrible mistake."

Catherine shook her head so hard that her silver earrings flashed in the sun. "Russell and this girl don't deserve one drop of your sympathy. You'd understand that if you met her, Mom. I hope to God I never have to see the evil little bitch again." She slapped down a twenty-dollar bill and stood up. "See you outside."

Eve stared, openmouthed, as Catherine slammed the door of the restaurant on the way out, rattling the glasses in their plastic racks by the drink machine.

Willow stared out the car window, glad she was in the backseat while Catherine and Nana talked about boring things, like what furniture to keep and what Realtor to call.

She couldn't believe they were selling the Chance Harbor house. It was so stupid. Nana was always so happy there. Everybody was.

But maybe Nana couldn't be happy there anymore. Willow got that. She didn't know if she could be happy in their Cambridge house again, either. Funny. She'd never really felt like Russell was her dad. But ever since he'd moved out, she missed him as much as she hated him. He'd been nicer to her than almost any other guy.

In some ways he was like Mike. Willow glanced down at the puppy, fondling its little triangle ears. She'd named the puppy for him because Mike was her real dad. She was sure of it! Mike was Mom's roommate in one of their apartments. The last good guy Mom was with. Maybe the only one.

Mike was tall and had wavy hair like hers. He was an artist like Willow, too. He had to be her dad, even though Mom always said no.

"It's okay," Mike told Willow once. "I would be honored to be your father and guide you through the rocky mountains, thorny thickets, and winding rivers of childhood and adolescence."

Mike always talked like that: funny and formal. Like a character in a book. He wore capes and top hats because he worked as a magician. She'd watched him perform at a few birthday parties for kids and loved watching him make doves fly out of a hat, grab a coin from behind somebody's ear, and twist balloons into swords.

Mike had taught her about colors and had given her a set of real watercolors in tubes. He showed Willow how art was everywhere: a picture of a house shutter, blue paint peeling right off it, could be as beautiful as a rainbow.

Then Mike had disappeared, saying, "Sorry, my little forsythia blossom, but your mom and I have agreed to disagree about her lifestyle." He gave Willow two art books and his own expensive camera before he moved out of the apartment, but Mom had sold the camera. She'd said she needed the money for food, but Willow knew better.

"Where's my dad going?" Willow had begged Mom to tell her, crying so hard that she was gasping and choking. But Mom pushed her away and curled up in a ball of misery on the couch, a joint in one hand. "He's not your dad. He's nothing to us," Mom said. "You need to forget about Mike. Pretend he's dead—why can't you? That's what I do when guys leave."

But Willow had never forgotten Mike, or the fact that she had a father. A good one. If Mike only knew Mom was dead, Willow knew he'd come back, but so far she'd tried everything to find him and it hadn't worked.

They were finally on that roller-coaster road between Bangor and Calais. Willow tried to ignore her lurching stomach and stared out the window at the trees. She'd been to Chance Harbor only in the summer, except one time at Thanksgiving, when the snow had blown everywhere and the road had disappeared out from under them. Now, in mid-September, some of the trees looked like they'd been dipped in red and gold paint.

The blueberry fields and marshes were starting to turn different shades of red and orange, too. Willow silently recited the colors for red she'd learned from her art classes: magenta and crimson, scarlet and burgundy, salmon and cherry, carmine and claret. She loved how nature had this whole unbelievable paint box.

"Did Mom used to like going to Chance Harbor?" she asked.

It was only when Catherine's head whipped around that Willow realized she'd actually spoken the question aloud; she'd meant to just wonder it in her head. She slouched in the seat. Catherine was doing a lot of blowing up lately. Scary. And she'd hate it that Willow had mentioned Zoe, especially since she'd called her "mom." Willow knew how much Catherine wanted to be her real mom.

Nana glanced at Catherine, then met Willow's eyes in the rearview mirror and smiled. That was Nana for you: always trying to save the day. "Yes, your mom was always happy at Chance Harbor," she said. "Zoe was meant to live in the wild."

"What do you mean?" Willow was excited to hear anybody say stuff about her mom. Nobody ever talked about her.

"Your mom used to say that Chance Harbor was the one place she felt safe," Nana said.

"Odd. She got into just as much trouble there as anywhere else," Catherine said to the window.

"Yes," Nana agreed. "But a healthier trouble, if there is such a thing."

"Like what?" Willow hadn't dared ask questions about her mom for years.

"Well, she loved jumping off that bridge at Basin Head with your grandfather," Nana said. "She did backflips and everything."

She had told her that before, but Willow loved hearing it again. She imagined her mom balancing up there on the bridge railing, where the sign said "Do Not Jump," and hurling herself into the river rushing below. Willow had been brave enough to jump off the bridge only once. The river carried you so fast into the Northumberland Strait that it felt like you were being washed out to sea. Instead, you ended up on a sandbar and waded back to shore, watching out for those green crabs that liked to nip your toes.

"What else did Mom do?" Willow asked.

She could hear the smile in Nana's voice. "Let's see, now. Every morning Zoe would take her bike out before the rest of us were even up. She rode all over the island by herself on those clay roads. I think she knew every tree and field. Or she'd go down to the beach and hunt for sea glass. Zoe used to make me crazy because she insisted on crossing the inlet and walking all the way to East Point. I don't know how many times we had to rescue her because she got trapped by the tide coming in."

"She was so brave," Willow said, awed.

"She was a thoughtless maniac," Catherine said. "God. Can't we talk about something else?"

Nana gave her a look that would have made Willow cry, it was so mean, but said, "All right. Let's wait and talk about this on the island, shall we?"

Willow sat back in the seat, determined to think about her mom the way Nana described her. Fierce.. Unafraid. Not like she was that last year before she went away—always sleepy, her arms bruised and scratched.

They crossed the border and drove through New Brunswick along the Bay of Fundy, stopping at Tim Hortons for a dinner of sandwiches and doughnuts. Willow slept for a while, then woke as they reached the Confederation Bridge. It stretched like a drawing sketched in charcoal, arching up to meet the sky.

The bridge went on for miles. Then they were on Prince Edward Island, arriving as the sun bled along the edges of blue sky.

They continued driving toward the easternmost tip of the island. At last they reached Saint Peter's Bay, where the mussel socks were laid out in tidy white rows, glowing like white marbles floating on the water in the purple dark. Half an hour later, they were pulling up in front of the yellow house with its steep roof and the sign that read CHANCE HARBOR even though all of the neighbors complained and said it should read CHANCE HARBOUR, the way everyone in Canada spelled it.

"What would be the point?" Grandpa used to say. "Everyone in Massachusetts thinks of me as Canadian, but here, they say I'm from away, even though I was born on this island. Might as well roll with it."

It took Nana two tries before she got the sticky front door unlocked. Then they stepped into the hallway and smelled musty basement, mothballs, red dirt, fields, wildflowers. Willow had always wanted to make a perfume out of PEI smells.

Bryan, the man who took care of the house when they were away—one of Grandpa's hundred cousins—had turned on the heat and lights for them; he'd even plugged in the fridge. The wood floors gleamed and Mike skittered around on them when Willow set him down. Willow staggered after him, saying, "I'm going to bed."

"Oh no, you're not," Catherine said. "You're helping us unload the car."

"Let her go," Nana said. "She's exhausted."

"And you and I aren't?" Catherine asked. "Remember, Mom. There's a lot more for us to do on our own now that Dad's not here."

Nana turned to face Catherine, her face cracking into seams like it had been stitched to her bones. "You think I don't know that?"

Willow went to her then and put her arms around Nana's waist. "I miss Grandpa."

Nana patted her back. "Me, too. But he'd be glad we're all here together."

Catherine snorted. "A lovely sentiment, Mother. But we're not exactly all here together, are we?" She went back out to the car, letting the screen door slam shut behind her.

"What a bitch," Willow muttered before she could stop herself.

Her grandmother snapped her head down to look at Willow. "My goodness. I guess we're all letting our hair down this week," she said, and smiled.

CHAPTER SIX

They spent the first morning in Chance Harbor sorting through dishes and linens until Catherine's fingers ached. She didn't care: she just wanted to get the necessary tasks done and go home.

Then, out of the blue, her mother had announced, "Beach break!" and led them outside to the steep wooden staircase descending down the rocky red cliff face to the beach. She had packed a bag of peanut butter sandwiches, apples, and three bottles of water. Like this was summer vacation instead of the kind of weather where you had to keep your back to the wind even in a fleece jacket.

Their house was located at the mouth of the inlet; Chance Harbor was the small area where people moored their sailboats and small outboards. It was just over a mile in one direction to East Point, though you had to wade across the inlet to get there, and a little over a mile the other way to Basin Head, recently voted as Canada's best beach in some tourist magazine. Her parents had worried that Basin Head's sudden media attention might cause an influx of people, but as far as Catherine could tell, little had changed.

Catherine shivered and jammed her useless phone back into her pocket. No service: she couldn't even e-mail or text Bethany to gripe.

She walked the beach, deliberately flicking up sand with the toes of her sneakers. Every morning of every summer of her life, she had walked along this beach. Now Catherine felt irritable, too restricted by her corduroys, stiff and tight against her knees, and by her coat, zipped to the neck. Suffocating.

Out on the water, the ferry was headed from Souris to Îles de la Madeleine. The long white boat looked flat against the blue horizon as it inched its way across the Northumberland Strait. Beyond it, Catherine could make out the humped shape of Cape Breton Island.

As she shaded her eyes against the glare to look at Cape Breton, she suddenly remembered a trip she'd taken there. She was little, maybe three years old. It must have been before Zoe was born. Now she remembered something else: her father standing on the dock at Wood Islands and crying as he waved good-bye to them. That had stuck with her all these years because it was the only time she'd ever seen Dad cry. God, she missed him.

Being at Chance Harbor made her miss Zoe, too, in a way she hadn't in a while. She and Zoe had been so excited every time they arrived that they'd jump on the beds, sometimes high enough to hit their heads on the slanted ceilings upstairs.

They'd ridden bikes everywhere, following red clay roads into pine forests and wide fields overlooking the sea. Every red road led to a secret cove. They'd come home with fingers and mouths stained from picking blueberries or raspberries, sick and giddy from too much fruit and sugar, because of course they always stopped for ice cream, too, at the little shop by the East Point lighthouse or at the corner store at the bottom of their road.

Where had that sister gone? She'd lost her long before Zoe had actually disappeared.

Zoe had started going off the rails in high school. The summer she was fourteen, for instance, she had actually stolen Dad's car. How did she even know how to drive? Somehow, she'd managed to get that car to Basin Head to meet some boy, another summer resident. She made it back in one piece except for an unexplained scrape on the passenger side. Their parents grounded her, as usual, and as usual that only caused Zoe to sneak out through a window after their parents were asleep.

Her parents were smart, yet Zoe always outsmarted them. Why hadn't they done more to stop her? To help her? Zoe might still be here today if they had.

Catherine wrapped her arms around her torso and stopped walking. No, that was wrong. Her parents had loved Zoe. They'd tried their best.

In fact, it had seemed like her mother had loved Zoe best of all. Standing here on the beach, Catherine thought about the time she'd gone swimming with Zoe on the other side of the island, where the surf could be ferocious and unpredictable. She and Zoe had gotten caught in the undertow. It was horrible, a moment when her world tumbled green and black and salty all around her. Catherine had screamed and then choked on water.

When she came up for air, her mother was swimming toward them with her long brown arms, calling their names, saying, "Hang on. Hang on!"

Catherine had gone under again, terrified as the undertow grabbed her ankles like a giant hand to pull her farther out from shore but convinced her mother would save her. Yet, when she came up again, she realized that her mother wasn't nearby anymore; she had Zoe under one arm and was swimming to shore, just the backs of their heads bobbing on the green water.

Uncle Ron had swum out a minute later to rescue Catherine. In retrospect, of course her mother's choice made sense: Catherine was older. Probably a stronger swimmer, though that was debatable. Her mother wasn't strong enough to rescue both girls and had to choose one of them. Yet Catherine had never been able to let go of the idea that her mother had chosen to save the daughter she loved more.

She finally felt warm enough to take off her sneakers. Her mother and Willow hadn't even bothered with shoes, of course; Catherine was afraid of getting splinters on the stairs. She squeaked her bare feet along the beach, shuffling to hear the famous singing sand as she watched the new game her mother had started with Willow. This one involved seeing how fast they could leap over a rapidly assembled obstacle course: a couple of huge chunks of driftwood, an ancient lobster trap, the prow of an old rowboat. They laughed whenever one of them fell.

This was a game Catherine remembered playing with Zoe. She'd loved it, too. But today she wasn't in the mood. Her mother always let Willow do whatever she damn well pleased, just as she had Zoe. This morning, for example, Willow had eaten only biscuits and honey for breakfast, followed by three squares of bittersweet chocolate. No wonder she was screaming like a seagull.

They spent an hour on the beach, Catherine occasionally interrupting their antics and trying to bring things down a notch. She pointed out a giant jellyfish—eggplant purple, as delicately transparent as glass—and suggested they collect sea glass. That quieted things down finally.

Still, no matter how adult and restrained she was trying to be, the island was working its magic on her. By the time they had walked up to Basin Head and back, Catherine's head felt clearer and her body was so relaxed that even her jaw felt unhinged.

They fried sausages for dinner and ate them with boiled potatoes. There were carrots, too, and spinach; her mother opened a bottle of red wine, but Catherine was afraid to drink it. Wine would make her weepy. Bad enough that everywhere she looked there were reminders of her childhood. Zoe's wakeboard was still leaning in the corner of the sunporch off the kitchen with her own. Her father, too, was present on the porch: his gardening tools and fishing poles, his floppy-brimmed sun hat, his birding binoculars. The sum of family.

Seeing these abandoned things made Catherine's throat tighten with grief. She didn't need any more reminders of how their family had shrunk. Yet her mother had seemed relentlessly cheerful as she'd greeted the flotilla of neighbors and cousins arriving this afternoon with snowflake rolls and pies, biscuits and canned fruit, homemade jams. Enough food for the whole damn winter.

As always, there was a great deal of talk about the weather, family, and house repairs: the steady tides of island life. "This summer was some hot," the women kept repeating, and several of the men pointed out the stains on the loose roof shingles and rotten boards. All of them offered to help with repairs, shifting uncomfortably in the kitchen chairs when Mom said she was putting the house up for sale. Catherine imagined them going home and turning over in bed to say, "Well, what can we expect? She's from away."

From away. Like her mother hadn't made Prince Edward Island her second home for the past forty-five years.

For Catherine, there were stories of cousins out west, mostly in Alberta. They asked vague questions about her job—everyone approved of her nursing career—and no questions at all about Russell. She wondered why, until her mother mentioned telling Cousin Jane, her father's oldest cousin, about Catherine's situation.

Cousin Jane was a square-bottomed, gray-haired woman of seventy who had been principal at the tiny elementary school that once occupied the site of the community hall at the end of the road. She was also the family's town crier. Catherine could imagine Jane calling each family member in turn, saying, "I'm bringing the pecan tarts, so you bring the rolls. But, whatever you do, don't ask Catherine about her husband. And for heaven's sake, don't you dare mention that wild daughter of Eve's, either."

Everyone knew your business on the island. Catherine knew she ought to feel relieved by that, but didn't. It was just more evidence of her failure as a wife and mother that here, generations of the MacLeish family still cozily inhabited seed and potato farms they divided into lots in case their children and grandkids returned from out west and needed a foothold on the land, while she couldn't hold on to her husband, keep her sister out of harm's way, or have a baby of her own.

And now her family was leaving the island completely. What would they do with all of these things in the house? Catherine's eyes roamed the kitchen as she finished dinner, taking in the egg cups shaped like hens, the baskets that had always held dried hydrangeas or fresh blueberries. Just leave them here?

Even without having had any wine, the thought of never being in this house again made Catherine feel overcome by the sorrow she'd been holding back all day. She covered her face with her hands and cried at the kitchen table. Grief was like the flu. You thought you were over the worst of it and then the fever and shakes returned. She longed for her father: his warm laugh, the way he read the newspaper aloud at breakfast, his capable square hands that could tame any machine. She mourned the absence of her sister's silly laugh and relentless energy.

Willow stood up and wrapped her arms around her shoulders. Her mother reached across the table to awkwardly pat her arm. Even the dog got into the act, dancing around Catherine's ankles and whining to be picked up.

"What is it?" Mom said.

"Everything," Catherine answered.

"I know exactly what you mean," Mom agreed. "Willow, how about if we do the dishes and let your mom go to bed?"

Catherine dropped her hands. "How can you be so functional, Mom? How can you not miss Dad every minute?"

"Who says I don't miss him?" her mother said. "Why do you think I can't stop functioning? Keeping busy gets me through the day. At least you still have a job. A schedule. Things to make you feel *important*." She turned her back on Catherine and started filling the sink with hot water.

Stung, Catherine watched in silence as Willow stood beside her grandmother, dish towel in hand. Willow was competent and quick, rinsing the dishes carefully before drying them and using a gentle hand to stack them on the open shelves above the counter. Her wavy hair was a tangled thicket around her shoulders. Catherine was shocked to realize that Willow was nearly as tall as Eve. When had that happened?

Soon Willow would be gone, off to college. And Catherine would be alone.

After dinner, Willow took the puppy outside and then tromped upstairs with a fat, musty mystery novel she'd found on the shelf beneath the coffee table. Catherine sat in the living room, listening to the clock tick and trying to read. She and Zoe used to play a memory game with their father where they'd stare at the objects in a room, then close their eyes and try to recite them all.

"It's like taking a picture with your mind," Dad had explained when he taught them the game. "If you do it enough, you'll have photographic memories and get good grades in school."

Catherine already got good grades, a fact she often hid from her sister, who did not. Now she played Dad's game, consciously noting every object in the room in case she was never back in this house again. Then she closed her eyes and recited the list of objects to herself: the ancient camel-backed sofa with its pair of needlepoint pillows, the pink ceiling lamp, the painting of milk bottles and eggs done by her great-grandmother, a floral pitcher on the end table.

So many treasures in this house. *Their* family's treasures. How could her mother bear to give them up?

When she'd asked her mother this question on the drive here, Mom had said, "Because sometimes you have no choice but to move forward."

Tonight her mother looked peaceful. She was knitting a dark green sweater, a complicated cable pattern that caused her to frown and keep recounting stitches. Those ticking needles had provided the rhythmic background noise throughout Catherine's childhood.

Catherine put down her book and went to the shelves. She pulled out a few jigsaw puzzles and settled on the five-hundred-piece puzzle of Nova Scotia. It was a map with various icons representing Nova Scotia's major industries: coal mines, fishing boats, lobster traps, logging trucks, paper mills.

She sat back down on the couch and dumped the puzzle pieces out of the box, then started flipping them right-side up on the coffee table. Maybe she and Willow could work on the puzzle together; she had to find a way to stop barking orders and simply enjoy being with her.

Catherine started piecing together the border of Nova Scotia. She and Zoe had fought about jigsaw strategies. Zoe liked to pick out the most interesting parts of the picture to work on, while Catherine did things in logical order: corners and borders first, then working from top to bottom.

They'd been fighting over nothing, of course. The puzzles got done. Neither strategy was faster than the other, though Zoe was careless and often dropped pieces, sometimes losing them under a chair or a table. Catherine had to help her scour the floor for them so Dad wouldn't yell.

She turned a blue puzzle piece between her fingers, glanced at the box, and noticed the section marked "Cape Breton Island." "Hey, I remembered something today, Mom," she said, fitting the piece into the top border with a flash of satisfaction.

"What's that?" Her mother smiled at her over the sweater, the needles still moving steadily in and out of the yarn, as if they were automated.

"Going to Cape Breton Island with you back when I was really little. Before Zoe was born."

Her mother raised an eyebrow. "Oh?"

Her voice was neutral, but something vibrated in the air between them. Wariness? Anxiety? "Yes." Catherine watched her mother's face closely now, looking for clues to her mood. "You and I went alone on the ferry to Nova Scotia, to Cape Breton. I was afraid of the ferry horn and all that black diesel smoke."

"I'm surprised you remember. I'd forgotten all about it." Her mother bent her head, counted stitches.

By her knotted shoulders, Catherine knew with certainty that her mother was lying. "No, you didn't," she said, wondering why she was bothering to challenge her mother on this, of all things. "You and I talked about that trip a few summers ago. We were on the beach with Willow, and she asked us what that land was we could see across the water. She asked if we'd ever been to Cape Breton and I said no. Then you reminded me of our trip. And that's when I remembered how Dad cried when he waved to us from the dock as the ferry left."

Her mother snorted. "You're delusional. Dad was never a crier."

"No, Mom. He cried. I remember because it scared me. It made me think we weren't ever going to see him again."

Her mother set the needles down. "Well, obviously you were wrong."

"Yes, but why did we go without him? We always did everything together as a family in the summers."

Her mother shrugged. "I don't remember. I suppose your father wanted to stay here to work on the house. You know how he was. He'd been to Cape Breton, but I never had, not in all the years we'd been coming to Prince Edward Island. Seemed stupid not to go. I was tired of just viewing the outline of Cape Breton Island from Chance Harbor. I wanted to see the place in person. But once your father got here, he never wanted to leave."

"Well, he did travel a lot for work. That's understandable."

Her mother picked up her knitting again, her usually generous mouth pressed into a thin line. "Of course."

Catherine fit another piece of sky into the border. She couldn't remember her parents ever fighting, other than their noisy disagreements about Zoe, but they must have. "So, what? You went off in a huff? To prove a point?"

"Oh, who knows now? I suppose."

"Were you arguing about more than that?"

"More than what?"

"More than about Dad wanting to stay home and you wanting to travel to Nova Scotia?"

Her mother wrapped the yarn around her needles and jammed the rubber stoppers onto the tips. "Catherine, why all these questions? What's this about? Are you asking if your father and I ever fought? Of course we did. What couple doesn't?"

"Did Dad ever cheat on you?" Catherine hadn't meant to ask, but the question had been nagging at her. She wanted to ask every wife in the world this question.

There was a long silence, broken only by the ticking of the pipes as the heat came on. Then her mother sighed. "Yes," she said.

The jigsaw pieces blurred on the table beneath Catherine's hands. She put both hands on her knees to steady herself. She hadn't really expected this answer. Dad? He had adored her mother. How was this possible?

"But you took him back, after."

"Yes, I did."

"So that's why you think I should work on things with Russell."

"I never said that."

"You did!" Catherine said. "You seem to think I can just overlook the fact that he fucked another woman—a student! a girl!—and got her pregnant. That I can just forget about Russell being a father to someone else's child, when he couldn't be a father to mine."

"Russell is a father to your child," her mother said. "You and he have Willow."

Catherine stared at her, eyes burning. "That's not the same and you know it."

Her mother stood up, walked slowly over to the couch, and sat down. She picked up one of the puzzle pieces—the tip of a lighthouse—and tucked it into another white piece. "I'm sorry," she said. "I don't have any doubt that you're in pain right now. But I can tell you from experience that things will get better with time."

"What happened with Dad? When did he cheat on you? Can you tell me?"

"If you really must know. If you think it would help you." Her mother studied the puzzle for a moment, then began fitting together pieces of a lobster trap.

Zoe must have inherited her jigsaw strategy from Mom, Catherine realized. "I do," she said.

"All right." Her mother leaned back against the couch. There were fine lines around her eyes, but otherwise, with her curly light brown hair and sharp profile, her long limbs and fluid grace, her mother could have been forty-six instead of sixty-six. She'd always been a youthful-looking woman, but in the past few years she had acquired the sort of elegance that had nothing to do with money or what she wore. "What is it you want to know, exactly?"

"How many times did Dad cheat on you? When did it happen? Was it with one woman, or more?"

Her mother flinched. They had never talked openly about personal relationships.

"I don't know," her mother said finally. "The first time, we'd been married about two years. You were just a baby. I found out about it in the usual way: credit card receipts for a hotel in New York that Dad forgot to remove from the pocket of a suit I was taking to the cleaners. I wouldn't have thought anything of it, except there were room service charges that were obviously dinners for two with some very pricey wine. And breakfasts for two as well."

"My God. You must have been so shocked. And angry."

"Of course."

"Did Dad deny it?"

"No. He cried, said he was sorry. And I believed him."

"Did you find out who it was?"

Her mother nodded, pushed aside a stray curl. "He'd been seeing a woman he'd known long before he and I were married. Marta. She was German, the CEO of one of the European software companies your father's company had acquired."

"So how did you forgive him?" Catherine asked, though really what she wanted to know was *Why did you*?

"I felt I had no choice at the time. I wasn't working, and you were still a baby. Besides, he seemed genuinely distressed by the prospect of losing me. He promised to never cheat again."

"Did he keep his word?"

Her mother averted her eyes, picked up another puzzle piece and examined it. "Not always. But his affair was only a blip in a long, productive marriage."

Catherine picked up another piece of sky and set it in place. She and her mother worked silently for a few minutes, but it was more tense than companionable. She should drop the subject. Wasn't it hard enough that her mother had to deal with Dad dying? But she was too shocked by this revelation to stop herself from saying, "I don't understand how you could stay with him if you couldn't trust him."

Her mother sighed, put down the puzzle piece she'd been holding. "Your dad and I battled on and off. You saw how we bickered. Over Zoe, especially. But I trusted him in the big things. Marriage—a long marriage like ours, especially—is about a lot more than just being faithful physically. Your father was my dearest friend. I trusted him with my life, and with the lives of you girls, too. Yes, it was difficult at times. But we got through it. And you will survive this, whether you stay with Russell or not."

"Even if I could convince Russell not to marry Nola, to stay with me instead, I wouldn't want that," Catherine declared. "I hear what you're saying, and I wish I could be that forgiving. Especially because I know our divorce will be another big emotional hurdle for Willow. But I can't be that generous. Not when that girl is carrying his child."

"Well. That's the way it is, then," her mother said, and leaned over to kiss Catherine's cheek. "You can only stay in a marriage until you can't stay anymore."

"That helps a little, knowing you understand." Catherine frowned at the puzzle. She'd put one of the pieces in wrong. She wiggled it out again, looked at her mother. "Were you happy with Dad? I mean, would you say you had a happy marriage, overall?"

Her mother hesitated only a fraction of a second before saying, "Yes. It was a good, solid marriage. A true partnership." Then she stood up and stretched, said she was going to bed. "This is a hard time for you," she added, "but you'll be fine. You've always been strong and resourceful."

"Thanks." Catherine watched her mother's narrow silhouette making its way up the stairs, one delicate, pale hand moving up the railing like a starfish, wondering why she felt oddly dismissed instead of comforted, and why she was so sure her mother hadn't been completely honest with her after all.

"I'm going into town," Catherine said as she came into the kitchen the next morning. "Coming?" she asked Willow.

Willow looked up from the book she'd been reading while she was eating oatmeal. "No. I'll stay here."

Catherine plucked her car keys off the hook. "Really? There could be doughnuts involved."

"No," Willow repeated. "You go." She had no intention of getting trapped in a car with Catherine, who would probably either yell or cry. She didn't need to hear any more about how their lives were going to be different from now on. She knew that already.

Catherine shrugged. "Okay. Suit yourself. Have fun."

Once she'd gone, it felt like Catherine had sucked an entire black cloud out the door with her. The kitchen filled with sunshine, and Willow was aware of the sound of the waves shushing against the cliffs below the house.

Nana had been making tea, but she must have caught Willow staring out the window, because she smiled. "Go down to the beach. Our chores can wait."

"Will you come with me?"

Nana shook her head. "I need to make some calls. But I command you to have fun."

Willow practically ran down the wooden steps, moving so fast that the rope railing burned her hand. The sparkling beach was empty and the tide was out, leaving long, shallow tide pools glinting silver under the morning sky. White clouds moved like scarves above her head. Mike followed at her heels, barking.

She raced up and down the sand with the dog, laughing and spinning like a maniac because there was nobody to see her, no adults to tell her to be quiet or slow down or stand in line or learn this or forget that. Maybe moving to the island was the answer. Forget school and Cambridge; Russell and stupid, slutty Nola.

Finally, Willow was tired enough to go back to the house. She rinsed her sandy feet and arms at the hose outside, shivering as the icy water hit her skin, then dried off with one of the rough towels Nana kept hanging from the pegs on the sunporch. Yesterday she'd volunteered to clean out the upstairs closets. Her grandmother was down in the basement when she got back to the house, so Willow brought a trash bag and a box up to the room that Nana said used to be her mom's.

Like all of the bedrooms, this one had a slanted ceiling and flowered wallpaper; the flowers were tiny pink roses with long green stems against an ivory background. The wood floor was painted light green. The only furniture, other than a double bed with a white embroidered bedspread, was a green nightstand and a white bureau. Maybe this really was the way to live, Willow thought: nothing to clutter your house, so your mind stayed free, too.

She began pulling stuff out of the closet. Everything was so dusty that she kept coughing. She pulled out all kinds of cool things, though, so she didn't mind the dust. Some of them, like the long fur coat in plastic, had probably belonged to her great-grandmother, Nana said when she came upstairs to see how Willow was doing.

"I'll give these old clothes to Cousin Jane, I guess," Nana said. "She'll know who they belonged to, and they might mean something to her."

"Except the gold hat with the peacock feather," Willow said. "You have to keep that, Nana! It looks awesome on you."

"Oh, Willow. Where would I ever wear it?" Nana said, but she smiled and set that box aside. "Want a snack?"

Willow shook her head. "No, I'm good."

"All right. I'm going down to make another cup of coffee. Shout if you need me."

She was almost done. Not much else in the guest room closet after Willow had dug through the clothing and shoes. Just a box of books, their pages so old and yellow and curly they looked like leaves, and a radio half-covered in the same pale pink paint that was on the trim in this room.

Only two of the bedrooms had closets, since people back in the old days just hung their clothing on pegs, Nana had told her. Nobody who lived back when this house was built could afford more than maybe two or three outfits. "They had their farm clothes and their church clothes," Nana said.

In the fourth and smallest bedroom, however, the one with the stained and peeling blue striped wallpaper, which Willow slept in, there was a blue wooden trunk. Inside it, Willow found blankets and a shoe box of photographs. She stacked the blankets in a neat pile and carried them downstairs, the box on top of it.

"What do I do with these?" she asked Nana, who was sitting at the kitchen table with a cup of coffee and making a list on the back of an envelope.

Nana glanced up. "Oh, those are the wool blankets your grandfather and I bought from that sheep farm in Scotland on our honeymoon. I should bring them home. Just put them in the corner of the porch."

"Okay." Willow did as she was told, then came back to the table and sat down with the box. "There are photographs in here," she said. "This is me, right?" She handed a picture over to Nana, who smiled and nodded.

"That's you, all right. What a little angel."

Willow made a face. "Mom used to tell me I cried all the time. And I'm so ugly! I never knew I was that bald and fat."

Nana laughed. "You're not fat. All babies have rolls of fat around their legs and wrists until they start moving around on their own. And every baby cries. That's normal. You weren't bald, either. You just had really light hair like your mom's. Almost white. It doesn't show in the photo. Trust me. You were a pretty baby. Almost as pretty as you are now."

Willow rolled her eyes, but she was secretly pleased. Nobody ever told her she was pretty. Usually she felt invisible, and that was fine with her. She knew what happened when guys noticed you. She suppressed a shudder, thinking of Tom touching her.

She squinted at the picture. "I remember this blanket with the cows on it—I had it on my bed until first grade—but not this room. Where am I?"

"In Worcester. That's one of the apartments you and your mother had after you stopped living with us."

"Did we live with anybody else?" Willow asked. "I remember Mom's boyfriend. Mike. He lived with us for a while, on and off." She was testing her grandmother, trying to trick her into telling her more. Willow felt bad about this, but her mom wasn't coming back. It was time she found her father. Mike would take care of her if Catherine and Russell didn't want her anymore.

"Yes, Mike was a nice guy," Nana said, looking up from her paper again. "I always hoped they'd end up together."

"He was a magician, right?" Willow was excited. This was the first time anyone had ever told her anything about Mike. "And his last name was Martin." She'd made that up on the spot, hoping her grandmother would correct her.

It worked! "No, no. He was only a magician on weekends for fun. Mike was a teacher at a Montessori school. His last name was Navarro, not Martin." Nana smiled. "I liked him, but your grandfather thought he was odd. He didn't believe teaching was an appropriate career choice for a man. But Mike clearly loved children. He loved you. I know that."

Willow felt her eyes sting. Her dad *had* to be Mike. He'd cared about her the way a father would. Like that time she was sick with the flu and got up in the middle of the night to throw up. She was little, maybe six years old then, and scared because it felt like a wild thing had crawled down her throat, clawing its way to her stomach. Mike was the one who got up and watched TV with her, gave her ginger ale and ice cream, stroked her damp hair. Mike. Not her mother, who didn't even wake up.

"Shhh," Mike had said, when Willow tried to call her mother's name from the doorway of the bedroom, not wanting to come into the room in her icky pajamas. "We don't want to wake your mom. I'm coming."

He'd helped her off with the nightgown—that was before Tom taught her that you couldn't trust some men, even if you were a little kid—and washed her face. He brought her fresh pajamas and wrapped Willow in his own big warm flannel robe, rolling up the sleeves and tying a big bow in it. "There," Mike had said. "You look just like a princess in her royal gown."

That had made Willow laugh, even though she still felt like puking.

Mike was definitely her father.

"What do you really think happened to my mom, Nana? Do you think she's dead?" Willow asked, setting the photo back in the box.

"No, I don't, honey," Nana said, biting her bottom lip as she looked at Willow across the table. "I think one day she'll surprise us all and walk right back into our lives."

Willow smiled and reached over to take her hand. "You're lying to make me feel better, right?"

Nana shook her head. "No. I'm hoping," she said. "With all my heart."

CHAPTER SEVEN

Eve thought she'd be tired enough to sleep after Catherine and Willow left Chance Harbor, but she was restless and finally got up with the sun.

She had taken Catherine and Willow to Charlottetown the previous afternoon for their flight to Boston. Catherine was skeptical when Eve said she wanted to stay on the island alone for another week to finish sorting through things and find workmen to do repairs before putting the house on the market. But she'd hugged Eve hard and left without looking back.

Now that Eve thought about the conversation with Catherine about her own marriage, she wished she'd been more honest. She could have at least shared the same story she'd told Russell. Maybe then Catherine would have a less absolute, black-and-white view of marriage and adultery. Of "good" husbands and wives.

But Catherine didn't ask whether you were faithful, Eve reminded herself. *Only her father.*

What had held her back from confessing her own infidelity? Shame, partly. And Eve knew that telling her daughter the truth had the potential to shatter their relationship.

Catherine had adored her father. They'd had a special bond, those two. Sometimes Eve had even been envious, watching as Andrew showed

Catherine how to bait a fishing line or taught her how to change the tire on her bicycle.

That close relationship between Andrew and Catherine had also bothered Zoe. Sometimes Eve wondered if that was why she'd been so protective, and perhaps too forgiving, of her younger daughter. Andrew, meanwhile, was often impatient with Zoe's silly antics, her dramatic flair, and later with her risk-taking. He had no time for such nonsense, he said.

"Maybe I'm just too Scottish and practical to have an artistic daughter," Andrew said with a sigh.

Of course, it was her own fault that Andrew couldn't really bond with Zoe. Eve knew that. She had come close to explaining all of this to Catherine but had pulled back at the last second. Why sully Catherine's memories of her father? Of their family?

Had she really trusted Andrew, as she'd told Catherine? In the big things—in sickness and health, for richer or poorer—absolutely, yes. She and Andrew had looked out for each other while he was building up his business and, later, as she was getting her career off the ground. They'd propped each other up through the early years of parenthood, his skin cancer treatments and her own breast cancer scare, the deaths of his parents and grandmother, her father's dementia and the deaths of her own parents, too. There had been challenges with their extended families as well, like the MacLeish cousin who was perpetually in jail and asking Andrew for money, or her own sister, a hoarder and recluse in Wisconsin.

But Eve did not trust Andrew to be faithful. What she didn't tell Catherine was this: after finding those hotel receipts and confronting Andrew, after hearing his story and his vow to end the relationship with his German colleague, she had met Marta.

It was at a company function where Andrew was receiving a major award. Eve hadn't expected Marta to be there, but by then Marta was one of the company's vice presidents—a promotion approved by Andrew, no doubt.

After Andrew first told her about his affair, Eve had imagined Marta as the sort of brisk, tailored, older woman who would be a top administrator at a high-tech company. Instead, Marta had been—how else to put this?—luscious, an ample brunette with creamy breasts spilling out of a red cocktail dress. A woman who spoke not with a clipped German accent, but in soft murmurs that caused everyone—the men, especially—to lean closer, to practically pillow their heads on her bosom, as if Marta were reading them bedtime stories instead of reciting sales figures.

Marta lived in New York, Andrew told her after that party, speaking dismissively, literally waving Eve's questions about her away with one hand as they drove home. "You have no reason to worry or feel jealous. Marta and I scarcely have reason to run into each other anymore," he said. "Anyway, that's all over now."

She had believed him.

After the affair, Andrew had insisted on scheduling regular weekend getaways. They both loved to cross-country ski, and so, for Andrew's birthday in January, she surprised him with a weekend at a hotel in Vermont. They'd spent the day skiing and had returned to their room exhausted, sore, and happy, making love in that languid way of couples who know there is nothing to interrupt them.

Afterward, Eve had gone down the hall for ice. When she returned, Andrew was sobbing in the shower, his body folded nearly double.

Alarmed, she'd opened the shower door and turned off the scalding water, worried that the red stains on his pale, freckled back might actually be burns that would blister. Andrew had been meek and quiet once she arrived, letting her bundle him into one of the hotel's plush white towels.

She'd ordered a hot toddy from room service, scotch with orange juice and hot water, a pat of butter melted on top. Once Andrew had drunk it, once he had collected himself and his teeth had stopped chattering, Eve had promised him that, whatever he had to tell her, it would be all right. They would get through it together.

She had believed this with all her heart. But she was blindsided when the truth turned out to be that Andrew hadn't stopped seeing Marta after all. They had met many times since then, in Europe and New York, even in Latin America, Andrew told her. "Now she has left her husband, and Marta says I have to leave you, too," Andrew said dully, pulling the towel around his shoulders like a cape.

"And what do you want to do?" Eve asked. "To stay with me, or be with her?"

"Stay," he'd said. "Oh, my love. You're the one who has my heart."

Eve had closed her eyes, trying to feel whether he was telling the truth. He was. Andrew had always loved her. Loved her, still. She knew that in her bones. She opened her eyes again. "All right, then. If you stay with me, you must promise to never see Marta again. Do you understand? This is your last chance."

"Yes," he said. "I understand."

"What's her number?" Eve demanded.

He'd looked up at her then. "Eve, you can't."

"I can. And I will."

Andrew had given it to her finally, and Eve had dialed Marta. There was a brief, terse conversation, where Eve told Marta that just because she was ready to end her marriage didn't mean Eve was ready to end her own. There would be no more threats, Eve added, or she would go to the police.

It had taken months. A year, maybe, before Eve would let Andrew touch her again. But she and Andrew had gotten through all that, and through Eve's affair with Malcolm a few months later. At the time, her own infidelity had seemed to be a far more serious betrayal than Andrew's; whereas he had always said he wanted to be with her, Eve couldn't honestly say the same to him. That was the real reason she'd gone to Cape Breton Island and left Andrew in tears: to decide.

Wednesdays were definitely going to suck big-time, Willow thought as she waited in front of the school for Nola to pick her up.

For some reason, Catherine was insisting on this stupid custody arrangement, and Willow now had to spend time with Russell every Wednesday. "It's important for you to keep up your relationship," Catherine had explained.

When Willow said no way did she want to waste even one more minute of her life with Russell, Catherine brought out some legal document about a gazillion pages thick to show her: the separation agreement.

"I'm sorry, but this is what he and I have agreed, and it's a legally binding document," Catherine said, pointing to the actual page where it supposedly said that. "Look on the bright side, can't you? I have to work late most Wednesdays. This way you'll get dinner. And it's the least you can do, if Russell's going to take care of that dog while you're in school. It's only fair."

Fair. Had Russell considered what was fair when he screwed Nola? He made her sick.

How was Russell so different from Tom, Mr. Real Deal, with his cold hand on her leg, sliding up her thigh? She was ten when that happened. Tom must have been, what, like twenty-nine? Nineteen years older than she was. Almost the same difference between Nola and Russell. Gross. Willow wanted to gag, thinking about how Russell might have put his chalky fingers up Nola's skirt when she was bending over his desk, asking for help on a history essay.

Except, knowing Nola, she'd probably worn a thong and put Russell's hand there herself. Last year Willow had a study hall with Nola. She remembered the effect Nola had on that Latin teacher who monitored the room, a guy with a name so long everyone called him Dr. Q. All Nola had to do was sit in the front row in a short skirt, crossing and uncrossing her legs, and the poor guy stood in front of her like he'd been turned to stone by a wizard. Once Nola had paralyzed him, she could use her cell phone all she wanted. Her hotness factor was like some kind of spider's web or magnetic force field. Guys could only make it in if she let them, and then they couldn't get out.

Nola was pulling up to the curb now, looking like a bitch in charge in her black Range Rover. The car was a present from her dad for her sixteenth birthday.

Willow scowled at a group of girls staring at Nola and the car. The only upsides to this whole custody thing were that Russell had picked up her dog earlier today, so now Mike greeted her by leaping from the backseat into the front, and people in this new school would leave Willow alone if they saw her with Nola, imagining Nola was her sister or cousin or whatever.

Or stepmother. Ew.

Willow focused on rubbing Mike's ears as the car slid noiselessly away from the curb.

"So how was school?" Nola asked, steering with one hand on the wheel and texting with her other. Willow had hoped Russell would pick her up, but apparently he had some kind of job interview.

"Fine."

Nola glanced at her. "Fine, fine? Or really fine?"

"Really fine. Nobody's beaten me up yet or stolen my lunch money, okay?"

"Well, you tell those pricks they'll have to deal with me if they bother you."

Willow glanced at Nola, surprised. Maybe because Nola had destroyed Willow's whole life to get what she wanted, she was going to be her fairy godmother now. Oh, goody.

"Need a snack before we go home?"

This must be Nola's way of practicing to be a mom. "No." Willow pointedly took a book out of her backpack and opened it.

She hadn't seen Nola's apartment yet. She'd been too busy "getting settled in school," as Catherine put it, though that wasn't actually what was happening. No, it was more like she was surviving by being invisible, something that was actually a lot harder to do than she'd thought it would be in a school this size.

Probably because she was the only kid who'd started at the wrong time of year. Everyone asked why. She said her family was traveling. Luckily, in Cambridge that excuse flew. About half the people she'd met in her classes so far had parents who were professors at some college or other; a lot of them had parents who did sabbaticals or were on fellowships.

They drove across the BU Bridge and down Commonwealth Avenue. Then Nola turned left and left again, finally pulling up in front of a brownstone on Beacon Street. "This is it," she said.

Willow glanced at her, shocked. They were maybe four blocks from Beacon Hill School. For the first time, she wondered what Nola was doing about school. They wouldn't let her stay at Beacon Hill, would they? Had they only kicked Russell and Willow out? Maybe, if Nola's dad gave the school enough money.

"How long have you lived here?" Willow asked, grabbing the dog's leash as she opened the car door.

Nola tossed her goddess hair. "Like, all my life since I was twelve," she said. "I mean, whenever my dad wasn't dragging us halfway around the world. He's in Dubai right now. Before that, my grandmother lived here and I lived with my mom in our house in Geneva, mostly, unless we were in New York."

"So your dad lets you live here by yourself now?"

Nola arched an eyebrow. "It's my house since I turned eighteen. It was my mom's before she died and left it to me. I was thirteen when she died. It was *her* mother's before that."

"Oh." Willow didn't know Nola had a dead mother; she had to work hard not to feel sorry about that. "Where does your dad live?"

"He lived here with me until I told him to get the hell out. Now he has a condo in Brookline. Come on. Russell's probably still at his job interview, but he'll be home soon."

Nola said her father's name like it was poetry. What job interview? Willow wanted to ask, but she didn't want to give Nola the satisfaction of knowing her dad told Nola more than he told his own kid.

Except I'm *not* his, Willow reminded herself. She had a real dad out there. Mike. He'd want her to stay with him instead of Russell if he knew what was happening. She had to find him.

She followed Nola along a stone path between two miniature but perfect gardens. The gardens still had a few raggedy flowers, and there was a curved stone bench in one of them next to a little pond. A miniature tree with branches falling like soft hair grew next to the bench.

They went through a glossy black door with a brass pineapple knocker. Inside, the house reminded her of the Gardner Museum, where she'd been a bunch of times with Catherine and once with her school: there were more paintings than walls, and the rooms were just as dark and cluttered with tapestries and rugs. None of the furniture looked meant to sit on.

"My mom was kind of an art collector," Nola explained. She pointed to one wall where the paintings were an inch apart and all had thick gold frames. "They're real and supposedly worth more than the house. I should probably sell them, especially if Russell doesn't get a job. But that would be like selling my mom's soul or something."

This talk was making Willow want to jump out of her skin. She wanted to hate Nola, but it was hard to hate somebody who was talking about her mother's soul. She narrowed her eyes at Nola's belly, trying to hate what was in there, but nothing showed. Nola was wearing a big sweater over leggings like everybody else.

"Go ahead and look around," Nola said, dropping her keys on one of the living room tables. "I have to pee. *Again*."

Willow went upstairs first—three bedrooms, one with a canopy bed, all of them decorated like rooms in a castle; and two bathrooms with black-and-white tiled floors, one with a bathtub big enough for an elephant—then came back downstairs. She followed the same hallway Nola had taken from the living room into a library alcove made to feel secret and cozy with pink silk drapes. No lie: she loved it.

From there, she entered a dining room with a massive table and then a narrow green kitchen, where a woman in a maid's uniform was doing something to a chicken, her hand right up its butt. The woman was dark-skinned and pretty. "Hello, miss," she said. "Miss Nola is outside." She gestured with her chin to a door off the kitchen.

"Come on, Mike," Willow said, and whistled for the dog to follow.

The door led into a pantry with shelves crammed mostly with Trader Joe's stuff. Through that was another door leading to a courtyard with a stone bench and a taller, but equally droopy tree. The leaves had fallen off the tree in a shower of gold confetti all over the bench and stone patio. There was another, bigger pond here, too, as if whoever had landscaped in front of the house was just practicing to put the same, larger versions of everything back here. Nola was filling a bird feeder; afterward she stood on her toes to hang it from the iron post at the far corner of the courtyard.

As she reached up, Willow was able to see the swell of Nola's stomach inside her black leggings. She looked away. "So is my dad living here now?"

"Yeah. He kind of had to, since he didn't have anyplace else to go after your mom threw him out."

"My mom only kicked him out because of you."

Suddenly, Nola covered her face with her hands and squatted down by the birdseed bag, sobbing like a rejected singer on *American Idol.*

What, did Nola actually feel *bad* now? Hell no. That was not okay. Nola should have felt bad before she spread her skank legs for somebody else's *husband.*

Willow wanted to leave, to show Nola that she couldn't manipulate the shit out of her like she did everybody else. On the other hand, it was sunny and warm in the courtyard, and what would she do back inside the house? Chat with the maid? Who actually had a maid, anyway?

She perched on the bench, crossed her legs, and watched some kind of little gold bird at the feeder. Amazing it wasn't afraid of people.

Eventually Nola wiped her face on the hem of her sweater and stood up. She put the bird feed away in the pantry and came back outside, where she sat too close to Willow and bent down to pat the stupid dog, who didn't know the difference between good people and lying, betraying sluts, and wagged his tail. "Sorry," Nola said.

"For what?"

Nola looked at Willow, her face a train wreck of smeared makeup. "For everything. You must hate me."

"I don't hate you," Willow lied. "I just think you're a stupid idiot."

"You're right." Nola reached up, broke a little stick off the tree branch hanging above them and tossed it. The dog attacked the stick like it was a rattlesnake, growling and shaking it. "But you can't always help who you fall in love with. You'll learn that someday."

Willow rolled her eyes. "Whatever."

"I mean it, Willow. Sometimes things just happen."

"Only if you let them."

"It's not that easy to say no to love." Nola's lower lip trembled. "Not when it's a guy as nice as your dad."

"Oh, no. We are so not doing this." Willow stood up and glared down at Nola. She wanted to head butt her. "Don't you fucking *dare* say you love my dad. You've known him for what, like, a year? A year of history class, plus a few special extra-help sessions or whatever? Never mind," she said when Nola opened her mouth to answer. "Don't tell me how you got with Russell. You're pregnant because he couldn't keep it in his pants and you were both too stupid to use birth control."

"You're right," Nola whispered.

Willow nodded and took a step away from the bench. "I am. And now you're *saying* you're in love so everybody will fucking forgive you or feel sorry for you. I don't want to hear how *in love* you are, Nola. Don't you fucking realize what you *did*? Jesus. You're worse than a stupid idiot. You're like this evil spell cast on my whole family. You make me sick just *looking* at you!"

"I make myself sick," Nola said, and pulled her sweater down over her knees, then tucked her hands inside the sleeves. "I'm so, so sorry."

She was making Willow want to puke her guts out with those fake apologies. Willow took the leash out of her pocket and hooked it to Mike's collar. "I am so out of here. Tell Dad I came like I was supposed to, like our agreement *says*, okay? But I have some serious homework. I'll get home on my own."

Nola practically jumped up off the bench. "Wait! You can't just go! How will you even get home? At least let me drive you."

"No. I'll take a subway like a normal person—not a fucking Range Rover," Willow said. "You can cover your ass. Tell Dad that Catherine wanted me to come home early or whatever."

"You can't expect me to lie." Nola looked around the courtyard, her eyes wild.

"Why not? Seems to me like you must be pretty good at it by now." Willow tugged the puppy back toward the kitchen. "You've been doing it long enough."

CHAPTER EIGHT

Catherine hadn't intended to date anyone. She had intended to fly solo, to be celibate the rest of her life. Yet here she was, having dinner with Seth Cunningham, breaking not only her own private vow, but the office rule not to date the parent of a patient.

Even worse, she had an ulterior motive. He was a divorce lawyer and seemed ethical rather than smarmy. Wary, still, of Russell, of what he might try to do (or not do) with Willow despite their custody agreement, she'd thought it would be a good idea to talk to Seth, so when he called her office to ask her out, she'd accepted his invitation.

How to bring that up was the tricky part, Catherine realized, as she and Seth made conversation over Indian food at her favorite place in Harvard Square. Seth was free because Brady was at his grandmother's house; he didn't mind when Catherine said she needed to be home by eight o'clock for Willow, because he had to pick up Brady by seven.

"I'm trying to get Brady on some kind of regular schedule," Seth explained. "I don't think his mom was into routines. Kids need that, right?"

He looked so anxious that Catherine understood now that Seth had called her for the same reason she'd agreed to see him: advice.

"Children definitely need a reliable routine," she assured him, "especially if there's been some upheaval in the past." She explained to Seth about Willow, telling him a little about her sister's chaotic history.

"Willow's still anxious if Russell and I leave her alone at night," Catherine told him, aware as she said this that she would have to learn to drop the phrase "Russell and I" from her vocabulary. "She had some terrible things happen to her as a child."

"Like what?" Seth asked. "Or shouldn't I ask? Is that the same thing as saying I'll show you my dysfunctional family if you show me yours?"

Catherine laughed. "I suppose, but it's kind of a relief to talk about it. Let's see. Once, Zoe's apartment caught fire because she fell asleep on the couch with a cigarette in her hand. Willow had to call 911. She was seven years old. Another time, somebody broke into the apartment while Willow was there by herself. She was nine."

"Where was your sister?"

"Working in a hotel as a bartender. Amazing tips. I think she made more than I did as a nurse back then. Luckily, the guy who broke into the apartment was apparently only after drugs and money. He left Willow alone. It was probably a friend of Zoe's," she added.

"Willow's dad isn't in the picture?"

"No. He never was," Catherine said. "It's so sad, really. Zoe ran with a tough crowd in high school—people who terrified me, and I was three years older—but she seemed to settle down a little once she got to college. We all thought Zoe was going to make it, but then she imploded. My mom was the only one who kept saying Zoe was just going through stuff and would grow up."

"An optimist."

Catherine stirred the curry around on her plate. "I guess. Dad was more realistic about Zoe. He emigrated with his parents from Canada when he was a boy. They had nothing. I mean, really nothing: a two-room apartment in South Boston. Dad helped support his family with everything from paper routes to landscaping jobs while he was in high school. He never understood Zoe's aversion to hard work. Me, either."

"Sounds like a tense household."

"Sometimes." Catherine pushed her plate away. "By the time she was in college, though, Zoe had a great boyfriend she'd met her senior year of high school and she was bringing home decent grades. She was even getting along with her roommate. I was a senior at the university when she was a freshman, and it was actually fun to see her on campus."

She paused, remembering Zoe as she was that last Halloween in Amherst. Zoe was living in one of the high-rise dormitories. They'd gone hiking despite the cold weather and returned to campus with windburned faces, laughing at the state of their hair.

Zoe had adopted a uniform of jeans and hiking boots. She wore them everywhere, even out to dinner, and never drank or smoked. She'd gained a little weight and even stopped doing molly, her favorite club drug.

"So what happened?" Seth asked.

"Mike broke up with her at the end of her freshman year, and all hell broke loose again."

Catherine stumbled into silence, remembering the sobbing phone calls in the middle of the night, Zoe's wild rants about throwing herself off a building or under a bus. She'd been afraid her sister might go through with it and called her parents. "Mom went to Amherst immediately and brought Zoe home, though our father was against it. After that, Zoe dropped out of school. She was pregnant."

"Was Mike the father?"

"We never found out. Zoe refused to tell anyone who the father was, and Mike denied it when my father confronted him. What's weird is that, a few years later, Zoe and Mike moved in together for a while, when Willow was little. But still there was no mention of paternity. Mike certainly never paid my sister any child support. Then he moved out when Zoe started doing drugs again. After that, she kind of bounced around between apartments and men."

"Zoe sounds as troubled as my ex," Seth said sympathetically. "My ex is—or was, anyway—an alcoholic. I kept talking her into checking herself into rehab programs, but nothing took. Eventually I walked out. I thought I'd get awarded custody of Brady, but the courts work in mysterious ways."

"Well. You have him now, anyway, and that's good," Catherine said. "For Willow and Brady, structure helps them learn to form loving attachments. It's a relief for them to feel like the adults are in charge."

They finished eating and moved on to talk about work, Seth's passion for distance running, and Catherine's summers in Chance Harbor. Finally, when the waiter had taken away their plates and brought them cups of Masala chai, Seth asked about Russell.

"So what's happening with your ex?" he said. "You seemed pretty upset the last time we saw each other."

Catherine laughed. "That's a very diplomatic way of saying that I was a puddle on the sidewalk. Thank you. Things are progressing quickly with our divorce. Maybe too quickly?"

"What do you mean?"

"We drew up a separation agreement with a mediator the week Russell moved out. He wants to expedite our divorce so he can marry this girl he got pregnant." When Seth looked startled, she said, "Yes, I did mean a 'girl.' She's only eighteen. One of his students."

"My God," Seth said. "There should be a special circle in hell for men like that. I'm surprised he wasn't arrested."

"Apparently, there's no law that prohibits teachers from dating students, only the policy of the individual school. Naturally, Russell was dismissed the minute the headmaster caught wind of things."

"That sounds very hard. I'm so sorry."

Catherine threaded her fingers together on her lap, wishing the napkin were paper so she could shred it. "It's difficult, yes. And it came as a complete shock. I thought we were happy." Her eyes burned. Impatiently, she pressed her fingers to them, hard. "Russell and I are trying to be civil. We've agreed to split our property down the middle. I'll buy him out of the house when I can. Meanwhile, he has agreed to let me live there with Willow. He's living somewhere with his girlfriend. Presumably in a place she pays for, since God knows we don't make enough to support two households."

"Okay," Seth said slowly. "Sounds fair so far. And I assume you're having the mediated agreement looked at by independent attorneys?"

Catherine nodded. "The only thing that worries me is the custody arrangement."

"Why? Does it look like Russell will fail to honor it?"

"I don't know," Catherine said. "I have physical custody, and we have shared legal custody of Willow as her guardians. Wednesday is supposed to be his night to have dinner with Willow. He also gets her every other weekend."

"A traditional arrangement, then." Seth sighed. "One that offends me as a father, I have to say, since it doesn't give dads enough access to our kids."

Catherine bristled. "Look, I'm not playing hardball or anything. I've told Russell that he can see Willow as much as he likes. But Willow has made it clear that she doesn't want to live with Russell, or even visit him regularly. I think this is partly because she considers Cambridge her home, but also because she's angry at him. Is she old enough to decide how often she wants to see him, or to refuse to see him completely?"

"No. There's no age at which a minor child can decide her own place of residence," Seth said. "Not in Massachusetts. And if there's a dispute over custody, a judge would have to decide the outcome."

"Even if Russell is only Willow's guardian, and not her biological father?"

"He has been her legal guardian for the past five years, though," Seth said, leaning back in his chair with a frown. "I think a judge would take that into account. Where are these questions coming from? Don't you trust Russell with her?"

"He's fine with her. But I'm anticipating problems down the road, like Willow not wanting to go there, and Russell with a baby, so he's not connected to her in the future. She needs a father."

Seth reached over and touched her hand. "You're worrying before there's anything to worry about," he said. "The opposite could happen, right? Maybe Russell and Willow will get closer as he spends more one-on-one time with her. Or maybe Willow will adore the baby and want to move in with Russell."

"That's a horrifying thought!"

Seth laughed. "I know. But that's the thing about family relationships: you can't predict how any of them will turn out. The only person you can control is you."

"That's not so comforting, either."

"No, but it is liberating. Since there's nothing you can do about how other people act, you might as well relax and enjoy the good times," Seth said. "Only worry if there's something real to worry about."

As they left the restaurant and walked along Mass Ave, Catherine felt more hopeful. Maybe things would be all right.

They said good-bye at Seth's door. He wanted to walk her home, but Catherine refused, insisting that she walked this route often. "I'll be fine."

"I'd insist, but I do have to pick up Brady," Seth said. "I should have planned this better. I'm woefully inadequate at parental multitasking." He bent down and pressed his lips to Catherine's hand. "Farewell. I hope we see each other soon."

"Wow," she said, laughing. "I haven't had anyone kiss my hand since my high school senior play."

He straightened, giving her an amused look. "Shakespeare?"

"Hardly. It was some farce where I was a damsel in distress. I was actually tied to train tracks at some point. My boyfriend played the hero, and his mustache literally fell off in the middle of the scene where he was releasing me from the tracks. I screamed because it looked like an insect flying down at my face."

Seth laughed. "That's live theater for you," he said. "We'll have to go see a play sometime."

"Maybe," she said.

Catherine enjoyed the walk home. She'd limited herself to just one glass of wine at dinner and felt fully awake, invigorated. The night was warm for early October and the sidewalks were buzzing with people. Even the bike lane was busy.

It wasn't until she reached Porter Square that she realized one of the figures walking ahead of her was Willow. Catherine wouldn't have recognized her—Willow had pulled her sweatshirt hood up over her head and wore a backpack like every other student in Cambridge—except her dog was trotting along on its leash beside her.

Where the hell was Russell? He'd said he would pick up the dog from their house, then get Willow from school and bring her home after dinner.

It occurred to Catherine again that she didn't know where Russell and Nola lived; she hadn't wanted to ask, and Russell hadn't volunteered that information. She frowned and hurried to decrease the distance between herself and Willow.

She grew angrier as she walked. How could Russell have let Willow walk home alone at night? She was only fifteen! There were all kinds of drug dealers and homeless people around Porter Square at night, like that raggedy beggar woman with dreadlocks following right behind Willow.

To be fair, Catherine might have let Willow walk home this late with so many people around, too. But the point was that Catherine had given Russell strict instructions about dropping Willow off at the house no earlier than eight o'clock, because that's when she had promised to return.

She intended to honor their custody agreement to the letter. Russell, on the other hand, had already turned Willow loose in the city at night.

Gritting her teeth, she increased her pace until she passed the beggar woman. Now she saw that the woman must be blind; she was using a white cane. Catherine muttered an apology as the woman, clearly startled, stepped to one side and hunched protectively over her tattered cloth shoulder bag as Catherine hurried by.

They'd reached their own block. Willow slowed as she neared the house, lifting her head to peer in the windows, probably checking to see if Catherine was home. The lights were on a timer and always came on at six o'clock. The car was in the driveway, but of course that didn't mean the house was occupied. Catherine typically walked or took the subway to work. No, the only clue Willow had to go on was the fact that Catherine had promised to be home by eight o'clock. And Catherine kept her promises.

Catherine hung back in the shadows, standing outside the pool of light cast by the streetlamp on the corner, as Willow unlatched the gate and walked up the steps to the front porch, whistling softly for the dog when the puppy stopped to nose around the hydrangeas.

The sidewalk was now empty of pedestrians, as if some invisible vacuum had hoovered them all up. Even the blind woman was gone. Maybe she wasn't a beggar after all and lived in one of the apartments around here.

Catherine deliberately made noise on the stairs and jangled her keys before inserting them into the lock. She didn't want to spook Willow by making her think there was an intruder.

Inside, she dropped her purse on the mission bench in the hallway and hung up her coat. The puppy ran up to greet her, tail wagging, squashed face grinning up at her.

"Hello, Mr. Mike," Catherine said, patting the little dog's head and smiling down at him despite her rotten mood. "How was your day?"

Mike rubbed his face against her black pants in response. Great. More dog hair to remove.

She poked her head into the living room, then went to the kitchen, her boots echoing on the hardwood floor. Catherine stopped for a minute, listening, and heard the toilet flush upstairs.

She went to the bottom of the stairs. "Willow?"

Her irritation with Russell was building like an allergic reaction, beginning with an itch in her throat and making it increasingly difficult to breathe. Had he even picked Willow up today? Did Willow eat dinner with him or not? Had she done her homework?

A door opened upstairs. "Hey, Mom," Willow called down. "I'll be right there."

Catherine went into the kitchen and grabbed a handful of tortilla chips out of the bag on top of the fridge. She wasn't hungry, but she needed to gnash her teeth on something.

Willow came downstairs wearing flannel pajama pants and slippers. She was carrying the puppy, nuzzling its head with her chin. "I didn't hear you come in," she said. "Did you just get here?"

Catherine eyed her daughter's sweet but wary expression; Willow's shoulders were folded forward with tension beneath the white-blond curls. She looked so much like Zoe right now that Catherine couldn't help but feel angry, remembering Zoe's willful misbehavior at this age.

Where had Willow been tonight?

With a sinking sensation, Catherine knew there would be days, even years, of this kind of uncertainty now that Willow was pinging between two houses. Times when she would have absolutely no idea where Willow was or what she'd been doing.

"I just got home," Catherine said. "Have you been here long?"

"No. I'm surprised I didn't see you on the street."

Catherine nearly said, *Ah, but I saw you*. "Yes, well, it's getting dark earlier now." She turned her back and rustled around in the bag of chips for another handful of tension tamers. "How was your day?"

"Pretty good. School's okay, I guess." Willow sat at the kitchen table, the puppy on her lap and gnawing on the string of her pajama pants. "Today I had photography for the first time. It's only twice a week, but the teacher seems pretty cool."

"How about dinner?" Catherine sat down across the table from her. "What did you have?"

Willow shrugged. "Some crap thing. I didn't really eat much. I'm going to have some cereal before bed." She put the puppy down and went to the cupboard, fished out a box, then got a bowl and poured the cereal and milk into it.

Catherine waited until Willow was back at the table before asking, "Did Dad cook, or did you go out?"

"Out," Willow said, chewing with her eyes fixed on the cereal box in front of her. "We had burritos from Fernando's."

This was plausible, but unlikely. Russell had always hated burritos.

Who hated burritos? Catherine should have known better than to marry him based on that alone.

"Sounds fun," she said. "Is Dad's place close to Harvard Square?"

"No."

Catherine waited, but Willow kept shoveling cereal into her mouth. Finally, she said, "So where is it?"

"Where's what?"

"Dad's new place."

"Why? You planning to visit?" Willow picked up the bowl and drank the milk from it noisily.

"Don't be mouthy with me. And we do not drink out of bowls. Put that down," Catherine said.

"Fine. I'm done anyway." Willow took the bowl to the sink and dropped it there with a noisy clatter, then stomped upstairs, the puppy at her heels.

Catherine was so shocked by this—Willow had never been the tantrum-throwing sort of kid—that it took her a minute to process what had happened. Once she did, she bolted up the stairs two at a time, but it was too late: Willow's door was closed. Catherine turned the handle, but it was locked.

"Open this door," she said. "Immediately."

Her command was met by silence. Catherine stood in the hallway, feeling chilly now in her bare feet, torn between wanting to pound on the door and longing to press her head against it and cry. Just then the doorbell rang downstairs. What the hell?

She galloped down the stairs, ready to tear into whoever would dare solicit at this hour. Just last week she'd had visits from Jehovah's Witnesses, high school athletes selling coupon books, and a reedy-voiced kid soliciting for some do-gooder environmental cause. She peered through the keyhole. Russell stood there, his face heavily lined beneath the bright porch light. Catherine opened the door, almost relieved. Maybe he could yell at Willow about her behavior. Then she remembered: Russell was the reason *behind* Willow's behavior. That made her furious all over again.

"What?" she said.

"I'm sorry to bother you so late. I need to see Willow. I texted her and she said she was here."

"You just saw her."

"No. I didn't." Russell looked tired but put together. He was dressed in his usual tweed jacket and tie and a white shirt, his khakis falling tidily around his expensive shoes. Why was he dressed like this?

A job interview, she guessed, and said, "Why not? What happened?" She opened the door wider and nodded for him to come in. "Willow got home just before I did. Like, twenty minutes ago. If she wasn't with you, where was she?"

"Oh, she was at my house. Just not with me." Russell stepped inside and stood in the hallway, gazing anxiously up the stairs. "Is she in her room?"

"Yes. Look, what's all this about?"

Russell started up the stairs. "It's between Willow and me. Sorry."

"Hey! You can't just waltz into my house and . . ."

Russell spun around on the stairs. At that height, he looked magnificent. And very angry. "As of now, this house belongs to me, too," he said. "But, more to the point, do you or do you not want me to have an ongoing relationship with our daughter?"

"I do." She felt her shoulders slump in defeat.

"Good. Now, is it all right with you if I go upstairs?" He waited, fingers drumming on the railing, until she nodded.

"Good luck getting her to open the door," she said.

So much for feeling proud about having had only one glass of wine at dinner. Catherine went to the kitchen and poured herself a generous glass of cabernet, then sat at the table pretending to read the newspaper. Eventually Russell came down.

"Willow's all right." He hovered by the table until she told him to sit.

"No, she's not. Willow's upset," Catherine said. "What's going on? How did she end up at your house but not with you?"

"You won't like the answer." He loosened his tie and took it off, tossed it on the table. When Catherine saw him looking at the wine, she got up and filled a glass for him.

"Try me," she said.

"I had a job interview, so I asked Nola to pick her up from school."

Catherine stared at him. "How is it Nola's job to take care of your child? And why on earth would you think that would fly with Willow?"

Russell held up a hand. "Look, I was desperate, okay? I knew you were working, and obviously I don't know any of the parents at Willow's school yet. I didn't know what else to do. I could have texted her and told her to come here, but I wanted to see her. Besides, that was our agreement. I wanted to honor it."

He drank some more wine, then went on. "I had no idea the job interview would take so long. It was in New Hampshire, at a prep school in Concord. Tim Bankhead, a friend of mine from high school, is the headmaster there now, and they're looking for a history teacher to replace someone who just became ill. I had to meet with a committee and explain why I was let go from Beacon Hill. Imagine how much fun that was. Then I ran into more traffic than I expected going home. By the time I got back, Willow had left and Nola was in tears."

That did sound like a terrible day, but Catherine wasn't letting him off the hook that easily. And she didn't give a flying damn about Nola. "Couldn't you have scheduled a job interview for a day when you didn't have to pick up Willow? You only have her one day a week, for Christ's sake."

He stared at her. "Can you hear yourself, Catherine? Get off your high horse! I am not ten years old. I know my responsibilities and I uphold them. But this was the only day they could do the interview, and I jumped at the opportunity. It's not that easy to find a job in this economy. Certainly not at my age."

"And certainly not after what you've done." Catherine tipped her wineglass toward her. It was empty. She wanted to refill it but wouldn't let herself. "Remind me. You uphold your responsibilities how, exactly? By doing something so *egregiously wrong* that you throw away your entire career, and our daughter loses her school, her friends, her whole life? Never mind me! God, forget about me. Oh, wait. You already have!" Catherine realized she was shouting, but she didn't care. It felt good to shout.

"Look, I never pretended to be perfect," Russell said. "You're the one who always pretended I was perfect. That *we* were perfect. So organized. So together. Our little house, our little life. Our little marriage."

"Little?" she spat out.

"Yes!" Now he was shouting, too. "Little! Small! Pathetic! Who are we, really? Nobody. And what have we done? Nothing much that matters. We gave Willow a stable home. Good for us. But we're just ordinary humans, Catherine. Flawed by definition. Remember Socrates: 'Be kind, for everyone you meet is fighting a hard battle.' Nobody's perfect. We tried to make our marriage work, and it did, for a long time. Who knows? Even now, if I weren't about to be a father, and if we both decided we wanted to work on our marriage, we might be able to put this thing behind us and keep going."

"That's what my mother says," Catherine said. "She keeps telling me that even though their marriage was rocky at times, and that Dad cheated on her, it was worth it for them to stay together. She and Dad were happy." She felt that knot of grief for her father, the sorrow that was always there, not diminished at all, only partly swallowed.

"Well, maybe that's because they were even."

"What do you mean?"

Russell scooped his tie off the table and stuffed it into his pocket. "Look, I don't know anything about your dad cheating on your mom. That's news to me. But your mother told me she had an affair. She fell in love with another guy, yet she had the nerve to call me pathetic! Your father could have thrown her out of the house. They decided to hang in there because of you and Zoe"

Catherine stared at him. "What the hell are you talking about? You're delusional. My father's the one who had an affair, not my mother. And it was brief and unimportant. A blip in their marriage, Mom told me. They *loved* each other! I've never seen two people closer than they were."

"Except when your mother was busy cheating on Andrew." Russell was looking down at her with something like pity. "You really didn't know?"

"Mom wouldn't do that. She would have told me!" Catherine tried to shout at him again, because that was the one thing that seemed to make her feel better, but her voice came out as a croak.

"Ask her, if you don't believe me," Russell said. "Maybe then you'll forgive me. Or at least not bite my head off. Remember, I still love you and Willow. Probably more than anyone else does. Or will." He left then, opening and closing the front door behind him with a rush of cold air.

Catherine put her face down on the table and closed her eyes, trying to make the chaos go away. Her whole imperfect life.

CHAPTER NINE

The dog showed up again while Eve was walking around the house with Red Allen, the painter that Cousin Jane had suggested.

"He's all the way in St. Peter's, mind," Jane had said as she'd written the painter's number on a scrap of paper for Eve. "And he's been known to indulge himself. You know what I'm saying." She made a tippling motion, as if tossing back a shot. "He did my son Bobby's house last year, and Bobby came home one day to find Red passed out on the lawn. Right under his own sign, if you please!"

"Why should I call him, then? Can I trust him?" Eve asked.

Jane nodded vigorously without dislodging a single strand in her tight gray cap of hair. "Oh, don't you worry. He'll get the job done. I'll come by every day, keep a close eye on him. And Red won't charge an arm and a leg because the man is family. A MacLeish through and through. Our second cousin, mine and Andrew's. You give him a call and say Jane told him to give you a fair deal."

Jane had brought her snowflake rolls; Eve stuck them in the freezer after she left. There was barely any room in there. Andrew's relatives had continued dropping by with biscuits, snowflake rolls, pecan tarts, and pies, all made with island butter and cream. She hoped it would all fit into the cooler for the ride home.

When Red showed up this morning, damp hair slicked back and smelling of cologne, she'd seen the MacLeish blood in him right away. He looked, at first glance, so much like Andrew and Malcolm that her breath caught in her throat as the painter climbed out of his battered blue truck. He had removed his cap to greet her with a funny little bow, revealing the familiar MacLeish blond hair and ruddy color, the nose turned up at the tip like a stubborn elf's.

"Whoa," Red said now, as Bear lumbered across the lawn, fanning the air with his tail. "That's some horse you got yourself there."

"Oh, he's a good pony, all right." Eve scanned the road for Darcy's truck as she rubbed the dog's head. Bear pressed himself against her thigh, blissful, nearly knocking her over. "I call him Bear, but his real name's Sparrow."

"Yeah, that dog's definitely no Sparrow," Red said. "Whose is it?"

"He belongs to a guy staying in North Lake. It's his son's, actually."

"Huh. He's a fair piece from home. Lucky that dog hasn't been hit."

"Or stolen."

Red scratched his head. "Doubt anybody could lift that animal."

She laughed, and they went back to discussing the work. There were clapboards to replace, most of which Red said he could do. He promised to call her with a quote by that night and suggested a couple of places to buy paint in Charlottetown. "You keeping it yellow?" he asked, one foot in the truck as he prepared to leave.

"I guess so. Andrew's family would kill me if I changed the color."

"Well, now, they're not the ones living here," Red said. "You want to change the color, you go ahead."

"We'll see," she said, not wanting to explain that she knew yellow or white were the colors that would probably appeal most to would-be buyers. Only people from away would be interested in buying this house. People looking for an Anne of Green Gables experience or a beachfront property they could tear down and replace with a glassy McMansion. Islanders were more likely to build new houses on family plots of land than fix up the old places. They were too practical to want a leaky old house like this one in winter.

Eve spent the rest of the morning pruning bushes around the deck and clearing fallen leaves out of the perennial gardens. Any other autumn, she'd be digging up the dahlias and storing the bulbs in the basement for winter; this year she'd have to leave them. Customs wouldn't let her bring them across the border. Or maybe Jane would want them?

Oh, it was all too much to think about.

For lunch she made a sandwich of cheddar cheese sliced onto a snowflake roll, sharing the food with Bear. Her shoulders and back ached from the yard work. The dog drooled as he ate, then flopped onto the wooden floor, lying on his side and stretching his legs out. She had to step around him to bring her dishes to the sink. She didn't mind; she was glad of the company.

Eve had just completed her next round of phone calls—to the plumber to drain the pipes for winter, to a roofer who could come tomorrow to inspect the shingles, and to a contractor who might be able to finish weatherproofing the basement—when she heard Darcy's truck rumble into the yard. Bear wagged his tail but didn't bother getting up.

"You sure are one lazy pony," Eve said as she stepped over the dog to open the kitchen door. "In here, Darcy," she called from the deck. "I promise I didn't kidnap your dog. He came of his own volition."

"Don't lie to me, now," Darcy said. "You picked up that beast and carried him into the house kicking and struggling."

She laughed, then gave him a serious look. "If you can't watch that dog more carefully, you might want to tie him up so he doesn't wander and get hit. Islanders drive this road like it's the autobahn."

Darcy shrugged his broad shoulders, which were clad in the same battered green jacket he'd had on the first time she met him. "I actually thought I *had* shut him inside before I went to the university this morning, but this dog can open doors."

"You've got to be kidding."

"Nope. Watch. Come outside."

Eve stepped onto the deck next to Darcy, who closed the kitchen door tightly behind her before calling the dog. "Sparrow! Hey, Sparrow! Let's go to the beach!"

To her astonishment, the knob turned and the dog stepped outside. He came over to Darcy and pushed his nose into the man's big palm.

"Not bad," Eve said, patting the dog's silky back. "There's only one problem."

"What's that?"

"Now you've made him a promise. And this doesn't seem like the kind of dog that would forget."

"I suppose you're right. I could use a walk anyway. Want to join us?"

"Sure. Let me grab a jacket." Eve went into the house and plucked her blue Windbreaker off the hook, then pulled the door closed and started toward the steps leading down the cliff to the beach.

"Wait," Darcy said. "How about if I show you a secret cove?"

Eve turned to look at him. "You forget that I've been coming here for forty-five years."

"I promise you haven't been to this place."

She hesitated as she thought about the work still ahead of her: phone calls, linens to pack and ship, clearing out the basement and the rest of the barn. The barn was taking forever because it had a second floor, and nearly everything she touched brought back fresh memories of Andrew and the girls. Plus, she kept having to make runs to the Waste Watch Drop-Off Center at Dingwells Mills twenty minutes away to dispose of things.

Darcy cleared his throat noisily, startling her. "You coming?"

She watched him cross the yard to the truck with his long loping walk. He let down the truck's gate, and the dog jumped in, surprising Eve with his agility. She followed. Was there really a beach on this eastern end of the island that she hadn't explored?

Darcy pulled onto the road and headed toward North Lake. As they passed the fields next to her house, Eve noticed that the potato harvesters were out, churning up the rich red soil, uprooting potatoes to be collected by the trucks that followed the diggers.

Potatoes were big business on PEI. Eve had always admired the beauty of the rolling fields, the deep green leaves dotted with white flowers interspersed with golden fields of wheat and the hypnotic, dizzying bright yellow squares of the canola crops.

But she also felt tense and vaguely guilty whenever she watched her neighbors work their fields. Many relied on farming for a living. They were laboring from sunrise until after dark, even on weekends, while most of her time on the island had been spent hiking, biking, swimming, or going out on a boat with one of Andrew's cousins.

Such long, lovely days in this place, and now those were coming to an end. Eve swallowed hard, reminding herself that this was Andrew's island, not hers. His family's home. Her own "home place," as the islanders called the houses where they were born, was actually a brick house in sensible, academic Madison, Wisconsin. Another place she'd stopped going. After her parents died, and her brother, too, of colon cancer just before his sixtieth birthday, there didn't seem to be much point. Not when her sister was such a hermit.

You got old enough, and the losses kept piling up. Eve studied her hands in her lap, the fingers still slender but the knuckles enlarged now, arthritis settling into her joints. Her hands were sixty-six years old, just like the rest of her. Her body was wonderfully functional. She was lucky, but she didn't always feel that way, too mired in grief to count her blessings.

"Penny for 'em," Darcy said, glancing at her.

"I was thinking those must be your windmills over there," Eve said to distract him—and herself. She pointed to the tall white turbines. She'd never paid much attention to them before; only noticed with a start, one day, that the windmills had gone up while she'd been away. The horizon had been drastically altered by their presence, yet somehow she didn't mind. The windmills were beautiful as well as practical.

"Not exactly mine," Darcy said. "But I'm proud to have played a small part in getting them to this part of the island."

"How?"

"I helped my PEI University colleague, Ed, write a grant proposal to fund them. I used to come up to the island with my parents to camp, and when I started studying wind energy in college, I always said PEI would be the perfect place for wind farms, with so few trees and all that water around us. I was one of the engineers overseeing the first big wind-power project in Vermont," he added. "Did you know the city of Burlington is now powered entirely by renewable energy? Wind power, wood chips, and hydroelectric."

"Brag much?" she said, but grinned. Darcy's enthusiasm was refreshing.

They were traveling along the north side of the island, the land flatter and emptier here than on the southern shore, feeling almost desolate. She asked Darcy more about his work—he was overseeing another wind farm being installed in southern Vermont—and about his children.

Eve felt relaxed for the first time on the island since Andrew's death. Maybe it was because someone else was planning her afternoon. Eve had always been independent—she'd had to be, given how much Andrew traveled for work and having had to juggle her career with children—but sometimes it was good not to have to be in charge.

Unfortunately, though, Darcy's next question was one she'd been dreading. "How about you?" he asked. "Any kids?"

Here was the point where she always had to choose how honest to be. She and Andrew had argued about this. Andrew's view was that people typically didn't want to hear about a dead or missing child. It made them uncomfortable, he said, because who knew what to say in response? And it made him sad as well, so why go there?

For Eve, though, it seemed dishonest to talk about only one of her daughters. Mentioning Zoe kept her daughter's memory alive, even if she really was gone for good, a thought that made Eve twist her hands more tightly in her lap. She would never accept that idea. Not without proof.

To Darcy, she said, "I have two daughters, Catherine and Zoe. Catherine is a nurse practitioner in Cambridge. Zoe has been missing for a while."

He glanced at her. "What do you mean? How long has she been gone?"

"Five years now. She ran off. Took a bus to D.C. and then, well . . . We don't know what happened." The problem with bringing up Zoe, of course, was that it often provoked questions she couldn't answer; she tried to head them off. "Zoe was struggling for years. Drinking, drugs, poor choices in men. We worked with the police and with private investigators, too, but nothing came of it. Catherine is raising Zoe's daughter. Zoe is presumed dead by the police."

Darcy gave her a sharp glance, steering with one hand on the wheel, the other propped on the window. "But you don't believe it."

"No."

"Why not?"

"Because I'd feel her absence." Eve kept her gaze fixed on the road ahead of them. "There would be some sign."

"From the universe?"

"Yes. For lack of a better word. That's exactly it."

To her surprise, Darcy nodded. "I'd feel that way if one of my kids were gone, too."

Relieved, Eve fell silent for a time and watched the horizon scroll by, the sky gleaming a fierce bright blue, free of the usual hazy clouds. She hadn't talked about her certainty that Zoe was alive with anyone in ages. Years. People were tired of the subject.

"I kept searching for her," she said. "I visited every place Zoe ever loved. I was so sure I'd find her. I even tried taking the same bus to D.C. she'd taken, and interviewed people myself. Nobody remembered her."

"I'm sure she was trying to fall between the cracks," Darcy said. "She must have been distressed. Depressed."

"Or scared and running from something. Or someone." Eve had uncovered more about Zoe's life than she'd ever expected—or wanted—to know: the arrests for shoplifting, the homeless shelters Zoe had lived in with Willow, the abandoned building in Worcester where Zoe had squatted for a week. But all of that was from before she ever got on the bus in Boston. After that, nothing. It was as if her daughter had never existed.

They were passing Campbell's Cove now. Eve deliberately changed the subject. "I suppose they're not selling ice cream here this time of year."

"Probably not," Darcy agreed. "Why? Is this one of your regular hangouts?"

"Anywhere that has ice cream is my hangout. You name it: this campground. Shirley's in Souris. Cows in Charlottetown."

"Oh, that Cows' blueberry ice cream!" Darcy moaned. "A dish of blue ecstasy!"

Eve laughed. "What's wrong with these places, that they don't sell ice cream all year?"

"What I always loved about Campbell's are those little wooden camping huts," Darcy said.

"Really? Huh. They always struck me as claustrophobic. Like wooden tents, only with less air."

"No, no. They're practical. Love them," Darcy declared, then pointed. "Here we are. My secret cove." He turned to her, gray eyes dancing. "You haven't been here, right?"

"No. I hardly ever come to this side of the island," she said, struck suddenly by the difference between Darcy's eyes and Andrew's. Andrew's had been blue and set slightly too close together on either side of his snub nose, giving him the sharp, intelligent look of a small, burrowing mammal.

Darcy's eyes were creased at the corners from laugh lines and too much time spent squinting outdoors, yet the irises were wide and a gray that looked warm instead of cool. Andrew assessed you with one glance. Darcy embraced you with a look.

"So, why haven't you?" Darcy asked.

"It's easier to go down the steps from our house and swim than it is to get in the car," she said. "The only beach we ever went to on the north side was St. Margarets, back when they had lobster suppers at the church."

"You've seen the Pioneer Cemetery there?"

"Oh yes. Andrew helped fund the restoration. He has people buried there. It's a beautiful site. I love the sandstone tombstones."

They had left the main road and were following a narrow gravel track between dormant blueberry fields. The fruit shrubs had turned a rose-tinted gold. The gravel soon gave way to red clay, and Darcy's truck jounced so hard over the ruts that Eve had to hang on to the door.

After another half mile, they arrived at a small turnout overlooking a pond surrounded by cattails. A great blue heron stood there, mirrored in the water. Eve loved the herons, their broad silvery wings and crooked necks, their long knobby legs. She loved it that such improbable, imaginary-looking creatures actually existed outside her imagination.

They climbed out of the truck and Darcy let down the gate for the dog. Bear led the way along a sandy footpath nearly overgrown with marsh grasses that whispered against Eve's jacket. It was like walking through shoulder-high water. She could hear the surf but couldn't see it, because of a tall dune ahead of them that seemed to rise from the ground as abruptly as a pyramid in the desert.

Darcy was ahead of her, carrying a blanket and a bag. Eve caught a glimpse of a wine bottle and hoped he wasn't getting any silly ideas. She had mentioned Andrew deliberately earlier to avoid all that nonsense. "How did you happen to have a blanket and wine in the car?" she said. "Are you always so prepared?"

"You mean, am I an alcoholic Boy Scout? No, darling. I packed some things in case you were home and happened to need nourishment. I know how busy you are. We could have eaten at your house, but it's always nicer at the beach."

"Tell me that if you're still up here in February," she said. "How did you even find this place?"

"Accidentally. Like I find most of my favorite things."

"Like what else?" She was breathing harder now that they were ascending the dune's steep slope. Luckily, the dog was slower than she was, so she could keep up her end of the conversation by pretending to wait for him.

"I ended up in Vermont by accident because my motorcycle broke down in the Green Mountains during one weekend joy ride. A farmer let me sleep in his barn and then gave me a job picking strawberries for the summer. I met my wife by accident, too. We literally bumped into each other on a street because we were both carrying things that blocked our view of the sidewalk."

Eve laughed. "What were you carrying?"

"In her case, books—she was an ESL teacher—and, in my case, a spoiler I'd bought for twenty bucks that I'd intended to attach to my Mustang."

Eve wondered about his wife, but maybe Darcy didn't want to talk about his wife any more than she wanted to discuss Andrew. He wore no wedding ring. There was something buoyant about Darcy's personality—he walked on the balls of his feet, as if he were still a young athlete, a distance runner, maybe—that made Eve think he wasn't bitter about whatever had happened.

"And this place?" she asked. "How did you find yourself way out here?"

Darcy gestured toward a stand of pines on a nearby headland. "I was headed to a concert there, at Rock Barra, but I turned left instead of right at the fork and ended up at this beach instead."

"A concert?" Eve didn't know there was anyplace to hear music on this part of the island.

"Yes. Rock Barra is a retreat. The musicians in residence give concerts on Sundays with guest artists."

"Wish I'd known," Eve murmured, though what good would it have done? Andrew hated going out and wasn't a fan of unnecessary noise. He especially disliked fiddle music, which was odd, given his Celtic heritage and the fact that so many people played it here. You could go to a ceilidh or a kitchen party every night of the week on Prince Edward Island.

"Ah. We've arrived," Darcy announced grandly.

It was grand, she had to admit: a length of pink sand bordered by steep red cliffs on either side. There was a bluff on top of one cliff with feathery yellow grass, a bright contrast to the burgundy rocks tinged orange in the sun. Pine trees topped the cliff on the opposite side.

"Okay," Eve said as they stood at the crest of the dune. "You managed to surprise me. This really is spectacular. Thank you."

Darcy looked pleased. "Good. I haven't surprised many people lately," he said, holding out his hand for her as they descended.

"Why not?" She ignored his hand and went first, taking little leaps as she descended, unnerved by his gesture and by his appealing body.

"Too old and slow these days," he said. "What's that line from Yeats?

'An aged man is but a paltry thing, a tattered coat upon a stick.' That's me. A bit worn-out and patched up. Though I hope I have a few years left in this coat."

"Careful what you say. I might be older than you." Eve ran down the second half of the dune, letting her weight carry her, whooping as she nearly lost her balance.

Darcy was right behind her, laughing. "You can't possibly be older than I am," he said when they'd stopped on the beach to catch their breath. He dropped the bag and toed off his sneakers.

"You'd be surprised. Plus, if you're worn and tattered, I'm torn to shreds." She took a deep breath, then added, "My husband died in May. I'm finding things very difficult."

Eve was horrified to hear the quaver in her voice. She began walking rapidly toward the headland side of the beach, to the red rocks piled there like a giant staircase.

Darcy was at her side in an instant, touching her shoulder. "Of course things are difficult for you. I already knew about your husband. I'm so sorry for your loss."

"How did you know?" She kept her head down.

"It's a small island. Forget six degrees of separation. It's more like two."

"My husband's cousin Jane keeps reminding me of that."

"She's the one who told me about Andrew, actually," Darcy said.

"Oh, hell no. Please, please don't tell me you're another MacLeish."

"No. But Jane is the sister of my friend Ed at the university, and she was a good friend of my wife's."

"Was?" Eve hadn't wanted to pry—if the wife was dead, she'd have to invite Darcy to her pity party, and if he was divorced, she'd have to speculate about why—but it seemed impolite not to ask.

"My wife has been gone five years now," Darcy said.

"Gone, as in divorced?" Eve said. "Or dead?" She covered her mouth, shocked at herself. "I'm sorry. That was so rude."

"Don't worry about it. You're entitled to be rude. You're a new widow and grieving. You get to sit on the throne of grief and dispense pronouncements without filters."

"I hope not," Eve said. "That sounds odious. Tedious, too."

He laughed. "Too bad. That's what losing a spouse does to people. And, in answer to your question, my wife died of cancer. It was a long haul. For both of us."

Eve walked quietly beside him, trying to time her breathing with the waves washing in and out so rhythmically along the shore. An old calming trick of hers.

So Darcy was one of the good ones, the sort of spouse who saw things through to the end. A caretaker. Would she and Andrew have done that for each other? Occasionally she found herself feeling relieved not to have been put to that particular test. And Andrew, for his part, would have been pleased by his own death. It was just the kind of ending he would have orchestrated for himself if he'd been giving the instructions: No pain. No drama. Just peace.

The only mistake he'd made was that he'd died at another woman's house. At Marta's.

Now Eve thought of something else. "Jane didn't send you to my house on some misguided attempt at matchmaking, did she?"

Darcy smiled. "No, no. That was all Sparrow's doing."

"Good. Where is he, anyway?"

They walked up and down the beach, calling the dog's name. Just as Eve was starting to worry, they found the dog asleep in the shade beneath a wooden staircase leading up one of the cliffs at the far end of the cove. The stairs were at nearly a ninety-degree angle, almost a ladder. "Sparrow knows this is where I play music," Darcy said. "He probably thinks that's what we've come to do. He just couldn't figure out how to get up the stairs, poor guy."

"I don't blame him," Eve said. "That looks like the staircase to heaven. Or hell. What do you play?"

He grinned. "The fiddle—what else? Want to see the retreat? We could go up there. Rock Barra is closed for the season, but it's still an interesting place."

"All right." Eve hauled herself up onto the first step with the thick rope that served as a railing and began climbing. She was aware of Darcy behind her, close enough that he blocked the wind. At one point she was warm enough to unzip her jacket.

At last they reached the top of the cliff. A circle of stones had been arranged on the headland around a fire pit. Darcy told Eve that people came here for seaside yoga retreats as well as songwriting and music workshops. Airstream trailers were randomly tucked among the pines, gleaming silver, and there was a wooden outhouse.

The main building was unlike any Eve had ever seen. About half of it was glass. The other half was cedar shakes, gone silver with age, and the roof had turf on it.

"The house was originally built as a movie set," Darcy said as they walked around the property. "I know it looks odd, but there's no better place to hear music."

"I bet," Eve said. "I would have loved coming here."

"Well, there's always next summer." Darcy offered her a hand down the stairs.

Eve shook her head and grabbed the rope railing, not wanting to risk touching him. The attraction was there, a buzz between them that made her imagine warmth, a red color. She didn't want to encourage it. What would be the point? She was a mess. And done with all that, anyway. Life was simpler alone.

"I don't know if I'll ever be back on the island again," she said as they descended with the dog's watchful eyes on them from the beach. "I'm actually getting the Chance Harbor house ready to sell."

"Give it time. You may change your mind." Darcy's voice was gentle.

They walked in silence back to where they'd left the bag and blanket. A few gulls wheeled overhead, but other than the birds and the dog, she and Darcy had the beach to themselves. Eve was aware of their isolation, of the thrilling sensation she so often had on this end of Prince Edward

Island—that she really had arrived at the end of the world. So much sky, unlike the brief glimpses of horizon between buildings and trees you got back home. It made you feel both closer to the heavens and insignificant.

Darcy uncorked the bottle of white wine he'd brought in the bag. He poured some into a plastic cup and handed it to her. Eve had meant to refuse the wine, but all of a sudden wine seemed like a fine idea here on this sunny beach, with this man. She felt oddly younger, her earlier bodily complaints and sorrows forgotten as she sipped the chilled wine and took a piece of cheese that Darcy cut for her with deft motions, using a knife with a curved olive-wood handle he'd bought in Italy on one of his consulting jobs last year.

They talked about Italy, where Eve had traveled twice with Andrew, comparing what they both loved about the country—olive groves, medieval villages, narrow winding roads, the abundance of good food and cheap wine—and what they didn't like, such as the scooters zipping up onto the sidewalks in Florence and the long lines at the museums.

"The mistake I made last time was inviting this woman I'd been seeing to come with me," Darcy said. "I thought it would be good to have a companion in Florence, but I couldn't have been more wrong."

Eve laughed and took another sip of wine. "Why?"

"Well, to begin with, this woman looked like a Barbie doll. She'd recently had breast implants despite being over fifty. And she wore so much makeup, it took her more than an hour to get ready anytime we went out."

Eve raised an eyebrow, trying to picture Darcy—so raw-boned and dressed as he always seemed to be, in practical, workman's clothes—with a woman like that. "Why did you even go out with her?"

"A reasonable question." He cut a cube of cheese and fed it to the dog. "I guess I didn't know how to say no. My wife had died and this woman was my sister's husband's niece, if you can follow that. We'd met at a few family functions and my sister encouraged the woman to call me. Let me tell you, there was some guilt on both sides, when my sister found out what a nutcase she was."

Eve laughed. "Do tell."

"You don't want to hear all that."

"Do I look bored? Try me."

"Well, for one thing, this woman was always telling me what gorgeous boobs she had. Maybe because she bought them and wanted to know if she'd gotten her money's worth. Who knows?"

"Or maybe she still felt insecure, even after the implants," Eve suggested. "I've always wondered what they feel like. Do they feel real?"

Darcy shrugged. "Fine. Firm. They have their appeal. Though I did find it odd to lie down next to a woman and realize part of her was still awake and aimed at the ceiling. But that's not the point."

"I would think that would be two points, actually," Eve said, laughing. "I'd love it if any part of me was still firm and bouncy."

He cocked an eyebrow at her. "You're doing all right. You're a very attractive woman."

"For my age, sure." Eve waved a crust of bread at him. "Don't worry. I'm not fishing for compliments. I'm glad to have all of my limbs working at this point. Go on with your story."

"Well, after a few months, she started migrating into my house without ever having discussed it with me. I'd come home and there would be a few pots and pans she'd brought over from her place, or a new blanket or something. I didn't say anything, but I didn't like it, either."

"Why didn't you stop her, if you didn't like it?"

Darcy sighed. "You're going to think I'm shallow if I tell you."

"I promise I won't."

"Well, for the first time in years, I was having regular sex. My wife had been sick for a long time, and it wasn't a gentle disease."

"I understand. So what happened after the woman moved in?"

"Well, we went to Florence—a disastrous trip—and when we came back, my father fell ill and I had to travel to New York to see him. I decided to wait there until he died. It was near Christmas, and I didn't want him to be alone."

"Of course," Eve said.

"Thank you. However, my new roommate didn't see things that way. When I told her what I was doing, she cried and said I'd ruined her Christmas."

"My God."

"Yes. I invited her to remove her belongings from my home at that juncture." Darcy cut another sliver of cheese and handed it to her. "Now. What about you?" he said, as they ate the last of the cheese and stood up to shake out the blanket.

"What about me?"

"You know. Marriage, sex, dating. Any good stories?"

Eve felt her face grow hot as she stepped toward him with her end of the blanket and their hands touched. She hastily moved away. "I'm not sure we know each other well enough for me to want to share that."

"Come on. I did. Why would you want a conversation that's a one-way street?"

"My husband hasn't been dead long enough for me to make an open book of our marriage, much less of our sex life."

Darcy reddened. "Sorry. I didn't mean to offend you. It's just that it's rare for me to be able to talk this openly with anyone." He tucked the blanket into the bag, then called the dog as they started walking back toward the dune. "Listen, though. I have a favor to ask."

"As long as it's not anything to do with sex, ask away."

Darcy laughed. "No, no. It's about my birthday."

"When's your birthday?"

"In ten days. And I've been invited to look at a potential wind farm site on Cape Breton Island that week. Have you been there?"

Eve shivered and rubbed her arms. "Once. Many years ago." She had a sudden image of Andrew, of his face turned up to watch her leave on the ferry, holding Catherine in her arms. She'd been so sick on that ferry. Pregnant with Zoe.

"So you know it's beautiful," Darcy said. "Good. I'd like to invite you to go there with me. I have to consult with someone in Baddeck for a couple of hours, and I'd love company on my birthday. My treat, of course."

"You want me to go to Cape Breton with you?"

"Yes. Just for one night. Separate hotel rooms," he added, seeing the look on her face.

"I don't know. It wasn't an especially happy trip for me, the one time I went there."

"You'd be happy on this trip," Darcy promised. "The leaves have turned and it's the perfect time to go."

"No. I'm sorry. Thank you for asking, but I couldn't possibly go back there."

"Because you're afraid of what you'd find?"

"No. Of what I'd feel," she said, and began climbing the dune ahead of him.

He caught up easily. "Maybe that's why you should go back," he said. "Not because of me or my birthday, as happy as that would make me. But because you haven't finished with that place. That's what this trip to Canada is really about for you, isn't it? Saying good-bye? One thing I discovered after Frannie was gone was that I couldn't move on until I'd revisited all the places we'd been and thought about the mistakes I'd made during our marriage. I had to forgive myself for them."

"What mistakes? You sound like you were the perfect husband." Eve moved away from him, climbing faster.

"No," Darcy said. "How does that old Springsteen song go? 'Sister, I won't ask for forgiveness. My sins are all I have.' That's it, right?"

"I wouldn't know," Eve said. "I only know it's late, and I need to get back."

She'd crested the hill and was walking ahead of him on the sandy trail to the car. The tall rushes seemed to grab at her clothes, threatening to halt her progress; she shouldered through them, not caring if the sharp leaves slashed at her cheeks. She needed to get back to Massachusetts. Away from Darcy.

Away from this island.

CHAPTER TEN

It took several days, but Willow had finally gotten up the courage to stay after school and talk to the photography teacher. Her classes were bigger here, twenty-five kids instead of eight or ten like at her old school. She'd thought she would hate this, but the chaos was a good thing. The teachers lectured and, as long as nobody pulled stupid shit or interrupted the class, left it up to the kids to learn or not.

Today, for instance, the two guys behind her in English said, "Dude, ow! My eyelids are, like, frozen shut!"

When Willow turned around, she saw they were using ChapStick on their eyelids. They made dumb faces, and what could she do but laugh? After class, they high-fived her and asked her to sit with them at lunch. She was wary at first, then realized these kids were part of a whole group that had known one another since grade school. One of them was the class president.

"Yeah, he ran on a platform of killing Meatless Mondays," one girl told Willow, smirking. "Gotta love it, here in crunchy Cambridge."

Photography was taught by Ms. Fiero, a stick of a woman with a crest of pink hair who wore striped leggings, like a Dr. Seuss character. She'd already taught Willow tons. Today, for instance, she talked about "the rule of thirds" and showed them how to divide a picture into a grid of nine squares.

"Most people think they should center every shot, but the human eye is naturally drawn to intersections of those squares," she said, and showed them cool examples.

Ms. Fiero was pretty pumped when Willow asked about hand tinting, and she admired Willow's photographs. Usually only juniors and seniors were allowed alone in the darkroom, but she would give Willow special permission, Ms. Fiero said. "You seem serious about photography, and being passionate about something trumps grade level in my book."

Willow stayed after school to develop her newest rolls of film. Then she walked home, shuffling through the noisy leaves on Cambridge Common until she was spooked by a tall shadow dropping onto the path in front of her.

She froze. A guy was blocking her way. He had a weird little beard and wore a sweatshirt so small that his huge hands stuck out of the sleeves. It was like somebody had jammed them in there: Mr. Potato Head hands.

"Yo, you got any cash money dollars, girl?" the man said.

"No. Sorry." Willow glanced around and, with a sharp little intake of breath, realized they were alone on the Common.

"C'mon, man," the guy said. "You gotta have some spare change. Or how about an iPod? I need money, man." He grabbed at her backpack as Willow tried to sidestep him.

Panicked, she tried to jerk out of his grip, but the man looped an arm tight around her waist and held her so close that she felt his belt buckle pressing against her hip. She flashed on Tom, the Real Deal, his fingers in her panties.

"Let go!" she said, and tried to stab him with an elbow.

"Why would I do that?" he said close to her ear. "You might have something I want."

It was like a gate opened to let out all those memories she'd been keeping locked up in her mind. Buried deep: all the times she'd been in bed and opened her eyes to find Tom standing next to her bed, his thing out, stroking it near her face. She always closed her eyes again and pretended to be asleep. Tom sometimes did it even when Mom was home. Willow had never told anybody.

"Get off me!" Willow pleaded. Her heart was knocking against her chest like a fist.

"Not till I see what you got." The man locked her in place with one arm while he used the other to unzip her backpack and rummage through it. He smelled gross, of sweat and something metallic. Blood?

Willow tried kicking his shin, but she was too close.

"Hold on. Hold on." Her attacker's voice was calm, but his breath was a hot flame licking her neck. "I'll let you go when I'm ready."

"You're ready now, you bastard," somebody growled behind them.

Willow heard a whacking sound. The man grunted and released her. Willow took off and kept running until she was halfway across the Common and had to stop because the stitch in her side felt like somebody had stuck a knife in there. She put her hand there to check: nothing.

She looked around. The guy was gone, but the blind woman who'd given her Mike was coming toward her fast, the cane swirling leaves up around her, like she was her own little tornado. "You okay, honey?"

Willow nodded, dropped the pack to the ground, zipped it back up, and pulled it onto her shoulders again. "Your voice," she said. "It sounds different."

The woman's voice sounded like a normal person's—not the grunting syllables she'd used when she'd given Willow the dog.

The woman waved the cane. "So?" she said. "Is your voice always the same? Different days, different voices, okay? Did that guy hurt you? I'll kill him if he did. I know where he sleeps."

Willow stepped away from her. Clearly, only crazy people hung out on Cambridge Common at night. "No. He just scared me. I shouldn't have been walking here at night. Mom always tells me not to."

"You should listen to her. Stay on the sidewalk after dark." The woman pointed her cane toward Mass Ave, as if Willow couldn't see the sidewalk between the Common and the street for herself, with its reassuring bright lights.

But wait, Willow thought. How could a blind person see the sidewalk? And how could she have attacked that guy, or followed Willow? Maybe she wasn't completely blind.

"You don't obey yourself, seems like," Willow said. "Why aren't you in a shelter after dark?"

The woman snorted, flipped a black dreadlock over one shoulder. "Shelters are crap. More thieves than anywhere. Anyway, do I look like the kind of woman worth mugging?" She rattled the coins in her guitar case.

"Still. You should be careful."

"Oh, don't you worry, honey. I was *born* careful," the woman said. "Now, go home."

If you're so careful, how come you're homeless and begging? Willow wanted to ask. But that would be rude, especially after this woman saved her life.

"Get going," the woman barked. "Go home."

"Okay, okay," Willow said. "Thanks for stopping that guy. See you."

She started walking toward Mass Ave. The wind had picked up; her sweatshirt hood blew off and Willow tugged it back up again. She was aware of the blind woman following, heard her moving through the leaves, but didn't stop. It was creepy, yeah, but she knew the woman was probably still trying to protect her.

Once Willow reached Mass Ave, the sidewalk was crowded and bright. Traffic clogged the street and the storefronts were lit up for Halloween, orange and white lights everywhere. When Willow turned around to wave good-bye before slipping through the wooden rails of the fence bordering the Common, she saw the woman standing with her arms at her sides, the guitar at her feet. Watching over her.

"Hey, want to come home with me and visit your dog?" Willow asked.

The woman shook her head. "I gave him to you so I wouldn't have to think about him anymore. I don't like to get attached, you know?" She turned around, the guitar case banging against her leg, and started walking back toward the inky center of the Common.

Willow didn't want her to go without thanking her in some way. She had granola bars. An apple, too. Snacks she always meant to eat but didn't have time to anymore, since you weren't allowed to eat in class at the public school the way you could at Beacon Hill.

"Hey! Wait!" Willow called. "I want to give you something!"

The blind woman stopped walking without turning around. Willow circled around in front of her and set the backpack on the ground between them. As she unzipped it, she said, "I want to repay you for helping me. I don't have any money. But maybe you can use something to eat."

She glanced up at the woman as she handed her the food. To Willow's shock, from this angle the face beneath the big sunglasses looked eerily familiar: the high, flat cheekbones, the wide-set eyes, the turned-up nose.

No. It couldn't be.

Willow's heart began hammering again, a drumbeat in her ears. Her tongue felt cottony and thick as she watched the woman silently tuck the food into the folds of her loose clothing, then begin walking away again, tapping the ground ahead of her with the cane.

She didn't need that cane, Willow thought, and called out, "Wait! Hold on. This is your real present!"

The woman turned around and shuffled back, grunting.

Willow removed the folder tucked next to her laptop inside the backpack, opened it, slid one of the photographs out, and handed it to the woman, careful to hide the rest from her—especially the photographs of her.

"What's this?" The woman's voice was muffled now by the red shawl, pulled up over her chin again.

"A picture I took of a boy skateboarding in Harvard Square," Willow said.

"Pretty good." The woman held it out for Willow to take back.

"No, you keep it." Willow stood up. It was more difficult to see the woman's features now that they were eye to eye. "Hang it in your room. I mean, if you like it. And if you have a room."

"Of course I have a room," the woman snapped, but the hand holding the photograph was trembling.

"You're not really blind, are you?" Willow said. Was she crazy? Or pretending to be blind to make people feel sorry for her and give her money?

There was one other possibility, too, but it was so out there that even imagining it for a second made Willow feel like she must be the crazy one. "Take off your glasses," she said.

The woman pulled her shawl up over the bridge of her nose and shook her head.

"Please," Willow said. "I need to see you."

"Not going to happen." The woman spun around, dropping the cane and guitar, gripping only the picture as she sprinted across the Common. After a moment of openmouthed shock, Willow ran after her, drawing breaths of cold air in gulps. She might not have caught her if the woman hadn't tripped and fallen. She went down with a soft thump on the carpet of leaves and tried to roll to a standing position. But her boot heel got stuck in her long skirt and she wasn't fast enough.

Willow practically fell on top of her, pinning the woman in place, saying, "Take off your glasses! Please!"

At last, when the woman stopped struggling beneath her, Willow sat up. "I'm sorry," she said. "I shouldn't force you."

The woman sat up, too, head bowed. "That's right. Just leave me alone."

With a sudden lurch, Willow leaned forward and grabbed the glasses off her face.

Even in that moment, even seeing the pale blue eyes, huge with fright now, and the familiar face with its tiny scar across the chin, Willow wasn't completely sure. Not until the woman slowly slid the rainbow tam and black wig off her head, revealing cropped, curly pale blond hair beneath it.

"Mom?" Willow said, staggering to her feet.

Her mother pressed her hands to her face while Willow stood above her, the ground tilting crazily beneath her feet.

. . .

Catherine's Saturday hours were all accounted for now: Zumba class with Bethany at the Y, God help her. Then dinner with Seth.

Three weeks into her separation with Russell, but plans were still crucial to her survival. Well. Only nineteen days, to be exact, yet she was exhausted. Catherine hadn't imagined how difficult it would be to keep a house—a whole life—going on your own. Planning meals and getting groceries, taking the trash out on the right day, laundry and vacuuming and walking the damn dog. What was that expression? *The devil is in the details.*

Other than the few days she'd spent clearing out the Chance Harbor house and the rare times she went out—usually when Willow went with Russell, like this weekend—Catherine had stuck to her routine. She saw Willow off to school and went to work, came home and made dinner, dropped into bed, failed to fall asleep. Did frantic sums in her head to see if she could pay the bills. Took an antihistamine to help herself drop off.

Every morning she woke feeling drugged. But she'd tried not sleeping and that was even worse. Bad enough getting through daylight hours without having to be awake at night, too, and reflecting on her miserable single state and on her mother's lies about her own marriage.

Catherine had mostly managed to forget that awful conversation with Russell about her parents. But then her mother had called this morning to say she was going to Cape Breton with a friend next weekend, and would be driving back to Newburyport the Monday after that.

"You and Willow should come up to Newburyport after I get home and spend a weekend," she'd said. "We'll go hiking or take out the canoe if it's still warm enough."

Who was this woman, who would just take off for Cape Breton with a friend? Who wanted to hike and canoe? That was not her mother, Catherine thought as she pulled on sweatpants and a T-shirt and laced up her sneakers. Her mother had been the quintessential career woman—tailored suits and late nights at the office, weekends spent catching up on household chores. Always with an agenda filled with work and chores, not fun. Like Catherine now.

Hearing her mother's voice brought back everything Russell had said. How could her mother have cheated on Dad? Catherine could understand Dad, with all of his traveling and business stress, having a brief affair. A blip, as her mother had said. But her mother, too? She didn't know what to make of that, other than to think she didn't know her mother at all.

Catherine blinked, shocked to find herself in the middle of the dance floor. Then she had to pay attention while following the teacher, a brunette in her fifties with the body of a teenage cheerleader. That was Bethany's point, exactly, when she'd forced Catherine to sign up for Zumba.

"You need things that keep you in the moment," Bethany had said.

Catherine had tried to stake out a place in the back row—too many intimidating twentysomethings up front—but Bethany had propelled her to the middle of the dance floor. Catherine was soon panting to catch her breath and clearing the floor around her as she tried to get the hang of basic salsa and cumbia steps. She stepped on at least three people.

"You made it!" Bethany teased as they grabbed their water bottles.

Catherine wiped her face with a towel. "I feel like I've been run over by a steamroller."

Bethany laughed. "It gets easier. I promise."

"That's what everyone keeps saying to me about everything. But nobody tells me when."

"Soon," Bethany promised. "I can tell you're better already."

Catherine made a face at her. "Only because I'm half-dead. How can class be an hour long? Ten minutes would have been enough," she moaned.

Back at the house, she did a few more chores, then showered and changed into a black dress she'd bought on impulse at the consignment store near her clinic. It was a simple, straight dress with long sleeves, but it had delicate beading around the collar. Catherine added her silver hoops and silver bracelets, examining the effect in the mirror, then removed the bracelets because they reminded her of the anniversary trip she and Russell had taken to Mexico, where she'd bought them from a woman on the beach.

She wondered what Russell was doing with Willow this weekend. (She never let herself think about Nola being with them, because the very idea of Russell making Willow spend time with Nola made her see red.) Willow had seemed alternately too quiet and too maniacally happy lately, especially the last couple of days; she was definitely feeling the stress of the separation and probably hating the idea of spending another weekend with Russell and Nola. She'd done nothing but complain about the last one.

"Nola acts like she's the only person in the world who's ever been pregnant," Willow had said. "She's all about aches and pains and peeing, even though she doesn't even *look* pregnant yet. I mean, she could be faking it—right? Just to get Dad to marry her?"

"Why in the world would she do that?" Catherine had said, though of course she'd considered that possibility. "Nola strikes me as the kind of girl who's had no trouble getting boyfriends in the past."

"Yeah, I know," Willow had said, sounding glum. "But she says Dad's the only guy who's ever treated her like a real person and been really nice to her." She'd given Catherine a sudden, stricken look. "Does this suck, when I talk about Nola?"

Catherine shook her head and issued her standard party line, the one she and Russell had agreed to use with Willow while they were hammering out the separation agreement. "No. What happened between your father and me is between us, honey. He wants me to be happy, I want him to be happy, and we both want you to be happy most of all. You tell me whatever you feel comfortable saying. I promise not to judge," she added, even though that last sentence was a lie.

Jesus, she thought now, as the doorbell rang. Willow had to see through that crap. She must know that Catherine was far from wanting Russell and Nola to be happy. Right now she wished a sinkhole would swallow up Nola's Back Bay brownstone with both of them in it.

Seth had brought her sunflowers, bright and bold. She smiled at the sight of them and invited him inside for a glass of wine while she put them in a vase. "How's Brady?"

"Still loving his preschool and breathing easy," Seth said, raising his glass of chardonnay to touch hers. "How about Willow? When do I get to meet her, anyway?"

Catherine sipped her wine, considering this. "She's fine, but I think Willow's got enough on her plate right now," she answered finally. "I don't want her to think we're dating."

"No, of course not," Seth said.

He'd answered so quickly that Catherine gave him a sharp look. "We're not, right? That's what we agreed."

Seth nodded, but his mouth—which Catherine had kissed exactly once, and liked well enough—turned down at the corners. He ran a hand through his thick auburn hair, pushing it off his forehead. "It's just that I don't meet many women I like as much as I like you," he said.

Catherine smiled. "I appreciate that. Right now I feel like I'm not great company, truthfully, so it means a lot to hear you say that."

Seth's eyes lingered on her face, but he finished his wine without saying whatever he clearly wanted to say and stood up. "Better go. The play starts at eight."

The play was a comedy, thankfully, a clever Oscar Wilde revival. Afterward they went for sushi in Harvard Square and browsed in a used bookstore. "You do realize we're the oldest ones in here," Catherine said, looking around at the college students.

"Well, except for that guy. He's our age," Seth whispered, lifting his chin in the direction of a man who'd fallen asleep in one of the aisles, his hat on his chest, his snores a noisy rattle. Because this was Cambridge, people just stepped around him and let him be.

As they walked home, Catherine shivered—she'd forgotten her hat, and the air was damp as well as chilly—and Seth put an arm around her. He didn't relinquish his hold even when they reached Mass Ave and the sidewalk was crowded. Catherine wasn't sure how she felt about this, other than warmer.

When Seth tried to kiss her good night in the doorway, Catherine let him, trying to surrender to the strange feeling of his broad chest and too-tall body against her own, but everything about it was wrong. She finally put a hand to his chest and gently pushed him away.

"I'm sorry," she said, and she was. How nice it would have been if, after Russell, she could so easily find a man whose company she not only enjoyed, but desired on every level.

"I'm sorrier," Seth said, and kissed the top of her head before he left.

She shouldn't have said yes. That was Eve's main thought as she hastily threw things into an overnight bag on Monday morning. But it was too late now.

Eve zipped the bag shut just as she heard Darcy's truck pull into the yard. Darcy had called her three times since their picnic on the beach, trying to convince her to come with him to Cape Breton Island. But the call that had actually changed her mind was Marta's. This was only the second time she'd spoken to Marta since Andrew's death. The first was when Marta had called to say she was in an ambulance with Andrew—Eve could hear the shrieking, bone-chilling sound of the siren over the phone—and that Eve should meet her at the hospital.

This time Marta caught her as she was painting woodwork in the kitchen. Eve hadn't bothered to glance at the caller ID, just plucked the phone out of the pocket of her work shirt with her free hand. She'd nearly dropped it when she heard Marta's voice.

"We have to talk," Marta said. "There are things you must know."

Eve had nearly toppled off the ladder. The audacity of this woman! She felt the tension, which had lifted from her shoulders after days of island air and hard work, return like an iron bar pressed across her throat.

"We have nothing to say to each other," Eve said.

"Oh, but I do."

Marta's voice was sultry and low, that German accent thickening every vowel. Eve pictured her as she'd seen her so many years ago, with her thick, shining dark hair, her red lips. That cleavage. If a jaguar could talk, it would sound like Marta.

"Just tell me over the phone, whatever it is, and let's be done with it," Eve said.

"I cannot do that. It is too complicated," Marta said. "Where are you? I could meet you today."

"In Canada," Eve said, and then, for good measure, added, "In Andrew's family's home. Where we were married."

There was a brief silence, during which Eve imagined Marta doing any number of things that would suit that cabaret voice of hers: smoking a cigarette, loading a pearl-handled revolver, pulling a knife out of her garter. Finally, Marta said, "It is something of grave importance."

"I'm hanging up now," Eve said.

"I will wait for your call when you return from Canada," Marta had answered, and hung up first.

That was yesterday. And last night Eve had called Darcy, feeling like she might go mad if she had to spend any more time alone, wondering what her husband's mistress was so determined to tell her.

Bear was in the back of the truck's cab, squeezed behind the seat. His tail thumped against the rear window as Eve climbed into the cab. "Somebody's happy to see you," Darcy said.

She laughed, but was quiet as they drove toward Souris, watching the sky lighten gradually, the spires of the pines emerging first from the hills, the white farmhouses glowing pink in the dawn light. Souris was starting to wake up, the trucks already in line for coffee at Tim Hortons. She and Darcy talked about the town as they waited in line with them, about some of the new restaurants and shops. "Do you know how Souris got its name?"

"No," said Darcy. "But I know it means 'mouse' in French."

"It was back in the seventeen hundreds. There was a mouse plague of some sort, and French sailors coming into port had to push their boats through waves of drowned mice that had swarmed into the water," she said.

"That might put me off swimming forever," he said, making her laugh. And suddenly, as Darcy joined her, his laugh low and rumbling, Eve felt her mood lift.

"So what do you want to do for your birthday?" she asked.

"I had a hike in mind, if the weather holds. Or maybe a boat ride out to Bird Island."

"Bird Island? Is that even a real place? Sounds like a cartoon."

"Sure it is. Might be too late in the season to see the puffins, but we'd see eagles for sure, and seals."

"Well. It's your birthday. You pick," Eve said.

"Hiking, then."

"All right."

He glanced down at her sneakers. "You're okay in those?"

"I brought boots, too. How old are you, anyway?"

"Old enough to know my own mind." He was grinning. "Old enough to know I got lucky, convincing you to come with me on this trip."

Eve rolled her eyes. "Come on. Just tell me."

"Sixty-six tomorrow."

"You're a babe. I'm way ahead of you. I turned sixty-six in February."

"Thank God. I was afraid I was robbing the cradle here."

The tide was out in Souris Harbor as they drove across the bridge. The sand glowed apricot, glittering with quartz crystals as the sun came up all of a sudden, the way it did here, as if hoping to surprise people. Then they were out of the city, the land gradually flattening out as they drove toward the southern shore and the Wood Islands ferry terminal.

There were hardly any cars in line when they pulled up and bought their ferry ticket. They waited about fifteen minutes, leaving the truck to walk Bear up the dirt road toward the lighthouse, then returned and drove down the clanging metal ramp into the belly of the ferry.

Dogs weren't allowed in the lounge area, so they had to stay on the deck with Bear. (Darcy, too, had dropped the ridiculous name "Sparrow.") Eve leaned over the port side as the ferry moved smoothly out to sea. She spotted a pair of seals on a sandbar, one of them a black U shape as it arched its back.

Darcy had brought a wool blanket for their laps and a picnic breakfast of egg-and-cheese sandwiches on wheat toast. Eve was suddenly starved. She ate all but her crusts, feeding those to Bear.

"So, are you going to tell me about it?" Darcy asked, leaning back against the bench when they'd finished their food, after first tucking the blanket in around Eve's shoulders and hips. He didn't look at her; he tipped his head back against the bench, his red wool watch cap pulled low over his forehead, his hands tucked into his armpits.

Eve glanced at him, startled. "About what?"

He opened one eye. "Your disastrous first Cape Breton voyage."

Unexpectedly, Eve found herself laughing again. Out here in the middle of the sparkling sea, with the red cliffs of PEI receding fast behind them and the sun a bright yellow disc against a gray sky mottled with clouds, her past problems felt small and insignificant. A storm could come up or they could hit a sandbar. The boat could go down at any moment and they would have to fight for their lives in the cold, choppy water of the Northumberland Strait. Today was what mattered.

What would be the harm in telling someone? Especially a man she'd probably never see again after this trip?

Eve tipped her head back, too, closing her eyes against the brightening sky, and gave in to the feeling of being on a boat, her hip and thigh warmed by Darcy's long body. Almost like being in bed, she thought, then shook her head a little. Really. At her age?

"I'm not telling you anything about my sex life," she warned.

"I'll just have to use my virile imagination."

She smacked his knee under the blanket. "Behave yourself, young man."

Darcy laughed, but kept his eyes closed, waiting.

It was surprisingly easy, once she'd begun. She told him about Marta first, about discovering Andrew's affair. About how he had continued to see her, as he'd confessed in Vermont. "I think he only told me because she'd threatened to tell me about them if he didn't," Eve said.

"Probably," Darcy said.

"Thanks a lot."

"I'm just being honest. That's what most people do, isn't it? Hide whatever they're ashamed of until some catalyst makes it impossible to hide anymore."

Bear stirred against Eve's feet; she glanced down and realized that the dog had thrown his big black body over not only her feet, but Darcy's, too, effectively anchoring them in place together. If the boat did go down, she had no doubt that this dog would tow them to shore.

She reached down to stroke the dog's silky back and said, "Anyway, after I found out he'd gone back on his word and was still seeing her, I was all of the usual things: hurt, angry, jealous. I had never felt so unsure of myself. I had a new baby and I'd given up my job with Andrew's company. I wasn't coping with anything well, really. So it was a relief to get to Prince Edward Island that summer, to just be in Chance Harbor with Andrew and pretend like we really had left all of our problems behind."

"I imagine so. The island has a way of making you feel like nothing can touch you," Darcy murmured.

"Yes. But then Andrew suddenly announced that he had to go away, to take care of some business in California and then in Berlin. I didn't believe him, of course."

"Because Marta's German."

"Right. We argued. I said some things I shouldn't have said, but Andrew kept telling me he loved me, he wanted to be with me, we were a family now." Eve caught the tremor in her voice and cleared her throat. "He was gone for two months."

"And you were alone with Catherine in Chance Harbor?" Darcy turned his head to look at her then, his face uncomfortably close. His gray eyes, she noticed, were flecked with gold, like the sea at sunrise. "That must have been excruciating, imagining what he was up to while you were stranded with the baby."

"Well, to be fair, I had plenty of company," Eve said. "Too much at times. All of Andrew's cousins were around, and it seemed like they were dropping in constantly. Catherine had plenty of little playmates, which was good, but I was exhausted, constantly making food and washing dishes and fretting about Andrew. This was before cell phones, of course, so we hardly communicated during that time."

She paused to take a breath and pulled the blanket higher. "One of his cousins, Malcolm, was a lobster fisherman," she went on in a rush, determined to finish the story before they docked. "Andrew left in July, and soon after that, it was Landing Day. I met Malcolm at North Lake while Catherine and I were watching the boats. He brought me some of his catch that night, cooked the lobsters for me. After that, he started taking Catherine and me out on his boat and coming around to the house at night."

She fell silent again, feeling the motion of the ferry and remembering Malcolm's boat. Catherine asleep in the cabin while she and Malcolm made love out on the deck, on top of the thick nets woven out of ropes, the sun beating down on their bare skin and the boat rocking them, amplifying their motions.

She shook her head and dropped her eyes, not wanting Darcy to read the memories there. "The thing is, I knew from the minute I saw Malcolm that I would sleep with him."

"Because you wanted a way to get back at Andrew?" Darcy suggested, rousing himself to turn and look at her.

"That was partly it, I'm sure," she said. "But I think it had more to do with me feeling so inadequate as a woman. Inferior. Because Andrew had desired Marta, I felt I wasn't enough for him."

"Sometimes desire is the last reason people have affairs."

"I understand that better now. But that's how I felt back then: undesirable, untouchable. Having Malcolm want me so openly, so unconditionally, well. That was a powerful aphrodisiac, just like you described feeling with that inflatable woman of yours."

When Darcy looked puzzled, Eve prodded him with her elbow. "You know. The Barbie with the implants."

"Ah," he said. "Go on."

"Right. Well, Malcolm and I started seeing each other. Only on his boat, or at night, of course, because the island is a small place, and he and Andrew have family all over East Point." She took a deep breath as the captain announced it was time for passengers to return to their cars.

"None of this sounds so sinful to me, you know," Darcy said, folding up the blanket and tucking it under one arm before picking up the dog's leash. "It sounds like a very common story, really, of a husband and wife who loved each other but hurt each other sometimes, too. We weren't meant to be married for decades."

"What?" Eve turned her head to look at him, nearly falling down the last three metal steps. "Why not?"

"Because humans originally lived to be only forty years old," Darcy said. "Now we're expected to stay *married* for that long, through thirty years of parenting and five careers? Come on. It's just not practical. I always thought there should be a renewable marriage contract."

Eve waited until they were in his truck again before asking, "What do you mean by that?"

"You know. I take thee to be my wife again, for another ten years."

Eve didn't know what she thought of this, so she was silent as Darcy navigated the truck up the ramp and off the ferry. Then they were on the road in Nova Scotia, and suddenly she didn't want to talk anymore, remembering her first trip to Cape Breton, how she'd wept while driving Catherine to Baddeck.

Which, ironically, was where they were headed now. Darcy's meeting was going to be in an office building in Baddeck, right on Bras d'Or, and he'd booked rooms in an inn overlooking the lake.

"You still haven't told me why you were afraid to come back here," he said, as they followed the traffic on the roundabout and headed out to the highway that would take them to the causeway bridge separating them from Cape Breton Island. "Why was the idea of returning so painful? Because you were afraid of thinking about all of this and wondering if you should have chosen Malcolm over Andrew?"

"Malcolm drowned," she said.

She kept her face to the window, but felt him turn to look at her. "My God, Eve. I'm so sorry."

"It's all right now. It was a long time ago."

"How did it happen? Was he fishing?"

She nodded. "He and a friend were going out for bluefin. A storm came up, and Malcolm drowned."

"That must have been horrible. Did anybody else know about the two of you? That must have been tough, if you had to keep your grief a secret."

"It was. Later, though, I found out that Malcolm's older sister had guessed about us."

Eve pictured Jane as she'd been after Malcolm's death, stumping up the steps to the deck of their Chance Harbor house the following year, when Eve had returned—against her wishes—with Andrew and the two girls. Andrew was out in his workshop.

Jane had thrust a pie in Eve's direction and said, "All sorted out with your husband, is it?" gesturing with her chin in the direction of the barn.

"Mostly." Eve waited for the rebuke, guessing from her expression that Jane knew about Malcolm.

None came. Instead, Jane had wiped her eyes and said, "At least Malcolm knew happiness before he went. His wife wasn't much for love. You gave my brother that. I'm grateful." Then she'd turned and hurried back to her car, shoulders hunched, without even saying hello to Andrew.

"Did Andrew ever find out?" Darcy asked.

Eve nodded and pressed her face to the window, taking a small stab of pleasure in the chilly slick feel of the glass against her forehead. "Yes. I might not have told him anything. Why would I, when it would only hurt him? I suppose I was a coward, just like you said before about all of us. But soon after Malcolm drowned, I realized I was pregnant. And Andrew would have to know the baby wasn't his, because he and I hadn't had sex in months."

She turned to glance at Darcy but couldn't read his expression. He was staring straight ahead at the road.

Eve focused on the road as well, on the trees covering the hills in a rich carpet of orange and red. She remembered this landscape now, how she had thought at first that this part of Nova Scotia didn't look that different from Vermont, with its lakes and rivers and hills. She'd been vaguely disappointed not to see something more novel despite her state of confusion and grief. But then, once she crossed the causeway to Cape Breton Island, the hills had begun to rise so steeply that they soon towered over the sea and tiny villages, the road reduced to a thin gray ribbon winding around them.

"I came here alone after I told him everything, because I needed to think about what to do, and I wanted to be in a place I'd never been before," Eve said. "A place I'd never been with Andrew. I was still trying to decide whether to stay with him. That's what Andrew wanted. He said none of it mattered, that he loved me and would raise the baby as his own. It was his cousin's baby after all, and Andrew was a good man. A man with a big heart. And he did try to love the baby. My younger daughter. But Zoe looked and acted so much like Malcolm, whom he'd known since they were children, that Andrew once told me it was the hardest thing he'd ever done, being her father."

Finally, Eve dared to look at Darcy. "Please say something."

"I'm sorry," he said softly.

"For what?"

Darcy reached over and took her hand. "That you had to go through all that. That you ever had to feel unloved or undesirable. That you had to feel alone and ashamed and scared. That you lost Malcolm. And that now you've lost Andrew and Zoe, too. I'm so sorry, sweetheart."

Eve couldn't speak. She looked down at Darcy's hand clasping her own. For this moment, she was not alone, and she was grateful.

CHAPTER ELEVEN

"Extreme Agony Weekends." That's what Willow had started calling her time with Russell. She didn't dare sneak out to see Zoe. Not with Russell trying to be all Dad of the Year and Nola throwing fits because Russell kept wanting to do things like play games that Willow was lots better at than Nola. Apparently Nola's parents had never played games with her. She had never even played Monopoly!

Meanwhile, there was Zoe—her mom, though Willow had trouble thinking of her that way—and having her come back had completely freaked her out. The night she'd figured things out, her mom had sat there on the ground and cried forever, tears and snot running down her face like she was a little kid. Finally, Zoe wiped her face on the shawl, which looked ridiculous once she took off the black dreadlocks and rainbow hat. With her real hair, which was cut short now but still blond and curly, she looked like a little boy dressed in old clothes for Halloween. Dressed like a hobo, which apparently she wasn't.

"I'm not really homeless," Zoe had said. "I'm not as much of a loser as I used to be. Promise."

It was her mother's voice, but a stranger's face. In Willow's mind, her mother had long hair and big blue eyes, smooth skin, and the kind of body you saw on movie stars who worked out 24-7. She was sexy and funny and unafraid, unless she was on something, and then she was either giggling like a maniac or nodding off and super calm.

Everything was wrong about this sad, scared person sitting on the damp grass of the Common. Willow's mind had buzzed with questions she wanted to ask but couldn't, because her mother looked like she might fly apart into little sparkling pieces of glass beneath the streetlamp. Zoe was trembling and talking too fast and trying to tell her everything was fine. She'd always been a great liar. Willow remembered that now.

"I know you've been having a hard time," Zoe said, "but I'm here now to take care of you."

"What are you talking about?" Willow said.

"I wasn't going to interfere in anything. But now I see I could make your life better."

How the hell would she do that? Willow wondered. Her mother had hardly managed to put food on the table and keep the electricity on even when she was working. Now she was homeless. "It's okay. You don't have to worry. I'm fine."

Zoe had blinked in surprise. "But you're not! You told me Catherine and Russell split up. That you had to change schools and leave your friends. That's why I gave you the puppy."

"I love the dog. But my life isn't that bad," Willow said, ticked off now because she was reassuring her mother like always. "I'm okay, Mom."

The word "mom" nearly stuck in her throat. She was used to avoiding it with Catherine, out of loyalty to Zoe. Out of some delusional—or *not*, as it turned out—idea that her mother wasn't really dead. Catherine would have a royal fit if she knew Zoe was alive and here, talking about taking care of Willow.

Oops. There was Catherine now, texting her, asking where she was.

"Shit," Willow said. "I need to go home." Desperately, she had grabbed her bag. "Will I see you again?"

Zoe had nodded without standing up. "I'm always right here. Every day, I'm waiting for you."

Okay, so that was a creepy stalkerish thing to say, Willow thought now, as she heard Russell calling her from inside Nola's house.

She didn't answer. She was tired of everybody. Of every pathetic, so-called adult in her life.

Right now she was hiding in the courtyard of Nola's house, sitting on the bench while Mike nosed around the garden, snorting like a piglet. Russell probably didn't even know this courtyard existed. Not with the maid, Carmen, always taking care of things in the kitchen. Carmen arrived early every day, even on Sundays, to make food and pick up after them. It was nice in a way. But also weird. Very weird.

Willow had lied to Catherine about staying after school and using the darkroom. Instead, she'd been seeing Zoe. She had brought her mother food, clothes, and things she'd made: a bright blue scarf she'd knitted in middle school, which Zoe immediately started wearing; a mug she'd made in pottery class last year.

She had learned to ask only a few questions at a time. Otherwise her mom got all speed freaky. So far Willow had discovered that her mother had hitchhiked to Florida after taking the bus to Washington. Since then she'd worked jobs under the table at motels and restaurants.

"If you speak English, you're a shoo-in," she had explained.

She'd told Willow about Key West, where she'd spent the first two years. About how she'd visited Hemingway's house and his double-pawed cats, and about the chickens that roamed the streets, even sitting on the tables in restaurants where she worked with Cubans and Dominicans and Haitians.

Then, when some detective came around, showing pictures of her, Zoe had moved to West Palm Beach and worked cleaning houses there for a while. Finally, she went to Homestead, a suburb of Miami. "It's the palm tree life," she said. "Can't complain. I even had a little house in a mango orchard. You could hear mangoes falling to the ground all night long. First time it happened, I thought there were monkeys in the damn trees."

Willow knew from the way Zoe pressed her lips together that she was trying to make her life sound postcard-pretty. Happy. Willow hoped her mother *had* been happy. But why hadn't her mom taken her south to live the palm-tree-and-mango life, too?

Her anger was mixed in a thick soup of other emotions more difficult to name, since her mom was so obviously trying to help her now. She'd given Willow the puppy and had scared off that guy trying to steal her money. And just yesterday after school, Zoe had explained how, in the bus station, she hadn't really left Willow alone.

"I wouldn't have done that, baby!" she said, blue eyes so wide and bright that Willow could see them gleaming beneath the sunglasses, which Zoe still wore, making Willow wonder if she was high and hiding it.

"I was really scared," Willow said. "Why didn't you tell me someone was with me? Who was it?"

Zoe shook her head. "I was afraid of being found. I had to disappear. My friend Sandra? You remember her, the one with the little boy who had that crazy Mohawk?"

"Yeah, sure." Willow pictured a gangly, dark-skinned woman with short black hair, but Sandra's face was blurry. It was the boy she remembered better. Sandra's son was a year younger than Willow and mean. He broke her stuff and once even hit her across the face with a metal travel mug while their moms got high together.

"Okay, well, Sandra stayed at the bus station with you until Catherine came," Zoe said. "I couldn't tell you she was there, because I was afraid you'd tell Catherine. And I knew Sandra would never keep her mouth shut if Catherine started asking her questions."

"Where was she?"

"Wrapped in a blanket and sitting on one of the benches near you. See? I never left you alone. I looked out for you any way I could, right?"

"Right," Willow had said, thinking, *That's a laugh.* Sandra was a crack addict, nodding off while her kid ran wild. "I still don't get why you had to leave without me."

"Oh, honey, because it was so much better for you," Zoe said. "I knew Catherine would take good care of you," she added fiercely.

Zoe had gone back to wearing her wig and rainbow hat, and yesterday she'd had that big red shawl on over some kind of men's baggy overalls. That bugged Willow. Why couldn't her mother dress like a normal person?

Then it dawned on her: maybe Zoe was in hiding from somebody. From the police, even. Was that why she'd really left? Had she done something that could get her sent to jail?

"I'm happy enough, Mom," Willow had said, and patted her mother's shoulder. "You did the right thing." She was still stuck reassuring her mom. But what else could she do?

Russell was calling her, his voice getting louder. "Willow? Willow, where are you?"

"Here," Willow said, finally giving up on having any time to herself. "In the courtyard with Mike."

"Oh." Russell appeared in the doorway. He had stubble on his face, and his white button-down shirt was wrinkled and untucked over too-tight blue jeans. Hipster jeans and suede sneakers. Jesus. Nola must have taken him shopping with her daddy's credit card, tried to make him look cool. It almost worked, except Russell still walked like a nerd, tipping forward over his feet.

"What's up?" Willow asked.

"Just wondered where you were, pumpkin."

"Please don't call me that."

"Right. Forgot. Sorry." As Russell stepped into the courtyard, Mike trotted over to greet him, stubby tail going like a pendulum.

"Mike's glad to see you, anyway," Willow said, hoping Russell got the real message: *I'm not. Leave me the F alone.*

"I'm glad to see him, too. Mike and I have done a lot of bonding while you've been at school, huh, big fella?" Russell scooped the dog up.

Mike licked his face and neck, his tail still sending that signal: *love me, love me, love me.* Or maybe it was *feed me, feed me, feed me.* You could never tell with dogs.

Russell set the dog down again and sat on the bench next to Willow. She scooted over so she wouldn't have to feel him touching her. God, why did guys want to be close to you all the time? She was never going to have a boyfriend. She was probably going to be a nun. Or maybe a lesbian.

"Where's Nola?" she asked.

"Taking a nap. Pregnancy makes women tired."

"Apparently." This was, like, Nola's third nap of the day. Unless she was doing something else in her room, like posting more Instagram photos of her stupid belly. Fine with Willow. She was just counting the hours until she could go home.

"Look, while we're alone, I just wanted to say again how sorry I am about all this," Russell said. "Especially about you having to change schools. How's it going in Cambridge?" He turned to face her on the bench, one foot crossed over his knee, putting his hipster shoe on full display.

Willow looked away and noticed how all the leaves on the ivy crawling up the bricks of the building had fallen off, leaving only the vine. It looked like the vine was trying to choke the building. Or maybe that's just the way she was feeling. "School's okay."

"I know it's not what you're used to," Russell said. "I'm sure it's a big adjustment. I went to public school for two years, and believe me, I know the difference. It's a factory, right? The upside is that if you can survive public school, you can survive anything in life."

"The corollary being that if I can't survive public school, I can't survive anything in life," Willow said.

Russell laughed. "Nice use of logic there. No. That's not what I'm saying. I'm sorry. I misspoke. I was just trying to convey my opinion that it takes real moxie to change schools, especially when you're going to a big, more impersonal institution. It wouldn't be surprising, or at all abnormal, if it took you a while to like it."

"I like public school," Willow said. "It's pleasingly anonymous. Nobody knows what a freak show I am."

"You're not a freak show!"

Willow rolled her eyes. "Joke, okay? Really. I'm okay."

"Good. Glad to hear it." Russell's voice was louder now. His confident classroom voice. He went on about the importance of a good education, saying, "Any school is what you make of it," and that Willow had to stay in honors classes and take a prep class for her SATs if the school offered one, *blah, blah, blah.*

"Of course," he added, "many fine colleges are now eliminating standardized testing from their admissions requirements. And you can always do an electronic portfolio to beef up your résumé—you know, send in your art and English papers and whatnot."

Willow stared at him. What the hell was he telling her all this for, when she was only a sophomore? And why was he sweating like that?

Finally she got it: Russell was having a mini panic attack. He was talking about school because school was all he knew, and he didn't know what else to say to her. Pathetic.

"How about you?" she interrupted suddenly.

"Me?" He touched his shirt pocket to be sure.

"Yeah. How are you doing?"

Russell straightened up on the bench beside her. "Fine, I guess. But I wish I had a job. I've never been without a job. Not since I was your age."

"Yeah? Are you interviewing at places? I mean, other than your friend's school in New Hampshire?"

He shook his head. "Nothing else has come up. But I'm hoping I'll get that job. My friend is the headmaster there."

Of course he was, Willow thought: all of Russell's friends were headmasters or deans. He was old and had been teaching for a long time. But who would want him, after what he did?

"How's your mom doing?" Russell asked.

Her mom? Willow's mind flitted around, trying to find a place to hide. Then she remembered: Russell didn't know. To him, "mom" meant Catherine.

"She's fine," Willow lied.

"Good. I'm glad."

Willow knew she shouldn't say more—why kick a guy when he was down?—but she couldn't help it: she wanted to pour salt on whatever wounds Russell had inflicted on himself. "You know she's dating somebody now, right?"

"No. I didn't know that."

Willow had read a description in some book about color draining from a person's face, but she'd never actually seen it happen. Now she did: Russell turned as white as the bench they were sitting on, as if he'd been transformed into stone, too.

She felt a little zing of fear. What if he had a heart attack and keeled over? She didn't even know CPR! Probably Carmen did. Carmen seemed to know how to do everything. Just yesterday she'd gotten a wine stain out of the carpet and made a chicken casserole that looked like it should be in a magazine.

Russell ran his hand through his hair. It was getting grayer, Willow noticed. Probably because he couldn't keep up with Nola in bed. Gross. "What do you know about this guy?"

"Not much. His name is Seth. He seems cool."

"Is he nice?"

"I don't know," Willow said, then relented: she could only torture Russell for so long. He was too easy. "I've only met him once. He came by the house a couple of nights ago to borrow a cookbook, and I was in the kitchen doing homework. I haven't had an actual conversation with him or anything like that."

"Oh. Well. I hope things are going well for her," Russell said. "Catherine deserves every happiness."

She did, Willow thought. And yet they were both cheating on her: Russell with Nola, and her with Zoe. She felt her cheeks go hot with shame.

Russell stood up and slapped his hands on his knees. "Well. I'm glad we had this little talk. Aren't you?"

"Sure."

"What do you want to do now? Want to play a game or something?"

Willow rolled her eyes. "You know you don't have to entertain me every minute, right? You could go work on your book or something."

Russell got this faraway look. "My book. Right. I'm actually a bit stalled on the manuscript at the moment. And I don't get to see you very often. Our time together should be extra special."

He leaned forward, putting his face so close that Willow could smell coffee. "I know you think I'm a shitty dad and a loser," he said.

Before Willow could come up with a response—as if there were anything to say to that but "yeah, duh" unless she lied again—Nola flew into the courtyard, her hair flying everywhere, her eyes big and dark. "You have to come!" she said, tugging on Russell's sleeve.

"Why? What is it?" Russell pulled her close. "Take a breath. Remember that stress is bad for the baby."

She jerked away. "The baby's fine. I'm the one who's not. Dad's here!"

"Your father? Here in the house?"

"Yes!" Nola was whimpering. "I told Daddy not to come over, but he never listens."

Russell's face had gone white again. "Does he want to see me?"

"I don't know," Nola said. "He just started shouting at me, so I ran."

Willow stood up. She was curious to meet this guy who hadn't even taught his daughter to play Monopoly. Who apparently thought it was perfectly okay to let an eighteen-year-old girl live alone in a house after her mom died, screw one of her teachers, and have his baby. He was an even worse parent than Zoe when she was high.

"Oh no," Russell said, pushing Willow's shoulder so she'd sit back down. "You stay here. This could get ugly."

"This is *already* plenty ugly," said the man standing in the doorway. "One ugly family." He gestured with his chin to Willow. "Your daughter, I presume?"

"Watch yourself. Nobody wants you here, Bill," Russell said, stepping in front of Nola and Willow. "Turn around and go home."

"Nobody wanted you to mess around with my daughter, either," Bill said. "Yet you couldn't help yourself. You fucked up her life. You know how much I've spent on private school and therapy and clothes for this kid? Hundreds of thousands! All down the toilet because you couldn't keep your prick in your pants."

Willow's armpits were tingling with fear. Bill was built like a square, his hips as wide as his shoulders. He wore a knee-length yellow wool coat and big rings on his fingers. His head was almost bald, and his ears stuck out like handles.

"Guess I'd better go do homework," she said. "You want to come, Nola?"

Nola nodded and stepped toward the door, but her father grabbed her by the arm and yanked her back. Meanwhile, Bill's eyes moved up and down Willow's body. It felt like bugs were crawling all over her. Or Tom's fingers.

"You stay right here, girls," Bill said, still looking at Willow. "You're a fine little package. Maybe we should double date. Tit for tat, Russell? You can get it on with my daughter while your girl and I hook up."

"Don't you dare speak about my daughter that way," Russell said.

Bill laughed, tipping his head back far enough for Willow to see his silver fillings. "Right. Like you're on moral high ground, buddy." He looked at Willow again. "What do you say, *sweetheart*? Want to have dinner with me tonight, since my own damn kid won't have anything to do with me? I could show you the town. It's a pretty nice place, Boston, as long as you've got money. And a job." He flicked a glance at Russell and stepped toward Willow.

She froze in place, panicked, but Russell charged him like a bull, head down. Bill sidestepped almost in time, but Russell caught him on the shoulder and the two men toppled into the shrubs.

"Dad, stop!" Willow screamed, just as Nola yelled, "Dad! Stop it, damn it!"

The two girls looked at each other, and Willow was startled to see Nola mirroring her across the courtyard, mouth open in shock. Then Nola stepped forward, grabbed Willow's hand, and tugged her over to the faucet and hose on the other side of the courtyard.

The men were still scuffling on the ground, Bill on top and trying to punch Russell's head. Willow ran over and leaped onto Bill's back, trying to pin his arms, but he shook her off. Finally, Nola managed to unfurl the black hose, and she turned it on full blast, aiming the water at her father.

"Jesus Christ!" Bill yelped, and covered his face.

In an instant, Russell was out from under him, scrambling to his feet, dripping and shouting.

Bill held up both hands. "All right, all right. Shut off the friggin' water! I can take a hint. I'm outta here."

"I'll show you the door," Russell said, his face red and determined.

The two of them disappeared into the house. Nola looked at Willow and shook her head. "Sorry about my dad. He's only half human." She smoothed her hair, shivering a little, and started to cry.

Willow went to her and towed Nola by the arm into the kitchen. Carmen was already gone for the day, so Willow rummaged around until she found some instant hot chocolate packets and two mugs. She dumped the packets into the mugs, added water, microwaved the drinks and brought the chocolate to the table after stirring it. She set one mug in front of Nola, who was drying herself off with a dish towel but still trembling.

"Thanks." Nola had stopped crying, but her eyes and nose were red. "You're as nice as your dad."

"My mom's even nicer," Willow said, but this time she was thinking of Catherine when she said "mom," not Zoe. She had no idea if Zoe was nice. A weird thing not to know about your own mother.

"Lucky you." Nola cupped her hands around the hot chocolate.

She looked so miserable that Willow blurted out the truth. "Actually, my real mom isn't that nice. She's kind of screwed up. You haven't met her. Only Catherine."

"Where is your mom, anyway?"

"Nobody knows," Willow said hastily, wary now. Zoe had made her promise not to tell anyone that she was back in Boston.

Besides, Willow had no idea if Zoe even planned to stick around. Zoe didn't seem to know, either. Which totally sucked. Nana should know that Zoe was alive, at least.

"How do you know your real mom's not nice, if she's not around?" Nola asked.

"I lived with her until I was ten," Willow said. "She did drugs. And she hooked up with some pretty creepy guys. Guys way worse than your dad, I bet."

"Doubt it." Nola made a face. "My dad belongs in jail. Anyway, at least you have Catherine and Russell, and they seem to really care about you."

"They're okay. Why do you say your dad should be in jail?"

Nola bit her bottom lip. "He's a prick," she said. "A perv. A self-absorbed asshole even when Mom was dying. Good thing we had Carmen."

"He seems pretty mad about Russell. He probably thinks he took advantage of you."

"That's what all men think when an older guy gets involved with a younger woman," Nola said, lifting her chin. "But I am so not a victim. I had a crush on Russell starting junior year."

Ew, Willow thought. *Gross.* "It didn't bother you that he was married?"

"I never really thought about it, because I never thought anything would actually happen," Nola said. "I know that sounds stupid, but it's true. Your dad didn't want anything to do with me at first. I pretty much had to throw myself at him for two years before he knew I existed."

"You shouldn't have done that." This was the least damning thing Willow could think to say.

"Duh. I know." Nola stared down at the mug between her hands. "Basically, I wasn't thinking. I was just, I don't know. *Being.* I didn't actually mean to get pregnant. Now I'm sorry. Sorry as shit. Not because I don't love your dad and want a baby—I really do—but because now I know you, and I can see that I fucked up your life. And I can say I'm sorry over and over, but that won't really change anything, will it?"

Willow had to work to keep her mouth closed, she was so shocked by Nola's admission and by the fact that she was actually starting to feel a little sorry for her. "No. But you didn't do this alone, remember. Russell helped get you pregnant. And he obviously loves you."

"You think so?" Nola whispered, swallowing hard.

"I do think that," Willow said, even though she wasn't absolutely sure.

"Thanks. Still. I would take it all back if I could." Nola looked like she might start crying again. But she took a sip of hot chocolate and made a face. "Ow. That's really friggin' hot."

"Because it's *hot* chocolate," Willow said.

And then both of them were laughing.

It was too early to check into their rooms, but Darcy and Eve dropped off their luggage at the inn. Eve wandered alone around the small town of Baddeck during Darcy's meeting, feeling strangely exhilarated to be here. Instead of remembering only the sorrow and confusion she'd felt, waving to Andrew as he'd wept on the dock, now she was thinking about how liberated she'd felt, too, coming here with Catherine, as if she'd put an entire country between herself and Andrew and the mess their marriage had become. She was happy today. Perhaps that was enough.

On impulse, she bought Darcy a few birthday presents: a green plaid scarf, a wedge of cheese, a small bottle of whiskey distilled on Cape Breton. Then she walked down to the lake, admiring its shoreline and the way the hills and boats were reflected in the water.

Eve watched a bald eagle swooping down from the surrounding hills to fish, still thinking about how different this felt from her last trip here, when she'd been alone with Catherine and in such turmoil. She'd been so sure she was going to leave Andrew, despite Malcolm's death.

When she returned from Cape Breton, however, her mind made up, Andrew had managed to talk her into staying with him. "Nobody said marriage would be easy," he'd said. "What I did to you by being with Marta was unspeakably hurtful. I know that. It's understandable that you felt compelled to turn to someone else. But I'm wholly committed to you, to Catherine, and to our marriage. Please. Give me a second chance, Eve. You won't regret it."

Eve had finally given in with equal parts relief and disappointment and said she'd stay with him. She did it mainly because it seemed unfair to deprive two children of a loving father when she could come up with no better alternative for their lives together. And she'd been happy with Andrew again, eventually.

Now, as she remembered Marta's recent mysterious call, Eve shivered in the breeze. She had stayed the course of her marriage and had believed that Andrew would remain faithful to her as well. Obviously, he hadn't been—and probably not for a long time. She'd been such a fool. Maybe that was the worst revelation of all.

Eve's mood was glum when Darcy returned, but he quickly cheered her up. He was in good spirits because he'd convinced one of the farmers who owned a tract of land in the hills above Baddeck to install an experimental wind farm. Besides, as they drove out of town and toward the national park, the scenery became more breathtaking with every passing mile and took her mind off everything else.

She had never made it past Baddeck with Catherine. Now, as they proceeded along the winding coastal highway toward the village of Ingonish on the Atlantic side of the island, Eve found herself nearly speechless as the mountains rose above the sea, eventually so steep that it seemed like the road was an afterthought between the rocky beaches and a solid wall of forest.

"We're not actually going to hike up there, are we?" she asked, pointing.

Darcy grinned. "Whose birthday is it?"

"Oh, all right, party boy. As long as you're prepared to carry me partway."

He waggled his eyebrows at her. "I'd carry you anywhere."

She laughed and turned her face back to the window.

Past Ingonish, they pulled into a parking lot and started up a trail that led up into the mountains. It had been cold the night before; the frozen grass crackled beneath Eve's feet. In several especially steep legs of the trail, wooden staircases had been built over the rocks.

It was eerily quiet as they paralleled a river meandering down the mountain. The water was iced over in places, glistening silver, but Eve could hear the rush of a distant waterfall. At one point she brushed against a pine tree and smiled when the branches sprinkled tiny ice flakes over her, a sudden miniature snowstorm.

She glanced above her now and then, hoping to see the trail finally flatten out around each corner. Despite her steady running habit, she grew increasingly winded as she followed Darcy, who kept up his chatter even though his backpack was big enough to carry a calf.

Bear kept wandering off the trail; he made Eve jump by startling a grouse into darting across the path right by her feet. The dog looked more surprised than anyone and made Eve and Darcy laugh with his bewildered expression.

"I can't believe you're still talking and walking," Eve grumbled after an hour of steady climbing. "How old are you again?"

"Old enough to know a good photo op when I see one. Here. Stand in the sun by that boulder."

She complied, glad to rest for a minute, removing her wool cap at the last minute and running a finger through her curls. Darcy lowered the camera after he'd taken the picture, shaking his head. "You must have been an adorable ten-year-old, with those freckles and curls."

Eve put a hand to her face, damp with sweat, embarrassed. "Now you're making me feel like my nose must be running and I have a milk mustache."

"You'd be cute even then."

"What were you like at ten?" Eve asked as they started up the trail again.

Darcy's answer surprised her: "Sad and lonely."

"Why?"

He glanced at her over his shoulder. "I was a little weirdo. Hyperactive—back in those days, schools dealt with the problem by pinning me in a corner with empty desks, so I couldn't bother anyone—and lonely at home. I was an only child and my parents were very close. The sort of parents who wanted time to themselves more often than not. The upside was that I spent a lot of time outside and still love to explore. I'm never bored, because I got good at entertaining myself at a young age. What about you? What were you like at ten?"

"Overprotected," Eve said. "My father was a professor at the University of Wisconsin. My mother could have been, but she stayed home with my siblings and me. My brother died a few years ago, but my sister still lives there in Wisconsin. I haven't seen her in years." She stopped. No need to tell Darcy about the hoarding.

"What were they like, your parents?" he asked.

"Oh, you know. Intellectuals. Liberals. My mother read constantly and wore her hair up in a French twist, like some sort of actress in an Ibsen play. She was very cool and removed and efficient. We were never close. She showed me only the finer things in life. Things that could come in useful at a dinner party, like how to use a finger cup and which fork to use."

"Good Lord. And here I've been licking my fingers around you like a savage."

"Yes, well. I've pretended not to notice. We've only ever eaten food outdoors. I've never seen you in a restaurant."

"And now you never will," he promised. "I'd be too terrified."

Amazingly, they had reached some sort of summit. To Eve's disappointment, there was just a field with short, scrubby pines and mottled yellow grass. Then Darcy pointed. "There's our view."

She turned and took in a sharp breath at the sight. The grass gave way to giant boulders and a drop-off beyond the rocky outcropping. Far below, she could see land jutting into the sparkling Atlantic, a peninsula with a white building on it. From here it looked like a toy castle.

"That's the Keltic Lodge," Darcy said, then guided her over the plateau to a narrower trail leading to another rocky seat. From here, they had a 180-degree view, not only of the sea, but of the canyon far below. The land fell in bright folds of color to a silver ribbon that snaked through the valley.

"Huh," she said. "It was almost worth that bloody climb."

"It's certainly no ordinary Monday, right? Happy birthday to me," Darcy sang. He put down his pack, unzipped it, and began unloading so much food that Eve started laughing, watching him arrange it all on a plaid blanket. "You were expecting twelve people, I see," she said.

"You never know who might show up at a party."

The array of food was astounding: several cheeses and sausages, two crispy baguettes, grapes and apples, shortbread cookies, dark chocolate truffles. And champagne, with fluted pink plastic cups, which Darcy produced with a flourish.

They sat against the rocks. The sun was warm enough that they shed their vests and fleece jackets. Eve ate more than she should have before reclining back against a sun-warmed boulder with a sigh.

"I might have to copy your birthday ideas," she said. "This is a great party."

"I'd have to agree," he said. "When's your birthday again?"

"February."

"Ah. A bit tricky to hike up here in the winter without snowshoes." He brightened. "I know. We can do Chile. The Andes would be perfect in February. Summer weather."

"All right," Eve said recklessly.

It happened as she leaned forward to clink her glass to his: Darcy kissed her, his mouth tasting of champagne and chocolate and all of the outdoors.

Eve was so taken aback that she let his lips touch hers without moving. Then, even more alarmingly, her body responded before her mind did. Heat rose in her belly as Darcy somehow pulled her over the food on the blanket between them and onto his lap without knocking anything over and without causing them to tumble off the cliff.

"That was quite a move," Eve said, pulling away just enough to glance over her shoulder at the drop below. "I'd say it's the champagne making me dizzy, but I suspect it's my fear of heights."

"I think it must be passion," he said, pressing his lips to her neck now, making her shiver.

"Me, too," Eve said, and kissed him properly this time, dizzy with the moment, with the champagne and the altitude and the feel of this man's body against her own most of all.

CHAPTER TWELVE

On Sunday Catherine began a systematic scrub down of the house. She started in her own bedroom, pulling dirty sheets off the bed and making it up with clean linens before hanging up the clothes she'd flung onto the chair throughout the week. After beginning a load of laundry in the basement, she huffed back upstairs to tackle the guest room.

That was a mess, too. Not from her mother's last visit—which seemed like years ago—but from her. She'd taken all of Russell's remaining belongings and piled them haphazardly into boxes. Now Catherine lugged all seven boxes down to the front hall to make sure she'd deal with them. She had to erase every bit of him from her life if she was going to move on.

Well, she'd make him take the boxes with him tonight when he dropped off Willow. Catherine texted him right then to say that was the plan, using firm jabs of her thumbs and imagining herself pecking at Russell's chest and face instead of at a phone screen.

If you don't clear out your stuff, I'm putting it on the curb tonight, she added. That should get his attention.

She pocketed the phone and scrubbed the upstairs bathroom, bagged the trash, then dragged the trash bags and cleaning supplies into Willow's bedroom. She hardly ever stepped foot in here anymore; she was so exhausted these days that she usually went to bed before Willow.

Now, surveying the room—an obstacle course of books, shoes, clothing, and even a few plates and glasses—Catherine realized she'd better devise a strategy for getting Willow to pitch in around the house, or she was going to end up being as irresponsible as Zoe. She remembered Zoe's room, how impossible it was to find anything.

"Oh, please, Catherine, help me get your sister ready for school," Mom used to beg, her eyes wild with panic as the minutes ticked by on the clock. "You know she doesn't listen to me. She'll make me late for work if you don't help. She'll do it if you ask her."

It was true. At least when she was young, Zoe had looked up to Catherine enough to comply when Catherine asked her to do something. Like find her own damn shoes.

Now, looking back on how often her mother had expected her to be mature while Zoe got away with murder, Catherine felt resentful all over again. Why hadn't her mother ever had the same expectations of her younger child that she'd so clearly had of Catherine?

She heaved a sigh and began plucking clothes off Willow's bedroom floor. She knew better than to go through a teenager's things—total violation of privacy, her friends assured her, and not worth incurring their wrath unless you suspected drugs or risky sex—but at least she could toss Willow's dirty clothes in with the next load of laundry.

Her arms were already full—jeans, T-shirts, socks, undies, all of it dirty—when Catherine bent over to pick up one last hoodie off the bed, Willow's favorite black one. Beneath it was a stack of photographs spilling out of a manila folder.

Catherine stopped cold. The top picture was of a woman with long black dreadlocks, a shawl, and a striped hat. Despite her giant sunglasses, she looked creepily familiar. There was something about this woman's features and posture that reminded her of Zoe.

Catherine shuddered a little, remembering her senior year at the university, when their parents had come to visit both of them on Family Weekend. "Zoe's herself again," her mother had said, taking Catherine aside, her eyes glistening. "We're so proud of how she's going to class."

How pissed off she'd felt, hearing that pride in her mother's voice. Why the hell was her mother crowing about a daughter who was only doing what she should? Catherine had been doing that all her life and never once heard about it.

Her father, too, was over the moon. "Zoe has completely turned her life around," Dad had said.

Only Zoe hadn't. In December of that year Mike had broken up with her, and by late spring Zoe had left school and moved home. She was pregnant. Hardly emerged from her room long enough to vomit and eat so she could throw it all up again. Hollow-eyed and silent. Zoe wouldn't tell them anything about school, Mike, or anything else, other than saying, "He left me. Screw him."

"Honey, you're both so young," their mother had said, trying to comfort Zoe one weekend when, in desperation, she had called Catherine to come home to Newburyport, to "talk sense into your sister." It was understandable, Mom had told Zoe, that Mike wasn't ready for a commitment. "Maybe the two of you need a break, that's all."

"No. I loved Mike and he left me," Zoe had said, burying her head in her arms. "It's over. I never want to see him again. I can't."

"Oh, don't be so fucking dramatic," Catherine had finally snapped. "Everyone goes through this. You think you're so special? You're not, Zoe. You're really not. Get a grip and move on."

Now, hearing her own harsh words replayed in her head, Catherine flinched. She had been deliberately cruel, thinking she could make Zoe angry enough to muscle her way through that breakup. Of course it hadn't worked. Zoe had always been fragile, beneath the bluster and manic daredevil stunts.

She sighed and dropped to the bed, dumping Willow's clothes to the floor at her feet. They were already dirty; what would it matter? She picked up the photograph and held it at various angles. This woman could definitely be Zoe. That pretty mouth, the sharp contours of the cheekbones beneath the big glasses. And there was a guitar at her feet. Zoe had played the guitar in high school. Maybe this was an old picture.

But where on earth would Willow have gotten it? And when had Zoe gone out in this disguise? Halloween, it must be.

Wait. There was something wrong here. Something Catherine caught only when she flipped through the rest of the pictures on the bed and realized there were more of this woman, some taken from farther away: this photograph couldn't have been taken at Halloween. The leaves were still on the tree above the bench, the grass lush and tall except for a few scattered leaves at the woman's feet. A boy walking along the sidewalk near the bench in one of the photos was wearing only a T-shirt and board shorts.

This picture had to have been taken in early September, at the latest. So who was this woman, and why was she dressed in this absurd costume?

Catherine tucked the photographs back into the folder and stood up, shaking her head. She picked up the heap of dirty clothes again. Right now she'd better keep cleaning. She could ask Willow about the pictures later.

Somehow, though, the evening got away from her. Russell showed up around seven o'clock, scarcely spoke to Catherine, and asked Willow if she'd help carry his boxes to the car. She complied, the dog trotting back and forth across the yard with them. Catherine watched from the window as Willow hugged Russell good-bye and turned away. They were getting along. That surprised her, and somehow pissed her off, too.

But she couldn't deny that Willow was in a good mood. She claimed to have done her homework and actually offered to help fold the laundry when she saw Catherine with the baskets in front of the TV.

"I should have washed my own clothes, Mom," Willow said. "Thank you."

Catherine felt her irritation evaporate. "It's no problem, honey," she said. They watched a brainless romantic comedy as they folded clothes on the coffee table. By then it was bedtime.

The next day was hectic at work, like every Monday, but there was only one real challenge: a teenage boy who'd stepped barefoot onto broken glass. Catherine had to remove the glass splinters with tweezers and put up with his swearing despite giving him enough local anesthetic to numb a hippo.

Her last two patients of the day canceled, so Catherine left earlier than usual, delighted to have some extra time in her day. She emerged from the clinic and zipped her jacket to the neck against the chilly air. She had driven the car today because she was running late. Now it occurred to her that she could drive over to the high school and pick up Willow, who spent most days after school working with the photography teacher. This would be a good night for pizza.

Maybe they should institute some new traditions, now that the weekends were disrupted by Willow going to Russell's, Catherine thought as she walked to the parking garage. Pizza on Mondays instead of Fridays. She liked that idea.

The high school was still busy and brightly lit, with students milling about in front of the main entrance and in the foyer. Catherine had to speak into an intercom to be admitted, a security procedure that surprised her only momentarily. Of course city schools had to take precautions these days. Maybe all schools, given the number of shootings in the past few years. She shuddered, hating the question that came next: Was Willow safer in a big school, because there were more targets to hit? Or in more danger because anybody could get into a public school, and the teachers couldn't possibly know their students as well as they did at Beacon Hill?

Jesus. What was wrong with her, having thoughts so warped?

She found the office and spoke with a gray-haired woman at the front desk who wore a suit too tailored-looking for a secretary. "Can I help you?" the woman asked, raising her head from a sheaf of folders with a smile.

"Yes. My daughter, Willow MacLeish, has been staying after school to work in the darkroom. I got out of work early and came by to see if she wanted a ride home."

"May I see some ID, please?" the woman said.

Catherine produced her driver's license and waited while the woman used the school intercom to buzz the darkroom. After a moment, a voice replied, also a woman's.

"Willow MacLeish's mother is here in the office, looking for her," the woman said. "Do you have her there with you, Aubrey?"

"No. Not today. In fact, I haven't seen her after school in a while. Sorry."

Catherine swallowed past a thick knot of apprehension. "Thank you," she said. "I must have been mistaken."

She hurriedly turned away before the woman at the desk could flash her one of those knowing looks that said, *Another dumb mother, too clueless to keep track of her own kid.*

Catherine blindly made her way out of the office and stopped in the foyer to text Willow. *Where are you? I need to see you immediately.*

She erased the second sentence—no need to alert Willow to how angry and scared she was right now, since that might put her off—and waited.

No response. Now Catherine's breath was coming in short pants and her mouth had gone dry. She thought about texting Russell to ask if he or Nola had picked up Willow. Was Willow sneaking out to see her father after school?

No. That was ridiculous. Willow wouldn't have to lie about that.

Maybe she had a boyfriend?

That thought actually cheered Catherine up a little. That, at least, would be normal. But why would Willow feel like she needed to hide that from her? They'd always talked so openly about dating. And, truthfully, Willow still seemed put off by the very idea of sex. Even kissing, she said, was creepy. "Why would I want somebody else's germs in my mouth?" she'd demanded once.

Catherine slowly walked out of the school to her car. It was completely dark now. She considered her options. She could drive home and see if Willow was there. That was probably the most logical thing to do. After all, Willow wasn't expecting Catherine to be home until her usual time, six o'clock. She could follow the route Willow usually walked home—or the route she thought she took, anyway—and see if she spotted her.

She drove down Broadway to Cambridge Street and turned left so she could circle the Common. Maybe Willow had gone to Burdick's with a friend for hot chocolate after school. She adored that place. If so, she would probably walk back this way, though Catherine hoped she'd have the sense to stay on the brightly lit sidewalk around the Common instead of cutting through it at night. The very idea of that made Catherine shiver with fright, though of course at Willow's age she probably would have thought nothing of doing it. Not when there were still so many people around.

So many, she would have missed seeing Willow if she hadn't spotted the girl's bright blond hair, loose and curly around her shoulders in the inky dusk as she sat on a bench near the playground.

At least I know where she is, was Catherine's first thought.

Her next thought was less coherent, as she realized that Willow was talking to the woman with black dreadlocks Catherine had seen in those photographs. The woman wore the same striped hat and sunglasses, too. Despite the odd clothing and near dark, this bizarre person looked even more like Zoe than she had in the photographs, right down to the way she was sitting on the bench and gesturing wildly with her hands as she said something that made Willow laugh.

Catherine's mouth was so dry that it felt like her lips had cracked at the corners. She could hear her heartbeat drumming in her ears, a steady whooshing sound, as if she were swimming in powerful surf. She felt like she was drowning. Just like she'd felt when she was caught in the undertow with her sister, all those years ago and their mother had chosen to save Zoe, not her: terrified and betrayed. Hopeless.

Catherine's vision blurred and the car veered toward oncoming headlights. A horn blared and Catherine regained control at the last minute.

No. That woman couldn't possibly be Zoe. Zoe was *dead*.

She parked at the only open space along the Common, in front of a fire hydrant, and watched. Willow was sitting on the bench next to the woman and talking animatedly. She looked engaged. Happy.

Willow must have met this woman on the Common and decided to do some portrait photography. Just a few months ago—though it seemed like a lifetime, given all that had happened—Willow had insisted on posing Catherine in the garden. The portraits were stunning in their detail, in the lighting, in the way Willow had caught Catherine's various expressions.

That must be it. Willow had met this homeless person and was doing a school project. Still, she shouldn't be on the Common after the sun went down, chatting up some vagrant. She needed to come home, have dinner, do her homework.

Catherine got out of the car and locked it, then started across the Common. She was perhaps twenty feet away when Willow and the woman noticed her approach. It was difficult to tell who was more panicked.

"What are *you* doing here?" Willow cried out, sounding nearly hysterical.

At the same time, the woman on the bench began running, leaving her cane and guitar on the ground.

Fortunately, there was a fence between the woman and the street, and her long shawl got tangled up in that as the woman tried to throw herself over the top rail. Catherine had been infused with some superhuman strength; she felt herself fly across the Common as if her feet literally weren't touching the ground. She was on the woman in seconds, yanking her back off the fence and onto the ground, then pulling the glasses off her face.

Catherine reared back as she stared into the defiant blue eyes. "Damn it, Zoe," she said. "What the hell are you playing at?"

Somehow, despite the number of times she'd teased Darcy about wearing a kilt, Eve had never expected him to go through with it. Yet here they were in a pub a few miles from Bras d'Or Lake, Darcy in his kilt and long tasseled socks, looking completely in his element as he joined a group of musicians by the fireplace and took out his fiddle.

They'd stopped at the inn to shower and change before coming here to have fish and chips for dinner in the pub, the fish unbelievably delicate inside its crispy coating. Now Eve sat with a glass of red wine at one of the round wooden tables, perfectly content as she listened to the music. Her face was chapped, windburned from the hiking they'd done all day, first for their picnic and then at the Skyline Trail, which traversed a bog, bright with red berries, through some scrub pines and eventually funneled them onto a headland. The wind was so fierce that Eve had to cling to Darcy's arm to avoid being blown off the cliff. They'd laughed and bent toward the wind, and Eve thought of all the trees she'd seen on these trails, gnarled and bent as they were now, strong enough to survive despite the elements.

As we are, Eve had thought, taking Darcy's face between her hands and surprising him with a kiss as they stood on the headland high above the sea, speckled pink and gold at sunset.

They returned to the inn from the pub just after eleven o'clock, wrapped themselves in woolen blankets, and walked down to a pair of Adirondack chairs positioned to overlook the lake. It was a clear night and very cold, the stars glittering in an illuminated spiderweb above the water, the moon's path white and so solid-looking that it was easy to imagine walking on it.

"Happy birthday," she said, and handed Darcy the gifts she'd bought him earlier. He laughed with pleasure as he opened each one and wrapped the scarf around his neck. He carved a few pieces of cheese off the wedge for them to eat, and they washed it down with whiskey they drank straight from the bottle.

"Is it my imagination, or can I taste peat in this?" Eve said, after she'd swirled the whiskey in her mouth.

"Whatever it is, it's perfect," he said. "As are you." He stood up from the chair then and came over to her.

She snorted. "If you believe that, you're in for serious trouble."

"My middle name is 'Trouble.'" He scooped her up out of the Adirondack chair too quickly for her to react and settled her onto his lap, now with his blanket over her, too.

"My goodness," she said. "Somebody's been taking his senior multivitamins."

"And doing my chair yoga, too," he said, and kissed her. "I'm thinking that the instructor might have more students if she included this particular exercise."

Eve laughed, and he kissed her neck, his breath hot against her skin.

They stayed until the fog came in over the water, a finger of white urging them back inside. Eve considered inviting Darcy into her room, but then what? Was she ready for anything like that? Would her body even know what to do, after so many months of mourning and solitude?

Of course, they never had to see each other again. She was planning to drive home the day after they returned to Prince Edward Island.

Except that wasn't what she wanted, she realized suddenly, with a jolt of understanding that was physically unsettling. She wanted to be with Darcy. In every way.

"Would you like to come in for a little more whiskey?" she asked, as she unlocked her room across the hall from his.

He cocked an eyebrow. "Not for whiskey, no."

And then he was behind her at the door, his arms around her waist, kissing the back of her neck and somehow unzipping her jacket and working his hands beneath her sweater, his fingers so cold against her skin that she gasped and wriggled free.

"Sorry, sorry," he murmured, and followed her into the room.

She'd just turned to face him, had reached up to put her arms around his neck—still a novelty, connecting her body to someone this tall—when her cell phone rang in her pocket, jarring them both and causing them to spring apart.

"Wasn't expecting that," Darcy said.

Eve shook her head. "I'm so sorry. It never rings. I don't even know why I carry it." She glanced down at the screen, though, and saw that it was Catherine. That was worrying. Catherine seldom called.

"I think I have to take it," she said after apologizing again. "It's my daughter. I'll just tell her I'll call her back."

"Take your time," Darcy said. "Do you want me to go? Give you some privacy?"

"No, no," she said, and pushed him lightly against the chest to make him sit on the edge of the bed. Then she perched on his knee and answered the phone.

"Catherine?" she said. "Is everything all right, honey?"

There was a silence—long enough that Eve wondered whether her daughter had already hung up—and then Catherine said in a small, shuddering voice, "Mom, you have to come home. Right now."

Eve stood up, alarmed. "Why? What is it?"

"Just come home! I found Zoe," Catherine said, and burst into tears.

Somehow, Zoe had managed to escape. Willow had watched, frozen in place, as her mother wriggled out from under Catherine and took off, leaving her sunglasses, guitar, and cane on the ground. They ran after her, but even in those layers of clothing and that stupid shitty wig with the dreads flopping around like octopus arms, Zoe managed to lose them as she slalomed her way through the people on the sidewalk along Mass Ave, all of them probably thinking, *Hey, there goes another insane homeless woman!*

Catherine wouldn't let Willow keep chasing her, even when Willow started crying. "There's no point," she said, taking a firm hold of Willow's arm. "Let's go back and get her things so nobody steals them. Does she know where we live?"

Willow nodded, unable to speak.

"Okay. So she'll probably come to our house after she calms down, at least to get her guitar," Catherine said. "We'll just have to wait."

But Zoe hadn't shown up at the house last night. And now, Tuesday morning, Willow was debating about whether to go to school or pretend to be sick—no easy thing, when Catherine was a nurse who'd seen it all. She lay in her bed after the alarm went off, staring at her phone and hoping her mom would text her; she'd given her the number days ago, but Zoe had never used it.

Did her mom even *have* a cell phone? She wouldn't just disappear again, would she?

That last thought was both aggravating and—Willow could admit this to herself, at least—almost a relief. She'd been thinking so much about her mom lately, worrying about where she was sleeping and whether she was still using, that a part of her wished Zoe would disappear again. What was the point of having a mother if she wasn't any more reliable than your ditziest friend?

Catherine knocked on her door, making Willow jump, and stuck her head into the room. "Time to get up," she said. "Breakfast is almost ready."

By the time Willow was dressed and had come downstairs, Catherine was putting bowls of oatmeal and mugs of hot chocolate on the table. "Sit," she said. "Eat while it's hot."

Like Willow was two years old! But Willow obeyed, picking up her spoon and taking a bite.

"Do you need me to make you a lunch?"

Willow shook her head. "I'll buy today. I have money." She didn't add that it was Russell's money. She wondered if Russell and Catherine even talked about things like who would give her lunch money.

Catherine sat down across the table but didn't touch her oatmeal. Why did adults give kids rules they didn't follow themselves?

The world was unfair—that's why.

Then, to Willow's surprise, Catherine apologized. "I'm sorry about last night," she said. "I shouldn't have yelled at you and Zoe like that. I was just really shocked and upset."

"I know, but you scared her off! That wasn't right!"

"Maybe not, but honey, I just couldn't believe Zoe would let us think she was *dead* this whole time." Catherine massaged her temple with two fingers, as if the noise in her brain was as bad as Willow's. "It almost killed Nana, thinking Zoe was dead."

"Except Nana never really believed that." Willow made herself take a bite of oatmeal. "Did you?"

"Of course! I mean, otherwise, why wouldn't she come back? What kind of person *does* that?" Catherine shook her head. "I'm sorry. I know that sounds harsh. But I can't forgive Zoe for abandoning you, never mind what she did to your grandmother."

"She didn't abandon me," Willow said, setting her spoon down. The oatmeal had gone cold; it felt like lumps of cold, gritty mud sliding down her throat. "Zoe had a friend watching me in the bus station. Sandra. She was there the whole time, until you came."

"I don't believe that. There was nobody else with you. I was there."

"I'm not lying! Sandra was dressed like a homeless person."

"Seriously?" Catherine folded her arms. "That's ridiculous. And stupid!

Why wouldn't Zoe take you to Sandra's house, if she felt so compelled to ditch you? Why go to all the trouble of leaving you in the bus station and scaring you? Why did she have to pretend to be *dead*? And why is she going around in that weird disguise?"

Zoe didn't completely trust Sandra, which was probably why she took her to the bus station, Willow thought, even as she felt the words "ditch you" like bee stings on her skin.

"She was afraid you might look for her," Willow said. "She had to leave her old life completely behind."

"Well, she certainly succeeded," Catherine grumbled.

"And also? She gave me to you because she felt sorry for you," Willow added.

"*Zoe* felt sorry for *me*? Oh, please. Why?"

"Because you couldn't have kids." Willow was just trying to make her mother's motives clear, but this was apparently the wrong thing to say. Catherine stood up and began clearing the dishes, clattering them into the sink and rinsing them full force beneath the faucet. After that was done, she turned around again, her face covered in blotchy red patches.

"I can understand why Zoe lied," she said. "Zoe has always been a first-class liar. But how could *you* lie to us, Willow? How *could* you, after all we've done for you? Didn't it occur to you that your grandmother, at least, might be happy to know her daughter's alive?"

"I'm sorry." Willow knew she'd been wrong to keep this secret from Nana, of all people. "But Zoe asked me not to tell anybody." She spoke slowly, trying to be careful not to trip up and say the word "mom" when she meant "Zoe." That would freak out Catherine even more. "She only came back because she wanted to see me. To know me a little."

"Oh, yeah? She wanted to see you and know you? And *then* what?" Catherine demanded. "Zoe wanted to gain your trust and ask you for money, so she could get her next fix?"

"No! She's clean now. Zoe never once asked me for money. It's not like that!"

Catherine took a step back and pressed herself against the sink, as if

Willow were cornering her. "Okay. Tell me, then. What is it like when you see her?"

"It's not like anything! We just meet up after school and, you know. Talk."

"And you can honestly say you never give her money?"

Willow felt her cheeks burn. She *had* given Zoe money. Five or ten dollars at a time. Nothing much. Just whatever loose bills she had from the money Russell and Catherine gave her. But Zoe had never asked for it: Willow was the one who secretly pushed money into Zoe's backpack.

Catherine was staring at her. Finally, she said, "I see," then came over to the table and pressed on Willow's shoulders, making her sit back down at the kitchen table. Willow felt like she was going to be pushed right through the chair and onto the floor.

"You have to get this through your head," Catherine said in a low, scary voice. "Once an addict, always an addict. Your mom is a drug addict and has been since she was your age. I know you're curious about her, and I'm sure you're happy to know she's alive. I am, too. But you can't trust her, Willow. I've known Zoe all her life, okay? And she has begged, borrowed, or stolen money from every single person I know, including me. She even sold some of our grandmother's silver, the silver that used to be in the hutch at Chance Harbor, so she could buy drugs. Who knows what she's up to now?"

"She's not up to *anything*!"

"Let's hope you're right. Maybe she won't even come back, now that she's seen you and satisfied her curiosity. Just promise you won't see her unless your dad or I come with you. Do not go anywhere with Zoe by yourself, okay?"

"Jesus. Okay, okay," Willow mumbled without looking at Catherine. She could never look people directly in the eye when she was lying.

The day dragged. Seven hours of school felt like seventy. Willow checked her phone so often—certain that Zoe would text or call, at least to get her stuff back—that her social studies teacher took the phone away.

"I need you to pay attention to me, not to your phone, Ms. MacLeish,"

Ms. Frangiapani said, pushing her blue eyeglasses up higher on her nose. "This information will all be on the test tomorrow."

Yeah, yeah, whatever, Willow wanted to say. *Test me now if you want.* There wasn't one thing she didn't already know about world history, thanks to Russell's stupid dinner-table lectures.

The upside of getting humiliated by a teacher in public school was that it gave you street cred. It wasn't cool to be too good. After her phone got taken away, two kids Willow had never talked to before invited her to sit with them at lunch. Fiona and Jasmine: Disney princess names, but they were all about fleeces and hiking boots. Like at any minute they might start climbing the school walls and rappelling back down off the roof.

Finally, the last bell rang. Willow racewalked to the office, where, before giving her phone back, the dean of students made her write a letter of apology to the teacher and the principal.

Only one message on her phone. It was from Henry, reminding Willow that she'd agreed to meet him in Harvard Square after school today. They'd met a few times after Willow left Beacon Hill, sometimes with Kendrick and Carly.

She'd worried at first that Henry was like some of the other kids at Beacon Hill; a lot of kids had e-mailed or texted to ask about Nola and Russell, looking to juice up their Twitter and Instagram feeds, a fact she didn't catch on to until it was too late. But after she told Henry she didn't want to talk about any of that, he was cool.

"I just like hanging out with you," he'd said.

Now Willow hesitated before texting him back. Catherine had given her strict instructions to go straight home. "I don't want you monkeying around alone on the Common while I'm at work," she'd warned. "And no seeing Zoe unless I'm there. Or your dad."

But she wasn't going to the Common, and she wasn't going to be alone, so she wouldn't be breaking any of Catherine's stupid rules. *OK,* Willow texted back, and started walking toward the square.

She met Henry at Newbury Comics. They hung out there until they got dirty looks from the manager, whose lip piercing was so infected it looked like a blood-swollen tick, then wandered back out of the store and started spiraling down the ramp to the first floor.

Ordinarily they spun around together, a not-really-dancing-but-sort-of thing. Today, though, Willow just followed Henry's tall twirling body at enough of a distance so his arms wouldn't whack her.

He stopped in the middle of the ramp and said, "How come you're just walking like a normal boring human? What's wrong?"

"Just everything," she said.

He came over and looped an arm around her shoulders. When most guys touched her, Willow freaked, but Henry was her own Big Friendly Giant, a fact they'd discussed so often that sometimes they even quoted the Dahl book to each other: "The human bean is not a vegetable," "Two rights don't equal a left," and, their favorite, "Don't gobblefunk around with words." Now she tucked herself into his armpit.

"Everything like what?" Henry asked.

"Like my mom."

She felt Henry's long arm stiffen up as he said, "Your real mom?" So he did remember.

"Yeah. As it turns out, she happens not to be dead."

They'd reached the bottom of the ramp; now they stopped in the hallway where a homeless man in a trench coat reminded Willow of her mother's weird disguise. Catherine was right to ask how Zoe thought it was okay to lie for such a long time. That was fucked-up.

"Tell me," Henry was saying, "but only if you want to."

She did. She had to tell *somebody*, and there was nobody she trusted more than Henry. Not even Catherine.

"Whoa," Henry said when she was done. "And you have no idea where your mom is now?"

Willow shook her head.

"Well, but at least you know she's alive, right? You could Google her."

"Not unless she has an address." Willow jabbed him in the ribs. "I don't even know if she goes by the same last name. She pretty much lies about everything."

"That sucks," Henry said. "You totally deserve better."

"Thanks," she said, and thought, yeah, she did, but that didn't mean anything better was going to happen. "What I hate most is that I can't do anything about this. It's not in my control."

Henry laughed. "So you've seen the light."

"What?" She tipped her head up to look at him, frowning. From this angle, she could see the red-gold stubble of his beard popping out on his chin. And his wide, smiling mouth. She liked Henry's mouth, Willow realized.

"I mean that you've come to the conclusion that nothing is in our control, as people have had to realize since the dawn of time. We're talking about human beans, here, remember?"

"And the human bean is not a vegetable," she said.

They both laughed, and then Willow had to stop laughing, because Henry was turning her in his arms somehow until she was wrapped against him, warm instead of cold, but shivering at the same time because of the way Henry made her whole complicated world seem easier.

They took the earliest possible ferry from Nova Scotia back to Prince Edward Island on Tuesday morning, and Eve was on the road back to Massachusetts by midmorning.

As she crossed the Confederation Bridge, Eve replayed Catherine's call in her head. Not the words as much as her daughter's strained voice. She'd heard that high note of panic in Catherine's voice only once before. It was a night when all three of them had gone searching for Zoe, not quite sixteen, who was out long after curfew. Catherine was home from her first year of college for the summer, and she had found Zoe passed out under one of the bridges in Newburyport near the rail trail. Bruises on her face, difficult to rouse.

Catherine had called 911 first, then Eve, her voice laced with that hysteria as she said, "Something really bad happened to Zoe, Mom. Come to the hospital. Right away."

This felt like that: driving as fast as she could down through New Brunswick, pushing the gas pedal to the floor and leaning forward, as if her body weight could give the car more momentum. It had started to rain. The visibility was poor and passing trucks sprayed the windshield, blinding Eve every few minutes. She felt like she was hallucinating, or maybe hypnotized by the red taillights swirling in front of her as her mind lit up with questions like some bell-ringing arcade game. Was Zoe all right? Where had she been all this time? Where was she living? What was she using for money?

After Catherine's frantic call, Darcy had held Eve all night long but nothing more. They didn't even undress. A kid crisis trumped lovemaking every time. Eve couldn't help this, and she was glad Darcy understood, but she was also sorry. Underlying her overwhelming wonder and relief about Zoe being alive was a shimmering slick of resentment that her fantasy life had been disrupted. This was probably the last time in her life she would ever feel young and desirable. Zoe coming back would age her by decades.

Darcy had helped her pack the car at Chance Harbor. At the last minute, he'd insisted that she take Bear for company. "In case you get stranded on the road," he said.

"A lot of good that dog would do me," she'd said. "If somebody tried to jack the car, he'd probably lick him to death."

"But he *looks* intimidating," Darcy had argued. "And talking to a dog makes you feel less crazy than talking to yourself. Trust me, I know. Plus, Bear will be safer with you looking after him. You've seen how he wanders. And I'll have an excuse to see you again if you take my dog."

"When?"

"As soon as I can." As Darcy kissed her good-bye, a light brush of his lips on her forehead, Eve caught a hint of the whiskey they'd drunk by the lake, a combination of peat and night sky. Darcy's cream wool sweater was itchy, but she briefly rested her head on his shoulder and let him support her weight in the circle of his arms.

Darcy was right: Bear *was* good company. It was a comfort to have his warm body on the front seat next to her, where she had invited the dog to sit after catching a glimpse of his morose expression in the rearview mirror. What must the poor dog think, being shunted from one person to the next?

Like Willow, Eve thought, and that's when the tears started to fall, threading down her cheeks until she had to pull over and search the car for napkins. This made Bear think she was getting something to eat; his tail thumped against the door, making her laugh and break off a piece of granola bar for him.

Eve somehow made the trip in just over ten hours. She ate in the car and stopped only when she needed gas. She drank seven cups of coffee and popped M&M's to keep herself awake. Once she crossed the border into Massachusetts, she zoomed past her usual Newburyport exit and breathed a sigh of relief as she wound through Cambridge's narrow streets. At least she was done with that hypnotic highway driving. So much easier to stay awake in a city, where you had lights and traffic to look at instead of that straight black ribbon of road.

Ten minutes later she pulled into Catherine's driveway and switched off the ignition. Bear whined and thumped his tail. "Now what?" she wondered, stroking his silky head.

The dog jumped out of the car when she opened the door for him and followed her up the stairs to Catherine's porch. The lights were on in the house. After a moment's hesitation, Eve rang the bell.

Catherine answered the door, her straight blond hair lifting in thin strands around the shoulders of her green sweater, her face pale and free of makeup. She'd lost more weight in the days Eve had been in Canada; her daughter's blue eyes looked enormous, like the eyes of some Japanese anime heroine, and her delicate nose and mouth were pinched and pale.

"Mom," she said. "Thank God you're here."

"Where is she?" Eve's heart was hammering hard enough for her to feel it in her throat.

"Come inside, Mom."

Eve stepped into the house, Bear at her heels. Catherine pressed her back against the wall to make way for the dog. "What the hell is that?"

"He belongs to a friend," Eve said. "Don't worry. He'll behave himself. But he probably needs some water."

"Mike's bowl is in the kitchen," Catherine said.

Just then, the puppy scrabbled down the steps and took a stiff, bowlegged stance, growling at Bear. The bigger dog sniffed Mike, wagged his tail, and lumbered down the hall toward the kitchen. Mike glanced at Catherine and then tore after him, barking.

"Will they be all right?" Eve asked.

"Mike can hold his own," Catherine said. "Here, come sit in the living room."

Eve shook her head. "No. Please. Just tell me about Zoe. You can't imagine how difficult it was, driving down here without knowing anything."

"I'm sorry." Catherine seemed, if anything, to shrink down another size. "I can't tell you more, because Zoe hasn't come back. I've told you everything. Zoe's alive, Mom. That's all I know."

"I still can't believe it," Eve said. "You're sure?"

Catherine nodded. "Willow had been seeing her for a while."

"My God. I really don't believe it." Eve felt something peculiar happening with her vision; everything was receding. It was as though she were looking at her daughter through the wrong end of binoculars suddenly. The kitchen beyond her seemed miles away.

"I know it's a shock, but it's true." Even Catherine's voice sounded muffled, as if they were speaking across a river. "Zoe's definitely alive and she's here. Well, not *here* here, obviously, but in Cambridge. Willow has been sneaking out to meet her."

"I wasn't sneaking!" Willow said as she padded into the hall from the kitchen to join them. She must have just taken a shower; her hair was wet and dark. "Zoe made me promise I wouldn't tell, Nana. I'm really sorry."

"It's all right. I understand how Zoe can be," Eve said, then felt the floor tipping beneath her. The wooden boards felt oiled slick beneath her feet. She was aware of a cracking sound and then a terrible pain at the back of her head before she blacked out.

When she opened her eyes, Willow was cradling her head and Catherine was phoning an ambulance. "No, no," Eve said. "Please don't call them. I'm all right." She must have fainted and fallen. She struggled to sit up, but had to lie down again when her vision swam. The pain felt like someone had slit the back of her neck open with a knife.

"Don't you dare move until we get you checked out, Mom," Catherine said, crouching down to tuck a living room pillow beneath Eve's head. "That was a nasty fall."

"Don't make such a fuss," Eve said, but she didn't try to sit up again. Not yet. She felt like she might vomit and there was a buzzing sound in her head, as if someone had turned on a fluorescent light in there. Willow was stroking her hair. This should have felt pleasant, but given the pounding in her head, Eve wanted to slap the girl's hand away.

"Tell me about Zoe," she said.

The doorbell rang before Catherine could answer. Eve knew, even as Catherine opened the front door, who it was. All of the love and worry and guilt and anger and loss she'd felt since Zoe disappeared were washing over her, emotions like a heavy surf pounding her against the wooden floor until she was numb with cold, breathless, and sick with fear.

Eve used all of her strength to sit up, pushing herself up off the wooden floor with both hands. She craned her head toward the door, biting her lip to keep from crying, to keep from shouting her daughter's name in joy and surprise, in relief and fury, knowing she was powerless to change anything that had gone on before, or was about to happen now.

CHAPTER THIRTEEN

"What's going on? Why is Mom on the floor? Mom, are you okay?" Zoe demanded, shouldering past Catherine and going straight to their mother, where she squatted down and took her hand.

"She fainted and fell before I could catch her. The ambulance is on its way." Catherine stared in disbelief at this new version of her sister.

Zoe had shed the black dreadlocks, sunglasses, and shawl. A stranger observing this scene would not see a gonzo woman pretending to be blind and homeless, but a pretty, slender woman with cropped blond curls, a curvy back end in snug jeans riding low on her hips, and an expensive-looking, stylish black leather jacket. To top it off, Zoe wore a black-and-white scarf with tassels. It was the sort of cotton scarf that hippie backpackers might wear to advertise the fact that they'd traveled through Asia on a shoestring.

Catherine had been angry at her sister many times in her life, for more reasons than she could list in a single breath. Still, even compared to all that, the anger bubbling up in Catherine now was lava-hot and threatening to spill out of her body. She could imagine spewing enough anger to burn everything in this room to a crisp. Especially her sister, the hot sun around which their family had always revolved.

Meanwhile, her deranged sister was making clucking and cooing noises over their mother. As if she knew one thing about falls or concussions. Zoe was even stroking their mother's hand like she actually cared, after nearly killing her with grief.

"I'm all right now," Eve was saying, but she didn't look it. The lines in her face were deep and her limbs looked brittle. Catherine didn't usually think of her mother as old. Tonight, though, she could see where Eve was headed. "I fainted and fell. But I'm perfectly all right. Just feeling silly." Eve stirred on the floor, as if to stand. Zoe and Willow both put their arms around her to help her up.

"Leave her there!" Catherine shouted, her voice echoing in the hallway. "Mom definitely has a concussion. She blacked out!"

"Please, Catherine. Let's not be dramatic," Eve said.

"Me? I'm a nurse practitioner! You're telling *me* to curb the drama?" Catherine sputtered.

Everyone ignored her. Eve had taken both of Zoe's hands in hers, saying, "My God. I can't believe you're here! Where have you been? Let me look at you. Are you really all right?"

"It's a long story. But yes, I'm fine," Zoe said, talking so fast that the words bounced noisily on the hardwood floor and echoed off the walls. She must have rehearsed this speech. "I'm clean. Healthier than I've ever been. I'm sorry I caused you so much pain and worry, Mom. Not only when I left, but for all those times before. Really I am. And I'm sorry about Dad, too. Believe me, I would have stayed here if I thought I could survive."

By now Catherine could hear the shriek of an approaching ambulance. "They're almost here," she said needlessly.

Eve turned to her, still gripping Zoe's hands. "For God's sake, do not let those paramedics in the house. They always find something wrong."

"Relax. We'll just have them check you out," Catherine said.

"All right. But don't let them take me to the ER," Eve said.

Zoe patted her hand. "We won't. Don't worry. It'll be fine," she said. "*You're* fine."

"Like you know squat," Catherine muttered as she went to open the front door. Getting there involved navigating around her sister, mother,

Willow, and both dogs, which had joined them and were now peacefully sniffing each other's backsides. She couldn't believe how many life-forms were breathing in her hallway.

She opened the door as footsteps thumped on the porch, expecting the paramedics. But it was Russell. Nola was standing behind him, peering over his shoulder. Catherine gritted her teeth. "What are *you* doing here?"

"Dad?" Willow said.

"Is that her?" Zoe demanded. "The little home-wrecking skank?"

Catherine's face felt hot with embarrassment. Willow must have told Zoe every embarrassing detail about their home life. "Stay out of this, Zoe," she said.

Russell waved a textbook he was holding in one hand and looked uncertainly at Catherine. "I just wanted to bring Willow's book. She left it in my car and I thought she might need it at school tomorrow. Nola and I were having dinner in Cambridge, so it seemed like a good idea to drop it off."

Catherine glared at Nola, who looked right past her and peered into the house. "Hey, Willow," she said. "Who's that?"

Before Willow could answer, Catherine shoved at Russell's chest and forced him back down the porch steps. Nola had to walk backward behind him to avoid having him plow into her; she stumbled as she misjudged the last step and her boot heel slid off the stone path. "Ow!" she said.

"Get out, Russell." Catherine's face felt as if it were on fire, and she had to keep blinking against the slap of the cold night air. "You know I don't want her here. We agreed! Get that girl off my lawn or I'll take out a restraining order. Go!"

Russell put both hands up in surrender. But he, too, was looking beyond her to the front door of the house. "Is that *Zoe* in there?" he said. "Is she *alive*? Jesus, Catherine. What's going on?"

The shock and concern in his voice undid her. Catherine had felt so alone, as if Zoe had coaxed her mother and Willow to one side of the moat and pulled up a bridge, leaving her stranded on the other side. When Russell said her name, she felt her knees wobble and stumbled toward him. Russell caught her in his arms.

For one blissful moment, Catherine let her exhausted body rest against his. It was so good to be held, to feel Russell's tweed jacket against her cheek and to be surrounded by his familiar spicy scent. Her husband was here. Everything would be all right now, she thought, as the ambulance pulled up in front of the house.

Her *cheating* husband, she remembered, and butted his chin with her head. Hard. "Let go of me!"

"Ouch!" Russell yelped, rubbing his chin. "Christ. What did you do that for?"

"Don't hurt him!" Nola said. "He was just trying to help you!"

"You shut up and get the hell off my lawn," Catherine said.

"Hey, hey, hey. What's going on, people?" A paramedic approached them, a young black guy in a reflective jacket. A woman stood behind him, a medical case in her hand, raising her eyebrows. The eyebrows were thin and black against her powdered face, like thread stitched onto her skin.

Now Catherine realized a fire engine had pulled up to the curb in front of her house as well. Neighbors were already stepping out onto their porches or standing on the sidewalk. Maybe she should just invite them all into her hallway.

"I'm fine. We all are. Well, most of us." She pointed toward the house. "I called because my mother fell. She's inside. I think she has a concussion." Catherine was so cold that the words emerged in clipped, icy syllables.

"You sure there's no problem with this guy here?" the EMT asked, stepping closer and essentially shielding her from Russell.

Catherine shook her head. "He's my ex. It's fine. He's leaving."

"He was just trying to help her," Nola said, sounding fierce. "He's a good person."

"Shhh," Russell said. "Don't work yourself up over this. You heard, sweetie. Everything's fine now."

Behind the paramedic, Catherine watched Russell wrap Nola in his arms. Even from here, she could see the bulge beneath Nola's short quilted coat. She did a quick calculation: January due date, so Nola must be six months along.

"Take her home, Russell. Please." Catherine wheeled around to lead the paramedics into the house.

Zoe had come outside and was staring at Russell, her eyes narrowed. "You piece of crap!" she yelled. "How *dare* you do this to my sister? And to Willow? And what gives you the balls to bring that little slut around here?"

Russell snorted. "Big talk from the drug addict who abandoned her child."

"At least I never *pretended* to be good," Zoe shot back. "At least I'm *honest* about who I am."

"Shut it, Zoe," Catherine snapped. "That's enough. Mom needs you."

Just then, Nola let out an agonized moan. Catherine turned back and saw that she was doubled over and clutching her stomach. Her forehead glistened. Russell was leaning close to her, stroking her hair. "Sweetheart, what is it? Talk to me. You okay?"

"I think I'm in labor," she gasped. "It really hurts."

"When's she due?" the male EMT asked, whipping out his stethoscope and going to Nola.

"January," Catherine and Russell answered together.

The female paramedic rolled her eyes. "I'll go check on the mother," she said, and trotted past them, bag in hand.

Catherine glanced once more at Nola as the male paramedic helped her over to the ambulance, where he began taking her blood pressure. Probably just Braxton-Hicks contractions, she told herself, but felt frightened. What if Nola lost the baby?

Inside the house, the female paramedic told Catherine to shut the door. "We've had enough drama," she said as she took Eve's vital signs, asked her questions, then helped her up. She led Eve to the couch and offered oxygen and water, took some notes. Eve refused to go to the hospital.

"She's probably going to be fine, but you might want to take turns sitting with her tonight to be on the safe side," the paramedic said, looking at Zoe and Catherine. "Take her to the ER if there's any deterioration." As she began explaining what to look for—vomiting, nausea, blurred vision—Catherine stopped her.

"I'm a nurse," she said. "I know what to do. But thank you."

Catherine saw the paramedic to the door. Outside, Russell was bundling Nola into the car. She waited until they were gone, and the ambulance, too, before coming back inside and shutting the door. The temperature in the house had dropped while the door was open; Catherine started a fire in the fireplace.

Other than the occasional crackle and pop from the flames, the house was eerily quiet. Willow sat on the couch with Eve's feet in her lap; Zoe was cross-legged on the floor next to Eve's head. Between them lay the big black dog, flopped onto his side, snoring next to the couch, Mike curled in a ball against him. The living room smelled like dog and wood smoke.

Catherine sat in the armchair across from them and tried not to think about how this chair had always been her father's favorite; he used to sit here and read the newspaper whenever she and Russell invited them for brunch. Now she remembered what Russell had said about her mother being unfaithful. Impossible to imagine. She never would have guessed that her parents had any serious problems. They seemed happy. Companionable. Respectful. She had tried to model her own marriage after theirs. How naive she'd been!

Catherine slumped lower in the chair, shivering a little from the shock of all that had happened despite the crackling heat of the fire, and studied her sister.

Zoe hardly looked older than when she'd left. Healthier and a bit heavier than before, but despite her extra weight, Zoe's waist was still well defined and her body looked toned. Somebody would have had to put Catherine in some kind of torture device to get her to flex her knees as much as her sister's were now. Maybe Zoe had been in a yoga retreat for the past five years. At this point, Catherine could believe almost anything about her sister's secret life.

Her irritation and anger had waned during the chaos. Zoe had come to her defense, really, going after Russell like a pit bull. That was a minuscule point in her favor.

"Anybody want a drink?" Catherine said to break the silence. "Coffee or tea? Brandy? Juice? Water?" She pointedly looked at her mother on the couch. A little brandy might do her mother good. If her sister asked for alcohol, though, Catherine would throw her to the curb. And if she disappeared again, good. It was nice to know she was alive—really, it was—but who among them would actually be better off if Zoe stayed?

"No, thanks," Willow said.

"I'm perfect," Eve murmured without opening her eyes.

"I'd take some OJ if you have it," Zoe said.

Of course Zoe wants you to wait on her, Catherine thought, aware of a bitter taste at the back of her throat as she filled a glass with orange juice in the kitchen and carried it back to the living room. What else was new? Zoe had always exhibited a debutante's need to be served. Or a dictator's. Part of her charm. But oh so exhausting.

"Thanks." Zoe did a graceful half spin on the floor without uncrossing her legs and reached up to take the juice. "So that's Russell's new squeeze, huh? Holy hell. What a dope."

Catherine said nothing. She didn't know whether by "dope" Zoe meant Nola or Russell. Either way, she didn't want to talk about it. Not because Russell was with someone else, but because knowing that Willow had probably already told Zoe all about Catherine's failed marriage and Russell's new life was humiliating. How much lower could anyone sink than to be the object of pity between a tenth grader and her homeless, runaway mother—who, P.S., was probably still a drug addict? She went back to curl up in the chair again.

"When's the baby due, Cat?" Zoe asked.

Zoe was the only one who'd ever called her by that nickname. As a child, Catherine had liked it because "Cat" matched "Zoe" in its snappy size; "Catherine" sounded like the name of a spinster in long taffeta skirts.

"January," Catherine said, "and no, I don't want to talk about it." She glanced at her mother, whose eyes were still closed, and wondered if they should wake her to make sure she wasn't slipping into a coma. No, that was ridiculous. Her mother was probably just exhausted after that long drive alone back from Canada.

"Fine by me," Zoe was saying. "But for the record? I never liked your husband. He always had a stick up his ass."

Instantly, Catherine was infuriated. It was fine for her to criticize Russell—she'd earned that right as the jilted wife—but not for her sister. "How dare you? Russell has always been kind to you! Even when you got drunk and nearly ruined our wedding because you thought it would be so, so funny to take over from the DJ. Even when you couldn't bother to show up at Willow's christening because you were too high. He's worth ten of you!"

"Probably. But he's dull as lint, Cat. No offense, girlie girl," Zoe said, glancing at Willow.

"It's fine," Willow said.

Catherine was about to light into Willow, too, ready to say, *Shame on you, after all Russell has done for you*. But by the way the girl was staring at her slender hands like she'd never seen them before, Catherine could tell Willow was hurt by Zoe's words. Russell had been her dad for five years.

"Willow, honey," Catherine said. "It's getting late. You should finish your homework and get ready for bed. School tomorrow."

Willow didn't move. "I've already done my homework. Can't I stay up a little longer?"

"At least go upstairs and pack your backpack," Catherine said, trying to muster up the energy to inject a little parental authority into her voice, despite feeling weird about doing this in front of Zoe.

"If I do that, then can I stay up? Please?"

Catherine nodded. She couldn't stand another confrontation with anybody. Not tonight.

Zoe didn't glance up as Willow slid off the couch. After she'd gone upstairs, though, she turned back around, her lips curving into a smile. "Willow looks good."

"No thanks to you."

Eve's eyes flew open, startling Catherine into wondering if her mother had only been pretending to be asleep. "Girls. Be nice," she said, before her lids fluttered shut again.

"*Yeah*, Cat," Zoe said. "Play nice. *God*. This is just like all those friggin' car rides up to Chance Harbor, right? Remember how Mom and Dad used to roll up a blanket to shove between us on the backseat, just to keep us from tearing each other's hair out?"

"Of course I do." Catherine massaged her scalp with both hands, trying to ease the tension. Her scalp was so tight, it felt as though it might crack open like an egg.

"I miss that place," Zoe said. "So beautiful up there. How's the house?"

"It's for sale," Catherine said.

"What? It can't be!"

Zoe looked upset, but she was a drama queen, Catherine reminded herself. A chameleon. "Yes. Mom feels like it's too much to keep up without Dad, and I'm in no position to take it on."

Neither are you, she wanted to add, but stopped herself. Instead, she said, "Where have you been, Zoe? What's kept you so damn busy that you couldn't at least let us know you were alive?"

Zoe shrugged, a movement so fluid that Catherine imagined muscles rippling beneath the black leather jacket. "I was busy surviving."

"Tell me," Catherine said, not nicely.

Zoe sighed. "Look, it's the truth. I was surviving. Struggling just to get by, you know."

Catherine willed herself not to lose her temper. "No. I don't know. Start at the beginning."

"Fine. After I left the bus station in Boston—"

"—after you *abandoned your daughter*, alone and terrified, you mean," Catherine interrupted.

"I did *not* abandon her!" Zoe insisted. "I've explained this to Willow. I paid one of my friends to stay in the bus station with her until you came."

"You *paid* her? Some friend. Why didn't you just leave Willow at your friend's house? I could have picked her up there."

"Her house wasn't safe at the time," Zoe said, then surprised her by adding, "Mine wasn't, either."

"Why not?"

"Trust me. You don't need to hear all the sorry details." Zoe tugged at the zipper of her jacket, yanking it down and then up again with a ripping sound. "Anyway. I knew Willow would be okay until you came."

"What if I hadn't come, though?" Catherine demanded. "What if I'd been away? Or too busy?"

Zoe rolled her eyes. "I knew you wouldn't be too busy. Not for Willow."

"All right. Go on. I still don't understand why you had to disappear."

"I couldn't get clean if I stayed here."

"But you had every opportunity," Catherine said. "Mom and Dad must have paid for rehab three times."

"More like six, over the years," Zoe said. "But every time I got out, I had the same friends. And I was weak."

"What made you think you could go away and be strong?"

"I didn't *think*," Zoe said. "I just hoped."

"Okay. But none of this explains why you let us think you were *dead*."

"I was afraid that if Mom found me, she could convince me to come back and I'd do it all over again. Also, I knew I couldn't leave Willow unless I left completely, you know? That was the hardest part." Zoe looked like she might cry; her cheeks had pink blotches beneath the delicate freckles.

Catherine looked away. She refused to feel sorry for her thoughtless, selfish little sister. "Did you have a plan?"

Zoe snorted. "Me? A plan? No. I just kept heading south. Not for any reason, except I was friggin' sick of being cold."

"Where? Virginia? Florida? Texas?"

"Florida," Zoe said. "I knew I couldn't waitress or do any job where I had to have papers. So I picked fruit and cleaned hotels. Sometimes I pretended I only spoke Spanish. That made it easier, if people thought I was illegal. Other times it was cool to speak English where nobody else did. I never had trouble finding work. And it's amazing how cheap life is if you don't have a car or rent, and if you're not supporting a habit."

Despite herself, Catherine was impressed by her sister's survival skills. "Where did you live?"

"Homeless shelters at first, when I could get a bed. Or I couch surfed with people I met. Everybody's got a couch, you know? After I found steady work, though, I got sick of putting up with other people's crazy shit, so I rented rooms by the week. Most people didn't ask questions as long as I had cash and looked like I washed my hair."

"Have you been in Florida this whole time?" Catherine couldn't believe it. If this were true, how was it possible that nobody had been able to find Zoe? Not the cops, not the private investigators. Not even their dogged mother, who had driven up and down the entire East Coast looking for Zoe.

She had felt sorry for her mother then, so strung out on sorrow, yet determined not to give up, even after Dad announced Zoe was a lost cause. Catherine had agreed with him. It must have torn her mother apart, being alone like that in her search.

Eve's lips were slightly parted in sleep, her face as relaxed and innocent as Willow's. Maybe this deep resting state wasn't due to her mother's head injury or the long drive back from Canada. Perhaps it was more to do with knowing that her youngest child was safe.

"Yeah, Florida was pretty good," Zoe was saying. "It's a place filled with people running away from something. Fit me like a friggin' glove. I hung out in the Keys for a while. Loved having water all around. People with planes instead of cars in their garages for a quick getaway. Lots of friends like that. Very useful. But I got spooked when some dick came around to the hotel I'd been working for and started asking questions. I knew the manager wouldn't out me—we were tight—but I figured it was time to move on. So I went to Miami, found jobs picking fruit on the farms, cleaned rooms in a hotel. Eventually I hooked up with some gypsies."

"Gypsies? You can't be serious." Even as she said this, though, Catherine could imagine it: Zoe in a turban, dancing with a tambourine. Not much of a stretch, considering how Zoe had looked in those dreadlocks and shawl when she first saw her with Willow.

"Totally serious. They were actually from Massachusetts, originally. That's how I made it back. I was working with this one girl at a hotel, Sadie. She and her brother had an extra room in their house in Homestead and let me crash. Perfect place, smack in the middle of an orchard, all the mangoes you could eat, nobody around to ask questions. They're gypsies.

Well, half. I think their dad's actually Cuban. Anyway, when Grey—that's Sadie's brother—said he was coming back to Massachusetts, I hitched a ride."

A shadow crossed her face, and Zoe abruptly stopped talking in a way that made Catherine wonder whether something had chased her out of Florida, too, just like something—or someone—had made her decide to disappear from home. "What made you come back? What's your intent and purpose?"

Zoe laughed. "What are you, a cop?"

"I want to know what you're doing here." Catherine glanced at their mother and lowered her voice. "What you're after."

"I'm not after anything!"

"You must be. I *know* you."

"No, you don't," Zoe said. "You know who I *was*. You don't know who I *am*."

"People don't change."

"Oh, really? Are you saying you haven't changed?" Zoe demanded. "Or Russell, either? That's rich. What about Mom, huh? Is she the same since Dad died?"

"Don't you dare bring Dad into this."

"Why not? What makes him so special? He was your hero, not mine. He never loved me the way he loved you."

"That's ridiculous."

"No. It's not. You were his princess." Zoe laughed, a harsh, grating sound. "You were 'everything a girl should be,' he used to say, 'and better than any son, too.' But Dad looked at me and saw nothing but trouble."

"Because you *were* nothing but trouble. You brought that on yourself! You made it very, very hard to love you, Zoe. You have to take some responsibility for that."

"Oh, I do. But you have to ask yourself why I did the things I did. Have you ever bothered to think about that?"

Catherine shrugged, uncomfortable now. This should be her domain—she had worked with children for more than twenty years—not Zoe's. "I believe kids are who they are at birth," she said. "I've seen some of my patients for their entire lives. And you know what? Their personalities are hardwired."

Zoe shook her head, the curls uncoiling like little yellow ribbons. "You can't discount environment."

"Fine. But you can't use your environment as an excuse for how you acted out. You and I had exactly the same one."

Now Zoe had the nerve to look smug. "Oh, really?"

Catherine was growing impatient. The last thing she needed was to hear Zoe rationalizing the foolish choices she'd made. "Get to the point."

"The point is that our parents never treated us the same."

"Of course not. You can't discount chemistry, even in families," Catherine said carefully. She knew she was treading on dangerous ground and really didn't want to be there. "That goes back to my argument, right? Personalities are hardwired from the start."

"But if a kid is rejected over and over, if a child is told so many times that she's bad or useless or even silly, what do you think happens?"

Catherine didn't think she'd ever seen Zoe looking so sad. She didn't like it. Or trust it. "Whatever," she said. "What happened to us in childhood is something we're all supposed to learn from and move on. Which brings me to the same question: Why are you here?"

"To see Willow, of course. And to let you and Mom know I'm okay. I felt bad about the way I vanished."

"And it only took you five years," Catherine said. "Golly."

"Don't be sarcastic. This is hard enough for me as it is."

"Hard enough for *you*?" Catherine asked in astonishment. "What about us? Did you ever think, even for one moment, about what kind of effect your little disappearing act had on us? Did you really believe you could just waltz back home and take over as Willow's mom? Or as the favorite daughter?"

Zoe smirked. "So you do admit our parents loved us differently."

"I never said otherwise," Catherine said, humiliated to know that her sister could bring her so easily to this same boiling point: *Mom loved you best.* Jesus. They were pitiful, both of them. "Go on. Tell me what you want. Money?"

"No, I don't want money." Zoe put her hands up as if Catherine were threatening her with a weapon. "Christ. You really are something. I told you. I came back for Willow."

"Well, you can't have her. You can't wreck her life again. I will fight you tooth and nail before that happens."

Zoe unwound her legs and stood up to stretch, revealing a flat, tanned stomach over her jeans. Catherine had to look away. There had always been something magnetic, even feral, about her sister. That hadn't changed. Zoe was graceful, but aggressive in her movements. Her eyes, a shade darker than Catherine's own blue, were watchful but commanding. It was unfair that she should possess so much power and abuse it.

She was like Nola that way, Catherine realized. Maybe that was another reason why she found it so hard to accept that Nola was now in her life.

Zoe wasn't much taller than Catherine, maybe five foot six. But in her black boots and leather jacket, and with her narrow features sharply defined by that short, tousled hair, she looked like a video-game street fighter. "I did not wreck my daughter's life." Zoe's voice was calm, but her lips were pressed into an angry line.

"Oh, no?" Catherine folded her arms tightly against her body, feeling her heart bump against her chest. "What do you call it, then, when a mother's lifestyle is so risky that her fifteen-year-old child is *still* anxious about being left home alone after dark?"

Zoe's hands were in fists; she shoved them into the pockets of her leather jacket. "I admit I made mistakes. But let's cut to the chase here, Cat. Is Willow's life with you really so perfect?" She looked pointedly around the room. "Do I see a husband here? A happy marriage? No. I see my daughter having to leave a school she loved and having to bounce between two households. I see a girl who's lost and practically a latchkey kid, because you work such long hours. You don't even know what she's doing after school."

"And you do?" Catherine demanded.

"I do now," Zoe said. "Who do you think has been making sure she's safe walking home from school after dark? She was attacked the other day.

Some guy jumped her and tried to steal her backpack. He might have done worse, except I was there. *Me.* Not you."

Catherine's throat was almost too tight for her to respond. Willow, attacked? "I don't believe you."

Zoe shrugged. "Ask her. Anyway, I'm not blaming you for that. It could have happened to any girl walking around at night in a city. But what I'm saying is that I was *there.* I protected her, not you. Willow needs me, Cat."

"Over my dead body," Catherine said furiously. "You will not take her from me."

Zoe had the gall to look amused. "Look, I didn't come here to interfere. I just wanted to get to know Willow, to make sure she's doing okay. I gave her to you because I thought you'd be a good mother and I was in trouble. But things are different now. That's all I'm saying. Anyway, it's not like you get to choose. She's *my* daughter."

"And I'm her legal guardian!" Catherine said through clenched teeth. Now her hands were in fists, too. She wanted to knock her sister off her stupid high-heeled boots, send her and her cool leather jacket back out to the street. "If you want money, fine. I'll give it to you. But that's it. Willow is staying with me. She's my daughter now."

"Relax," Zoe said, watching Catherine warily. "I didn't come here to fight."

Catherine had no intention of relaxing. But then she became aware of a movement behind her. She turned around and saw Willow standing there in her blue bathrobe. How much had she heard?

"Sorry, honey," Catherine said shakily. "You shouldn't have had to hear that. Everything is fine. Did you brush your teeth?"

"It's okay," Willow said. "You don't have to hide stuff. And, yeah, I brushed my teeth. But you really don't have to ask that question anymore, either. *God.*"

She sounded so normal, so wonderfully adolescent, that Catherine wanted to kiss her. But she didn't want to kiss her in front of Zoe.

"You should probably go now," Catherine told her sister. "It's getting late."

To her surprise, Zoe nodded and walked across the room, stopping to briefly rest her hand on Willow's shoulder before opening the front door and letting another blast of cold night air into the house. "We'll talk later," she said.

"When?" Willow said, turning to watch Zoe with her face alight, hopeful.

"Soon," Zoe said, and closed the door behind her.

Willow turned back to Catherine after Zoe had gone, looking panicked. "What's going to happen? Will she come back?"

"I think so. Right now, though, all that's going to happen is that you and I are going to bed," Catherine said. "It's been a long, long day."

"What about Nana?" Willow asked, giving Eve an anxious look.

"I'll come back down and check on her every couple of hours. Don't worry."

She followed Willow up the stairs with an effort, feeling like someone had attached lead weights to her ankles. She noticed that Willow's bathrobe, bought for the new school year a couple of months ago, was too short for her now.

Things were going to change whether she wanted them to or not. In fact, they already had. But she'd meant what she said to Zoe: she would fight for Willow, and she would win.

CHAPTER FOURTEEN

Two days after seeing Zoe at Catherine's, Eve crossed the Route 1 bridge from Newburyport over the Merrimack River in search of her. Most of the boats had been pulled out of the water for the winter. Instead of the usual forest of masts, the river was a shimmering bolt of indigo silk unrolling toward the ocean, which lay just beyond the mouth of the river.

Zoe lived on the other side of the river, in Salisbury, and that's where Eve was going, even though Zoe hadn't given her the address and had no idea that her mother was coming. Too bad. Zoe couldn't expect to be the only one with surprises up her sleeve. And Eve didn't have a way to call her daughter anyway.

Bear was in his customary pose, seated on his massive haunches in the passenger seat and panting with pleasure, turning his head to grin at Eve from time to time. He was tall enough that his head nearly hit the ceiling.

She probably shouldn't have brought him. But she'd grown so accustomed to having Bear's company that she couldn't stand the thought of leaving him home. It would be difficult to give him back. Bear was her link to those last carefree hours with Darcy. Oh, Darcy had called twice already, but she didn't want to see him again. Eve knew that her feelings for him were misplaced. It was the island, or maybe all of the Canadian

Maritimes, that Darcy and his dog represented to her. It wasn't *real*, what she felt.

And even if it were, what was the point of entering into another relationship at her age? In a few years, God, she'd be seventy. Not many good years left. She enjoyed her conversations with Darcy. She enjoyed *him*. But who were they fooling, talking on the phone like teenagers? Where could all of that lead?

To intimacy. Maybe even love. But then? More grief down the road. No, she couldn't take that. Better to live on her own.

She'd explained all of this to Darcy on the phone, in very plain language, but he'd only laughed. "Well, even if we have only a few good minutes left, wouldn't they be better if we spent them together?"

She didn't agree. Couldn't. Her heart had been broken too many times. Besides, she was too focused now on Zoe, on finding her and keeping her close, if possible, to think much about Darcy.

Eve cracked the window open, letting in a rush of salty air and causing Bear to swivel his giant head her way and threaten to scramble onto her lap until she opened his window, too. She thought again about Zoe, wondering why her daughter had come back now.

Unfortunately, Catherine was right about one thing: in the past, Zoe had typically put herself first. Eve hoped Zoe wasn't here to extort money from them. Or to threaten Catherine in any way about taking Willow back.

Eve could kick herself for fainting and then conking out on Catherine's couch before having a proper conversation with Zoe. What had happened between the two girls while she was asleep? And why hadn't Zoe tried to get in touch with them since then? She felt sick, thinking that Zoe might disappear again.

She remembered waking on Catherine's couch. Zoe was gone. She had immediately panicked. What if she had only dreamed about Zoe's return, as she had so many times before?

Eve had cried out Zoe's name, but it was Catherine who appeared, rising out of the armchair across the living room. Apparently she'd gone upstairs to tuck Willow into bed, then had come back down to the living room to sleep in the chair, determined to keep an eye on her after the fall.

"Silly girl," Eve had said, smiling.

She had felt hugely comforted when Catherine had shushed her the way a mother quiets a small child and told her it wasn't a dream. "Zoe's really back and she's okay, Mom," Catherine said. "I'm sure you'll see her again soon. Sleep, now."

The next time she woke, it was still dark, but Catherine was making coffee and Willow was eating breakfast before going to school. Catherine had looked fragile, her skin almost translucent in the sunny kitchen, her hair pulled back severely from her forehead with a red hair band that didn't suit her. She was clenching her jaw.

As they drank coffee in the kitchen, Catherine filled Eve in on what Zoe had said about her itinerant life in Florida.

"And that's it?" Eve had asked desperately. "Zoe didn't tell you how long she's staying here? Or where she's living?"

Catherine shook her head. "I'm sorry, Mom. I really don't know anything else. You know Zoe."

That was the problem, Eve thought. None of them knew Zoe.

Fortunately, Zoe had given Willow her address, and Willow had shared it with Eve before leaving for school—but only after making Eve promise not to tell Catherine.

"I don't think Zoe's ready to see her," Willow had said solemnly while Catherine was upstairs, getting ready for work. "She told me to only use her address if it was for something really important." She had flashed a sweet, unexpected smile. "I think you're something really important, Nana."

"Bless you," Eve said, pulling Willow against her in a sudden fierce hug.

She'd given Zoe an entire day and night to get in touch. When she hadn't, Eve had decided to look for her. Now she checked the GPS again, despite knowing exactly where she was. She couldn't believe Zoe was right across the Merrimack River in Salisbury, of all places.

Back when the girls were small, Eve used to bring them to Salisbury Beach on hot days after school or even at night. It wasn't the same as the deserted, singing white sand beach at Chance Harbor, but it was still better than sitting at home in the stifling September heat. Andrew claimed to be too Scottish to ever agree to air-conditioning. They'd come here and have a picnic dinner after Eve got out of work, sometimes eating pizza and fried dough on the boardwalk.

Then they'd go down to the water. Eve usually settled on the beach with a book, glad to have the sea air clear her head after whatever PR crises she'd faced at the hospital. Catherine typically hung back for a bit, then waded into the icy water with a grimace. Zoe threw herself into the waves as if into a mother's arms, shrieking with laughter.

Catherine had always been afraid of whatever might lie beneath the water—sharks, crabs, rays—while Zoe teased her sister, even swam underwater and pinched her legs, pretending to be some crazy biting beast. Which, looking back now, she was.

Eve knew she should be angry with Zoe for vanishing. For coming back so secretly. For not making it home before Andrew died. And now for deliberately not giving Eve a way to contact her. But she was still too relieved to find Zoe alive to allow herself the luxury of anger. Her daughter was home and safe. That trumped everything.

Her GPS led her to a mobile home park a few blocks before the Salisbury boardwalk. She was surprised to see, even off-season, how many cars and trucks were parked in the driveways and how permanent some of the trailers looked. Many had patios and decks, screened porches, and even stone walls and birdbaths or garden statues.

Eve couldn't imagine what had brought Zoe here, of all places. She anxiously navigated the narrow streets—well marked, another surprise—until she found Arrow Lane and turned onto it, looking for 27, the number Willow had scrawled on the paper.

This trailer was white and smaller than some of the others, but it was tidy. A picket fence enclosed a garden of perennials gone by. A stone birdbath stood next to a brick walk leading to the front steps, and the windows were adorned with ornate shutters, painted red. A motorcycle was parked in the driveway.

The sight of the motorcycle made Eve even more nervous. She knew nothing about Zoe's living situation, and women didn't usually ride Harleys that size.

When Eve knocked on the trailer door, a man answered it. He was tall and magnetic-looking, with broad shoulders and a stubborn chin. His tangled blue-black curls fell to his shoulders. His wary dark eyes were rimmed in lashes so black that at first she thought he might be wearing eyeliner, and a scar beneath one eye gleamed pale against his toffee-colored skin. He wore black jeans and a black leather jacket similar to the one Zoe had on last night. This couldn't be the same jacket, though, Eve thought in confusion, because this guy was much larger than Zoe.

So large, in fact, that he easily blocked her view of the trailer's interior. "Can I help you?" the man asked, in a way that made it seem as if he wasn't really interested in doing so.

"I'm looking for Zoe." Eve pulled her purse more tightly across her shoulder.

The man's dark eyes narrowed. He had a long, elegant nose, and this expression, along with the gleaming black hair and the almond shape of his eyes, made him look regal and foreign despite his workman's clothing. The kind of regal that heralded another time. Alexander the Great, maybe, prepared to go into battle to unite ancient Greece.

"Is she here or not?" Eve pressed as the silence lengthened and become uncomfortable.

"Depends who's asking."

"I'm Eve MacLeish. Zoe's mother." She held out a hand. "And you are?"

At her name, the man's expression had altered. He was smiling now, his eyes warm and a lighter shade of brown. Chocolate, maybe. "Nice to meet you. I'm Grey Boswell. Zoe didn't say you were coming."

"She didn't know. I wanted to surprise her."

"Sure. Come on in."

Eve hesitated. Grey had said nothing to indicate his connection to Zoe, though he must be her boyfriend, if they were camped out here on the beach together. At least he didn't look wild-eyed or sleepy or red-eyed or angry, all of which Zoe's other boyfriends had been. With the exception of Mike, her sweet high school and college boyfriend, Zoe had demonstrated universally awful taste in men.

To Grey, she said, "Thank you. But I think I'll wait outside while you tell her I'm here."

"You sure? Might be a while."

"Oh."

Grey must have read the disappointment in her face, because he added, "She's just taking a shower. I'm about to go to work. Sure you don't want to wait inside?"

The fact that this man was leaving gave Eve the courage to say that she'd come inside after all.

"Good. I'll tell her you're here," he said, and disappeared after she'd stepped through the door.

Grey went down the hall to speak to Zoe, then gathered his things—a wallet retrieved from somewhere and tucked into his jeans pocket, a backpack slung over one shoulder, a motorcycle helmet—before shaking her hand good-bye and leaving. She watched through the front window, arms crossed, for Grey to straddle the bike and roar away before finally turning around to examine her surroundings.

The trailer's living room wasn't exactly neat—there were magazines and newspapers strewn about, and a few empty mugs and plates—but it smelled clean and the rugs were in decent condition. The living room was painted pale yellow and was separated from the kitchen by a low Formica counter with a retro pattern of black-speckled white like the old composition notebooks her daughters used in elementary school.

The kitchen cupboards were white with bright red knobs, continuing the retro theme, and the living room furniture was inexpensive but serviceable—a green cloth couch and a leather recliner. It looked like a seaside condo, really, Eve thought, feeling better now about Zoe's living situation.

She sat on the couch to wait. A few minutes later, Zoe hurried into the living room, still toweling her hair, looking bewildered. "What's happened? What are you doing here, Mom?"

"Nothing. I just came to see you."

"How's your head?" Zoe draped the towel over one of the kitchen stools and finger-combed her short blond curls. She wore no makeup, but her skin was mostly unlined, her cheeks pink from the shower, her nose sprinkled with freckles. She looked younger than her age, which—and Eve was mortified to have to do a deliberate calculation here—must be thirty-four.

"My head's fine."

"I'm glad," Zoe said. "Want something to drink?"

"Water would be nice."

"How did you even find me?" Zoe asked, filling a glass from the tap and adding a couple of ice cubes from the freezer. She held the glass out to her mother, rolling her eyes. "Never mind. I can guess. Willow."

"She made me promise not to tell Catherine."

"Well, that's a relief. Want anything to eat?"

Eve shook her head. "Why is it a relief? And why didn't you give Catherine and me any way to contact you?"

Zoe snorted. "You were asleep when I left. And the last thing I need is to have Catherine bulldogging her way into my life. Jesus. She's wound tight as a top. What a scold."

Eve agreed, but didn't want to say so. Funny how quickly she reverted to her old mothering stance of trying to treat the girls fairly and evenly. They were always so quick to find fault with each other. "Things aren't easy for her since Russell left."

"Yeah, no kidding. What a dick." Zoe's head was in the refrigerator and her voice was muffled.

"I'm surprised to hear you be that judgmental," Eve said carefully. "Russell was always good to you. And he has been very good to Willow."

"He wasn't good to me! He was condescending. And how is he being good to Willow now? Remind me." Zoe came back to the living room with a bag of carrots and proceeded to eat one of them, crunching loudly. "Oh, right. He's dragging Willow through another mess. What a nightmare."

You started Willow's nightmare, Eve thought, but contained herself.

"Russell loves Willow. He's doing his best to stay connected to her. Seeing her on weekends and some weeknights."

"Hooray for him." Zoe bit into another carrot with a snap.

"Do you have to eat those now?" Eve said irritably. "While we're trying to have a conversation?"

"Sorry. No, guess not." Zoe set the bag down on the table beside her. "So, is this the part where we play twenty questions? I bet I can guess what they are."

"Probably. But let's start with that guy on the motorcycle. Is he your boyfriend?"

"He's hot, right? But, sadly, no."

Eve wondered why not, but let it go. "All right. I would like an account of what you've been doing for the past five years." Somehow, the anger she'd thought wasn't there had started working its way up from her belly and into her throat. How *dare* her daughter be so flip about everything?

"Oh my God. That is *such* a boring story," Zoe said, her eyes skittering toward the carrots. She twisted her hands in her lap.

Once an addict, always an addict, Eve thought suddenly. Zoe probably needed something in her mouth 24-7 to stay clean. She'd always been high-strung. Drugs and alcohol were her way of self-medicating.

"Go ahead and eat your carrots," Eve said. "Maybe try to chew with your mouth closed. And tell me everything. You may think your story is boring, but your mother will not. I promise."

To her relief, Zoe laughed. She took another carrot and said, "I already told Catherine pretty much everything. She must have told you."

"No. Not much."

Zoe told Eve how she'd hitchhiked to Florida and lived hand-to-mouth on the street or in shelters while she worked at whatever she could, most recently cleaning hotel rooms.

"People are pigs," Zoe added.

"And that's a surprise to you?"

Zoe bit into another carrot, slowly. "I guess not. I mean, look how I lived, right?"

"You had a drug problem." Eve took a deep breath, then added, "You're an addict, Zoe." Andrew would be proud of her, she thought, for speaking her mind.

"Yes," Zoe acknowledged. "I am."

"Are you using anything now?"

"No, Mom. I'm clean."

Eve nodded. "I'm glad. How did you quit?"

"By almost dying a few times. The last time was the worst."

Eve winced, imagining Zoe nodding off on somebody's couch, or maybe in a gas station bathroom. Being found, rushed to a hospital by strangers. Machines keeping her alive.

"I'm sorry you had to go through that."

"Yeah, well. I brought it on myself. I had to get scared straight, right? That's what everybody says. You and Dad tried your best, but you couldn't have gotten me off drugs. I had to do it." Zoe stood up and carried the carrots back to the fridge, put them away. She came back with a glass of water and sat back down on the opposite end of the couch, cross-legged and facing Eve.

"How long ago was this?" Eve asked.

"Two years ago. I met Sadie, Grey's sister, at work. She offered me an empty room in her house so I could stay off the streets. It was Grey's doing, really. He'd come down to Florida to look after his sister and thought I'd be a good influence on her, believe it or not. They're gypsies, so Sadie lived part of the year down there, part of the year here."

"Gypsies? Really? I'd call them snowbirds," Eve said.

"Nope. They're gypsies for real. Their mom is a fortune-teller here on Salisbury Beach. Madame Justine."

Eve had seen Madame Justine's signs—tarot card and palm readings for ten dollars—but had never been tempted. "If Sadie's a gypsy, then isn't Grey one, too?" She thought about the mobile home park, about all of the cars and trucks here. Of course: the gypsies in this area were itinerant workers, roofers and driveway pavers. They schooled their children sporadically and married them off to one another. Why would Zoe want to hang out with them?

Look at her, though, Eve reminded herself. Zoe was clearly healthy. And happy. The gypsy lifestyle must agree with her.

"They're only half gypsy," Zoe was explaining. "Sadie was more into the lifestyle than Grey ever was. Grey's a boatbuilder. He has a shop in Salisbury and a house, too, but his mom lives there, since Grey travels so much. Now he's fixing up another house for himself."

Eve was trying to take all of this in and failing. Oh, what did it matter, anyway, if Zoe's friends were gypsies or boatbuilders or kangaroos? The only thing that mattered was Zoe. What she was doing now and what she intended to do next.

And Willow. What about Willow? If Zoe was living like a gypsy, clearly they'd have to prevent Willow from living with her. Willow needed stability.

"Why did you decide to come back now, after all this time?"

"Timing, I guess. When Sadie died, I realized how alone I felt, and that made me think about how much Willow must have been missing me, at least at first. Grey was driving north and said he wouldn't mind some company. And I'd been thinking about things. I didn't want to come back too soon; I felt like my head was finally on straight. Though of course I wish I'd been here for you when Dad died." She covered her mouth, whispered, "I can't believe I didn't get to see him, Mommy."

Eve felt terrible, seeing her so upset. And how much worse would it be for Zoe if she knew she'd lost not just one father, but two?

Still. Eve had decided: she had to tell Zoe about Malcolm before she disappeared again.

"It's all right. Dad knew you loved him."

Zoe nodded, her face pink. It looked like she was struggling, trying not to cry. "Were there a lot of people at his service? I bet there were."

"Oh yes," Eve said, and tried to describe it for her: the people crowding into the wake, the church service in Newburyport, and the memorial service a month later at the church in Chance Harbor.

"He was well loved," she said, remembering Marta like a thorn she'd forgotten was embedded in her foot.

Marta had had the nerve to show up at the funeral in Newburyport, and even came to their house for the reception afterward, saying, "I'm so very sorry, Eve, about all this. It wasn't meant to be this way."

What had she been talking about? At the time, Eve was too numb with grief to ask, much less to throw her out of the house, which was what she should have done. What had Marta meant? That Andrew hadn't meant to *die*? Or that he hadn't meant to die on her couch instead of his wife's?

Meanly, now, Eve decided she could be glad in one way: at least she hadn't had to deal with the shock of finding Andrew, of trying to do CPR and failing to revive him, as Marta had done. (Marta had told her this at the reception.) Eve hadn't had to ride in the screaming ambulance, knowing the trip was futile.

No. By the time Eve made it to the hospital an hour after Marta's call—Marta's house was in Brookline, a suburb of Boston, forty miles south of Newburyport—Andrew was already gone. Just the rapidly cooling shell of his body on the gurney. Marta was a shadow in a black coat disappearing down a long, antiseptic-smelling hallway.

Beside her on the couch, Zoe was weeping quietly. "I feel so awful about Daddy. About all the things I did to disappoint him. God, if only I had another chance, I would take it all back. Or I would at least have made it home in time to tell him I was sorry."

You used up all the chances he gave you, Eve thought sadly, remembering Andrew storming out of the house once when he discovered that Eve had been secretly giving Zoe money after Zoe moved out of the house with Willow. A lot of money. She had done it because she was terrified that her daughter and granddaughter would end up on the street. Andrew, on the other hand, had been determined "not to fall for any more of Zoe's damn drug addict tricks."

He could be so harsh. But he was right: Zoe had probably used that money for drugs.

"Daddy loved you, honey," Eve told Zoe, finally daring to slide over to her daughter on the couch and stroke her hair while Zoe cried on her shoulder.

Zoe's head felt as it had when she was a girl, heavy and hot. She had only ever let Eve hold her when she was sick or upset. Eve had treasured those moments, the feeling of her daughter's solid weight against her. Zoe's hair was always long. So odd to feel it cropped short now. As short as Eve's own.

Zoe had been high-strung as a child, easily upset. When she was tiny, the least thing could spark a tantrum: a wrinkled sock, peas for dinner, having to wear a jacket. High school was even worse. Then the tantrums built into tsunamis with terrible consequences. Once, they'd tried to ground her for breaking curfew in ninth grade, and Zoe had run away. They'd found her with the help of the police, living in a tenement house in Revere with a man ten years older than she was. The man had overdosed before they could charge him with anything.

The truth was that Zoe had never really fit into their family. Zoe had said that herself one Christmas. Screamed it, really, at the dinner table. Zoe was a junior in high school, while Catherine had come home from college, filled with excitement about her classes, her professors, even the food and her crazy roommate.

At dinner, Andrew had praised Catherine. "You've taken an important step toward independence," he'd told her. "I'm proud of you."

That's when Zoe, already sulking because they'd told her she had to eat Christmas dinner at home with the family before going out with friends, lost it completely. Said she might as well leave the family, because they obviously didn't need her, with Catherine around.

"I don't even fit into this stupid perfect TV family!" she'd shouted. "I'm not like *any* of you!"

Then she'd stormed out in the way only Zoe could storm, making the china rattle in the cupboards. They didn't see her for two days. Of course, that was before they knew she was not only drinking and smoking weed, but doing ecstasy—molly, they called it now, MDMA—and cocaine, too, as well as whatever pills she could get. Zoe swung between euphoric highs and crippling depression, depending on what drugs she was taking. How could she and Andrew have been so stupid? To have missed their daughter's addiction for so long?

Because nobody wanted to think a beautiful, middle-class girl would become a drug addict, least of all her parents.

"Zoe," Eve said quietly, "Daddy did love you. You have to believe me."

Zoe turned to look at her without lifting her head off the couch, so that her hair snagged on the green tweed fabric. The trailer was so quiet that Eve heard the shushing sound made by Zoe's head rubbing on the couch. "Come on, Mom. You don't have to pretend. You know he didn't love me unconditionally. Not like Catherine."

"He was concerned for you. He wanted you to grow up to be good. Responsible. Every parent wants that for their children."

"Not every parent," Zoe mumbled. "I've seen the other kind."

Eve thought back to the apartments Zoe had shared, to the shelters she must have gone to when she was desperate. She probably had seen plenty of the other kind. Somehow, this didn't seem the time to tell her about Malcolm, so Eve stayed on more familiar ground. "We were upset when you drank and did drugs, when you let your grades slip. We were certainly disappointed when you got pregnant and dropped out of college."

To her shock, Zoe leaped off the couch and turned on her. "You and Dad had *no idea* the kind of shit that happened to me in college!"

For a moment, they stared at each other, Eve willing Zoe to stay in the trailer. She knew by the way her daughter's body was trembling that Zoe's instinct was to run away. "Why don't you tell me, then?" she said quietly. "I'd like to know what really happened to you in college."

Zoe sat down again, but shook her head. "I can't. You'll only tell Catherine, and she might tell Willow."

This was about Willow's father, Eve realized with a start. Oh, good Lord. What was Zoe saying? That she'd been raped? "I won't tell Catherine," she said. "I promise."

Zoe shook her head, adamant. "I don't want to talk about any of that." She turned to her then and said something unexpected. "I need to see Chance Harbor again before you sell it, okay? Promise? I was always happy there."

"Of course," Eve said. "I was planning to go up again anyway, to finish up some work I started." Maybe that would be the right time to tell her about Malcolm.

"Can I ask you something else?" Zoe said.

"Why not?" Eve said, steeling herself.

"Could we bring Willow to Chance Harbor with us?"

"I don't know." Eve frowned, considering. "Catherine probably wouldn't want her to miss school," she said, silently adding, *And she certainly doesn't want Willow spending time alone with you.*

"Willow's miserable at school," Zoe said with an impatient toss of her head. "Catherine doesn't know anything about my daughter's life."

Eve stared at her. *My daughter*, Zoe had said. Oh, dear. If Zoe wanted custody of Willow and Catherine fought her on that, what would happen?

Maybe, now that Willow was fifteen, she'd be allowed to choose. Who would she want to live with, if it was left up to her? Eve knew how much Willow hated having to spend time with Russell and Nola. Would those visits continue? Russell was her legal guardian, but could that be overturned?

She was jumping to conclusions, Eve reminded herself. Maybe Zoe wouldn't even want the responsibility of raising her daughter.

"I certainly do think you should spend some time with Willow," she said. "Still, we ought to discuss the logistics with Catherine, since she knows Willow's school and social schedule." She hesitated, then asked, "Are you working?"

Zoe nodded. "Grey helped me find a job with a friend of his who owns a car dealership. It's an Internet dealership; I drive the cars to the buyers. It's fun. Yesterday I took a Range Rover to Maine. This afternoon I get to drive a Mini Cooper down to the Cape! I work my own hours and get paid off the books," Zoe added. "Twelve bucks an hour."

She said this with pride. Zoe probably loved the fact that she was off the radar and free of ordinary burdens, like paying taxes, Eve thought. "And how long will you be staying here?"

Zoe shrugged. "I don't know. I just came to see Willow, you know?" she said in a rush. "I never meant to even *talk* to her. But she seemed so unhappy. So lonely. I couldn't help it."

"What do you want now, then?"

"To know Willow," Zoe said quietly. "And to let her know that her real mom loves her. Catherine is good to her, but she can't be that, right? Her real mom?"

"No, honey. Only you can be that." Eve reached out to put a tentative hand on Zoe's knee. Zoe smiled at her.

They were silent then, the two of them sitting close together, Eve's hand resting lightly on Zoe's leg. She slowly became aware of the faint ticking of a clock in another room and of the fact that her daughter was finally sitting still, as if she were a wild animal and Eve had, with great patience and skill, managed to quiet her so she wouldn't run.

CHAPTER FIFTEEN

Catherine had made Willow promise to go to Russell's on Thursday and then come straight home after dinner. She couldn't go anywhere else. Like she was ten years old!

"I don't care if you don't like it," Catherine had said when Willow tried arguing.

"I don't see what gives you the right to manage my schedule," Willow had said. "My usual day with Russell is Wednesday. It's not my fault if he was busy yesterday!"

"I have every right to manage your schedule because you've betrayed my trust too many times now," Catherine reminded her. "You were meeting Zoe after school all those times and didn't tell me where you were. You walked across the Common after dark when I expressly told you not to, many times, and you were almost mugged! How can I believe anything you say? No. You'll have to earn my trust before I grant you that kind of freedom again. I need to know where you are at all times, even when I'm working. *Especially* when I'm working. So today you're going to Russell's. End of discussion!"

Willow couldn't believe it. She'd never fought with Catherine. Now, ever since Russell had left and her real mom was back, Catherine was morphing into some kind of stupid drill sergeant you couldn't please no matter what. She'd even started harassing Willow about making her bed. She'd never made her bed! Not unless company was coming for a holiday or something. What was the point of making your bed in the morning anyway, if you were going to be out all day and then just drop back into it at night?

So after school Willow didn't think twice about texting her dad to say her mom had made a doctor's appointment, sorry, and she couldn't make it to dinner with him and Nola after all. Nobody was going to boss her around anymore.

Briefly, Willow thought about how scared Nola had looked when the ambulance came and everybody was shouting on the lawn. She was glad Nola hadn't lost the baby. Nola seemed to really want a child. At least *some* babies ought to be lucky enough to have moms who actually wanted them. Unlike her. Yeah, Zoe was back, but did she want Willow with her?

If so, Willow needed to check out her house first. She wasn't going to move into any dumpy apartment like they had before, where sometimes the lights didn't even work and there was nothing in the fridge.

Willow took the subway to South Station, where she got a bus that took her as far as Newburyport. From there, she wasn't sure how to get to Salisbury.

Then a solution pulled up right in front of her: a yellow school bus from some prep school in Maine, delivering kids with sports bags and musical instruments to their moms. The moms were waiting in practically matching SUVs, all with ski racks. She watched until she saw an older kid walking to his own car, a scraggly looking guy with more zits than skin, and followed him. It was easy to talk him into giving her a ride to Salisbury. Clearly, he didn't have a lot of girls talk to him. He was super jumpy and wouldn't look her in the eye.

Willow kept a tight grip on a pen in her pocket in case he did something funny and she had to stab him in the throat. The boy seemed as scared of her as she was of him, though, so gradually Willow relaxed and they talked about movies and video games.

The boy dropped her off at Salisbury Beach, where she said she was meeting a friend. When the kid looked like he didn't believe her, Willow waved and turned around, acting like she was going into one of the big arcades.

After a few minutes, she came back out and consulted the GPS on her phone. Her mother's house was only a few blocks away. An easy walk, though it was getting dark fast and she had to pull the collar of her coat up against her neck to keep out the oceany dampness.

Salisbury Beach was full of skaters and drug dealers and drunks. Everybody knew that. But there were new restaurants and condos, too. Willow hoped her mom lived in one of those nice places as she walked fast along the sidewalk, feeling the cold wind suck the heat right out from under her jacket. Why hadn't she brought a hat?

Catherine was always trying to make her wear one against her will, that's why.

All she wanted to do was check out where her mother lived. Zoe still had secrets, no matter what she'd said to Willow about being clean and all that crap. Her mother was the world's best liar. For a minute Willow flinched, wondering if she'd turn out like that. She was lying to Catherine and Russell right now. Was this how it started?

No, she was on a mission. This was for a good cause. Willow had to know how her mom lived. To picture herself there. Maybe her mother was shacked up with some guy and had three other kids. Wouldn't that be a fun surprise.

Willow kept her head down against the wind and finally turned onto a street of houses that kept getting smaller and smaller. Capes, then ranch houses, and finally a mobile home park. She glanced at her phone again. Oh, great. Mom lived in a trailer. That made Willow official trailer trash. Nice.

She found the right street, then the right number. A huge motorcycle was parked out front, as hulking and black as a buffalo.

Willow stood for a few minutes, staring at the white trailer and wondering what she'd find inside. Her mother zoned out on a couch? Her legs up around some guy's bony ass? Two screaming babies in a playpen?

She couldn't move. It felt like her feet were encased in cement. Now she wished she'd told somebody where she was going. Henry, maybe.

God. She should turn around. Leave right now. This was a total mistake. Why find out anything about people, if they only disappointed you in the end?

Then the door to the trailer opened and a man came out. He was the kind of guy you had to run from in the movies. He looked like he should be wearing a patch over one eye. "Hey, kid!" he said. "What are you doing out there?"

Willow glanced at the address on her phone. Had she put it in wrong? Maybe that was it. Her mother probably *did* live in a nicer place. One of the condos by the beach. She'd made a mistake.

She began to walk away. "Sorry," she said. "I was just looking for somebody."

"Who?" the guy called. "Who do you want?"

My mother, Willow thought miserably. *I want a real mother. Somebody who cooks and cleans the house and asks how my day was at school. Somebody like Catherine, only more permanent and less bitchy.*

"I asked you a question!" the guy yelled. He had a deep, scary voice. "Maybe I can help you."

"I doubt it," she said, and broke into a run, her backpack bumping against her like somebody hitting her spine with a fist.

In a minute she heard a revving sound, which made her heart race with it. She ran faster. It was no use, though. In seconds the guy was next to her on his motorcycle, somehow keeping it upright on two wheels even though they were going, like, one mile an hour.

"Who are you looking for?" he yelled over the engine.

Willow could feel sweat prickle her armpits as she kept running. She tried to calm herself down, rationalizing that it would be virtually impossible to mug somebody from a motorcycle, wouldn't it? It wasn't like people couldn't hear you screaming. She glanced nervously around the trailer park to reassure herself that there were lights on in some of the other windows.

"Just tell me!" the guy said.

"My mom," she finally answered, watching him out of the corner of one eye and sticking to the sidewalk. He'd have to jump the curb on his bike to get to her. "I'm looking for my mother."

"You mean Zoe?"

Willow stopped dead on the sidewalk. "You know her?"

The guy pulled to the curb and cut the engine, letting the bike idle. "We live together."

So that was it, then: her mother was trailer trash and had a druggie boyfriend on a Harley. What else could go wrong? Willow thought miserably. "Do you have kids, too?"

He laughed at this, tipping his head back. Who the hell was this guy? His hair was to his shoulders and tied in a ponytail. And shouldn't he be wearing a helmet?

"No kids," he said. "It's not like that with us. Your mom and I are friends, that's all."

"Oh," Willow said, almost sick with relief. "How did you know I was looking for Zoe?"

"Because she told me she had a daughter your age, and you look like her. You're Willow, right?"

Willow nodded. "Who are you?"

"My name is Grey. Your grandmother stopped by this morning," he added. "But you missed your mom. She had to go to work."

"Nana was here?" Crap, Willow thought. Why hadn't Nana told her she was going to look for Zoe? Willow could have come with her.

"Yeah. Your grandmother seems like a nice lady."

"She is," Willow said. "Where does my mom work?"

"At a car place just up the road. But she's driving a car down to the Cape right now," Grey said. "She won't be back until late."

"Oh." That sounded like a cool job. Better than dealing drugs, anyway. But this guy sure looked like a dealer. Willow had seen a lot of long-haired guys in leather jackets come and go in her mom's life.

"So, you want a ride home?" Grey asked.

Willow shook her head. "I took the bus here."

"There aren't any buses from Salisbury to Boston."

"I know. I got a ride from Newburyport." She was eyeing the bike. Maybe she could just let him give her a ride to Newburyport. Catherine would have a fit. This was a total stranger. On the other hand, he lived with Zoe and had met Nana.

"I could take you to Newburyport if you want," he said. "But I really don't mind going to Boston. It's a nice night."

Willow shivered. "It is not. It's cold."

"It's a nice night on a bike if you're wearing leather," Grey amended. "Come on. I'll get you outfitted. Then we'll head south. I'd like to meet Catherine."

That's what did it: He knew Catherine's name. Grey was practically part of the family, Willow told herself, as she straddled the bike and put her arms around his waist.

Seth was out of town at a conference when Zoe showed up. Catherine had waited to call him until Thursday night, squeezing in the call on her cell phone between patients at the clinic. "I need to see you tonight," she said.

She could hear the grin in Seth's voice. "I like the sound of that," he said. "What did you have in mind?"

Nothing, other than talking to him about Zoe's reappearance and the possibility that she might fight for custody. Catherine needed Seth's legal advice as much as his friendship.

She decided to come clean and told him this, knowing he was hoping for something else. He'd made his interest in her clear enough. But to his credit, Seth listened, then said he'd come to dinner.

"Takeout, my treat," Catherine said in relief. "Chinese or Indian? Bring Brady, too, if you like."

Seth assured her that Brady could go to his mother's and said he'd bring the food, not to worry. She felt better by the time they hung up and managed to get through the day. With luck, she and Seth would be able to talk before Willow got back from Russell's.

Catherine paced the living room nervously after work, a glass of wine in one hand as she waited. Seth arrived promptly at six, carrying two grocery bags stuffed with food. "What's all this?" Catherine said as she opened the door.

"Dinner. I thought it might be nice to cook for a change."

Dear Lord. That was the last thing Catherine wanted to do. But she obediently followed Seth's instructions, chopping vegetables and fishing out her biggest pan. He was making a chicken mango curry with rice; he'd even found fresh mangoes at the little market near his house.

Catherine's spirits lifted as they sat down to eat. Of course, that might have been the second glass of wine, but why couldn't she fall in love with Seth? He was nice, better-than-average-looking, a good father from all she'd seen. Employed. And he could cook! She took a bite and chewed, savoring the mix of spices.

"So tell me about Brady," she said.

Seth said Brady was doing fine. "The new inhaler really lets him run around," he said. "It's such a relief for him. For me, too."

"I'm so glad," Catherine said warmly. Stories like that reminded her of why she'd become a pediatric nurse practitioner in the first place.

"So let's talk about you," Seth said, clearing the table.

Catherine watched him move comfortably around the kitchen. He really was adorable. Why had that nutty wife of his dumped him? What on earth had she been thinking?

She hoped people were saying the same thing about her whenever they saw Russell: What on earth was he thinking?

And then Catherine was weeping. Seth was at her side in an instant, an arm around her shoulders, urging her into the living room and onto the couch, ordering her to prop her feet up and tell him what was going on.

She told him then about Zoe showing up, about Russell coming at the same time and Nola's miscarriage scare. That led to telling him about her own miscarriages and about how hard it had been lately at work. "So many babies with thoughtless mothers," she said. "And then. And then! My own sister shows up and wants Willow back!"

"Did Zoe actually say that?"

Catherine put a hand to her mouth. "I don't know with Zoe whether she's telling the truth or lying, no matter what she says, so it wouldn't really matter."

"She isn't doing drugs anymore?"

"No. At least, I don't think so. But, again, this could be an illusion."

"Or her being on her best behavior."

"Right." Catherine bit her lip, thinking. "I love Zoe. I do. I'm glad she's in one piece. I did really think she was dead! For years I thought that!"

Seth nodded, his brown eyes serious. "I know you did. And that must have been awful. But let's deal with the here and now. Your fear is that Zoe will want Willow to live with her now, correct?"

Catherine nodded, thinking, *If that happens, what will I have left?*

"And you're Willow's legal guardian."

Catherine nodded, mute with despair. What right did she have, really? If Willow wanted to go with her mother—and why wouldn't she prefer the excitement of Zoe's life—how could Catherine stop her?

More than Eve, and certainly more than Catherine, Willow had been mourning the loss of her mother. This was her chance to have her back. How could Catherine deny Willow that?

"I want you to tell me the worst-case scenario," she said. "What happens if my sister wants to get rid of me as Willow's guardian?"

"First, Zoe would need to go to court and file a motion to vacate guardianship," Seth said. "If you contested that—which I'm assuming you would—Zoe would have to argue in front of a judge that it's in Willow's best interest to live with her. That would mean showing she has an income and decent housing, for starters."

Seth explained that the court would appoint a neutral GAL—a guardian ad litem—in the meantime for Willow, so she'd have an independent advocate speaking on her behalf and helping her make decisions. "She's fifteen, so of course her opinion would be considered as well," he said. "The GAL would then file a written report with the judge, suggesting a resolution."

"That all sounds so complicated. And hard on Willow, if she felt she had to choose between us," Catherine said miserably.

"I'd be happy to advise you through the process. Free of charge."

"I couldn't ask you to do that," Catherine said. "Besides, wouldn't it be a conflict of interest?"

Seth shrugged. "Why? You and I know each other, but we don't have a relationship. Not really. Unless?"

He looked so hopeful that Catherine had to smile. "No, you're right," she said. "We don't. And I don't think we will. I wish I felt that way about you, Seth. I really do. You're a wonderful man. But I don't. I'm so sorry."

"It's all right. Maybe you'll change your mind if you hang around me long enough." Seth smiled, too. "In the meantime, let me know how I can help you through this, if it comes down to a legal dispute."

"Thank you," Catherine said, and leaned over to kiss his cheek, which smelled of spices and lemon. "You're very dear."

He rolled his eyes. "Now you sound like my mother."

The doorbell rang, startling them into separating. Another of those MassPIRG kids soliciting, probably. Catherine went to the door and opened it without looking through the peephole, confident with Seth in the room behind her.

It was Russell. Early as usual—they must eat dinner at four o'clock—and he looked angry. His car was parked in the driveway; it was too dark for her to see Willow in the car. "Hello," she said, not opening the door all the way. The last thing she needed was for Russell to see Seth.

Then again, why not? Why shouldn't Russell think she was dating? Catherine let the door swing open, revealing Seth, who was standing behind her now. Checking to see that things were all right.

"Where's Willow?" She peered around him.

At this Russell looked startled. "I was about to ask you that. Willow texted me to say you'd made an appointment for her after school, despite our arrangement for today."

"What?" Catherine's heart started to race. "Oh my God."

Now Russell was alarmed. "She's not here? Where is she, then?"

"I don't know!" Catherine said miserably. "I thought you were getting her after school. I told her to come straight here after dinner with you, because she's grounded. I called you, remember?"

"Yeah, but that was earlier. Then Willow texted me to say the plan had changed. Wait. Why is she grounded?"

"Because she was seeing Zoe behind my back. Sneaking around. What did she text you, exactly?"

"Only that she had a doctor's appointment and couldn't come over."

Catherine shook her head. "I can't believe this. It's like the minute Zoe shows up, Willow starts acting like her. She's never been devious before."

Inwardly, she was kicking herself: it was her own fault that Willow had disappeared. She should have embraced Zoe's return, even invited her to stay at the house with them. Willow was probably with Zoe right now, God knew where. And doing God knew what.

Russell's tone was glum. "Well, I guess we need a better system."

"What do you mean?"

"You know. From now on we'll need to cross-check with each other to make sure Willow's where she's supposed to be. Every day."

Catherine shot him a grateful look. "That's a good plan."

Russell was looking over her shoulder. "You have company." His tone wasn't accusatory, but nearly.

Seth held out his hand. "Nice to meet you, Russell. I'm Seth Cunningham."

As the men shook hands, Catherine actually felt sorry for Russell. He looked so wistful and lost, standing there on the steps of his own house, where he was no longer welcome. It must be demoralizing, to be out of a job and not having anyone to come home to but a pregnant teenager who couldn't possibly understand what a midlife crisis looked like.

But she didn't have time to consider Russell's plight. Catherine pulled her cell phone out of her pocket and called Willow. No answer. Next she texted Willow and waited, while the men made uneasy conversation about Cambridge real estate.

"Anything?" Russell asked her anxiously.

Catherine shook her head. "I wish I had a number for Zoe. I don't even know if she has a phone."

"I'm really sorry," Russell said miserably.

"This isn't your fault," Catherine said, thinking, *For once.*

Just then a motorcycle rocketed down the street, did a sharp turn, and pulled into the driveway beside Catherine's car. There were two riders on it. One looked like a woman.

Zoe? Catherine felt her mouth go dry. If Zoe was here, where was Willow?

The passenger dismounted the bike, took off the helmet, and shook out her hair. It wasn't Zoe: it was Willow. Willow, riding a motorcycle! What next? And who the hell was *that*? Catherine narrowed her eyes at the man, but he had his visor down against the cold and she couldn't tell anything about his appearance.

She hurried down the steps, calling Willow's name. Russell and Seth were on her heels. "Where the hell have you been? And what are you doing on a *motorcycle*?" she yelled at Willow.

Willow looked at her as if she had two heads. "I was getting a ride home. *Jesus.*"

Later, Catherine would ask herself what the tipping point was: Willow looking so much like Zoe? Or was it the way Willow had talked to Catherine as if she weren't a good enough parent for her?

Whatever it was, Catherine's temper erupted and she had to shove her hands into her pockets to keep from slapping Willow's fresh mouth. "Go to your room!" she shouted, stepping close enough to put her face almost nose to nose with Willow's. "You lied to me, Willow, and you lied to your father. You *scared* us. What is *wrong* with you?"

Catherine stomped over to the motorcyclist. "And *you*! Who the hell are you? And what gives you the nerve to give a fifteen-year-old girl a ride on the back of your motorcycle?"

Slowly, the man unclasped the helmet and slipped it off his head. He hung it from the handlebars and nodded at Catherine and the two men behind her, standing guard. Though neither, she noticed, stepped in front of her and took over.

The motorcyclist wasn't smiling, but Catherine got the impression that he was amused by the scene. By her, maybe. He definitely did not belong in Cambridge. He was enough to give any composting Prius owner a solid fright, with his leather jacket and black jeans, that Harley, and those glittering dark eyes. His long hair was black and tied in a ponytail.

"You must be Catherine. I'm a friend of your sister's," he said. "Grey Boswell." He held his hand out for her to shake. When Catherine didn't take it, he nodded again and said, "Willow showed up at our house to see Zoe. She apparently took the bus up to Newburyport, then hitchhiked. I didn't want her to hitchhike home, so I gave her a ride."

"We appreciate that," Russell interjected before Catherine could say anything.

Catherine glared at him, but nodded at Grey. Even riding on a Harley was probably safer than hitchhiking these days. "Where's Zoe?"

"Work."

"She works?" Catherine couldn't keep the astonishment out of her voice.

Behind her, Seth cleared his throat. "Hey, sorry to do this, Catherine, but I have to go pick up Brady. I'll check in with you tomorrow, okay?"

She smiled at him. "Thanks," she said, aware that Russell was watching closely as Seth kissed her on the cheek before leaving.

Grey was watching, too. He cocked an eyebrow. "I suppose I'd better get going, too, unless you want to introduce me."

Catherine folded her arms, feeling the cold wind cut through her thin blouse. November was the wrong month to stand outside without a coat. "This is Russell. Willow's legal guardian and my ex-husband."

"Not yet," Russell interjected, but he shook hands with Grey. "We're separated." He turned around to walk back toward the house. "I'm going to have a word with Willow."

"Wait," Catherine said. "I think we should let her cool down. You and I are both too upset to talk with her now."

Russell hesitated, then nodded. "I guess you're right. You and I can talk tomorrow, come up with a plan for consequences. I should just go. Early day tomorrow. I'm substituting up at the school in New Hampshire. Trial run. Wish me luck."

"Luck," Catherine said softly, and meant it.

Russell kissed her cheek, too, and then drove off. She and Grey stood in silence, Grey still straddling the bike, as Russell started up Nola's BMW and drove off.

"So," Grey said. "This all looks very complicated. If that's your ex, who's the other guy kissing you?"

Catherine rolled her eyes. "A friend. You're saying *my* life's complicated, and you live with Zoe?"

"Right," he said, and began to put on his helmet.

"Wait," Catherine said. Maybe this guy knew what Zoe was doing back in Massachusetts. What her sister's life looked like for real. He must have some clue about what was really going on. "Do you want to come inside for a few minutes? You've got a long ride back. I could give you some coffee first."

"Sure. Sounds good." Grey dismounted the bike in one fluid motion and followed her into the house.

As they entered the hallway, Catherine remembered: Zoe had told her all about Grey, the gypsy. He was the brother of one of Zoe's drug-addled pals in sunny Florida. And, apparently, Zoe's live-in boyfriend.

She offered Grey his choice of coffee, tea, or wine. Grey chose tea, to her surprise. She put the kettle on and leaned against the counter while he sat down at the kitchen table, his eyes roving around the room. "Nice woodwork," he said. "Solid maple."

She nodded, feeling unexpectedly nervous. Grey was so tall and well built that it was hard to know where to look. She wanted to look only at him. "That's why we bought the house. I loved it because it reminded me of our family's summer place on Prince Edward Island. Same general era. Zoe's told you all about our family's place at Chance Harbor, I imagine."

He shook his head. "Zoe doesn't talk much."

This puzzled her. All their lives, Catherine had been the shy, serious one. They used to tease Zoe for being a motormouth. "That girl could carry on a conversation with a deaf-mute for six hours," their father had said.

Grey didn't seem to talk much, either. He sat in silence, still surveying the room with those alert dark eyes, while she made the tea and brought it over in two mugs with a plate of teddy-bear-shaped cookies. She was embarrassed to have them on hand, but they were Willow's favorite. She watched, fascinated, as Grey picked up a tiny bear between his long fingers and popped it into his mouth.

"So, you and Zoe live in Salisbury Beach, you said?"

Grey nodded. "I've got a trailer there," he said. "I'm a boatbuilder. My shop's down the street. We're just friends," he added hastily. "Roommates."

"Oh." She digested this. She could not picture this guy living in a trailer. It was easier to picture him in a castle. "What sorts of boats do you build?"

"Classic wooden skiffs and dories, mostly."

"Was that what you were doing in Florida? Building boats?"

He looked at her, his cup halfway to his mouth. "No," he said.

"Sorry," she backtracked. "It's none of my business what you were doing."

"That's right," he agreed easily.

Now Catherine was irritated. "I only asked what you were doing because you met my sister in Florida. I'm curious about her life there. We haven't exactly been in close contact over the past few years, and I've been raising her daughter. If Zoe's going to be in Willow's life, it would be nice to have more information."

Grey nodded. "I'm sure." He popped another cookie into his mouth.

"You're not very helpful."

"What do you want me to say?" His tone was mild. "I don't talk about other people. Whatever Zoe wants to share with you about her past should be her choice. As for her future plans, ditto. I don't know what they are, anyway. I doubt if Zoe knows what she's planning to do, either. She's a seat-of-the-pants kind of person."

"Oh, yes."

Grey brushed the crumbs off the table and onto his plate. "But you, you're different. Zoe says you live by schedules. You uphold your responsibilities."

"You make that sound like a bad thing." Catherine's skin was prickling all over, as if she'd slipped on a wool sweater. Why did being called responsible make her feel defensive?

"See, I don't judge," Grey said. "I don't say that's bad or good, what anybody does. I mean, unless they're obviously out to hurt another person, right? Otherwise, I try to cut people some slack. Assume their intentions are good until proven otherwise."

"Are you saying I should do that with my sister?"

Grey put his hands up and smiled. He had a magnificent smile. A movie star's generous mouth and white teeth. "I'm not telling you what to do. But it sounds to me like you're brewing up trouble where there isn't any. You and Zoe probably both want what's best for Willow. Start there, and see what happens."

Catherine scowled at him. To her surprise, Grey laughed, and she couldn't help smiling. "All right. I'll try," she said. "If Zoe will see me again, that is."

"Oh, she will," Grey said. "I'll make sure of that. Besides, she's got a good job now. She'll probably stick around awhile." He stood up. "I'd better get going and let you talk to Willow. Don't be too hard on her," he suggested as he zipped his jacket. "She wasn't being bad. Just curious. She's trying to find out more about her mom and dad. About herself, too."

"Join the club," Catherine muttered, following Grey to the door. "Zoe hasn't ever said a thing about Willow's dad. Not in fifteen years."

Grey gave Catherine an intent look. "She has her reasons," he said. "Trust me on that."

Catherine found that she did. She also discovered that she couldn't look at this man too long without feeling a burn of attraction that started low in her belly and rose to her face. She turned away and said, "Thank you for bringing Willow home. More than anything else, I'm trying to keep her safe."

"You're doing a good job of it," he said.

She stood in the doorway watching him ride off, feeling more curious and confused about her sister than ever. For a brief moment she imagined following Grey, certain that he must know the answers to so many questions about her sister's life. Then she closed the door and went upstairs. Willow needed her. Her questions would have to wait.

CHAPTER SIXTEEN

On Friday morning, Eve drove over to Amesbury and hiked around Woodsom Farm with Bear to clear her head. They walked down to the Powwow River, where the dog plunged into the water and paddled with such a joyful look on his face that Eve had to laugh.

Afterward, she toweled him off and he napped in the car while she went grocery shopping. It was late afternoon and starting to get dark by the time she got home, but she recognized the truck parked in her driveway. Even if she hadn't, the island's red dirt nearly covered the bottom half of it, a definite clue. Eve climbed out of the car in a hurry and opened the passenger door to let Bear jump out of her Subaru.

Darcy was resting his head against the seat and looked like he might be asleep. Eve rapped on the door, startling him awake. He grinned at her in a way that made her skin buzz and opened the door.

"Thought you'd never show," he said and rubbed Bear's head. "Well? You a Massachusetts dog yet? Or are you going to come back with me to Vermont?"

At the idea of Darcy taking Bear, Eve's spirits fell. But of course he'd have to, since Bear wasn't even his to keep, but his son's. "I'll miss him," she said.

He studied her. "You mean that? Because I have a solution."

"What?"

"My son says he wants to stay in Los Angeles after his MBA. You know, because they have so much spare water and so little traffic."

She laughed. "And?"

"And he thinks Bear might not like the heat. I travel all the time, so I was wondering if you might want to have custody of this dog, and I'll have visiting rights."

She hugged him. "You made my day," she said.

"Shoot. I thought I did that when I showed up."

"You're the second best thing that's happened today." Eve looped her arm through his as they walked up to the house. "Did you drive straight through?"

"Yep. And I have to get back to Vermont for a meeting on Monday."

"You must be exhausted." She hesitated, then added, "You're welcome to stay here if you don't want to drive straight back to Vermont tonight."

"Music to my ears. Which reminds me!" He opened the car door again. "I brought you something."

She laughed when he pressed a fiddle case into her hands. "But I don't know how to play!"

"You have great natural musicality," he pronounced, and winked. "And an even better teacher."

Inside, she poured them each a glass of cabernet and laid out a platter of cheese, bread, and slices of salami. It was chilly enough to light a fire; they caught up about Darcy's work before Eve filled him in on Zoe. Once again, she was struck by how intently he listened, never interrupting or offering to fix things. In her experience, most men were better problem solvers than listeners, so this was a relief.

Bear was snoring in front of the fire by now, having enjoyed his own small plate of salami and cheese rinds. "He looks right at home," Darcy said. "Thanks again for looking after him. I don't know what I would have done if you hadn't taken him off my hands. Work really exploded. I'm going to have to go back up to the island again before Christmas."

"Me, too," Eve said happily, envisioning more walks on the beach with Darcy. She wouldn't have a relationship with him; she'd decided that. But it would be wonderful to have another chance to enjoy his company before the two of them went their separate ways.

"Good to know." Darcy poured her a second glass of wine and refilled his own glass. "Your place up there has been busy."

She nodded and told him about the roofing work and plumbing being done. "I need to get up there again before winter and do some more work on the house myself," she said. "It's too difficult to pick out wallpaper and trim paint long-distance. I have to stand in the rooms to decide what I really want."

And to say good-bye one last time, she thought, but didn't want to say. Why bring down the mood?

"Sounds like you've had a tough go of things with Zoe, but I'm glad for your sake that she's all right."

"Me, too." Eve pinched the bridge of her nose, unwilling to cry. Where was all this emotion coming from? She had cried her fill when Zoe disappeared and again when Zoe returned. Zoe was here now. She seemed healthy. There was nothing to cry about.

Darcy was watching her closely. "Did you tell her about her father yet?"

"No. I've been waiting to see how stable she is."

"Makes sense."

Eve leaned against him. "I have made so many mistakes," she said.

"Mistakes by the dozen?" he suggested, a smile in his voice.

"By the thousand!"

He laughed. "You and me both, baby."

Eve made a face. "Don't laugh. I mean it!"

"So do I." Darcy turned on the couch so they could face each other. "Don't you think anyone who lives to be as old as we are has made mistakes? That's the beauty of life! We get to screw up over and over, always believing we'll do things better the next time around. Sometimes we do, and sometimes we don't. But the human heart never stops hoping. If it did, it wouldn't keep beating."

"You are a silly old fool—you know that? A hopeless romantic," she said. "Though I never really understood that phrase. Shouldn't it be 'hopeful romantic'?"

"Either sounds better than being a hopeless cynic. Or a hopeful one."

"Now you're talking nonsense."

"No," he said, "I'm talking to you, Miss Eve." He put his hands on her waist and pulled her onto his lap, then lay back against the sofa so that Eve was lying on top of him, resting her head just beneath his chin.

"You're so tall. You're built like something meant to climb," she teased.

"I was hoping you'd say that," he said, and kissed her in a way that made her forget that they were too old and wise, too foolish and broken, to be this hopeless and hopeful all at once.

Willow had expected to be grounded for the rest of her life after last night. But Catherine seemed different in the morning. Nicer. She packed Willow's lunch for her and gave her extra money for the snack bar.

"What's going on?" Willow finally asked.

Catherine turned from the counter, where she'd been loading the dishwasher while Willow ate her favorite kind of cheesy scrambled eggs with a piece of raisin toast. "What do you mean?"

"You're being so nice."

Catherine dried her hands on a towel and came over to sit at the table across from her. "I feel bad about how I blew up last night. I'm sorry."

Willow shrugged. "You were worried. I get it. But I'm not a baby anymore."

"I know. And I get that you went to Salisbury last night because you want to find out stuff about your mom. I don't blame you. I have questions for her, too."

Catherine looked pretty today, Willow thought. More relaxed. Her hair was in a bun and she wore Willow's favorite green sea glass earrings from Prince Edward Island. "So why don't you invite her here, then?"

"You're right. I should. Maybe she'd come over for dinner one night. Would you like that?"

"Yeah. I'd even help you cook." Willow frowned. "What happens if my mom decides she wants me to live with her?"

She was immediately sorry she'd asked, because Catherine's face closed down, like someone had turned out the light in her eyes. "I don't know. I'm trying to find out what Zoe wants. Why she's here."

"She came to see me," Willow said, stung. "She told me that."

"I'm sure that's true, honey. But the thing about Zoe is that she's a very impulsive person." Catherine put her hand over her mouth and shook her head. "I shouldn't say that about my sister. I don't really know who she is anymore, you know? For a long time, Zoe was a risk taker. But I don't know how much of her behavior was from the drugs she was taking."

Willow curled her feet around the rungs of the chair, feeling miserable. "Do you think she still takes drugs?"

Catherine wiped her eyes. "I hope not. She seems okay, right? But you can bet that if you ever wanted to live with her, or even *stay* with her for an overnight, I'd make sure she was clean and sober first."

"Is that what you want?" Willow asked, swallowing hard even though there was nothing in her throat. "For me to live with my mom again?"

"Oh, honey girl. How can you even think that?" Now Catherine was crying for real, the eye makeup running so that her eyes were circled in black streaks. "You're the reason I do everything. You're my *family*. I want you to live with me. Always and forever, okay? But the truth is that I'm not sure what would happen in court if your mom wanted you back, or what I'd do if you really, really wanted to try living with her again. Do you want that?"

In answer, Willow threw herself out of her chair and into Catherine's arms, even though she was far, far too old to sit on anybody's lap. She didn't know what she wanted, other than to stop Catherine from crying any more.

Work was busy, even for a Friday, with a slew of kids coming down with a virulent stomach virus that kept the mothers coming in for advice on rehydration that they probably could have gotten over the phone. Catherine found herself feeling patient with them, though, after Willow's surprising show of affection this morning. Maybe she hadn't screwed up everything after all. And each of these moms, no matter how misguided, was trying to do her best by her child.

It was so easy to judge parents from the outside, she thought, as she tamed a squirmy toddler by pretending he had an elephant in his ear while the mother sat, white-faced with fear because her son had his third ear infection in two months. She could tell this mother that her son would be fine, that tubes were no big deal, that someday he'd outgrow all this. She could tell this mother that sometimes ear infections went away by themselves with no antibiotics at all. That was her job, advising parents. Infections and viruses and broken bones, yes, she knew about those. She took pleasure in sharing that knowledge. But about the big things, like whether a child would turn out to be good or bad, happy or sad, she knew nothing. Look at her own sister and herself. They'd been raised by the same parents in the same house. Yet it was as if Zoe and Eve—the people with the "fun" names, as Catherine used to think of it when she was young—were one family, while she and Andrew—serious names—were in another. Who knew what, or where, the tipping point was, when it came to a child's personality?

Willow had been flip-flopping lately between affectionate and critical, honest and not. How would she turn out? And would her fate—or even her personality as an adult—be determined by who she lived with or by her biology?

These questions were making Catherine feel fogged in by anxiety. So when Alicia, the receptionist, offhandedly invited her to a spin class during lunch hour at the local Y, she surprised them both by accepting; she happened to have her gym bag in the car and desperately needed to clear her head.

Catherine had never tried a spin class. She was startled by the ferocity of the instructor, a guy in his sixties who looked and acted like he was in the Marines. He barked commands at them over the throbbing music: "Catch that bike in front of you. Come on. The chase is on. You can do it! Pedal, people, pedal!"

Ridiculous, she thought, staring at Alicia's bobbing ponytail and tight buns perched on the stationary bike in front of her. *We're not even going anywhere.*

But then something kicked in. She pedaled faster and faster, determined to catch Alicia, to outpace her and her youth, too. To prove that she was still in the race.

Afterward, Catherine was spent and so sweaty that she braved the slimy floor of the Y showers to quickly rinse off before going back to work.

Her thighs and calves were still burning when she got home. The doorbell rang as she was gathering up a load of wash. Mike's sharp barks echoed up the stairs. She glanced at the clock. Too early for Russell. He was teaching in New Hampshire today; it was his weekend with Willow and he had arranged to pick Willow up in time for dinner; it wasn't five o'clock yet and Willow was still at school. Catherine had even called the photography teacher to check.

The doorbell rang again before she reached it. Someone must be feeling impatient. Mike was still barking.

Catherine opened the door, expecting Mrs. Hurley, an elderly neighbor who seemed to routinely lock herself out of the house, or maybe the UPS man. But it was neither.

"Oh," she said, stepping back.

Russell stood on the porch, looking sheepish. "I know I'm early," he said. "I just thought it would be easier if I came straight here from New Hampshire to pick up Willow instead of fighting traffic into Back Bay first."

"That's fine. She should be home soon. Want some coffee?"

"Sure."

"I've got beer, too, if you'd rather."

"No, no. Coffee's fine."

Catherine started the coffee, her mind scrabbling for small talk that wouldn't incite either of them to say anything they might regret later.

"How's it going at the school? Do you like it?" she asked finally.

"It's good, actually. Not the same caliber of student as at Beacon Hill, but the faculty's nice enough, and Tim has done a great job of introducing me around so that I'm not a pariah."

"You must be relieved." Catherine stared at the coffee dripping into the pot, surprised at how easily Russell had found another teaching job and wondering how she felt about that. He wasn't exactly a predator, but he had taken advantage of one of his students. She still had trouble reconciling that fact with the husband she'd loved.

On the other hand, Nola was a young woman of eighteen and very independent. She could see where, in a contest of wills between Nola and Russell, Nola would win.

"You bet I am. So how is she?" Russell asked.

Startled, Catherine realized that she didn't know who Russell meant: Nola, Willow, or Zoe?

It was liberating to feel so disconnected from him. But she was wary about it, too. Where had her self-righteous ire gone? How had it evaporated so suddenly, without her even noticing? And what did that mean if it had?

It means you're moving on emotionally. That's what Bethany would say. And a therapist, if she could have afforded one.

She brought the coffee to the table with a plate of cookies and sat down across from Russell. "How is who?" she asked. "Willow?"

"Of course, Willow. Who did you think I meant?"

"I was thinking about Zoe, actually." Sort of a lie: just then she'd been thinking about Grey, Zoe's gypsy, and how ridiculous these bear-shaped cookies had looked in his hand. She'd found herself thinking of him more often than she would have admitted to anyone, even Bethany, picturing Grey's black hair, his dark eyes, the way he'd looked on that motorcycle. Bad-boy alert! Luckily, she'd never been attracted to that sort of man, beyond her obvious and ridiculous physical response, unlike poor Zoe.

"Ah." Russell stirred sugar into the coffee. "How are Willow and Zoe getting along? And how are you doing with it all?"

Funny, Catherine thought, watching Russell stir sugar into his coffee.

He never used to take sugar. She was glad. The way his spoon clinked against the cup would have driven her mad through the years.

"I think they're doing fine," she said. "I was angry, of course, that Willow was sneaking off to see her. But then I realized how wrong that was. Why wouldn't she want to see her mom, maybe get some answers? I'd like answers, too. I got Zoe's address from her. I'm planning to see her tomorrow."

"Really? Good luck with that." Russell set the spoon down. "I imagine Zoe is as terrified of having a real conversation as you are. Does she know you're planning to visit?"

"No. Not because I'm trying to ambush her, but either Zoe doesn't have a phone or won't give out her number, remember?"

"Christ." Russell shook his head. "I'm sorry you're going through all this, Catherine. But I'm glad for everyone's sake that Zoe's alive. So strange that she could pull off that total disappearing act. I wonder how she did it."

"It couldn't have been easy. She must have been looking over her shoulder every minute. It makes me wonder if she was running away from something."

"Like what?"

Catherine shrugged. "With Zoe, the possibilities are endless. A drug deal gone sour. A gambling debt. An abusive boyfriend. A landlord suing her for back rent." She sipped her coffee and winced; still too hot. "Anyway, my main concern is keeping Willow safe. I want to check out Zoe's living situation before I give Willow permission to visit her alone, especially overnight."

Russell frowned. "Willow wants to *stay* with Zoe? After everything her mother put her through?"

Catherine shrugged. "It's an obvious next step. Willow is curious about her mom. I think, on some level, that Willow wants to take care of Zoe so she doesn't leave again."

"We can't let her do that," he said emphatically. "It's dangerous. Zoe can't be trusted." His voice was rising in alarm.

"We don't know that," Catherine said, but she had to sweep her own panic into a dark corner of her mind. She'd visited Zoe in Worcester once, when her parents had pleaded with Catherine to talk her into a new rehab program. Willow must have been about three years old, a chubby preschooler with tightly coiled ringlets. It was a disaster of an apartment with scarcely any furniture.

Zoe was clearly high, grinning like a jack-o'-lantern and speeding around the filthy apartment, pretending to clean but really only moving clutter from one corner to the other. She'd asked for money right away, started sobbing when Catherine refused. Then she'd asked for vodka. Again, Catherine had said no, appalled.

"I need alcohol with my molly. You don't get it. You just don't get it. I'm going to crash!" Zoe had shouted, picking up one of the sofa cushions and flinging it hard across the room.

Catherine had taken Willow home with her, had given the girl supper and a bath. Willow had slept with her that night, her small sticky fist keeping such a tight grip on Catherine's hair that she couldn't turn over.

To Russell, she said, "Zoe told me she left Massachusetts because she couldn't quit her lifestyle if she had the same friends. I think a social worker was threatening to take Willow from her, too, if I'm remembering right. Anyway, I don't know how Zoe will do now that she's back. She's living in Salisbury Beach, not far from the people she partied with in high school. I think, in a way, that she came back not only to see Willow, but to test herself."

"That sounds risky," Russell said.

"I know. But all we can do is wait and see what Zoe's next move is, right?"

"I guess. But I don't like this a bit."

At her feet, Mike circled between her chair and Russell's, finally settling by Russell's feet and looking up at him with a gaze groupies reserve for stage icons. She smiled. "Do you give that dog food from the table at your place?"

Russell reddened. "Sometimes. Accidentally. Maybe." He glanced down at Mike and laughed. "It's hard to resist that face."

"I know. But that dog's going to be the shortest two-ton pony on the planet soon. Hey, how's Nola doing? Only two months to go, right?" There. She'd done it. All right, so she'd compared Nola to a two-ton pony, but still. She'd brought Nola up in a civil tone.

Russell shifted in his chair. "About that, yeah. I've got something to tell you. That's the real reason I came by early."

Catherine grew very still. "What is it? Twins?"

"No. It's Nola. She's kicking me out."

"What?" Catherine had to force herself to close her mouth. "Why?"

Judging from the circles under Russell's eyes, it was more than financial pressure and his job loss making him look older: he was unhappy. "She thinks we're rushing into things by getting married so soon," he said.

"But what about the baby?"

"Nola wants the baby. And she loves me, I think. It's just that she doesn't feel like I really love her."

"Do you? I hope to hell you do. You threw away fifteen years of marriage for her! Willow, too. You jeopardized your career for that girl. Doesn't that count for anything in her eyes?"

He looked at her in surprise. "No, actually. She's young. Romantic. Passionate. What matters to her is love. Nola says we don't have any sort of true love built on longevity or deep emotions. She's a smart girl and a thoughtful one. Now she's questioning everything, and I don't blame her. Nola's parents got divorced before her mother died. Her dad abused her, I think, though Nola won't talk about it. Anyway, Nola knows what Willow went through with Zoe and what Willow's going through now with us. She doesn't want to put her child—our child—through that kind of pain, she says. She only wants us to get married if we're very, very sure of each other."

"But aren't you?"

"I thought so." Russell rubbed his face again and blinked hard at her. "Now I don't know."

Catherine felt on high alert, as if the refrigerator were humming inside her skull. "Why not?"

His voice was gentle. "Because I miss you. I miss *us*. And our life together."

"Of course you do," she said slowly, trying to gather her wits. "You and I were habits for each other." Could he possibly be serious? Or was this just Russell's way of trying to reel everything back, as his life was spinning out of control? She must represent safety to him, as he did to her. "I miss it all, too, what we had. But I'm beginning to think you were right."

His brow furrowed. "What do you mean?"

"You were right when you accused me of not being interested in your work or your biking or in most other things you do. I was putting more of my energy in Willow and in keeping up with my work and the house than I was in you most of the time. And I'm sorry about that."

"That hurts," Russell said.

"I'm sorry," she said. "But I don't think you and I have been in love for a long time. We were working on staying married. There's a big difference between that and love. Somehow, when we weren't looking, our love morphed into something else, like resigned contentment."

"I don't know about that," Russell said. "It nearly killed me when I showed up here the other night and that guy was here, Seth. Seeing you with him made me wonder what the hell I'd done, letting you go. What kind of fool am I?"

She thought of Grey on his motorcycle. "One thing you don't need to worry about is Seth. I promise."

"That's good." Russell reached out and took her hand. "Because that wasn't a rhetorical question. I really have been a fool, Catherine. Maybe there's a way we can fix this. What would you say if I moved back home and we gave things another shot?"

Catherine felt the smile fade from her face so abruptly, it was as if a hand had suddenly covered her mouth. "You can't be serious."

Russell was looking at her steadily. "I am. Think how good it would be for Willow if I moved back in."

"But what about the baby?"

"I'd support the baby. I'd make sure I had joint custody. And I know how much you've always wanted a baby. You could help me raise mine." Russell was warming to the idea now, leaning forward so that she could practically count the lashes around his brown eyes. "Besides, if I moved back in, Willow would feel more secure. You'd have a better shot at keeping her if Zoe decides she wants to fight you for custody, too. What judge would rescind the guardianship of two loving parents who have always given Willow the best of everything, in favor of a drug addict who abandoned her kid for five years?"

"Former drug addict," Catherine said.

Russell shrugged. "So she says. Zoe would have to go a long way to prove that." He put his other hand over Catherine's, too, effectively trapping her hand on the table. "What do you think? Can we start over, maybe add a baby to our household?"

Privately, Catherine had her doubts about Nola wanting her baby anywhere near their house, but that wasn't her main objection. "I don't know." She was having trouble breathing.

"Come on. You know it's the best thing for us. For Willow, too. Just say yes!" He was smiling now, his brown eyes creased at the corners.

She'd always loved Russell's smile, but her hands were sweating inside the cage he'd made of his palms. She pulled out of his grasp and wiped her hands on her jeans. "It's not that simple."

"Why not?" Russell's voice was patient, but she could tell he was agitated by the way he was bouncing one knee.

Catherine didn't realize she'd been holding her breath until she blew it out again, trying to relieve the pressure that had built in her chest. "Because I don't think I love you anymore."

"What?" Russell sat back in his chair.

For one absurd moment, Catherine nearly laughed at Russell's shocked expression. Had he really expected to convince her so easily?

A faint and nauseatingly petty voice inside her was saying, *See how it feels, buddy? Huh? See how it feels?* But she had to ignore that voice and give Russell's suggestion serious thought. This was their marriage they were discussing, after all. The rest of their lives. Everyone was allowed to make mistakes. And if it came down to a custody battle with Zoe, Russell was right: the court might be more likely to let them keep Willow if they were a couple.

"I'm not saying I don't love you," Catherine said, wishing she could sort through her words and feelings more easily. And alone.

"Yes, you are. You just said exactly those words!" Russell argued. "How could you say that? I've said all along that I still love you!"

"You sure have a funny way of showing it," Catherine snapped. "Look, Russell. Don't rush me. I need to think. This is very sudden, and not at all what I was expecting."

"I know. I'm sorry." Russell wrapped his hands around his coffee mug again, his expression contrite. The portrait of a well-behaved man. Mr. Manners. "I got carried away. I love the idea of a new start with you, Catherine."

Russell was feeling at a loss because Nola was rejecting him, Catherine reminded herself. "I appreciate that," she said slowly. "We've been through a lot together. It's tempting to say yes. But I can't just jump back into bed with you."

"We wouldn't have to," he said quickly. "We could be roommates. I'll stay in the guest room. I mean, while we work things out," he amended, catching her expression. "We'll take things slowly."

She shook her head. The thought of Russell moving in was making her feel claustrophobic, as if the kitchen walls were moving in toward the table. She stood up and went to the sink to get a glass of water. "We can take things slowly without living together. I'm sorry," she repeated, relieved to hear the front door open and Willow's voice.

"Hey!" she called. "I'm home. Where are you?"

"In here, waiting for you," Catherine called, and went to the hallway to meet her with a hug.

The excitement on the couch led them to the floor, and then, when both of them admitted they might be too old for that, to the bed.

At first Eve was hesitant about bringing Darcy into the bed she'd shared with Andrew, but none of the other beds were made-up. *A bed is just a piece of furniture,* she told herself as Darcy slowly undressed her. *It can't have any meaning you don't give it.*

But, oh, how wrong she was, Eve thought, her skin still humming as she and Darcy walked Bear down to Plum Island Roasters by the waterfront the next morning, where they had coffee and scones outside in the bright November sunshine. She would never look at that piece of furniture in the same way, now that Darcy had shown her all of the marvelous ways there were to not sleep in a bed.

They wandered through downtown Newburyport with silly grins, hands and hips touching. It was too early for the shops to be open, but they stopped here and there along State Street anyway, so Bear could drink out of the water dishes shopkeepers put out for dog visitors.

Back at the house, she came up behind Darcy and wrapped her arms around him. She wondered even as she did it who this new woman was, reaching for him. Andrew had always been the one to initiate. Malcolm, too. Not her.

She steadily unbuttoned Darcy's shirt as he tried to do up the buttons, playing this game until they were both laughing hard, the same kind of stupid giggles she used to get with her sister when they were children and having a contest of faces. That giddy laughter of childhood, that mirth. Where did it go when you grew up?

It was still inside her, Eve was relieved to discover, as Darcy, still laughing, turned in her arms and said, "If you insist, madam," and led her back to bed.

She did insist. Oh, yes, she did.

Willow and Nola had finished their homework by noon on Saturday. Russell was at the grocery store when Nola dropped her newest bomb. "So, Russell's moving out," she said.

"What do you mean?" Willow's body froze in place.

"He's moving out of my house." Nola looked like she always did, saying this. A cross between pretty and smart, sweet and mean. Like she couldn't decide who to be. Even in a blue striped maternity top that made her look, well, like a top.

Sometimes, looking at Nola was like looking at those drawings her art teacher had shown them that could look like different things depending on your perspective: an old lady or a young woman, a flower or a tiger.

"But *why*? And where's he going to go?" Willow felt a hummingbird flutter of fear in her throat. Where would *she* go, if not here? Catherine always said she wanted Willow to stay with her, but would Catherine still want her if it meant having her all the time, now that she was used to having some weekends free and going out with Seth or Bethany?

Maybe Zoe would just take her someplace, like Florida, if Catherine and Russell didn't want her. Willow pictured palm trees and alligators. She didn't know if she wanted that. In fact, she was pretty sure she didn't.

"I need my space. Guess Russell didn't tell you like he said he would, huh? Figures." Nola rolled her eyes. "He's a nice guy, but kind of a coward, your dad."

"He's not my dad," Willow said automatically, then felt guilty. Russell did everything a dad should do for her. Well, except be predictable. Predictable might be nice for a change.

"Whatever. He still should have told you."

"Is it you or him?" Willow asked.

"Me, I guess. But sort of both." Nola was sitting cross-legged on her Yogibo, where she'd been watching videos to help her study for her GED test; once she earned her high school degree that way, she was going to the community college part-time, she'd announced earlier today. Willow had been studying at Nola's desk and was turned around now, straddling the chair. In this pose, Nola looked like a Buddha, with her belly sticking out and resting on top of her legs like it was a pillow shoved up under her shirt.

Her stomach wasn't fake, though; Willow had seen the ultrasound photos. Nola had put them on Facebook and Instagram, even Twitter. Pretty much the whole world had seen how the baby was sucking his thumb inside

Nola, his eyes closed. And, yeah, it was definitely a boy. That much was embarrassingly obvious.

Willow had felt the baby move, too. Nola had made her put a hand on her belly when it was happening. It was terrifying, like that ancient movie *Alien*. Willow had imagined Nola's body splitting open and the baby coming out, all head and snapping jaws on a long neck.

"Why?" Willow asked again.

"I'm just not sure this is absolutely for me, you know, this whole playing house thing. Marriage." Nola waved a hand. "I mean, I definitely *want* a baby. That's cool. But marriage? Not so much. Every marriage is a train wreck waiting to happen. Just look around."

Willow hated to admit that Nola was right, but she was. "What about Russell, though? Don't you love him?"

"I don't know. What is love, anyway?" Nola said, nibbling on a cuticle.

Love, thought Willow, meant knowing somebody would be on your side no matter what, which was what Russell had totally done for Nola. "So what's going to happen?"

"No clue. I mean, I felt bad when I told him, no lie," Nola said. "I really did. I know I pretty much fucked up his whole life. Yours, too. I get that. But it is what it is, right? That's what my dad always says. He thinks it's better to cut your losses before you get in too deep. Daddy says he'll pay for a nanny. Carmen can't do *everything*, I told him, and Daddy totally agrees with me. Plus, Russell will take care of the baby sometimes, like on weekends. That way I can still have a life."

Willow wanted to choke her, but she reined it in. One thing she'd learned lately was that (1) you couldn't change crazy, and (2) she'd better take care of herself. Her best bet now was to find her backup parent. Mike. It was time for him to know she existed.

"Okay, well, good luck," she said. "I've been thinking about finding my real dad, anyway. Maybe spend some time with him."

"That's cool. Where does he live?"

"I don't know. I guess I'll have to look online or something." Willow knew this was like feeding catnip to a cat. Little Miss Internet Addiction would grab at it.

Sure enough, Nola lit up and said, "Let's do it! That bastard should at least give you college funds. What's his name?"

Willow told her. Nola tapped Mike's name into her iPad. Google brought up a bunch of junk. She tried Facebook next. There were tons of Michael Navarros, though, even when they typed "Massachusetts" into Facebook's search bar. Willow felt discouraged. "This is harder than I thought. Maybe we should give up."

"Hell no. What else do you know about this deadbeat?" Nola said.

"Don't call him that. He might not even know I'm his."

Nola's eyes practically popped out of her skull. "Whoa. Your mom was a total player."

"She was a total drug addict." Willow bit her lip, feeling guilty about outing her mom that way. But nobody seemed to be playing by the rules anymore. Why should she? "My dad was a teacher and a magician," she remembered.

By now she'd moved over to stand next to Nola, close enough to smell her strawberry lip gloss. It was funny how she'd stopped seeing Nola as sexy hot. Now she saw Nola as a hot mess. Like, that lip gloss probably drove guys insane with lust, but personally? Willow thought lip gloss was beyond gross. Wearing it made her feel like her mouth was glued shut.

Plus, she could see the baby moving under Nola's shirt. The alien. So creepy. Definitely not hot. At all.

Willow fixed her eyes on the screen as Nola scrolled through Google searches, and wondered what this baby would think when he got old enough to know his mom was once the hottest girl in high school, until she screwed a teacher and got knocked up. Would she and Nola even know each other then? Probably not.

Weirdly, that thought made her sad. At least Nola, unlike most of the other people in Willow's life right now, was always honest. You never had to guess what she was thinking.

As Nola next tried searching Mike's name plus "teachers," Willow suddenly remembered something else. "Try Montessori schools in Massachusetts with his name," she said. "How many of those could there be?"

Not many. Most had Web sites listing the faculty with photographs. And there, in one of the Montessori schools in some town called Framingham, was a Web site listing Mike Navarro as the middle school science teacher.

"Where's Framingham?" Willow asked, almost chewing through her cheek with excitement.

"An hour away." Nola bent over to squint at the thumb-sized profile picture. "Holy shit. Your real dad's hot."

Willow yanked on a piece of Nola's hair. "Stop. Be good."

Nola laughed. "Yeah, yeah. Anyway, who'd want me now?"

So Nola knew she was over. Willow wondered if she minded. She didn't think so. In fact, the more Willow thought about it, the more she thought that maybe Nola was glad. It must get pretty tiring to look like Nola.

"So all I have to do is get to Framingham." Willow used her phone to search bus and train routes. "There's a bus in an hour from South Station," she said. "But then what would I do? We know where he works, but not where he lives."

Nola was still moving her hands across her iPad like spiders. "White pages," she said when Willow came over to watch again. "Here's his address. And look. We can Zillow his house."

Another few seconds, and there was the house, a white Cape.

"See?" Nola said, obviously pleased with herself. "Wow." She squinted at the photo. "Looks like a doll's house. So cute. I'd say your dad's doing pretty good for a teacher. Zillow says it's worth six hundred and seventy-five K. Trust fund?"

"Yeah, like everybody in the universe has one of those," Willow said, rolling her eyes.

"Okay, so maybe your dad married somebody rich. That's good, right?"

Nola looked up at her expectantly. "You need to get some of that, girlfriend. You don't want college debt."

Willow felt uncomfortable. "That's not why I want to find him."

Nola was indignant. "It should be, though. Your mom didn't get pregnant all by herself. That would be like saying Russell shouldn't support his son." She rested a hand on her belly.

Privately, that was exactly what Willow thought: Why should Nola get money from Russell, if she was the one who seduced him and then dropped him without a blink? Nola had plenty of money and now she was kicking him out. The poor guy wouldn't even get to live with the kid he was paying for.

Then Nola took her by surprise again, saying, "We should go right now and catch your dad at home. It's Saturday. He's probably mowing the lawn or whatever."

"Oh no. You are *so* not coming with me," Willow said. "We'd probably give Mike a heart attack. And I can't go now. Russell would kill me even if Catherine didn't. I'm already in huge trouble. And I don't have bus fare."

"No probs. I'll give you a ride." Nola put the iPad on the pillow, where it always lived, stood up, and pushed her feet into a pair of striped Toms. "We'll get back before Russell does. He said he was going to the store after the gym, and that guy can take a long time to pick out a chicken."

"I don't think this is a good idea," Willow said, but she was already tucking her phone into her pocket and looking for her shoes.

CHAPTER SEVENTEEN

On Saturday morning, Catherine finished cleaning the house, exploring the sensation that she was scrubbing not just mold off the shower and dirt off the floor, but removing Russell, too. As she tried to picture her husband moving home again, or to imagine Russell in bed with her or even cooking in the kitchen, she had trouble breathing. It felt as if a heavy animal, maybe a raccoon or a monkey, was sitting on the back of her neck, a dead, itchy weight that made it difficult to move.

It took a few hours of housework before the strange sensation disappeared. Her body was telling her what her mind had been having trouble acknowledging: She didn't want Russell to move back in, no matter how logical that step might seem in terms of making a home for Willow.

She'd been too busy cleaning to eat anything. By noon she was starving, and her arms and legs were trembling the way they had when she'd had to take steroids once for poison ivy. She inhaled a quick lunch of canned soup and half a ham sandwich, washed down by more coffee.

Within a few minutes, she knew the caffeine was a bad idea. She was even more jittery. Or was that just nerves, now that she was finally ready to see Zoe?

Catherine had lied to Russell about Zoe giving her the address. The truth: she'd found the piece of paper after doing a thorough search of Willow's room. Yes, she felt guilty, but she was desperate. And the paper wasn't even hidden; it was folded in half and tossed onto Willow's desk. She knew it was the right address because it was in Zoe's round, loopy handwriting.

Salisbury made sense. Zoe used to surf that beach with one of her boyfriends, a guy from California with ear gauges as big as quarters. His earlobes had practically hung to his shoulders. Catherine had met him after tracking Zoe down on the beach one summer weekend when her sister had refused to come home. Zoe was only seventeen; their parents were out of their minds with worry.

"They treat me like a baby," Zoe had fumed when Catherine found her on the beach. She was wearing a wet suit, and her blond ringlets curved in gold commas around her face. "They won't let me live my life, so I have to run away and live it myself!" she'd cried, then whooped and ran into the crashing waves with her board.

Catherine had watched her sister surf for a few minutes, furious but envious, because she'd scheduled that entire weekend around studying for the SAT exam. Why did Zoe get to have all the fun?

Because you chose to be good, she reminded herself then and now. Zoe had made her parents so miserable that Catherine couldn't rebel.

To Zoe, Dad would say, "You want to do *what*?" whenever Zoe described some of her outlandish plans for the future: to be a rock star, a fashion model, a doctor. "But that doesn't even make sense," he'd say. "Pick something sensible. God knows you probably won't even get into college with your grades. Maybe it's time you looked at hospitality programs, Zoe. Or secretarial schools."

Catherine had tried to pick something sensible, a job she could do even while having a family. A career that would give her the flexibility to work part-time. She was thinking ahead, she told her parents. Nursing was perfect.

"I don't want to have to go to school forever, so forget medical school. And I don't want to have to work long hours like Mom," she'd added pointedly. She had hated it that her mother's job in public relations meant she was hardly ever home, even in the evenings.

"Now, that sounds like a sensible plan," Dad had agreed about nursing.

Meanwhile, Zoe's transgressions grew in number and severity as she got older: an arrest in middle school for shoplifting, a drunk-driving charge in high school, drug possession. Catherine couldn't understand what propelled her sister to keep screwing up.

"Why do you always make the wrong choices?" she'd screamed at Zoe once, after Zoe lost her license for drinking and driving at seventeen.

"Why are you so *boring*?" Zoe had shouted back.

Thinking about all of this made Catherine decide to stop in Newburyport on the way to Salisbury and invite her mother to join her. Zoe would be less hostile if their mother were present for their conversation.

Besides, if Zoe was living rough, Catherine wanted her mother there as a witness and an ally. It was easy to imagine her sister holed up in one of those welfare motels along Route 1, maybe the one near Tiger Cubs, the strip club that advertised "Mini Mary" and "Tiny China."

It took her less than forty minutes to drive north from Cambridge to Newburyport. The seaside town was all but deserted now that the summer day-trippers were gone; the Christmas shoppers hadn't yet descended. Driving down High Street, past the stern white Federalist houses and the curvy Victorians with their turrets and grand porches, Catherine pictured women in long skirts and bonnets, their hands tucked into muffs, wandering the brick sidewalks beside men in stovepipe hats.

Catherine's father had bought their Victorian on Water Street before the town experienced its resurgence in the 1970s and began attracting tourists and Boston commuters. It was a Queen Anne style and painted in three colors like the Painted Ladies in San Francisco: yellow clapboards with green and red trim. Her favorite was the turret overlooking the Merrimack River; this round space jutted out from one corner of her parents' bedroom.

Her father had built a window seat there. As she approached the house, Catherine remembered now, with startling clarity, a morning spent sitting there with her mother. Both were in their bathrobes. They'd read the newspaper while snow fell on the river, pockmarking its smooth surface. The reason Catherine remembered this particular morning was because her mother had been so tense, chewing her nails as she read, biting them to the quick. Eventually her mother had started crying and had sent Catherine away. She still had no idea why.

Now she thought back to the strange conversation with Russell weeks ago, the one in which he'd claimed that her mother had had an affair, too, as well as her father. Catherine still had trouble believing this. Shouldn't she have suspected? And yet she never had. As a child, and even as a teenager, Catherine had viewed her parents' marriage as a foundation, one as immovable as their Victorian house. A house that had withstood countless storms since it was built in 1880, including one that had sent boats crashing up onto the riverbank when she was ten years old.

"Don't you worry," her father had said during that storm, as the wind howled and the windows rattled around them. "This house was built to take a thrashing. You'll always be safe here."

That's exactly how she'd always felt with her parents: safe. How silly. They must have been unhappy with each other, at least during some of their long marriage. Otherwise, why would they have sought out other lovers? Now she wondered, on the heels of Russell's offer, how they'd resolved those affairs and trusted each other again.

She pulled into the circular driveway and parked behind an oversized pickup truck with a Vermont license plate. What sort of workman would her mother call to come down from Vermont that she couldn't find locally?

Catherine was also surprised that anyone would show up on a weekend. Yet, there he was, a guy in a green jacket up on a tall ladder. He appeared to be clearing leaves out of the gutter. Well, good. At least Mom was taking care of the house.

She didn't bother knocking, just opened the front door and went in. Catherine smiled at the familiar homey smells of coffee and bacon. That was a good sign, too. For weeks after Dad died, her mother hadn't cooked. Had hardly eaten. Grief must be loosening its grip on her as time passed, especially now that Zoe had reappeared.

"Mom?" Catherine called.

She heard footsteps on the second floor, a startled series of light thumps, and went to the bottom of the staircase. "Mom? It's only me!" she called. "Are you decent?"

"Not exactly." To her shock, her mother appeared at the top of the stairs in an unfamiliar bathrobe, something ivory and silky. Her mother's short brown curls were tousled and her face was free of makeup despite the fact that it was early afternoon.

"Hi," Catherine said. "Are you sick?"

"No, no. What are you doing here?" her mother said. "Did we have a date and I forgot?" She pushed the hair out of her eyes.

"No," Catherine said. "I stopped by on impulse. Were you sleeping?"

"Yes. Just resting." Her mother's laugh was a nervous giggle. "Hang on. I'll be down in two seconds. There's coffee in the kitchen if you want."

Catherine went into the kitchen, puzzled by her mother's odd behavior. Her mother was usually up with the sun and never greeted company unless she was fully clothed, yet today she had a workman here and was wearing lingerie after lunch.

She poured a cup of coffee and went to the refrigerator for milk, then took a spoon out of the drawer. It was only as she started to put the spoon in the dishwasher that she noticed the two mugs and two plates on the counter. That was strange, too. Her mother had never tolerated dirty dishes in the kitchen.

She was rinsing the plates when she heard footsteps behind her. She turned, smiling, expecting her mother, but it was the man she'd seen up on the ladder. He was rangy and tall, well over six feet, with an angular, patrician sort of face and intelligent gray eyes. He smiled and stuck out a hand in greeting. "Hello. I'm Darcy."

"I'm Catherine. Eve's daughter," she said, shaking his hand. Maybe he'd come in for a glass of water. Nervy guy, but at least he looked clean enough. "Can I help you? Did you need something?"

"No, no. I was just looking for Eve," Darcy said.

"She's upstairs getting dressed. She'll be down in a minute."

"I'm right here," Eve said, coming into the kitchen, looking breathless, her hair combed but still not tidy. She'd misbuttoned her blue flannel shirt. "Hello, sweetie."

When she saw the way Darcy was looking at her mother, Catherine suddenly got it. "Oh," she said, feeling foolish. "You're not here to work on the house, are you?"

"What? Why would you think that?" her mother said. "Oh! You saw Darcy outside. On the ladder. No, no. He's not working on the house." Her mother was blushing, even her neck bright red now. "Well, he is, but only as a favor. Leaves were clogging the gutters. He volunteered to clear them for me."

"That was nice of you," Catherine said, as the big black dog her mother had brought to her house wandered into the kitchen and gazed up at them hopefully, smelling bacon. "I like your dog."

Darcy laughed and glanced at her mother again. "Not mine. My son's. And now he's your mom's. Likes it here and plans to stay." Darcy looked like he was about to reach for Eve's hand, but she sidled away, broke off a bit of bacon, and fed it to the dog.

"What are you doing up this way?" she asked Catherine. "Nothing's wrong, is it? Where's Willow?"

"She's with Russell this weekend. I'm on my way to see Zoe."

"Oh?" Her mother's voice held a note of warning.

Catherine ignored it. "Yes. I just, you know, want to catch up a little. I stopped by to see if you want to come with me."

"Actually, I've already been there," Eve said. "She lives in a trailer near the beach. It looks clean enough. I think she's doing all right. I believe she's telling the truth about not doing drugs."

Catherine felt a ripple of tension across her shoulders, as if someone had dragged a wire across her skin. As usual, her mother was going to side with Zoe. She should have predicted that.

"My wild monkey," Eve would call Zoe affectionately, whenever her sister ran around the yard, hooting and out of control. Their mother loved that streak of abandon in Zoe. She'd encouraged it. "Zoe's not afraid of anything," Catherine had once overheard her mother saying to a neighbor. "Catherine's another story. She's afraid of her own shadow, poor thing."

"I hope you're right about Zoe cleaning up her act," Catherine said. "If she's not, no way will I let Willow even visit her. I'm going to check things out for myself."

"She's living with someone now," Eve said. "A man."

"I know. I met him." Catherine looked again at Darcy, whose weight was resting on one foot more than the other, so that his body listed slightly toward her mother's. Yes, they were definitely lovers. God, this was uncomfortable.

"So, do you want to come with me?" Catherine asked.

Her mother shook her head. Her body had responded to Darcy's subtly; she had cocked her hip in his direction while still looking attentively at Catherine. "No. It might be better if you saw Zoe on your own. Did you call her? She works odd hours."

"No," Catherine said. "I wanted to surprise her."

"All right. Good luck. Let me know how it goes."

"I will," Catherine said, but as she left the house and the realization sank in that she was truly on her own, she felt slightly nauseated from fear. Hurt, too. Her mother had apparently moved on from her father and had easily embraced Zoe's return. Catherine felt like she was inhabiting a completely different reality. Alone.

She found Zoe's place without difficulty. Her mother was right: the trailer was well kept, at least the outside, and the trailer park appeared to be quiet, just a few modest vehicles parked in front of the mobile homes, children's toys and bicycles in some of the yards.

Catherine stepped out of the car and smelled the bittersweet tang of the ocean. She could hear the surf in the distance. Tall, tawny marsh grass hemmed the trailer park. The grass shivered and whispered in the breeze. Seagulls wheeled overhead, like white boomerangs flung into the sky. The bright day mocked her dark mood.

Grey's motorcycle was parked in the driveway, the only vehicle. So maybe Zoe did have a job. Catherine sensed that her sister wasn't here. She should probably leave and come back later. On the other hand, this was her chance to see the real state of her sister's new life.

She squared her shoulders and walked up the path leading to a narrow wooden deck that ran the full length of the trailer. It was easy to imagine sitting out here in nice weather, listening to the ocean and the trills of red-winged blackbirds.

The door opened before she could knock. Grey stood there in a white T-shirt and jeans, his hair loose around his shoulders, black and silky. Catherine took a step back and tucked her hands into her jacket pockets, embarrassed by her desire to touch him.

"Hi. Sorry to bother you. I came to see Zoe," she said.

"She's not here." Grey didn't invite her in.

Catherine wanted to see the inside of the trailer. To know how her sister lived with this part-time gypsy. She still couldn't believe Grey was only a friend. Zoe didn't know how to be just friends with a man. She screwed them for fun or used them for something more tangible—money, drugs, a place to crash. Catherine had seen her do it all.

"When's she coming back?"

"A couple of hours."

"Mind if I come in and wait?"

Grey's impassive expression finally gave way. Now he looked surprised. "That's a long time to wait."

"I drove a long way. Look, I need to talk to her. Does she really not have a cell phone?"

"She does, but she doesn't like to give out the number to people she doesn't trust."

Of course that would include her only sister, Catherine thought irritably. "If I wait, will she see me, do you think?"

"Only one way to find out, I guess." Grey finally opened the door wider and gestured for her to pass through it.

The living room was ordinary and clean, except for a few scattered magazines, mostly devoted to boats and motorcycles. A flat-screen television dominated the wall across from the couch, and in one corner by the window was a desk with a laptop open and humming.

The combined dining/living room was separated from the kitchen by a narrow counter. The feeling was more bungalow than trailer; the space was bright and comfortable, welcoming, with red knobs on the cabinets picking up the bright red poppies on the taupe rug beneath the dining room table.

"This is nice," she said. "Are you renting it for the winter?"

"I own it." Grey closed the door behind her. "I own the park, actually. I bought it as an investment. I have a house on the beach between here and Seabrook. My mother lives in that house now. I'm fixing up another place now. I'll move in there soon."

"Oh," Catherine said, confused. "So you spend most of the year here?"

He laughed at her expression. "Zoe told you I was a gypsy, huh?"

She nodded. "I thought you must spend most of your time on the road."

"Not all of us do. Can I get you a coffee?"

Catherine's stomach was still sour from the coffee at her mother's house and the shock of meeting Darcy. "No, thank you."

"Want to sit down?"

She shook her head. "I think you're right. A couple hours is too long to wait. I should go."

Grey eyed her curiously. "You don't look like you should drive. Are you feeling all right?"

"I'm fine. I might take a walk on the beach or something, then stop back, if that's all right."

"Anytime."

"Thanks." She turned around and opened the door again, welcoming the cooler air.

"Wait." Grey grabbed his leather jacket from a peg near the door. "Why don't I go with you? I could use some air, too. I've been working all morning." He gestured toward the computer.

They followed a quiet street that paralleled the main road, and after a few blocks arrived at the beach. It was nearly empty, except for a lone surfer and a dog walker, and the tide was out, the beach wide and flat.

As soon as she saw the water feathering out on the sand, leaving silver tide pools behind as the waves retreated, Catherine felt homesick for

Chance Harbor. How silly that she hadn't stayed longer there with Willow and her mother to make the most of what could be their last days on Prince Edward Island.

The wind was stronger as they began walking along the packed sand toward the main State Park reservation. The dunes were gold in the sunlight and the water mirrored the deep blue autumn sky. The simplicity of these colors mocked Catherine's complicated thoughts. She couldn't think of anything to say to Grey. They walked for several minutes in silence. Finally, she asked him how long he and Zoe had been living together.

He didn't turn to look at her, his profile fierce-looking with its black eyebrows and prominent brow and nose. "A few months."

"And you were living with your sister down in Florida?"

He was silent for so long that Catherine thought he mustn't have heard her. Finally, though, Grey said, "Yes. For a little while. Just until the end."

"The end of what?" she asked.

Grey stopped walking so abruptly that Catherine took several steps beyond him before she caught on and turned around. "The end of my sister's life," he said.

Catherine opened her mouth, then closed it again, too shocked to speak for a moment. "But I thought Zoe worked with her," she said finally. "I thought that's how she ended up living with you guys."

Grey nodded. Now he was looking away from her and toward the water, squinting a little. "Zoe and Sadie were friends from work, yeah. One day my sister went to a bar and nearly overdosed. A guy at the bar found Zoe in her contacts on her phone and called her when they took Sadie to the ER. Sadie didn't want anyone to call and tell our mother what she'd done, so Zoe called me to come down to Florida to help. I got Sadie into rehab, and I invited Zoe to move into our house in Homestead. I thought that having Zoe there would be good for Sadie when she got out of the clinic. Someone who could understand what she was going through. For a while it worked. Then it didn't. And then Sadie was gone." He stopped talking and bowed his head, kicking at the sand with the toe of one black boot.

Catherine stood quietly beside him, facing the sea. A pair of cormorants surfaced, then dove and surfaced again, their narrow heads and skinny necks like black umbrella handles sticking up from the blue water.

"What happened?" she said softly. This was always the story she'd been afraid she might hear about her sister. It still was.

"Sadie overdosed. She was alone in her car, in the parking lot of the restaurant where they both worked. Zoe's the one who found her and called the police. Sadie had gotten some heroin tainted with fentanyl."

"I'm so sorry."

He nodded and finally turned to look at her. His skin was brown with an undertone of gold, the same color as the damp sand they'd been walking on, as if Grey had grown up from the beach fully formed, like a tree springing forth from the earth. "It could have been your sister," he said. "That's what you're thinking, isn't it? But Zoe is stronger. And luckier."

"At least so far," Catherine said. The wind had picked up. She shivered and wrapped her arms around her body. "Zoe has always had luck on her side."

"So far." Grey smiled, but the smile didn't quite reach his eyes. "All addicts are lucky until the one time they're not," he said. "Come on. Let's go back. You look like you're freezing."

"No. I'm fine. Let's walk some more."

They went on for another few minutes in silence before she said, "So do you think there's any chance Zoe will relapse?"

"There's always a chance."

"How big?"

"I don't know," Grey answered. "Zoe had been clean for several months by the time she met my sister. Sadie's death really shook her up. She and Sadie were close. Like sisters." He glanced at her. "Sorry. I shouldn't have said that."

"No. It's fine. I know we're not close. We never have been. I'm glad Zoe had somebody in her life who felt like family."

"Why weren't you?" he said. "Was it the drugs?"

Catherine thought about this. "Partly. We were close sometimes, as kids. Then Zoe changed."

It was true. She had fond memories of her childhood with Zoe. At

Chance Harbor, making cities for the snails and crabs they caught, jumping off the bridge at Basin Head Provincial Park, or looking for bottle caps and sea glass.

In Newburyport, the early mornings on weekends were theirs because their parents slept in. She and Zoe had made forts, invented pancake recipes with everything from chocolate chips to hot peppers. Dared each other to stand on their hands on the couch or go down to the basement alone in the dark. Despite being younger, Zoe won almost every contest. She was smart, quick, and fearless.

"Zoe could have done anything with her life," Catherine said. "Something happened in middle school to change her. A boy, maybe. The wrong friends. We never really knew what it was. But by the time she was fourteen, Zoe might as well have been a stranger living with us."

"She says she always admired you," Grey said. "But I get the impression that she was afraid of you, too."

"I was a snitch and never any fun," Catherine said, hearing Zoe's voice in her head. "She called me a flying monkey." When Grey glanced at her, she said, "From *The Wizard of Oz*. Zoe accused me once of always swooping out of the sky to snatch her up whenever she was having fun. One year she even made me a hat like those monkeys wore, a cap trimmed in red felt cut in a zigzag pattern." She smiled. "Zoe gave it to me for a birthday present and I thought it was pretty. Then she told me what it was and I cried. But Zoe was right. I *was* a snitch. My parents relied on me to help control her. I was more like another parent than a sister to her."

"I get it. I had the same role with Sadie in our family. You can never let your guard down."

"Exactly."

By now they had reached the breakwater at the end of the reservation, near the mouth of the Merrimack River. So funny, Catherine thought, that they were standing across the river from Newburyport. From her mother's house.

Her mother and Darcy. *My God*. Her mother had a lover. She felt the corners of her mouth turn up. Such a weird thought.

"Why are you smiling?"

Catherine felt her cheeks burn. She hadn't realized Grey was watching her. "My mom. I stopped at her house on my way up here from Cambridge, and I surprised her with a gentleman caller."

Grey's dark eyes danced. "Good for her."

"I know. I couldn't get out of there fast enough." Catherine was laughing, and then she wasn't. She was crying, crazy salty tears rolling down her cheeks.

"What is it?" Grey said.

"I don't know," she said. "I'm not sure I can even explain what's wrong. It's just that I don't recognize our family anymore. Everybody's so different. So far apart."

Grey reached out and pulled her close to him with one arm around her shoulders. Brotherly and warm. Zoe was so lucky to have him, she thought.

"Tell me," Grey said. "Everything." He tugged her gently until they were sitting next to each other on the sand and leaning against the stone breakwater overlooking the river. The rocks protected them from the wind and the sun was surprisingly warm.

Catherine leaned her head against his shoulder. Somehow it was easier to talk freely if she didn't look at him. "My dad died in May—Zoe told you that, maybe—and it seems like my mother is moving on. She's seeing this other guy, apparently, and she's selling our summer house on Prince Edward Island."

She stopped and swallowed hard, then went on. "It's weird. I'm at work or whatever, doing just fine. Then I see someone who reminds me of Dad, you know, an older guy in the grocery store or walking his dog, and I fall apart. Or I hear one of his favorite songs and can't move until the song ends. I can't seem to get my head around the idea that he's not with us anymore."

"It'll take time," Grey said. "My dad died while I was in high school. I still have those moments when I see him walking toward me, looking just the same as he always did."

"I'm sorry. That's a tough age to lose a parent."

"Any age is a tough age to lose a parent."

Catherine felt sleepy and leaned in to him a little more. "Now Zoe's back. I know you think of her as your sister's friend, but she'd been gone for five years without a trace. I really thought she was dead. I'm happy she's okay, of course, but everything seems very uncertain now."

"Like what?"

She suddenly wondered if she could trust him. "Oh, I don't know, like what Zoe might do next," she said, and stopped talking.

"What else?" Grey said, nudging her with an elbow. "You might as well pour all of your worries and sorrows into the sea and let them be washed away by the tides."

She smiled. "Is that some kind of gypsy creed?"

"It's mine," he said.

"Okay. Let's see. There's my husband, Russell. Well, maybe my ex, now," she said. "That's confusing, too."

"Which one was he, that night I came?" Grey asked.

"The shorter one with the dark hair."

"Who's the other guy? The one who looks like a runner?"

"Seth. Just a friend."

"He wants to be more, though," Grey guessed.

Catherine turned to look at him, surprised. He met her with a grin. She jabbed him, not so gently, with her elbow. "He's just a friend," she repeated. "I met him when I treated his son in my clinic."

"All right. Russell?"

"Russell was having an affair with one of his students. Now she's pregnant and he's living with her. But suddenly he's saying he wants to move back home and give things another try with me. His girlfriend is kicking him out." Catherine took a long, shaky breath. "I can't believe I just told you all that."

"I can't believe you're *living* all that," Grey said, but his voice was calm and deep, as if the surf itself were speaking, washing gently over her.

Catherine closed her eyes for a moment, letting the rhythm of the surf dictate how she breathed. In. Out. In. Out.

"Thank you for this," she said. "I guess I needed to vent."

He laughed. "Clearly. How do you feel now?"

"Much better." She glanced at her watch. It was nearly three o'clock. "Do you think Zoe's back yet?"

"Only one way to find out," he said, but didn't move.

She didn't move, either, aware of a slight shift in Grey's posture. They were still sitting side by side, leaning against the rocks, but he was no longer simply supporting her weight against his shoulder. He was embracing her, curving his arm around her in a way that held her close to his body.

Her own body was responding, a warmth starting in her feet, oddly, that moved up, as if someone had put her feet close to a fire. Soon she was burning up, almost feverish, despite the fact that she hadn't moved.

But Catherine wanted to move. She wanted that more than anything: to move from where she was next to Grey and straddle him, to look into his black eyes and hold on to his silky hair, to tip his head back so that she could put her lips and tongue on his throat, to feel him grow hard under her and slide her jeans down from her hips. To take him inside her.

All of that went so much more smoothly in the movies than it would go in real life, though, and she was being ridiculous. She didn't even know this man. This boatbuilder and trailer park dweller. This friend of her wayward sister's. This motorcyclist. This *gypsy*. She wouldn't even know how to have sex with somebody who wasn't Russell, whose every move in bed she could predict with 99 percent accuracy.

Catherine stood up and brushed off the seat of her jeans, looking down at Grey from a safe distance.

Except it wasn't safe, not at all. Because he was looking back at her, and then he reached up and drew her back down, as if he were reading her mind, placing her gently on top of him and kissing her mouth, her neck, her collarbone. "Is this all right?" he murmured.

She glanced around the deserted beach and then rested her lips against his warm, sleek black head. "More than all right," she whispered back, and began slowly unzipping her jacket, inviting him in.

CHAPTER EIGHTEEN

Framingham was a confusing jumble of stores and car dealerships and traffic and strip malls. Mike's street was one-way. When Nola dropped her off at the corner a little after four o'clock, the first streetlamps were flickering on.

As Willow watched the taillights of Nola's car blur into the distance, she wished she'd asked her to stay. But Willow knew it would be better if Nola just went home.

Nola had promised to lie to Russell about what Willow was doing. She'd say that she'd driven Willow to the Northshore Mall, just twenty minutes away, to meet friends from her new school, and that Willow was getting a ride back with them. "Brittany and Crystal," they decided, giggling.

"They sound like stripper names," Nola said.

"Yeah. Mall strippers," Willow agreed. "Like there's a kiosk for lap dances right next to the one with iPhone cases."

That got them both laughing so hard that Nola had to pee. They stopped at a gas station and Nola bought them each bags of chips and sodas. "I'm going to be as big as a house," Nola said, happily tearing her bag open with her teeth.

As they reached Mike's street, Willow told Nola to pull over to the curb and let her out.

"Why?" Nola demanded. "I should come with you."

"No, you should not," Willow had said. She'd realized, when dealing with Nola, that the trick was to be definite about things. Nola usually listened then. "This is my deal. Besides, if you hang around, Russell will come back from the grocery store and start worrying. I don't need him calling Catherine. You have to cover for me, remember?"

For the first time, Nola had looked uncertain. She pursed her lips like a pop singer and tossed her hair. Now that her face was puffy from pregnancy, she looked like a three-year-old having a tantrum. "I really don't like the idea of you going to see a guy you never met."

"I've met him," Willow said. "My mom and I lived with him, remember? He's a nice guy."

"You don't know guys like I do, girlfriend," Nola said. "Believe me, the ones who seem nice can be something else when they get you alone. Even dads."

Willow had stared at her in horror. "*Your* dad?" she said, almost whispering, because she felt like the words were toxic, burning her lips and tongue.

Nola nodded. "Not for a long time," she said. "But that's why I don't live with him. Otherwise? He seems like a totally stand-up guy. That's why he's not in jail."

"That sucks," Willow said.

"Yeah, well. It started after Mom died. Said he couldn't help it; he was sad and lonely—cry me a river. Then I threatened to tell everybody and he moved out, gave me the apartment. Carmen looked after me. Now I only see Daddy when I want money. Guys can really screw you over, even the ones you're supposed to be able to trust, right? Russell's one of the few guys I've ever met who wasn't, you know . . . all freaky."

Willow nodded. Russell had always been good to her, too. Nothing weird. Not ever. She remembered Tom, her mother's Real Deal, and how he used to stand next to her bed at night. How he'd touched her. She shuddered a little and pulled her jacket closed, zipping it to the neck.

How could you have the upper hand over a guy if you were just a kid?

She had no idea. Willow was glad she wasn't little and helpless anymore. Fifteen was a lot different from eight. Or even ten. She could take care of herself now.

Before getting out of the car, Willow had reached over and rested her palm on Nola's belly. "You won't let your baby be alone with your dad, right?"

"No way," Nola said, shaking her head hard enough that her long hair made a broom-sweeping noise on her nylon jacket.

"It happened to me, too, you know," Willow said.

Nola's eyes widened. "Who?"

"One of my mom's boyfriends."

They had looked at each other for a minute, and Willow felt something in her chest loosen. She had always known she wasn't the only girl that kind of thing had ever happened to, but still, it felt good to tell somebody who really got it. Plus, if it could happen to Nola, it could happen to anybody. It wasn't her fault.

Nola fished a can of pepper spray out of her pocketbook. "Take this," she said. "Just in case."

Now Willow made her way down a nearly empty sidewalk on Mike's street in Framingham, checking the numbers to make sure she was headed in the right direction.

She walked fast. She couldn't wait to see the look on her dad's face when he saw how she'd figured out it was him, Mike, all along. A magician: who could ask for a better dad than that?

Willow recognized the house instantly. It looked exactly like the picture on Zillow, right down to the bright red door. A car was parked in the driveway, an old black Toyota. Maybe Mike had spent all his money on the house. Or maybe that car belonged to his roommate.

Or to his wife.

Willow walked up to the door, trying to own the moment instead of letting that shrinking feeling in her gut make her feel sick. She needed to shut out the little voice in her head screaming, *You're stupid. If your real dad wanted to find you, he would have done it by now, moron.*

Nobody heard her knock. Either that, or nobody was home. Willow searched for a bell and found it beside the black mailbox. She pushed it, hard, and held it for several seconds, until the ringing seemed to be inside her head.

The door finally opened. A scowling man she didn't recognize said, "Who are you and what are you selling?"

"I'm looking for Mike."

This man in the doorway was bald and built like a professional wrestler, his forearms bulging and tattooed beneath the sleeves of his blue T-shirt. "Mike!" he bellowed. "One of your kids is here!"

"Hang on," Mike called back. Then he appeared in the hallway. "Why are you yelling? Don't be so rude!" He was scolding like he was the other guy's mom.

To Willow's astonishment, the guy at the door grinned, and his face changed from mean and ugly to sweet and kind of hot, like a dumb jock might look in a bro comedy. She could picture him getting to Las Vegas with his pals and coming home with his underwear on his head.

Mike didn't look much different. He had less hair, but Willow knew him at once, recognizing his goofy grin. He wore a red sweatshirt and black workout pants, and he was drying his hands on a yellow dish towel.

"Who do we have here?" he asked.

The other guy still had his dumb face on. "This one isn't yours?"

"No, no. Too old to be one of my students. Go back to the kitchen, Sammy. You're scaring her."

Sammy, Willow thought, considering the way Mike said the name, like it was some delicious drink he was sipping through a straw. Wait. Was Mike *gay*? Was that why he and her mom split up?

"Now," Mike said when they were alone. "How can I help you?"

She had rehearsed this part a thousand times in her mind. "Hi," she said. "I'm Willow. Zoe's daughter. You used to live with us. Or we lived with you—I'm not sure. I was pretty young." She had barely stopped herself from saying *I'm your daughter*, even though in her head that's how it had worked out. Just like in a movie.

"You're *Zoe's* daughter? Oh. My. God." Mike walked out onto the steps with Willow and scanned the street. "Where is she, honey? Tell her to come on in!"

Mike wasn't much taller than she was; he'd been much taller in her mind, maybe because she remembered him wearing a tall hat and practicing magic tricks in the house. His brown hair was prickly; Willow had a memory of that in her fingertips. When she was little, she used to love patting Mike's head and saying, "Ow! Ow! You're a porcupine!" and pretending his hair hurt her hand.

How old was she then? Five or six? Mike used to pick her up from kindergarten when her mom was asleep and couldn't wake up, or when her mom forgot to come home.

"Mom's not here," Willow said. "Just me."

"Oh." Mike raised his eyebrows at her. "Is everything okay with you guys?"

"Sure," Willow said. "Mom's working today, but I wanted to see you." Mike's eyebrows were thick and leggy, like caterpillars. They were okay eyebrows for a magician, but Willow was glad she hadn't inherited them.

"You did, huh." This seemed to amuse him. "Set another place, Sammy," Mike called into the house. "We've got company for dinner."

"It'll be another twenty minutes," Sammy yelled back. "You can't rush genius."

Mike rolled his eyes at Willow. "I can't even go in the kitchen when that man is cooking, or he'll bite my head off," he said, and finally invited her inside. "We're having cocktails. Would a Shirley Temple float your boat? I suspect you're still too young to have developed a gin habit or an affinity for wine."

"A Shirley Temple would be good." Willow remembered that, too: Mike mixing Shirley Temples for her with as many cherries as she wanted.

"I hope you like fish. We're on an omega-3 kick around here. We are very invested in living forever."

"Fish is fine," Willow said, making a face behind his back at the smell.

"You like mashed potatoes, I bet," Sammy said when they came into the kitchen, where he was shaking a silver cocktail shaker.

"I like everything," Willow declared. She would prove to Mike that he would be glad to have a daughter. "Want me to set the table?"

Mike showed her the silverware drawer. Willow laid out knives and forks on the kitchen table while he poured ginger ale over ice and mixed something pink into it. He added cherries, saying, "I remember you used to eat these like candy," making her laugh as Willow rolled up gold napkins Sammy gave her out of a drawer and pushed them into napkin rings shaped like peacocks.

They lit blue candles in brass candlesticks of all different heights, so that it felt like they were eating in church. Willow didn't usually like fish, but this was fine, all covered in butter and lemon and little green things that looked like balls of snot but Mike said were capers.

"So. Why did you want to see me?" Mike asked, his brown eyes dog friendly beneath the thick eyebrows.

"Just, you know, to see how you were doing. It's been a long time," Willow said.

"That it has." Mike's eyes were wary now, but he didn't ask her anything else.

As they ate dinner, they talked about Sammy's job—he was some kind of tax guy—and Mike's school, where his kids were doing a project on beavers and trying to build their own dam. They finished dinner before Mike began asking her questions again. He started out with the usual stuff, like where did she go to school and what grade was she in.

Willow didn't bother telling him about Nola and Russell and why she'd had to leave her old school. Mike wouldn't want to hear about some other guy raising her. Instead, she said she'd tried private school, then decided public school would be better for her. "You know. More like real life."

Sammy and Mike looked at each other across the table. "Well, I can tell you that real life is overrated, in my humble opinion," Mike said, and pulled a deck of cards out of his pocket as Sammy started clearing the table. "Here," he said, "pick a card."

Willow tucked her hands under her thighs. "I should help do dishes."

"Come on. Humor me. Pick a card and prepare to be amazed."

Willow pulled a card out of the deck. "Do I show it to you?"

"Absolutely!" Sammy yelled from the kitchen, where she could hear the teakettle starting to whistle.

Willow turned the card over. "A six of hearts."

"Perfectly done," Mike said. He held the deck out to her. "Now put it back in the deck."

"Anywhere?"

"Anywhere at all."

She kept her eyes fixed on Mike's hands as she inserted the card in the middle of the pack.

"Good job," Mike said, and started shuffling the cards so fast that they blurred. "Now. Do we agree that your card is lost in the deck?"

"Yes," Willow said, grinning. She was buzzing with happiness. This was her dad, and he could do magic! It was coming back to her now, the tricks Mike used to do for her at breakfast or at night, when she was having trouble sleeping. Sometimes she'd wake up and find a card on her pillow. Always hearts.

"Do you bet I can't find it?" Mike asked, almost yelling. "Do you doubt my amazing abilities?"

"I bet you can't find it!" Willow said, giggling.

"How dare you doubt me, the great Magical Mike?" he said, and turned the top card over to reveal her six of hearts.

"Every time," Sammy said, and brought cups of mint tea to the table.

Mike tucked the cards back into his pocket and watched Willow sip her tea. Then he said, "Honey, why are you really here? Does your mom need help?"

She shook her head. "Mom's doing really well," she said. "She stopped using drugs."

"Really?" When Willow looked up, Mike apologized. "Sorry. Didn't mean to sound quite so astonished."

"But you are," Sammy said. "I remember Zoe. I only met her twice, but both times were very, very memorable."

"Shush," Mike said. "Tell me about your mom, honey. I want to know. We used to be good friends."

"I know," Willow said. "You guys started dating in college, right?"

"High school, actually." Mike looked at Sammy as he said this. "Before I knew anything."

Willow understood what he was trying to say. "You can say you're gay, you know. I won't be shocked."

Mike's shoulders sagged a little and he smiled at her. "You are wise beyond your years, little cricket."

"Why did you leave, though?" she blurted. "I know my mom didn't want you to stop living with us. She cried all the time after you were gone."

There was a small silence filled with the scent of mint, and then Sammy stood up. "I've got some work to do before bed," he said. "Nice to see you again, Willow."

"Thanks for dinner," she said, wondering when she'd seen him before. She didn't remember Sammy and, after he left, said so to Mike.

"You were a little kid," Mike said. "Maybe seven. And Sammy never slept over."

"But now he's your boyfriend."

"My husband, actually."

Willow nodded. "Is that why you left Mom and me? Because you found out you were gay?"

"Partly." Mike traced a finger on the tablecloth. Figure eights. "I also couldn't watch her destroying herself."

Willow nodded. She remembered something else now: hiding in a closet while her mother fought with some guy who stole her drugs, until Mike came home and kicked him out. Mike was the one who found Willow in the closet. His nose was bleeding, but he picked her up anyway and took her somewhere, shouting at her mom, who kept trying to throw things at Mike and calling him names.

"Where did you take me, that night you found me in the closet?" Willow asked. "Do you remember that night?"

Mike made a face. "Of course. That was toward the end, when things went from bad to hell-o. I took you to my mom's house for the night because I was afraid that guy would come back. I tried to get Zoe to come with us, but she went after her boyfriend."

"So you weren't her boyfriend anymore, but you lived with us?"

"Yes. Zoe and I broke up in college, when I discovered I wasn't exactly prime boyfriend material, unless you count advice tips on shoes. But she needed a roommate to help her with rent and expenses after she had you, so I invited her to live with me."

"What made you stop being friends? Was it me?"

Mike's caterpillar eyebrows practically crawled up his forehead, he looked so surprised. "Oh, honey, no. It was never, ever because of you. You were the reason I stayed as long as I did."

"Because you were my dad?" There. She'd said it, and it wasn't nearly as hard as she'd thought it might be.

But Mike looked shocked. "What did you say?"

"I know you're my dad." Willow smiled, trying to reassure him. Of course he'd have to feel guilty for leaving. He was a nice guy. "It's okay that you weren't around. You took good care of me when I was a little kid. I'm glad I found you again. And I really like Sammy. I don't care that you're gay. It's cool."

She could definitely live here, Willow thought, if neither Catherine nor her mom wanted her anymore, and if Russell and Nola split up and Russell couldn't afford a big enough place for her to visit. It would be cool, having gay dads. Plus, Sammy could teach her to cook, and Mike could teach her magic tricks. She could use some magic.

"Honey, I'm so sorry, but you've got the wrong idea," Mike was saying. "I wish I was, but I'm not your dad."

Willow clenched her hands and dug her nails into her palms. "But it *has* to be true! You and I are both artists. We both love photography. You even gave me a camera before you moved out! I tried not to let Mom sell it!"

"No, no, no," Mike said, his face sad. "If I did have a child, Willow, believe me, I would want her to be as beautiful and as smart as you are. But Zoe got pregnant after she and I broke up in college."

"That's not true," Willow whispered, but Mike kept talking.

"It really hurt your mom when I broke up with her, I know. I still feel bad about that. I tried to be her friend after, but it was tough." He sighed. "When your mom was using drugs, there wasn't much I could do to support her. I finally moved out because I couldn't stand to see what she was doing. Not just to herself, but to you."

The room was silent then, except for the ticking of computer keys from the other room. Willow realized that Sammy could probably hear everything they were saying. She wanted to get up and slam his door shut, she was so ashamed, but what did it matter now? She hadn't found her dad. She'd only found more evidence that she was alone.

"Who is he, then?" she demanded, folding her arms.

"Who? Your dad?"

"Of course my dad! I need to find him!" Willow said. "If my mom got pregnant in college, you must know who he is. You were there."

"Sorry to break this to you, but I wasn't in the room when she got pregnant, sweetheart," Mike said.

Willow gave him Nana's evil eye. "Don't make fun of me. Can't you see how much this *sucks* for me?"

Mike pulled the deck of cards out of his pocket again and busied himself shuffling them. "Want to see another trick?"

"No," Willow said. "I've seen enough tricks. Life is one big trick." She buried her face in her hands.

Mike came around to her side of the table and sat on the chair next to her. "Hey, now," he said softly. "Everything will be fine. I'm not your real dad, but I can be your friend."

"I don't need any more friends!" She dropped her hands. She was too pissed off to cry.

"Not even friends who can do this?" He pulled a quarter from behind her ear and put it on the table in front of her. "Come on. We're friends. And, in my book, that's better than family. Friends are together because they want to be, not because they have to be, right?"

"I guess," Willow said, staring at the quarter flickering in the light of the candles in front of her and wishing there really was such a thing as magic in the world.

Eve had finally arranged to meet Marta at a coffee shop in Newburyport at Darcy's insistence.

"It's like facing Cape Breton Island again," he had said, holding her one last time before he left for Vermont late on Saturday afternoon. "Remember: memories can't control you unless you let them."

"I'm not in control of anything," Eve said. "Obviously." She tipped her face up to his, scowling. "Otherwise I might have scheduled Catherine's surprise visit a little differently."

He laughed. "Lucky for me, I'll be gone before she starts asking questions."

"A lot of good you are."

At least she could walk to the coffee shop. Eve didn't even want to waste gas on this woman. It was a nice walk, though she missed having Bear tug her along. She'd left him at home, not wanting to share even that much of her life with Marta.

The day was cooling down. The river glittered beneath the sun, sparking silver, and she spotted a pair of loons as she followed the boardwalk to the coffee shop.

Marta was already there, as glamorously out of place as ever. She wore her rich chestnut hair (dyed, it must be, to have that monochromatic look, Eve thought with a petty stab of glee) in a sophisticated twist high on her slim neck. Her black wool coat was belted tightly around her slim waist. She had on lipstick, bright red, that matched her fingernail polish, and she carried a black briefcase.

"Thank you for coming. I am so delighted to see you," Marta said in her rich alto, and held out a hand.

A man would be tempted to kiss the back of that hand, Eve thought, but she ignored it. "I needed a coffee anyway."

Marta nodded toward the line at the counter. "Go ahead. I will score us an available table."

Eve had forgotten how much Marta, with her deep voice and slightly robotic German accent, sounded like Arnold Schwarzenegger in *The Terminator*.

She stood in line for an impossibly long time as the tattooed girl behind the counter played with designs in the foam. The back of her neck itched, a sure sign that Marta was watching her.

When she sat down, Marta pretended to be absorbed in one of the free newspapers, taking her time about glancing up at Eve. Finally she did. "You are looking well," she said.

Eve pushed a hand through her curls and wished she'd put on makeup, or at least worn something besides black pants and her old bomber jacket. "We don't need to make small talk," she said. "I'm sure neither of us wants to be here."

"That is not true. I am glad to be here," Marta said. "This visit is something I owe to Andrew. I am sorry you are not curious. But maybe you will change your mind and be glad when you hear what I have to tell you."

"I doubt it." Eve took a long, deliberate sip of the coffee, just short of a slurp.

"First, please let me apologize."

Eve held up a hand in warning and leaned forward across the table. "Do. Not. Say. You're. Sorry. It's too late for that. You slept with my husband," she said in a low voice. "You tried to get him to leave me. You continued having an affair even after meeting me and my children in our own home. Now my husband dies on your couch, and you're finally trying to *apologize*? It's probably *your* fault he's dead!"

She sat back in the chair again. She had tried to keep her voice low enough to avoid being overheard, but the few people in the café—a pair of young moms with sleeping babies in strollers, an elderly woman in a crocheted beret with a French bulldog on her lap, a guy scribbling in a journal—were all staring at them. Eve felt her face flush. She had meant to be civil, not hostile. But she certainly wasn't going to apologize.

Marta looked completely unruffled. She'd probably had years of practice at deflecting emotions from disgruntled employees at the company.

Andrew's former company, where Marta was still a VP and probably in charge of firing people whenever someone needed to be let go. She nodded and picked up the briefcase, set it on the table. "To begin with, you should know that your husband was finished with me."

"I don't believe you," Eve said. "If he was done with you, why did he die at your house?"

"It was completely my fault. I called him and said I was having a breakdown, that I might end my life. I am ashamed to admit that, but I fully believed it at the time." Even this, Marta said without emotion, as if she were half machine.

"So he came to your rescue."

"Yes. That is precisely what Andrew did. He knew I would not call him unless I was serious. We were good friends, despite everything that came after our involvement. We shared things that we couldn't with anyone else."

"He couldn't give you up," Eve said. "He was in love with you."

Marta seemed to think about this. "He was for a time," she agreed, her voice surprisingly gentle. "But not in the way you think. He loved you more. Think about it. Otherwise, why would he have stayed?"

"Because of the children," Eve said.

"No. Because of you," Marta said firmly. "That is why Andrew ended our love affair after that time you and I talked on the phone."

"Really?" Eve was stunned. She had certainly thought otherwise, when she arrived at the hospital and Marta explained how she'd come out of the kitchen and found Andrew dead on her couch.

"That is correct. We did see each other, many times through the years, but not for the reason you think. We were never intimate again. We had a friendship. And Andrew had no choice about that." Marta was watching her steadily. "You must believe me when I say your husband loved you more than anyone. Despite your affair with Zoe's father."

Eve was startled, and horrified, too, that Andrew had confided so much about their marriage to this person. On the other hand, hadn't she done the same with Malcolm? Poured her heart out about her loneliness, her uncertainty about whether she could stay married to a man she couldn't trust?

Marta was sitting quietly, watching Eve's face. Finally, she unsnapped the latches on the briefcase. "I came here to show you something." She pulled out a slim black photo album.

"I have no interest in seeing any of your pictures," Eve said, her stomach churning.

"Just look." Marta opened the photo album and turned it so that Eve could look at the pictures right-side up.

"I don't understand," Eve murmured.

But she did. She couldn't take her eyes off the images. Infant photos, first. A baby sleeping in a crib, on a sheepskin blanket on a floor, then growing into a toddler in overalls, a little boy laughing up at the camera in almost every shot: at a playground, a beach, a preschool where he'd smeared finger paints on his face. And then a boy in elementary school, ruddy-faced and blond, snub-nosed, sturdy.

A MacLeish.

"Your son," Eve said, a dull headache starting between her eyes. "Andrew's son."

"Yes. You see? You won, Eve. Andrew loved you. He didn't just stay with you because of the children." She continued to turn the pages. "He and I had a child as well. But my son never knew that Andrew was his father. Andrew came to see us sometimes, but that was our agreement: that I could never tell my son his father's name."

Eve's headache had reached cataclysmic proportions. The noise in the café seemed deafening and she felt an attack of vertigo coming on. She was barely holding it together. Yet she couldn't look away as Marta kept turning pages, as Andrew's son went from being a small boy in a Spider-Man costume at Halloween to kicking a soccer ball, growing leggier and leaner by the year, though his face kept Andrew's elfin proportions. Only his dark eyes made him resemble Marta.

Finally the boy was in a graduation robe, throwing his hat in the air. The last shot was of the boy, now a man with a blond beard shot through with red, turning to laugh at the camera as he hiked away from it down a wooded path, the leaves a blur of gold and orange around him.

"He is gone now," Marta said simply, and closed the photo album.

There was a roaring in Eve's ears, as if she were underwater. She knew what Marta meant. A mother always knows. "What happened?"

"My boy was caught in an avalanche in Nepal," she said. "He was trekking there for his twenty-fifth birthday. Doing what he loved. But since he is gone, my heart is broken."

"Yes," Eve said. "Of course." She reached over to touch Marta, to feel the woman's warmth beneath her coat.

The other woman turned her head away, but not before Eve saw the tears. "That is why Andrew came to me the night he died. Because it was our son's birthday, and I didn't want any more birthdays without my boy."

"I am so sorry," Eve whispered, and she was, for all of it: for Andrew giving up his own son for her, for this woman's pain, and for her own, too.

The two of them sat in silence, united by the knowledge that no matter how well loved, a child can still be lost and a mother's heart can never completely heal.

Catherine finally left Grey at five o'clock, when the light had washed out of the sky and it was clear that Zoe wasn't coming home. They'd made love on the beach, with her on his lap, sheltered by the rocks and noisy surf. He had wanted to take her to bed again in the trailer, but that felt too close to Zoe. Instead, they passed the time by eating eggs scrambled with cheese and scallions and a salad made with avocado and tomatoes.

"What do you mean when you say you're a gypsy?" she'd asked.

"I'm only half." Grey looked uncomfortable. "On my mother's side. My father grew up in New Hampshire. He had a car dealership up there and met my mother on the beach. She told his fortune. She still does that here in the summers."

"So what kind of gypsy are you? Romany?" That was the only sort of gypsy she'd heard about, and that was from some television show about gypsy weddings that Willow made her watch once.

Grey told her that all gypsies were descended from people in India who fled the Ottomans and moved to Europe. “My family, the Boswells, are descended from the Romanichals. English gypsies.”

“I’ve never heard of English gypsies,” Catherine said, then remembered the time her parents had taken them to England and Scotland, and the brightly painted caravans they’d passed once in a field. “Gypsies,” her father had pronounced with disgust. “You can’t trust them. They don’t know the meaning of hard work.”

Grey was telling her how the Romanichals had immigrated to New England in the 1850s as horse traders. “Then, when people didn’t need draft horses as much after the First World War, the Romanichals started making furniture or telling fortunes to make a living. My people were nomadic, so they took up businesses like roofing or paving. Anything that let them travel. There are something like a million gypsies living in the United States.”

“Are you nomadic?”

“No.”

“But you were in Florida,” she said. “Now you’re here.”

“I live here. I went to Florida because Sadie needed me.” He sighed. “Not that I did much good.”

“She knew you were there for her,” Catherine reminded him. “The rest was up to her.”

“Is that what you tell yourself about Zoe? That you were powerless unless she decided to change?”

That stung, but it was true. “Eventually, yes.”

“You’re smarter than I was, then.” Grey stood up, cleared the table.

Catherine helped him rinse the plates and stack them in the dishwasher, conscious of his hip and thigh close to hers. She wanted to lean against him at the sink but didn’t. What would be the point? She’d had her fling. Now it was time to go back and get her real life sorted out. Grey clearly belonged to Zoe, even if he was only a friend. Zoe needed friends.

She dried her hands and glanced at the clock. “I should be going. She’s obviously not coming home.”

"And then what happens?" Grey had whispered, his lips close to her ear as they stood beside her car afterward. "Will I see you again?"

"I don't know."

"Don't say that." He bent down and kissed her, pressing her against the car.

"You live with my sister," she said. "I don't want to come between you and Zoe."

"You'll work things out with her. I'll wait. As long as it takes."

"We'll see." She couldn't imagine it, though, Catherine thought as she walked up the steps of her own house now, an hour later.

She hung up her jacket on one of the pegs in the hall and was aware, suddenly, of the quiet in the house, reminding her again that Willow was no longer only hers. No more pretending that Willow was her daughter. She had to play the part of loving aunt from now on, sharing Willow not only with Russell, but with Zoe as well.

Furiously, she started snapping on every light in the house, going from room to room as she stomped her way upstairs and into the shower. She would get into her pajamas and drink wine and watch a stupid movie. No romantic comedies, either. Only bloody action flicks. No more tears. No more pleasure. Just action, damn it. Time to embrace being on her own.

Catherine showered and wrapped herself in the soft pink fleece robe her father had given her one Christmas. She poured a glass of wine, wondering whether any of the Barbie doll outfits she and Zoe played with had included wineglasses as accessories. She should patent that idea, she thought, as she made a generous bowl of popcorn.

She was sitting in front of the television, pouring popcorn directly from the bowl into her mouth as she flipped through the movies on demand, when the doorbell rang. Catherine glanced at the clock. It felt like midnight; she was shocked to see it wasn't even eight o'clock.

Willow, she thought, fear hitting her gut like a fist. She hurried to the door and looked through the peephole. Zoe stood there, her hair a halo of curls. She was one of the few women whose short hair didn't make her look like a PR executive, Catherine thought, despite her shock at having her sister materialize on her porch after she'd been waiting in vain at Zoe's trailer for hours.

Well. Not completely in vain. She felt her cheeks flame as she yanked open the door. "I was at your house," she blurted. "Looking for you."

"I know. Grey told me. That's why I'm here." Zoe stepped inside and began appraising Catherine's appearance as only her sister could.

Catherine remembered this from their childhood, how Zoe had this habit of looking her up and down, always finding fault. "Are you trying to bore people to sleep with that dress?" Zoe had said once when they were in high school.

"Want a glass of wine?" Catherine offered, then remembered. "Sorry. I've got cider. Or tea?"

"I don't need anything." Zoe was still looking at her with those keen blue eyes. She'd rimmed them in black eyeliner and black mascara; she looked like a cabaret singer. "Are you sick or something? Why are you already in your pajamas?"

"I was cold. I took a shower and I was about to watch a movie."

"Sounds like another thrilling Saturday night," Zoe said, not quite smirking.

"Shut up. What can I get you? Popcorn?"

"I said I don't need anything."

Catherine turned around, aggravated by her sister's bullish tone. "Fine. Why are you here?"

"You came to see me, remember?"

"It's an hour's drive, Zoe. You should have called. What if I'd been out?"

"I could say the same to you."

"I would have called, but you never gave me your number! Apparently I'm not in your trusted inner circle."

Zoe crossed her arms. "Can you blame me? I knew you'd come spying on me. Just like you used to do. How the hell did you find me? Did Willow give you my address, the little traitor?"

"Don't call her that. And no." Catherine flopped down on the couch, turned off the television, and took a gulp of wine.

"What, then? You spied on Willow? Stole it? What?" Zoe remained standing, her legs apart. A gunfighter's stance.

"Something like that."

"God. You are too much. No wonder Willow doesn't trust you."

"What do you mean, she doesn't trust *me*?" Catherine shot back. "*You're* the one who took off on her! *You're* the one who won't tell anybody what you're doing here, or what your plans are for the future!"

"Because I haven't figured them out yet!" Zoe yelled back. "Jesus Christ. I'm not you, Kitty Cat. I don't have my ducks lined up in a pretty row. I'm living my life one scary day at a time." She fell onto the other end of the sofa, legs outstretched, and stared at the TV's blank screen. "What were you going to watch?"

"Something stupid to take my mind off my life."

"Oh, boohoo. Poor you. Nice house, great job, never a night on the streets. My heart bleeds. Write me when something bad actually happens."

My husband left me and you're going to steal back your daughter, Catherine wanted to say, but she pressed her lips together because she was still thinking about what Zoe had said about living life a day at a time. It was probably true that Zoe barely had her feet back under her. She'd given up Willow, fought her addiction, and lost Sadie, not to mention all of the other terrifying things that must have happened to her while she was in hiding. How alone she must have felt.

But it was her own fault, Catherine reminded herself sharply, thinking of how much anger and grief Zoe had caused everyone. "Plenty of bad things have happened to me," she said.

Zoe glanced at her. "You really do look like shit."

"Thanks. I can always count on you to prop me up when I'm down."

"Seriously. What's going on? Headache?"

"What the fuck do you think it is? My *heart*, okay?" Catherine said. There had never been any way to hide things from Zoe. When she wasn't high or zonked out on whatever, Zoe was always the keenest observer in their family. That's what had made her so good at shoplifting and sneaking out of the house: she always knew what the rest of them were doing, and even thinking, while they were clueless about her.

"Why?" Zoe pressed. "What's wrong with your heart?"

Catherine turned to look at her. What to say? She didn't want to begin any conversation around Zoe taking Willow. She couldn't go there yet. "I miss Willow when she's at Russell's," she said.

To her surprise, Zoe nodded. "That must be tough on you," she said. "I knew Willow was with Russell this weekend. That's why I decided I'd better come now instead of waiting until tomorrow."

"Who told you I was alone? Grey?"

"Willow. She gave me her cell number a while back. I realized it was probably better if we had some regular contact. I didn't want her taking any more chances to come out to Salisbury on her own."

Catherine flinched. She hated the idea that Willow and Zoe were communicating directly, but said, "Thanks. You're right. It's probably better if Willow knows how to reach you. She's pretty anxious about you suddenly disappearing again."

"I've promised her I won't do that, and I won't. So what's up with you and Grey?"

"Nothing," Catherine said too quickly.

Zoe laughed. "Right. Remember, Grey's like my best friend, my brother, and my guru all wrapped up in one tidy package. I know him. He's obviously crushing on you."

Catherine touched her chapped lips. "I like him, too. But he's not exactly my type."

"How do you know? You've only ever been with Russell. And look how that turned out."

Catherine made a face. "Russell wants us to get back together."

"*What?* He's out of his gourd."

Zoe sounded so indignant that Catherine had to smile. "Apparently the girl has changed her mind about getting married. I think Russell's just floundering now."

"Too bad for him, but you're not seriously considering a reboot of that relationship, are you? Because if you are, I might have to kidnap you and take you back to Salisbury with Grey and me." Zoe toed off her boots and pulled herself up to sit cross-legged on the couch.

"How can you sit like that?" Catherine grumbled. "It hurts my knees to even *look* at you."

Zoe grinned and flexed her thighs down even more, until her knees nearly touched the couch cushion. "Om," she chanted, putting her palms together close to her chest.

"You are such a show-off. Have you been doing yoga?"

Zoe nodded. "Grey's sister, Sadie, taught me. She was into meditation and all that crap."

Catherine waited a beat, then said, "I'm really sorry about Sadie."

"Grey told you?" Zoe lowered her eyes, played with the frayed hem of her jeans.

"Yes. That must have been awful for you. For him, too."

"And for his mom. I still can't believe it. We tried so hard to save her."

"I'm sure you did."

"I nearly died, too," Zoe said, her voice soft. "A couple of times before I met Sadie. That made it worse, finding her. I could picture myself." She shuddered. "I wish I hadn't gone to work that day. Maybe she'd still be alive."

"You, of all people, should know that Sadie had to save herself, Zoe." Catherine hesitated, then added, "Anyway, I'm glad you didn't die."

"You don't need to say that," Zoe said. "I would deserve it if you felt differently. I knew I was risking that when I got on the bus in Boston."

"I'm not trying to be a hard-ass or punish you in any way. What's done is done. You're back now. That's the important thing." Catherine finished her wine and stood up. "Want a sandwich or something? I'm starving."

"Maybe. I don't know. Make me one and I'll see."

"You are still such a spoiled brat."

"And you're still an easy touch. Why are you even offering to make me a sandwich if you resent doing it? That's a little passive-aggressive, don't you think?"

Catherine sighed. "I offered because you're my guest. That's what's done."

"I'm not your guest. I'm your sister."

"And I was born to be a caretaker."

"I don't buy that, either. That's like saying I was born to be a drug addict," Zoe said, following her into the kitchen. "One thing I've learned is that a lot of things happen by chance, but we also make choices."

"We agree on that. Truce, okay? Jesus. You're exhausting me!"

Zoe sat at the counter while Catherine rummaged for turkey, lettuce, and cheese. She slapped mayonnaise on two slices of bread, assembled the sandwich, and cut it in half. She put half on a plate for Zoe and pushed it over. "Here. If you eat that, I'll make you another one."

"Fine." Zoe took a bite and chewed thoughtfully, looking at Catherine. "You might look like hell, but I bet it's a relief to give up on being the perfect womanly half of a perfect couple."

"That's a horrible thing to say." Catherine felt the bread ball up in her throat and focused on swallowing past it. "I'm still devastated that Russell left me." As she said this, though, Catherine realized it wasn't quite true anymore. She could still feel the sharp hurt and anger, but it was buried now beneath other concerns. She was moving forward. Approaching life differently. She thought of Grey, of his body beneath hers on the beach, and turned away so her sister couldn't see her expression.

Zoe was wolfing down her sandwich. Afterward, she wiped her mouth on her hand and went to the sink, where she drank noisily from the faucet.

"God," Catherine said. "It's like having a wild dog in here, watching you eat."

Zoe belched and grinned, then sat down again, her face suddenly serious. "I came here today because Grey says I owe it to you, and to Mom, to tell you some things. I don't know if Mom can handle it. I thought I'd test out what I have to say on you first."

"Lucky me," Catherine said, feeling the color drain from her face.

What if this was the moment when Zoe announced her plan to take Willow back? What would she do then?

She couldn't afford a custody fight. Not only financially, but emotionally. She didn't know how she'd keep putting one foot in front of the other without Willow in her life, not after five years of committing her whole heart, body, and soul to the girl. But what if the court declared Zoe a fit mother because she seemed clean and had a reasonable place to live?

And—the most frightening thought of all—what if living with Zoe was the one thing that Willow wanted more than anything else in the world? Could she actually deny Willow that?

Catherine didn't know the answer to that. Or to anything. "I need to sit down for this," she said, and put the plate, with the remains of her sandwich, in the trash.

"You're throwing away the plate, too?" Zoe asked.

"I can't deal with one more thing." Catherine drifted back to the couch, cinching the belt of her bathrobe tighter.

In the kitchen, she could hear Zoe opening the drawer with the trash can, removing the plate, scraping it, and rinsing it. So odd to have her sister be the functional one. But Catherine really did feel helpless at this moment. If only she'd brought the wine bottle into the living room with her. Anything to knock her unconscious.

Was that how Zoe had felt about drugs, all of those years? Like she couldn't wait for that next fix so she could leave her life, and even parts of her thinking, feeling self behind?

When Zoe returned to the living room, she sat on the opposite end of the couch again. Catherine turned to face her, forcing herself to fold one leg under the other. The pain would help keep her upright.

"Okay," she said. "What is it?"

Zoe's Florida tan was fading, Catherine noticed, and her face looked both younger, even childlike, and more worn, with her lips pressed tightly together and her blue eyes rimmed in black. "I need to tell you why I left," she said.

"You already did that," Catherine said, surprised. "You said you had to leave the people you were hanging out with if you were going to stay clean. I don't necessarily appreciate how you cut off all contact, but I'm willing to forgive you."

"I didn't come here asking for your forgiveness."

"Oh." Catherine pressed her back against the nubby fabric of the tweed couch. "Fine. I won't forgive you, then."

"Don't be a jerk," Zoe said automatically, without rancor. "This isn't easy for me."

Like it was so easy for us, everything you did, Catherine thought, but waited.

"It's true that I left Massachusetts because I had to jettison certain people from my life," Zoe said. "One guy in particular. But the main reason I left was to protect Willow."

"Oh, come on. We've been through that. Don't waste my time with that delusional horseshit rationalization again, Zoe. You left your ten-year-old daughter *in a city bus station*!" Catherine erupted. "In the middle of the night, all alone! You let her think you were dead. How was that *protecting* her?"

Zoe put a hand up. "Stop. I know I should have done things differently, okay? I made mistakes, and believe me, I'm sorry. But I wasn't thinking clearly at the time. I was too panicked."

Catherine wanted to slap her, to say, *If you were panicked, what do you think Willow was? And me? Or our parents?* "What where you protecting her from?"

"That same guy who was after me was after Willow." Zoe's trembling had increased; her teeth were chattering.

Catherine unfolded the blanket on the back of the couch and tossed it over Zoe's lap. "Why was he after you?"

"I owed him money. He wasn't a nice guy, but I could have handled him," Zoe said. "I had ways to get money when I needed it."

Catherine didn't ask what those were. She didn't want to know. "Okay. So why did you have to protect Willow from him, then? Was he threatening to hurt her to get money from you?"

"No."

"I'm still not getting the picture here." Catherine stretched her feet out, tucking them under the other end of the blanket, wishing she didn't have a sister whose every story made her hair stand on end.

"This guy—his name was Tom—he was my boyfriend," Zoe said. "I'd started to get my life together when I met him at this place where I was a bartender." Zoe ran a hand across her face, then left it pressed to her throat, swallowing noisily enough that Catherine could hear it. "I thought he was the real deal, you know? The guy had a job—he was an accountant—a car, a decent family. Tom even took Willow and me to meet his parents one Christmas. They were good people. Married fifty years. I didn't love him, but I liked him. A lot. It had been a long time since a guy had treated me like I wasn't garbage, you know?"

"Did I ever meet him?"

"Yes. Once."

Catherine frowned, thinking. She'd met so many of Zoe's so-called boyfriends that she'd eventually stopped trying to keep track. But now she did remember Tom: an ordinary dark-haired man with a slight build. The only thing that stood out about him was his car. "He had a red Corvette, right? A convertible?"

"Yes. I brought him to Newburyport once. It was a birthday party for Dad. I wanted you all to meet Tom, to see that I'd finally started digging myself out of that black hole I'd been in for so long. What a laugh."

"Why?"

"You have to understand. I had no idea it was happening, not until it was too late." Zoe's voice was so soft that Catherine had to lean forward a little to hear her. "Tom was after Willow. That's why he was with me, I think. Because of her."

Catherine reared back against the arm of the couch as if Zoe had struck her. "You mean he *molested* Willow?" Her stomach twisted.

Zoe's nod was barely perceptible.

Catherine put a hand to her mouth, feeling like she might retch. "How did you find out?"

"Willow told me. He didn't rape her, but he did touch her."

"You left him alone with her?"

"Only a few times, because *I* trusted him, but Willow didn't like him. She begged me not to let him babysit, but I didn't figure out why. All she'd tell me was that he annoyed her and she was old enough to stay alone in the apartment. I usually told Tom not to come over while I was working. But this one time he dropped by while I was at work. After that, Willow told me."

Catherine didn't want to hear any more. "You let a pedophile take care of her," she said. "Instead of calling Mom or me, you left Willow with a strange man!"

"I thought he was good!" Zoe said, huddling her knees up to her chin, her face miserable. "I was trying to be independent, like everyone said I should be. I had no idea he'd hurt her!"

"Because you didn't deserve to be a mother!" Catherine threw the blanket off her legs and got up so fast that she knocked the empty wineglass off the coffee table in front of her. She paced the room. "You still don't. You have no judgment at all! Your mind is too addled from drugs, and you've always been selfish besides! Willow never should have been left alone. And she certainly shouldn't have been left with a pedophile."

"I didn't know Tom was like that!" Zoe shouted back. "I tried to do my best. It's not easy, being a single mom with no education."

Catherine stopped in front of her sister and pointed at the door. "Get out! I don't want to hear how hard things were. You had the same start in life I did, and better than most people. Our parents gave us everything we needed. We all tried to help you, but you just threw your life away, and Willow's, too."

"I did not!" Zoe's face was blotchy, her voice sharp-edged with desperation. "I tried to save Willow's life by leaving her with you!"

"No," Catherine said, jabbing a finger at her. "You ran away to duck out on your debts, maybe, and to leave the past behind, but only after putting your daughter in danger over and over. I'm ashamed to be your sister." She went to the front door and held it open until Zoe walked through it, her shoulders hunched and narrow, then slammed it shut behind her.

CHAPTER NINETEEN

From the crash outside, Eve thought raccoons must have gotten into the garbage and tipped over one of the metal trash cans. She'd been watching television, nearly asleep in her chair. Now she sat bolt upright and muted the sound.

Her heartbeat drummed in her ears as she waited, listening. She hated dealing with raccoons. They terrified her, with their black masks and humanoid hands. Plus, they always looked like they were laughing at some secret joke. A joke at your expense. She didn't want to go outside and chase them away from the trash, make sure the lids were securely locked in place. That had always been Andrew's job.

Andrew. She closed her eyes and pictured him as he'd looked greeting Marta in their home, Marta towering and magnificent in her heels and red sheath. Then she remembered Marta's grief-ravaged face as it had looked in the coffee shop.

Marta and Andrew had had a son. Had her husband offered Marta child support? She hoped so. Andrew had insisted on handling the family's finances. Their investments. Retirement plans. Eve never would have suspected a thing. Idiot.

She should be angry at Andrew. Monumentally angry. Instead, she felt a creeping sorrow, a helpless compassion for both Andrew and Marta.

Oh, what fools they'd all been. Andrew had loved Marta. He would certainly have adored their child, his only son. And then he had lost his child in the end.

With so much pain in the world, Eve thought, it was a wonder that human beings had the courage to keep putting one foot in front of the other.

A series of loud thumps from outside startled her into action. She jumped off the couch and grabbed the broom in the kitchen. Slowly, she opened the back door and peered outside. The trash cans were still upright. What, then, was making all that racket?

Then she saw the body lying on the ground. Eve gasped and slammed the door shut, locked it, and went to grab her cell phone. Just as she was about to dial 911, though, the contours of the prone figure re-formed in her mind: a narrow waist encased in leather, a gentle curve of hip, a small white hand.

Zoe?

Eve raced back to the door, unlocked it, and yanked it open. She approached the figure tentatively as her eyes adjusted to the darkness. Then she squatted down next to the blond head and said her daughter's name.

Zoe was lying facedown on the cement sidewalk that led to the side door of the house. She was breathing, thank God, her hands curled into fists on either side of her head the way Eve remembered her doing in her crib as a baby. Zoe was angry even as an infant, protesting every nap and bedtime, raging with her howls and fists. Of course, that was the age of letting your babies cry themselves to sleep; Eve used to stand in the shower until the crying stopped to keep herself from picking Zoe up.

How differently she would do things now.

"Zoe? Sweetie, are you okay?" Eve said, feeling for the cell phone in her pocket.

Just as she was again about to call 911, Zoe lifted her head, turned to blink slowly at Eve, and smiled. A sloppy grin. Drool on the pavement beneath her face. Or was that vomit? Eve sniffed and moved back a little. Definitely vomit. Was she sick? Drunk?

"Come on! Talk to me, Zoe," Eve said more sharply now.

"Mommy," Zoe said, and dropped her head again. "Nice Mommy."

Eve swore under her breath, grabbed beneath Zoe's arms, and managed to turn her and hoist her to a sitting position. "Can you stand up?"

"Stand up?" Zoe said happily, her head bobbing like a rag doll's. "Stand up, no way!"

"Yes way," Eve muttered. She used her legs—thank God for all that running—and managed to get Zoe to her feet, then half dragged her daughter into the kitchen. She propped Zoe up on one of the chairs by pushing it all the way in to the table, until Zoe was half lying with her head on her arms the way she used to fall asleep if anyone tried to make her do homework.

"I need another drink." Zoe picked her head up again and looked dazedly around the kitchen.

"No. You need coffee," Eve said.

She kept checking Zoe as she made the coffee. Her daughter seemed stable, even peaceful. Her face was damp; Eve wiped it off with a paper towel before tipping a glass of water toward Zoe's lips. It didn't work. Zoe just grinned, and the water ran down the side of her mouth. "Funny," she said.

"Not really," Eve said.

The coffee was ready. She put an ice cube in a mug and poured coffee over it, adding two teaspoons of sugar. She fed the coffee to Zoe by the spoonful, until her daughter was sitting straighter in the chair and looked shell-shocked rather than comatose. Finally Zoe picked up the mug at Eve's prodding and drank the rest of it down. She did the same with a second mug, and even nibbled at a piece of dry toast with cinnamon sugar.

"Yummy," Zoe said. Then her eyes filled with tears. "Sorry. I'm so sorry, Mommy."

"I know," Eve said, and patted Zoe's hand. "What happened? Why are you here?"

"To see you, because Catherine, she hates me." Tears were sliding down Zoe's cheeks, rinsing the rest of the mascara out of her eyelashes. Her face looked like she'd crawled out of a coal mine, streaked black with angry red patches, a nasty bruise on one cheek.

"Oh, honey, your sister doesn't hate you," Eve said.

"Yes. She does."

"Why are you saying this? Did you see her?"

Zoe nodded in slow motion. "I told Cat what happened with Willow, why I really left. That guy, the bastard who hurt her. He's why I left, you know? I told Catherine that, and now she says she's ashamed to be my sister. She says I shouldn't have Willow and I don't think she's right—is she? I'm her real mom! I took her baby blanket from when she was born everywhere, to Florida, even, to the shelters where I told everybody they couldn't steal it or I'd cut them. But Cat says I don't deserve Willow, because I keep putting her in danger. She doesn't get that I'm not like that anymore."

"Hush, now. Everything is going to be all right." Eve put a hand on Zoe's cheek to break into her dizzying monologue, remembering all of the times that Zoe had come to her like this, high or drunk or just in despair. Rambling. "Standing at the brink," as she and Andrew said to each other: "Zoe's standing at the brink again."

"You need a shower and some pajamas," Eve said. "Things will look better in the morning."

Zoe did that slow blink at her again, processing this. "Morning is the fun time," she pronounced, and giggled, though one fat teardrop still clung to her long lashes.

Eve sighed. "Let's hope so, honey."

She stayed in the bathroom while Zoe showered, finally turning off the hot water when she realized Zoe had fallen asleep standing up and was leaning in one corner of the glass enclosure. She noted two new tattoos—an owl on her lower back, Chinese letters scrawled down one arm—as she helped her into a clean T-shirt and sweatpants. Zoe's head was heavy on her shoulder as Eve walked her into the bedroom and tucked her in, sitting on the chair next to the bed for a while to make sure Zoe wouldn't vomit again.

Downstairs, Eve fished in her handbag for the business card Grey had given her with his number on it. She hesitated; it was late, after ten o'clock. But then she dialed with trembling fingers. Grey was close by and seemed like the only real friend Zoe had right now. She reached him on the second ring and explained the situation.

"I want us to talk to her together," Eve said, pressing the phone hard enough against her cheek that she could feel her molars beneath her skin. "Can you come here tomorrow morning?"

"For an intervention, you mean?" he asked.

"Let's call it a conversation. We need to help Zoe stay straight. She's come this far. I can't let her go again."

"Agreed. I'll be there," Grey said.

"Thank you."

Next, Eve dialed Catherine. She sounded groggy and irritable and was far less amenable to Eve's suggestion that she come to Newburyport in the morning. "Mom, it's almost eleven o'clock and I'm in bed," she said. "Couldn't this have waited until morning? I can't think straight. And it's not like this is an emergency."

"You don't know what kind of state your sister was in."

Eve could practically hear Catherine's eyes rolling as she said, "Oh, I think I can imagine it. Hardly a news flash if she's drunk."

"Catherine, that's unfair. She's been sober for months. Something must have happened to make her relapse."

"Not necessarily."

Eve heard it in Catherine's voice, though: a note of guilt. "What happened between you two?"

"You don't want to know, Mom. And I don't want to talk about it. You're on her side. I get that. It's always been that way: you and Zoe, Dad and me."

"No," Eve said, though of course Catherine was right.

"Yes," Catherine insisted. "And now you're asking me to come over and help fix Zoe like I always have. To be her second mother. Well, I'm sick to death of that. I am beyond done with being her caretaker. Nobody has ever held Zoe accountable for her actions. That's why she's the way she is."

"Are you implying that your father and I are responsible for your sister's behavior?"

Catherine sighed. "Go to bed, Mom. I'm not playing the blame game now."

Eve swallowed what was left of her pride and said, "I need you to be here tomorrow morning to talk to Zoe with me. Please. Do it for me, if not for your sister."

"I don't know if I can stomach that. I really don't."

"Catherine, please. Grey is coming, too. We need to work this out together. I'm not letting Zoe slip away again. I want Willow to be here, too."

"Absolutely not," Catherine said fiercely. "Willow's at Russell's for the weekend. She texted me to say she's going straight to school from there on Monday. Anyway, I refuse to subject her to one more second of her mother's irresponsible behavior. You have no idea how much danger Zoe has already put her in."

Eve shivered, feeling the icy floor through the soles of her slippers. "What do you mean? What kind of danger?"

"Ask Zoe," Catherine said, and hung up.

Catherine didn't sleep well. How dare her mother ask her—no, *expect* her—to give up her Sunday to drive all the way the hell up to Newburyport, for some family intervention with Zoe that would be just as useless as anything else they'd ever tried?

She felt hot beneath the covers. She was so irritated with Zoe and with her mother, too, that the sheets might as well have been woven out of fiberglass. Her skin was on fire.

She got up and took a shower, then finished the book she was reading as the darkness finally started to lift and the sun stained the gray sky a watered-down pink. She made scrambled eggs and read the newspaper, waiting until midmorning to get dressed. She refused to kowtow to Zoe's needs, not ever again. Especially not after her sister's horrible revelations about Willow's abuse.

Now she and Russell would have to deal with that, too, on top of everything else. They'd have to take Willow to see another therapist. Someone who specialized in sexual abuse. Her stomach turned at the thought. What, exactly, had the poor kid been subjected to?

It didn't bear thinking about. Yet Catherine knew it had to be dealt with and that she was the one who would have to do it. Otherwise, Willow could end up with bigger trust issues than she already had.

Meanwhile, what good was Zoe? None whatsoever. She'd followed her usual pattern: obliterated herself with alcohol or drugs, then gone to their mother for absolution. *Oops! So sorry, Mommy! I was bad!*

Fine. Let Zoe live her miserable life. Catherine wanted no part of it. She was an adult. An adult in charge of a girl, now a teenager, who was more troubled, even, than Catherine had suspected when Willow had first come to live with her. No matter how much it cost, she vowed to fight Zoe for custody if things came down to that.

Her phone rang as Catherine was leaving to meet Bethany for a walk. She was relieved to be walking outside and breathing in the cold air. "Hello?"

It was Russell. "We need to talk about Willow." His voice was grim.

Catherine had forgotten her Bluetooth; she pressed the cell phone to her ear as she navigated the crowded sidewalk and tried to hear Russell over the steady throbbing noise of traffic. "Why? What's going on?"

"That's what I want to know. Willow gave Nola some lame excuse about needing to leave our place early yesterday so she could study instead of spending the day. She took off while I was at the grocery store yesterday morning. I wasn't going to make a big deal out of this, but after thinking about it more last night, I decided that was a mistake. I need you and Willow to understand that when it's my weekend, I call the shots."

"What are you talking about? What are you accusing me of, exactly?" Catherine stopped walking so suddenly that a man behind her bumped her shoulder. He muttered something and kept moving past her while she stood there.

"You let her come home yesterday, and it was my weekend," Russell said angrily. "That's not playing fair, Catherine. You always accuse me of bringing Willow home too soon when it's my night for dinner, but when it suits you, when you're lonely on the weekend, you let her come home whenever she pleases."

"I do not! Russell, she's not here!" Catherine said, feeling her heart start racing. "Willow never came home yesterday. In fact, she texted me to say she planned to spend Sunday night at your place because you were going to help her with a paper. I thought you were taking her to school tomorrow morning. Why? What did she tell you?"

"She didn't tell me anything!" Russell roared. "That's what I was saying! Willow texted me while I was at the store yesterday morning and said she was leaving to study with a friend at your house."

"Oh my God," Catherine whispered. "So where is she?"

"I don't know. Jesus. Where's Zoe? Could Willow have sneaked off to see her?"

"That must be it," Catherine said. "Mom called last night and asked me to come to Newburyport to speak to Zoe. Apparently Zoe had some kind of relapse and was drinking. She's at Mom's house in Newburyport right now, and Mom wanted Willow to come with me to talk to Zoe. Some kind of family intervention, I think. Mom asked Zoe's friend Grey to be there, too. I told Mom I didn't want to do it, but maybe Mom called Willow and asked her to come anyway."

"She wouldn't do that," Russell said. "Your mother would never tell Willow to come up to Newburyport alone. And, anyway, that still doesn't explain where Willow was last night."

Catherine was having trouble breathing. "With another friend, maybe? So she could go to Mom's this morning on her own without telling us? She knows how we feel about Zoe. And, if Mom thought it would help Zoe to hear Willow ask her to stay sober, Mom would do it."

"Did she have money?"

"I don't know," Catherine said. "But the bus doesn't cost much. She'd figure out a way. Look, I'm hanging up now to call Mom. I'll call you back."

"All right," Russell said.

Catherine dialed Willow's number. When there was no answer, she called her mother; when Eve picked up, she barked into the phone, "Is Willow there?"

"No, of course not," her mother said. "You said she was at Russell's."

"I thought she was, but Russell just called me to say that Willow didn't spend the night at his house," Catherine said, fumbling for the right words. Her throat was tight with fear as she explained what was going on.

"Could she have spent the night with a friend?" Eve asked.

"I don't know! Did you talk to her? Tell her what happened with Zoe last night?"

"I didn't tell her about Zoe's behavior, but Willow did call me this morning. She wanted to know if she could come up here next weekend and maybe see her mother at my house, since you don't want her seeing Zoe unsupervised. But I would never, ever tell Willow to see her mother without your permission. I certainly didn't tell her to come up here this morning."

Catherine thought about this, biting her lip hard enough to hurt. "Did you tell her Zoe's at your house, though?"

"Yes."

"All right. Keep Zoe there, will you, please? I'm betting Willow might try to come up and see her. I'll head up to Newburyport and catch up with her there."

"That doesn't make sense, honey. Willow wouldn't come up here without you, would she?"

"Why not? She went to Salisbury by herself," Catherine said. "I don't know what Willow's capable of anymore, Mom. Look, I've got to go. I'll call you when I know something." She hung up and dialed Russell as she hurried back up her porch steps. She told him what her mother had said, adding, "Can you stay home today, in case Willow shows up back at your place? I'm going up to Mom's. Zoe's there, and Willow talked to Mom this morning, so she knows that. I'm betting that Willow's on her way to Newburyport."

"Wait," Russell said.

Catherine heard a voice in the background: Nola. She waited several moments before he came back on. "Nola says she knows where Willow might have spent last night."

Catherine unlocked her front door, grabbed the car keys off the table in the front hall, and let herself out again. "Why would Nola know?"

"She took her there, apparently," Russell said. "They drove out to Framingham. Willow wanted to meet her real dad. Some guy named Mike Navarro. Have you heard of him?"

Catherine swore under her breath. Nola's fault, again! "Yes. He used to be Zoe's boyfriend. Then they were roommates for a while. I don't think he's really Willow's dad. Did Nola give you his address?"

"Yes. She's finding the number for me online right now. Hopefully the guy has a landline. Wait for me to call him before you start driving north, all right? Otherwise you might be on a wild-goose chase."

"All right. But hurry," Catherine said, because she couldn't imagine waiting at the house and doing nothing if Willow was in some kind of danger.

But maybe she wasn't. Maybe—in the best of all possible worlds—she really *had* found her father, and it was as simple as that: locating Mike Navarro, whom Catherine vaguely remembered as a skinny nerd who used to love playing Ping-Pong with them in the basement of their house in Newburyport. Mike had come up to Chance Harbor with them once, too, and entertained them with magic tricks.

Russell called a few minutes later. "All right," he said. "I talked to Mike. He says Willow spent the night at his house. She told him she'd cleared that with us."

"That little sneak." Catherine felt a pulse start in her temple, like someone was pushing something sharp there. "Why is she lying to us about everything all of a sudden?"

"I don't know," Russell said, sounding grim, "but I'm sure you're going to say this is all my fault."

Catherine wanted to blame him. To blame someone. But she said, "No, it's not all you. It's everything."

They were both quiet for a moment. Then he went on. "Mike thinks you're right that Willow's trying to see Zoe. He says he dropped her off at the bus station in Framingham this morning. She told him she was taking a bus to her grandmother's house."

"Did he know which bus?"

"No," Russell said. "But according to what he told me, and to the schedule I found online, she probably got on the eight o'clock from Framingham to Boston. If she got directly on the nine o'clock bus to Newburyport after that, she'd be there by ten ten."

"I'm driving up there," Catherine said. "Oh, and tell Nola thanks very much for continuing to make my life such a fucking nightmare."

Zoe sat bolt upright in bed, as if an alarm had gone off. Her short hair was pushed to one side of her narrow face, giving her the look of a molting bird. The bruise on her cheek was an extravagant blossom of red and purple. "Why am I in my old room?" she asked in astonishment.

Eve had been sitting beside her since Catherine's call, the cell phone in her hand, about to wake Zoe and ask if she'd talked to Willow last night. "I put you to bed here. What do you remember about last night?"

"Not a lot." Zoe looked quickly around the room, then stared intently down at herself, as if checking for wounds.

Eve waited quietly beside her. She imagined this must be a routine that Zoe had developed over the years. She shuddered a little, thinking of all the times Zoe must have been as out of it as she'd seemed to be last night. So much could have happened to a young woman in that vulnerable state. Probably *had* happened, in Zoe's case.

Then Eve remembered what Catherine had said about Willow. The poor child. What had she seen and heard through the years? And where could Willow be now? Eve had to hope that Willow was sensible enough to keep herself safe.

Zoe took a deep breath and looked at her now with troubled eyes. "I remember you finding me outside," she said. "I was pretty drunk."

"Yes. Did you do anything else?"

"What do you mean?"

"Drugs, honey."

Zoe shook her head. "I was on my way home from Cambridge, but I was upset, so I stopped at a bar in Newburyport. Some guy kept buying me drinks. I made myself throw up in the ladies' room because I realized I'd had too much, but I knew I still shouldn't drive. I walked here. God. I don't even remember where I left the car."

"Where were you before the bar?"

"Catherine's." Zoe put a hand to her mouth for a minute, wincing, then said, "We had a fight. A bad one. She threw me out of her house."

"What was it about?"

"Willow." Zoe lay back down on the pillow and pulled the covers to her chin. "Cat hates me now because of some things I told her."

"What things?"

Zoe closed her eyes and thrashed her head hard against the pillow. "I don't want to tell you. I shouldn't have even told Catherine. I was just trying to explain why I left Willow. How I was trying to protect her. But Catherine told me I've fucked up Willow's whole life." She opened her eyes again and stared up at Eve. "Do you think that's true?"

"No," Eve said with as much certainty as she could inject into her voice. "Willow is resilient and smart and loving. Anyone who knows her can see that."

"I'm not sure. That's what Willow *lets* us see," Zoe said miserably. "I think she might be unhappy, Mom. Really unhappy. And that's my fault."

She could be right, Eve thought, but there was no point in speculating about that. "Did you talk to Willow last night, honey?"

Zoe shook her head. "No. Why?"

Eve debated about whether to tell Zoe that Willow was missing, then decided there was no point in saying anything about that, either, because it might upset Zoe. She couldn't chance that now, with Grey on his way. She could only hope that Willow had spent the night with a friend and was perfectly fine, just feeling rebellious because Catherine wouldn't let her see her mother.

Not that Eve blamed Catherine for being protective, but the sisters were going to have to work something out that would allow Willow more regular contact with Zoe, at least if they could keep Zoe on the straight and narrow. Which was her main goal this morning, in asking Catherine and Grey and Willow to come to Newburyport: Eve wanted to convince Zoe that her actions affected all of them, not just herself.

Finally, Eve said, "No reason. I just wondered. Anyway, I'm glad you came here last night. I've been trying to find time to see you alone. I need to tell you some things that might help you. I fucked up, too."

Zoe gave her a sharp look. "Mom! I can't believe you said the F word."

"I meant it, though. I royally fucked up."

"Quit saying that! It doesn't sound like you!"

"I'm sorry, honey. But there really isn't another word for what I did. For so many mistakes I made."

"Like what?" Zoe challenged, then instantly raised both hands to ward off an answer. "No. I don't want to know."

"Yes, you do." Eve sat up beside her. "And I don't have any choice. I have to tell you these things because they concern you. You and your father," she added.

"Daddy," Zoe said mournfully. "He hated me as much as Cat does."

"No, sweetie. He just couldn't see you as a person."

"What does that even mean?" Zoe chewed on a thumbnail.

Eve put a hand on her daughter's wrist, tugged Zoe's fingers away from her mouth. "Daddy wasn't your real father."

"*What?*"

Eve had never actually seen someone's mouth drop open in surprise before, but her daughter's did now. It was almost comic.

"See?" she said. "You're not the only one who fucks things up." Eve watched as a series of complicated emotions passed over her daughter's pretty freckled face. Waited for the inevitable questions.

Finally, Zoe said, "Did Daddy know I wasn't his?"

"Oh, yes."

"So you had an affair after Catherine was born? Wow. Why?"

Eve hesitated as she formed a response. She was so sick and tired of lies. Lying had obviously never done their family any good at all. "Your father was seeing another woman and I was hurt. Devastated, really. I thought it was somehow my fault that he wasn't satisfied. I had an affair because of that, only the affair turned into something more. I fell in love with that man and got pregnant with you."

Zoe's face was pinched with shock. "Who was he?"

"Your dad's cousin Malcolm. He was a fisherman on PEI."

"Did I ever meet him?" Zoe looked panicked now, her eyes darting about the room.

"No." Eve felt the weight of her old sorrow, heavy and damp, as if she were lying facedown in a chilly field, a boot on her neck.

One therapist she'd seen after Zoe disappeared, when Andrew was trying to convince her to have a memorial service for her, had tried to explain to Eve that each person's sorrows harken back to some original pain. The past is always with us, the therapist said, so there's no point in ignoring any of it. "Love yourself as you were in childhood, during adolescence, and as a young woman, and you will love yourself now," she had promised.

Eve hadn't ever tried following that advice. But now she knew that the therapist was right. She could see in Zoe's adult face how she'd looked as an infant, her cheeks round, her hands chubby. She remembered the satisfying physical sensation of Zoe clinging to her neck when she cried, hot with fever or murmuring in her sleep.

At the same time, Eve could picture Zoe exactly as she'd looked as a skinny girl in elementary school, wearing a hot pink snowsuit and tunneling through snowdrifts with Catherine. She could also envision Zoe as a teenage girl in tight jeans and tank tops with armholes cut dangerously low, a girl who'd learned the power she had to attract boys and men, and as a harried single mother scraping by in an apartment where every day there were noisy arguments in the apartments around her, the sounds of despair and anger filtering through the floor and ceiling.

Yes. The past was with her, and with Zoe, too, going all the way back to Eve's own feelings of anger and abandonment with Andrew, to her affair with Malcolm and Zoe's beginning, to Eve's love for this daughter and her mistakes winding through Zoe's life, through Zoe's own love for Willow and mistakes as a mother, all of that twining together like strands of the same rope.

"Mom?" Zoe said, startling Eve into wakefulness again, though she'd been sitting there with her eyes open. "What happened to my real dad?"

"Malcolm drowned before you were born," she said.

Zoe's eyes swam with tears. "Oh."

"But he does have family. They would love to see you, if you wanted that."

"I'm not sure I do. Did Daddy know it was Malcolm?"

"Yes. He said he didn't care. Daddy just wanted me to stay with him. He wanted *you*, too," Eve added.

"But he didn't really, did he?" Zoe raked a hand through her hair. "That's why everything I did drove him crazy. It makes sense now. Why he couldn't love me like he loved Catherine."

Eve waited. She had thought Zoe would be angry: furious that her father had died, or that Eve had stayed with Andrew, or at the very least, that they'd kept this information from her. "I wanted to tell you before," she said.

"I bet." Oddly, Zoe didn't seem angry. She simply drew her knees up to her chin and clasped her arms around them, rocking a little on the bed. "Thank you for telling me now," she said. "That must have been hard, Mommy. All of it."

"It was," Eve said. "Especially because one of your father's—I mean Andrew's—conditions for our marriage was that we didn't tell you. He was afraid you might not accept him as your father if you knew."

"Maybe he was right," Zoe said as the doorbell rang.

Eve glanced at the clock on the bedside table. "Good God," she said, "it's getting late."

"So? Are you expecting someone?"

"Yes." Eve scrambled out of bed and dashed across the hall to her room, calling, "I invited Grey for breakfast."

"What? Why?"

"Because I thought you could use a friend," Eve said, hoping this would go over well, that Zoe wouldn't feel tricked or ganged up on when Catherine showed up, too.

And Willow? Where could Willow be? Eve wondered, her palms slick with nerves as she dressed quickly and made it downstairs just as the doorbell rang a second time. When she opened the door, she was startled to see a woman with Grey.

"This is my mother, Madame Justine," he said. "She cares a great deal about Zoe. I thought it might help if she was here, too."

"It's nice that you both made the trip," Eve said. "Thank you. Please come in."

Madame Justine was short and round, with her son's deep olive complexion and intelligent dark eyes. She wore a long black skirt and a short blue jacket with a brightly patterned purple shawl wound at her neck. Her long black hair was silvered with gray and she wore silver hoops in her ears.

"Please, sit down," Eve said.

"You have a lovely home." Madame Justine's voice was a rich alto, almost as deep as a man's.

"Is Zoe still here? Is she all right?" Grey asked.

"Yes. She is now. But she wasn't in great shape last night."

Before Eve could say more, Zoe came downstairs, wearing a pair of Eve's leggings and one of Andrew's white shirts. Andrew wasn't a big man, but the shirt hung nearly to Zoe's knees. She wore the sleeves rolled up.

"Hey, Mama Justine," she said. "What are you doing here?"

Zoe didn't sound alarmed, only curious, Eve was relieved to see. Now she regretted her decision to call Catherine. Perhaps, given what the sisters had gone through last night, it would be better not to involve Catherine.

"You sit down right here, Zoe," Madame Justine commanded, patting the couch cushion between herself and Grey. "You gave your poor mama a scare, daughter."

Eve started at the word, feeling immediately defensive. This woman knew more about Zoe's life, past and present, than Eve did, and that rankled. "Can I get anyone coffee or tea? Something to eat?" she offered.

Zoe and Grey both asked for coffee. Madame Justine shook her head.

Eve was glad to escape to the kitchen, where she started a pot of coffee and then, still not ready to return to the living room, made toast and put it on a tray with butter and jam. As she brought everything into the living room, Zoe was laughing at something Madame Justine was saying about telling a couple's fortune at the Salisbury Beach boardwalk.

Once she'd sat down on the chair across from Zoe and Madame Justine, Eve fumbled for words. "Thank you both for coming," she said.

"Why did they, Mom?" Zoe said. "I have my car in Newburyport. I can drive myself back to Salisbury. I mean, as long as I can find it and the car hasn't been towed." She looked momentarily chagrined. "It isn't even my car. I'm supposed to deliver it to Maine tomorrow."

"I'm sure it's fine," Eve said. "Anyway, that's not why I called them." She took a deep breath, wondering how to begin the conversation.

"You sure you don't want me to pick you up?" Nola had hissed into the phone when Willow called her Saturday night to say Mike wasn't her real dad but she was spending the night there anyway. "You don't even know this guy."

"He's gay," Willow said. "Don't worry. Nothing bad's going to happen."

"I still don't get why you want to stay there," Nola said.

"Because Mike was with my mom at the university. He says he doesn't know who my dad is, but I think he has to, since she got pregnant right after they broke up," Willow said, thinking things through as she talked to Nola. "Anyway, I'm going to find out whatever he knows. Just cover for me, okay? You owe me that much for all the shit you've pulled."

Nola had finally promised, so Willow had hung up and told Mike she was tired. "Is it okay if I spend the night? Mom says it's fine." She waved the phone at him. "I was just talking to her."

He had frowned. "How will you get back?"

"Oh, no probs. I told my mom I'd meet her at my nana's house in Newburyport. We go there almost every Sunday. To visit her, you know, since my grandpa died. If you drive me to the bus station in Framingham, I can just take the bus to Boston and get another one to Newburyport."

On Sunday morning Willow woke to the smell of pancakes and bacon. Sammy served her a plate with a pancake made up to look like a face, with a bacon smile, banana slices for eyes, and whipped-cream hair. Mike was still in the shower, he said, and then Sammy went to the gym and Mike came downstairs, wearing a striped shirt and jeans.

They ate together and looked at the newspaper. Finally, as Willow helped Mike clear the table, she said, "You must remember the guy my mom dated after you broke up, right?" she said.

Mike shifted his feet at the sink and looked worried. "I know what you're trying to find out, Miss Nancy Drew, but I don't know a thing. Your mom wasn't really dating anybody steadily."

"All right. Who did she hook up with, then?"

Mike sighed. "You need to ask her that."

"I can't!" Willow said in desperation. "My mom'd been gone for five years. If I start bugging her about things now, I'm afraid she'll leave again!"

Mike put his arms around her, drew her close. "That's the risk you'll have to take if you bring up this subject. But I know your mom. Zoe is always honest if she's not on anything. If she does choose to answer your questions, she'll tell you the truth. Wouldn't that be better than me guessing who your dad is and getting it wrong?"

Willow wanted to resist being near him. Being near anyone. But Mike smelled good—lemony from the shower or the dishwasher soap, she wasn't sure. She rested her head on his shoulder for a moment before pulling away again. "I don't see why this has to be such a big secret."

"Me, either," he said. "But Zoe obviously feels uncomfortable talking about it."

"Maybe she doesn't even know which guy was my dad," Willow said. "Maybe she was hooking up at parties."

By the way Mike's arms stiffened, she sensed she'd stumbled onto the truth at last. "Oh God," she said softly, and pulled away to look up at him. "That's what happened, isn't it?"

"Willow, I cannot discuss this with you, truly," Mike said. "It would be disrespectful to your mother, for whom I still feel a great deal of, perhaps misplaced, affection. Please do not ask me again."

He dropped her off at the bus stop. Willow boarded the next bus to Boston like a robot, handing the driver her ticket blindly and dropping into the first available seat next to a fat old guy with his nose practically resting on his phone. He smelled like coffee and bananas. Willow bit the inside of her cheek to take her mind off the stink, tasting salt and blood, swallowing hard.

At South Station, she got off the bus and called Nana before going in to look at the schedules. She had to see her mother—her real mom—alone if she was going to find out any more about her dad. When she asked Nana if she could meet with Zoe at her house in Newburyport, there was a hesitation.

"What is it, Nana?" Willow demanded. "Has something happened to my mom?"

"No, no, honey. She's fine. She's right here, in fact. Zoe spent the night at my house last night. And I think it's fine if you want to meet her here next weekend, but you have to ask Catherine. She's still your guardian, and it's her job to look out for you. We have to respect that. Please don't make a plan with Zoe behind Catherine's back. That's all I'm asking."

Willow was infuriated. Who were these so-called adults in charge, telling her what to do? None of them could even manage their own freakin' lives. Why should they be allowed to manage hers?

"Fine," she said. "Listen, I've got to go. Talk to you later."

She hung up and wandered into South Station. It was noisy with weekend travelers this morning, but it had been nearly empty the night her mom left. Willow's teeth had chattered so hard that night that she was scared other people could hear them. She'd been so cold and scared, and her jacket had been wet from the rain. She'd pressed her forehead into one corner of the wooden bench after calling Catherine, praying for her aunt to come fast even though she didn't believe in God. If he existed, why would he let her end up in a bus station with a mom who hated taking care of her so much she ran away?

Of course, now she knew why: It was because her mom wasn't in love when she got pregnant. Hadn't wanted a baby at all.

Why didn't Mom have an abortion? Maybe she wanted one but she was too broke or found out she was pregnant too late, Willow thought miserably.

She didn't want to go back to Russell's. She didn't want to go back to Catherine's, either. Most of all, she didn't want to face anybody's questions about her life. Her life was her own now.

Willow stared up at the departures board. Where could she go, just for the day? She felt around in her pocket and came up with fourteen dollars. Where would that take her?

For the first time, she imagined her own mother doing this: running away. Picking out a new place and just getting on a bus to go there so she could start over.

Willow wanted a new start. She wanted to feel in charge of her own life, instead of always being at the mercy of the adults.

Maybe just for today, she'd pretend to be a girl who didn't have a home. Plenty of kids her age figured out how to live on the street. And this would be good practice for a time when her mom wigged out again, Catherine decided she couldn't keep her, and Russell had no place for her anymore.

It was time she learned to fend for herself in the world. She'd be fine. She had fourteen dollars and pepper spray with her. More than most people had.

Willow studied the bus station departures board again and made up her mind: a one-way bus ticket to Salem. Not too far, but not too close, either. Nobody would think to look for her there. She'd pay cash when she bought the ticket so she couldn't be tracked. Just like her mother.

She turned off her phone and went up to the counter, keeping one hand on the pepper spray in her pocket.

CHAPTER TWENTY

By the time she arrived in Newburyport, Catherine's palms were so sweaty that she had to keep wiping them on her coat. She was only a few minutes ahead of the 10:10 bus from Boston; people were already lined up to take the southbound bus, holding their places in line on the sidewalk with odd objects while they went inside to buy tickets: a pen, a thermos, a tiny plastic alien. She called her mother to see if Willow had been in touch, but she hadn't.

Catherine remained outside the station, shivering in the November wind. When the bus arrived and disgorged its passengers, she scanned the faces anxiously for Willow's.

Willow wasn't on the bus. Jesus. Had they gotten things wrong? Maybe Willow had decided to take the train instead and was walking to her mother's house from the commuter rail station across town. Or had she, God forbid, run out of money and tried to hitchhike? Or gone somewhere else entirely?

Catherine was nearly panting with fear, feeling like she might pass out. She paced outside of the bus station for a few more minutes, trying to decide what to do, then got back in the car and drove to her mother's.

She wouldn't let herself entertain the possibility that Willow might be somewhere else entirely. Willow knew Zoe was in Newburyport. She had to be coming here next! Willow had seen Mike, and now she would demand answers from Zoe about her father

Catherine intended to get answers as well. This mystery about Willow's father had dragged on long enough. Willow was a teenager and deserved to know the truth, for medical information if for no other reason. If Zoe was going to remain in Willow's life, she would have to tell her daughter who her father was; otherwise, Willow's curiosity would continue to eat away at her.

A stranger's car, some kind of low-slung black Porsche, was parked in the driveway behind her mother's Subaru. At the sight of it, Catherine's breath caught, the air trapped as suddenly as if someone had pushed a fist against her throat. Her sister had a job delivering exotic cars. Zoe must still be here.

She marched up the porch steps, her pulse roaring in her ears. Catherine wished she didn't have to go inside; in her current state, it felt as if the house walls might not contain her. She wanted to stand out here on the front lawn and scream her sister's name, make Zoe come outside.

And then what? In her worst imaginings, she saw herself slapping her sister. Or demanding that she go back to whatever pitiful life she'd been living in Florida. Anything but have Zoe stay here and make trouble.

Catherine entered the house without bothering to knock or ring the doorbell. "Mom!" she yelled, deliberately fixing her eyes straight ahead to avoid seeing her own white-hot reflection in the hall mirror.

Her emotions were so intense at this moment that it felt as if she might be dreaming, the sort of dream where the unthinkable happened: she would melt in the energy of her own gaze, or her body could float up to the hallway ceiling and then, in a strong gust of wind, be sent out the door like a balloon. Fairy-tale feelings.

The kind of fairy tale where witches cooked children and trolls lived under bridges.

"Mom!" she yelled again. "Where are you? And where's Zoe?"

"Right here." Zoe materialized in the kitchen doorway at the end of the hall, facing Catherine with her shoulders and feet squared.

She looked good. Catherine narrowed her eyes at her sister, taking in every detail. Zoe didn't appear to be hungover or beat-up, other than a bruise on her cheek. She looked strong and calm. Focused.

"Where's Willow?" Catherine demanded.

Zoe crossed her arms. "Not here."

"You're lying." Catherine's first instinct was to push past her and search the house.

"Why would she be here?" Zoe said. "She lives with you."

"Because she wants to talk to you!"

Zoe shifted her stance but kept her eyes locked on Catherine. "Well, she's not here. Look around if you want."

Now Catherine's chest was painfully tight, her breathing shallow. "You really haven't talked to Willow today? Or texted her?"

"No," Zoe said. "I came straight here last night after I saw you. Well, after a few drinks at the old watering hole, which apparently nobody thinks was a good idea. Including me." She gave an odd, forced little chuckle. "Remember you and me at the Thirsty Whale? That time we pretended to be twins? That place hasn't changed. Same sad sacks at the bar."

Catherine nodded impatiently. Her memory of that night had more to do with trying to stop Zoe from going home with a man twice her age. "Give me your phone."

Zoe pulled it out of her pocket and held it up so Catherine could look at it. "It's dead as a door knocker. I forgot the charger."

"Give it to me!"

Zoe tossed it over. Catherine pressed the buttons and discovered she was telling the truth. Another woman, short and stocky and dressed in peculiar clothes, appeared behind Zoe and stepped forward to stand next to her. The stranger was shorter than Zoe and had a strong face with a broad, flat forehead and round chin.

The woman stared at Catherine with unnerving dark eyes that looked solid to the touch, like fruit pits, and slipped her arm around Zoe's waist. "You must be the sister," she said.

"Yes. Who are you?" Catherine asked, though now she remembered that her mother had said Grey would be here. This woman must be Grey's mother. The pulse beating at her temple had increased to a stab of pain behind her right eye, the first symptom of the blinding headaches Catherine got now and then, usually accompanied by vertigo so intense that she had to lie down, preferably on a cold tiled floor.

"I am Madame Justine." The woman drew herself up another half inch. "Zoe's friend."

Zoe visibly relaxed as Madame Justine put an arm around her waist. "Catherine, what are you doing here, anyway?" Her sister's tone was almost cordial. "Did you really drive all this way looking for Willow? Why didn't you just call Mom?"

"Mom called *me*," Catherine said. "She wanted me to come up here and take part in some kind of intervention with family and friends. She wants us to talk you into staying on the straight and narrow."

"Oh. Sweet of her, but you're too late. We did that already."

"Doesn't matter. I wasn't going to bother coming for that," Catherine said. "I mean, why would I? There's never any point. But then Russell called and said Willow didn't spend the night at his house like she was supposed to, and now we're looking for her."

"You must be out of your mind with worry," Eve said, joining them in the hall and standing behind Madame Justine. The color had been rinsed from her face and she looked exhausted. "No word from her yet?"

Catherine shook her head. "Not unless Zoe's lying."

Zoe rolled her eyes. "Why would I lie? And why do you and Russell think Willow wants to see me so badly that she'd sneak up here by herself to do it?" she asked Catherine.

"Because Nola took her to Mike Navarro's house yesterday. . . ."

"What?" Zoe interrupted. "*Mike's* house? Why?" Now she looked worried, too.

"Willow thought Mike was her real dad," Eve said. "She told me that when we were up at Chance Harbor. But he's not, is he?"

"Oh, God," Zoe said softly. "Mike? No." She looked wobbly suddenly, and Madame Justine squeezed her waist to keep her upright.

"Come and sit down, daughter," she said, guiding Zoe back into the living room.

Daughter? Catherine thought, following them.

She stopped at the sight of Grey, who was entering the living room from the kitchen, carrying a pot of coffee. His gaze felt hot on her skin. She felt her cheeks burn.

"Hello, Catherine," he said. "I was hoping you would decide to come this morning."

Zoe looked at Grey and rolled her eyes. "Oh, Jesus," she said. "I should have known you'd fall for the virgin."

"Shut up, Zoe," Catherine said automatically. "I need to talk to you."

Zoe shrugged. "So talk. Who's stopping you?"

"Not here. Alone." Catherine pointed to the stairs, determined not to look at Grey.

"I don't think that's a good idea, honey," Eve said, looking from her to Zoe. "Say what you want. We're all family here. That's why I wanted us all together today."

"I didn't come here to help you with Zoe," Catherine said. "I came because I'm worried about Willow and Zoe owes me some answers. I need to talk to her alone."

"No, thanks." Zoe dropped onto the couch next to Grey and folded her arms. "Mom's right. Whatever you want to say to me, do it here. No more secrets. We're all worried about Willow. Meanwhile, everybody here should know just how supportive my sister is."

"That is true," Madame Justine said. "We are all very eager to hear this." She perched on the arm of the couch next to Zoe.

Grey, to Catherine's shock, now put an arm around Zoe's shoulders. "Eve's right," he said. "Say your piece, Catherine, whatever it is. Let's all work things out together. We need to show a united front where Willow is concerned."

"This is none of your business!" Catherine said, finally daring to look at him square on. He didn't flinch.

"Of course it's his business," Eve corrected her impatiently. "Grey cares about Zoe. He lives with her. Zoe was his sister's friend. And he cares about Willow, too." She was standing in the living room doorway, effectively blocking Catherine's exit from the room.

Catherine felt trapped. She might as well have been a rabbit surrounded by coyotes, quivering in the middle of a field as the other three stared her down. She felt anger rise like heated mercury up her spine. How had it come to this—that she, who had done everything right all her life, had ended up on the outside of her own family, looking in?

Catherine swiveled to face Zoe, hands fisted at her sides. "All right. I'll say what I came to say: I hate you," she told Zoe, speaking under her breath at first, her words steadily gaining volume as she continued. "Know why? Because you're a selfish little bitch. You always have been, and you haven't changed. Anything for attention, right? Tantrums when you were two. Night terrors in elementary school, or climbing too high or running too fast. Always falling down and crying your head off, because it never failed: Mom or Dad came running to pick you up. Or I did!"

"I was clumsy as a kid," Zoe said, not taking her eyes off Catherine. "And adventuresome. Not a great mix."

"Yeah, well, who was there to pick you up? I was! All my life I've been trying to keep you from hurting yourself. From killing yourself! Drugs, alcohol, screwing all the wrong guys: you kept making sure you fell down, didn't you?"

"It wasn't all my fault," Zoe said. Her eyes were glazing over, as if a fog were coming in now over the blue irises.

"I don't care," Catherine snapped. "The point is I'm sick to death of always having to be responsible for you. I'm done! If you want to run away again or get wasted, be my guest. I. Don't. Care. But I do care about Willow, and if you dare try to take her back, you'll have a real fight on your hands!" She was shouting by now, her fists curled so tightly that her nails dug into the fleshy pads of her palms like talons.

Zoe jumped to her feet, ignoring the pleas by Grey and Madame Justine and even their own mother to please sit down, stay calm, talk this out.

"You think you're the absolute shit, don't you?" She took a step toward Catherine. "You always have. Just because school was easy for you and Dad thought you were the bomb, and you pussyfooted around with guys and married the first decent one who stuck his dick in you, you think you're better than me. Better than anyone! And that's a laugh, because your life is as fucked-up as anybody's!"

"I do not think I'm better than anyone," Catherine said. "I only know I'm better than *you*."

She heard a sharp intake of breath from her mother. "Girls! Please, that's enough! You're *sisters*. We need to support each other, not tear each other down."

"Fine," Catherine said, not taking her eyes off Zoe, whose cheeks were pink now. "I'll support Zoe in anything she wants to do that doesn't involve Willow."

"Willow's *mine*," Zoe said. "I carried her for nine months. I raised her for the first ten years of her life. What claim do you really have?"

"I'm her legal guardian! More importantly, I'm the only constant in her life," Catherine said. "Face it, Zoe. A dog can have puppies the same way you had a kid. Any bitch in heat can do that. But you kept running away. You're doing it now, even. You might be physically present, but you're drinking and refusing to commit to anything. How can Willow trust you, when you won't even say whether you're going to be here next *week*, never mind for Willow's sixteenth birthday party, her first heartbreak, or her college applications?"

"Please, Catherine," her mother said. "You're going too far. Zoe doesn't deserve this."

Catherine ignored her. "And what about down the road, Zoe?" she went on. "How about the night Willow gets drunk at a college party and calls, crying, for you to pick her up? Or when she gets married and has kids of her own? Where will you be then, Zoe? Will you be here? Will you even be in your right mind? Or thumbing around paradise under another fake name?"

"That's enough," Eve said.

"And guess what?" Catherine said. "I missed you when you were gone. I still miss the sister I had. I miss *you.* Again and again, I lost you. How hard was that for me, do you think? Oh, wait. You didn't think, did you?" she cried, and then she was moving, dodging past her mother, whose mouth was open with shock, and running out the front door.

In the car, she locked the doors and then, realizing she'd forgotten her purse and keys inside, sobbed with her forehead pressed hard against the steering wheel.

A minute later Catherine heard a sharp rapping sound on the window beside her. She pressed both hands to her eyes, wiping away the tears before turning her head to the window.

It was Grey, his black hair loose and gleaming in the sunlight, his face unreadable as he held out her cell phone. He must hate her now, too.

She cracked the window and took the phone. "Thanks," she said. "I know I acted like an asshole in there. I'm sorry."

"Never mind that. You have a call," he said. "It's Willow. She's at the police station in Salem."

CHAPTER TWENTY-ONE

When Grey came back inside to say he needed Catherine's purse and that he was driving Catherine to Salem to pick up Willow, who had apparently been caught shoplifting, Zoe insisted on going, too.

"I don't know if that's a good idea," Eve said, still so shattered by Catherine's outburst that she hadn't moved from the middle of the living room.

Grey came up with a quick solution: If Zoe and Eve wanted to go to Salem, too, they could take the Porsche. "I don't think Catherine should drive alone, the way she is right now," he said. "And I don't know if it's a good idea to put her and Zoe in the same vehicle."

"No, you're right about that," Eve said. "Thank you, Grey."

"Oh, great. Now you can be Catherine's knight in shining armor, since I apparently don't need you anymore," Zoe said, sounding sullen.

"Grow up," Grey said mildly. He handed Zoe the keys and left with Catherine's small blue purse dangling absurdly from one muscular arm.

Riding in the Porsche with Zoe at the wheel was terrifying. The car's slitted headlights and low, compact shape made Eve feel like she was trapped inside an insect's carapace, and the car surged forward every time Zoe touched the accelerator.

It didn't help that Zoe's face looked stitched to her skull, the way she was squinting and pressing her lips into a thin line, or that she was taking the corners at top speed. She'd chosen a different route to Salem, not following Catherine's sensible Honda from Route 97 to Route 1A, but using a mysterious warren of narrow side streets, threading her way through Beverly. How did she even know where to go? Eve wondered.

She couldn't shake the image of her daughters facing each other in the living room, saying those horrible things to each other. This rift felt primal and permanent. How could they do this to each other, especially when Willow so clearly needed them to put her first right now? Eve couldn't stand the idea of Willow feeling so lost and angry that she'd done something as stupid as shoplifting, especially since this was an echo of Zoe's poor choices as an adolescent.

To calm herself down, too, Eve started babbling, saying, "This is a wonderful car. What an interesting job you must have, driving cars as exotic as this one." She clung to the dashboard as Zoe careened around another corner. "You must have to be so careful with them, though. So expensive if you crash."

Zoe rolled her eyes without looking at Eve. "I won't crash. Anyway, this isn't a work car. This is Grey's."

Somewhere in Eve's cluttered mind, she still managed to feel shock. This car had to be worth a hundred thousand dollars. "What do you mean, it's Grey's? Does he work for the same place you do?"

"No. It's his Porsche. He owns it." Zoe's eyes flicked to the rearview mirror. "Right, Mama Justine?"

"He has many cars," Madame Justine said.

Eve had forgotten she was in the backseat; the other woman had somehow managed to squeeze into that tiny space. Madame Justine's voice sounded slightly muffled, as if she'd covered her face with her scarf. Maybe she had to, going around these corners. She was probably carsick.

"I thought Grey was a boatbuilder," Eve said.

"He is. But that's mostly for fun," Zoe said. "A hobby. Really what he does is invest in real estate. He's loaded." She braked so hard for a light that Eve felt Madame Justine's bulk press against the back of her seat.

"But I don't understand. Why does he live in a trailer with you?"

"We're friends," Zoe said.

Madame Justine spoke up again. "And because I am in my son's house," she said. "Grey, he is now building another one for himself. A house on the water like he always wanted."

This was too confusing, so Eve let it go. "I'm sorry about your daughter," she said.

"I am happy about yours, that she is here," Madame Justine said. "That is why I made Grey bring me this morning. To tell her so." She leaned forward to rest a hand, plump as a pigeon, on Zoe's shoulder. Zoe patted it and accelerated through a yellow light.

People stared at the car: pedestrians, other drivers, even a cop. Eve supposed that must be why people bought cars like this one, to be noticed. Frankly, she hated the attention. Why hadn't she driven them in her own Subaru? So what if Grey's car was parked behind hers? She could have asked him to move it. It's not like this was an emergency. Willow wasn't in any danger now that she was in police custody.

But why had she shoplifted? Eve didn't realize she'd asked the question aloud until Madame Justine responded.

"She is crying for help," Madame Justine suggested.

"I used to shoplift," Zoe said. "Maybe it's genetic. Maybe she's going to be a bad girl like me. A rotten apple." She tucked a stray blond curl behind her ear and then shifted abruptly into second gear as the car in front of them slowed unexpectedly.

Eve glanced at her. "Honey, I don't think Willow has bad genes. She's just acting out. Protesting the changes in her life. You're going to need to talk to her."

"I've talked to her. Maybe that's the problem. Maybe I'm Willow's biggest problem, right? That's what you all think."

"We don't think that!" Eve said.

Zoe kept her eyes on the road without answering. Her face was bathed in sunlight, her hair and skin nearly the same shade of pale caramel. She was a beautiful woman. Even when she was this hungover and upset, she managed to look serene and sexy, Eve thought. Like those actresses who dominated every movie scene they were in. The light was drawn to Zoe.

Unlike Catherine, who in the living room had appeared nearly unrecognizable, in the grip of such strong emotions that her face and shoulders had been pinched tight, her skin mottled with anger.

"You haven't really been honest with Willow," Eve said. "She needs you to guide her. You're her mother."

"Ha. Tell Catherine that."

"It doesn't matter what Catherine says or who Willow ends up living with in the long run," Eve said. "She will only ever have one biological mother, and that's you. It's time you told Willow who her father is, now that she's older."

"I can't do that," Zoe said.

Her daughter's lips were pressed tightly together again. But maybe that was because the police station had come into view.

"But why not?" Eve was determined to learn the truth, no matter how ugly it might be, mainly because she thought sharing that truth, and having people accept it, might be a way for Zoe to start moving forward in her life. "Was her father married? Was he gay? Was it a one-night stand?" She took a deep breath, then added, "Were you raped? You can tell me, Zoe."

"Stop it, Mom," Zoe said. "I can't talk about this with you."

Eve shifted in her seat to look at Zoe. She took in the white knuckles on the steering wheel, the twitch in her daughter's eyelid, the set of her jaw: pain personified. "I'm sorry this is difficult," she said. "Whatever the circumstances, I promise we'll figure out how to present them to Willow in the best possible light. But you have to tell her about her father before her curiosity gets her into even more trouble."

Zoe was driving more cautiously now, easing the rumbling sports car down ancient-looking streets between brick buildings. "Look. Here's the truth: I don't know who her father was, okay?"

"You know what happened that night, though," Madame Justine said from the backseat. She leaned forward, bringing her spicy scent with her. "You have not yet told your mother about this?"

Zoe shook her head. Her face was no longer serene. "I didn't want you to know, Mommy."

"Tell me," Eve said, despite the fear fluttering in her own chest, a bird trapped beneath her ribs. Frantic, now that it had seen light but found a window covered in glass. "Please."

"You must share this thing with your mother," Madame Justine urged. "It is the only way. Remember what you and I talked about after Sadie died."

To Eve's shock and relief, Zoe nodded once, then took a deep breath and began.

"It was the end of freshman year. Mike broke up with me, and I felt so . . . I don't know. Lost," Zoe said. "I'd done everything Mike asked. I stopped drinking and doing drugs. I even kept going to classes and studied. I loved him, Mommy. I thought he loved me. But he couldn't stay with me."

"He did love you," Eve assured her, the dread building. "I saw him with you. How he looked at you. Something must have happened. But that's natural. You were both so young."

"He was gay," Zoe said.

Eve thought back: Mike's precise magic tricks, his formal speech, his courtly manners at dinner, his strange clothes. Of course. Why hadn't she seen it?

"Oh, honey," she said. "That must have been difficult."

"It was horrible!" Zoe said. "He was the first guy I ever loved! I couldn't believe I'd been so stupid. How did I not know he was gay, especially when all my friends said so?"

She went on talking: about being so depressed she couldn't go to class and how a friend had suggested going to a party. About how she was determined to stay straight after the breakup. "I thought that if I could just convince Mike I was doing okay, I wouldn't look pathetic and he'd change his mind about wanting to be with me," Zoe said. "I didn't even care about him being gay. I told him he could have boyfriends and we could still live together."

Eve didn't know what to say to that, so she simply said, "You still loved him."

"Yes! But I didn't know what else to do, so I went to this party one night with my friend Gaby. It was at a fraternity house in Amherst. A house I'd never been to before, but a nice place. Not one of those firetraps. I don't know what happened. Oh, God. I can't tell you this, Mommy. I really can't." Zoe was crying, the tears shining silver against her freckled skin.

"But you must be strong and finish," Madame Justine said, leaning forward again, this time touching Zoe's cheek. "Secrets can destroy you from the inside. We have talked about this, daughter. Think of Sadie."

Zoe nodded. They'd reached the police station parking lot. She pulled into a space and shut off the engine, staring straight ahead, her face bleak.

"Somebody at the party must have spiked my drink," she went on, "because suddenly I couldn't control anything I did. I got really, really dizzy. Then I felt so tired I couldn't move. I tried to tell my friend I needed to leave, but she was off dancing and I couldn't get my arms and legs to follow my orders. I finally blacked out." She stopped talking, put a hand over her eyes as if to shield them from whatever was on the other side of the windshield: the sun, a car accident, a beast in the woods.

"Oh, Zoe," Eve said, wanting to cover her own eyes. "I'm so sorry." She swallowed hard. "What happened then?" She didn't want to hear the answer, but she knew Zoe had to say it.

Zoe took a shaky breath before going on. "I woke up in a dark room. This guy was on top of me, pulling down my jeans. I tried to move, but he had me pinned, and my head wasn't right. I just let him do whatever."

"Oh, God." Eve felt like she might be sick and fished for a tissue in her purse.

"Yeah. That wasn't the worst of it, though," Zoe said. "After he was done, there were other guys. I don't know how many. Three? Four? I kept blacking out. I woke up at one point and two of them were on me, even though I was hurling over the side of the bed. It was like being trapped in a nightmare. Finally I passed out for good. When I woke up, I was on the lawn behind the house, in the bushes." She shuddered. "I wasn't wearing anything except a T-shirt. It wasn't even mine. I don't know who put it on me."

Eve felt her own face with one hand. Sure enough, her flesh was literally crawling with horror, doing just what Zoe's had earlier: crumpling, the skin sinking in around her cheekbones and jawbone. "Why didn't you tell us?" she said. "Your father and I would have done something. Pressed charges! Gotten those bastards thrown in jail!"

"I didn't know who they were! Anyway, I didn't want anybody to know. Any girl I'd ever heard of who accused a frat guy of rape lived to regret it. Everyone talked about them and hassled them, called them sluts. My roommate knew one girl who had to leave school, it was so bad. Plus, I felt stupid, getting myself into something like that. I'd always had better street smarts. And I was afraid of Mike finding out, because he'd just think I was drunk or using again. That's the worst thing, Mommy," she whispered. "I really wasn't. For the first time in my life, I was actually trying to be good."

"Oh, honey. You have always been good," Eve said, unfastening her seat belt so she could slide across the seat and put her arm around Zoe. "You're my girl. You have a big heart and a big life. You've made mistakes, just like we all do, but you're here now and trying to fix them. You're still my girl, my baby, no matter what happened to you. Those bastards have to live with what they did on their consciences, and I hope it eats away at them. But you weren't to blame, okay? You didn't do anything wrong that night."

"Except be stupid, stupid me," Zoe said, unfastening her seat belt and flinging herself out the door as Catherine's car pulled up next to theirs.

Willow had told the policewoman not to call anyone. She'd already phoned Henry after the security guard caught her and made her wait in his tiny office behind the drugstore pharmacy. The security guard wasn't that much older than she was. Twenty, maybe, with a constellation of pimples on his face and a haircut his mother probably did in the kitchen.

"Sorry. Gotta do my job," he'd said after catching her. "Next time, don't run."

The boy's office stank of potato chips and farts. Willow tried the door, but he'd locked her in. She wanted to cry, but didn't let herself.

This whole day she'd been asking herself what her mom would do, trying to imagine Zoe's life. "WWZD?" she whispered to keep up her courage when the man sitting next to her on the bus fell asleep and his head landed like a bowling ball on her shoulder. Willow had shoved the man so hard, he almost fell out of the seat. He woke up with a snore. Then she'd switched seats, stepping on his foot almost on purpose.

Unfortunately, the security guard had been standing on the other side of the door when she'd tried to pick the lock of his door with a bent paper clip. He opened the door and there was the cop, Officer Martinez, shaking her head. "I'm taking you in," she said, "before you can get yourself into any more hot water."

When Willow called Henry, he showed up in half an hour. He'd driven his Dad's Audi without asking, even though he'd had his license less than a month. His parents were at the movies.

"How are you old enough to drive?" she asked. "You're in the same grade as me."

He looked down at his big hands and shrugged. "Had to repeat kindergarten because I couldn't sit still in my chair."

It was a miracle that he could make her laugh, but he did. Henry took her hand and held it even when the policewoman gave them a mean look over her glasses and said she still had to call Willow's parents.

"But it's okay. I have a ride now," Willow said.

The officer shook her head. "You're going to be formally cautioned by the police, and for that we need a parent or guardian present," said Officer Martinez, whose blue uniform was so tight that you could see the bunches of flesh over her belt. She looked too out of shape to run after anybody. Why hadn't she been the one to chase her, instead of that punk store security guard, obviously a track star in his high school glory days? Willow might have gotten away then. She could still be wandering around Salem and pretending she was Zoe.

"Who do you want me to call for you, sugar?" Officer Martinez said.

"Nobody," Willow insisted.

"Come on," Henry said softly, looking down at her with his butterfly lashes. "The sooner somebody comes, the sooner we can go."

"I'm the one who's locked up. You can leave anytime," Willow said.

"Right. But you don't want to spend the night here—do you? I'm betting those cells aren't too comfortable. Plus, you'd have to pee standing up over some metal tube or something."

She had no idea what he was talking about, but she didn't care. "It's fine. I don't want anybody to find out. Not my mom or Catherine or Russell."

The policewoman overheard this. "No chance of that, sweetie," she said. "They're going to know because we won't let you out until they do. I can track down your information if I need to, but believe me, you do not want to make me do extra work and get on my bad side. So just give me a damn number."

Willow sighed and scrolled down to Catherine's contact info, then handed the phone to Officer Martinez. Catherine was the only person who might actually come and get her. Russell would be busy with Nola and pissed off that she left, and who knows where her real mom was or whether she even had a car?

"So why'd you do it?" Henry said, as they waited and played hangman in some kind of conference room with those mirrors that were probably windows. The policewoman had brought them Cokes when Henry turned his doe eyes on her and asked if maybe they could have a drink. Life was easy for Henry. Nobody could resist him.

Willow suddenly wondered if that was how her mom felt: that life was easier for everybody else. Especially for Catherine.

"I don't know, exactly," she said. "I guess I was trying to see what it felt like to be bad."

To her relief, Henry didn't seem too freaked-out by this. "Interesting. How did it feel?"

"Good. Well, sort of good and sort of scary."

"What did you steal?"

She thought back. She'd been in a drugstore, the huge kind that was practically a Walmart. She'd gone there because it was too cold and windy to walk around Salem and the museum she'd wanted to go to, the Witch Museum (which Russell and Catherine never took her to no matter how much she begged, saying it was "worse than Disney, not even good special effects; read *The Crucible* instead") cost, like, a zillion dollars.

That's when she asked herself what Zoe would have done in Salem at her age, if she were on her own with no money.

Drugs, probably. But Willow didn't want to fry her brain the way she'd seen her mom do.

Then she realized Zoe must have stolen things to trade for drugs, since she always had trouble with jobs. What would it feel like, Willow wondered, to take what you wanted? To stop being good, to quit worrying about grades or whether people liked you? To be in your skin and apart from the world, and the world's rules, which her mom often thought—and said—were stupid? "The world is run by dickheads with too much money and no taste, kiddo," her mom used to say.

So Willow had followed her mother's impulse to see what it would feel like to be free. She'd blindly reached out while she was walking down the cosmetics aisle and grabbed a tube of lipstick. Not a good color for her—it was the sick pinky-red of grapefruit—but that wasn't the point. The point was to take, take, and take some more. She'd prowled the aisles, feeling giddier as the minutes ticked by and she got away with putting stuff in her pockets.

"A lipstick, eyeliner, a package of cool pens, a jar of nuts, some skin cream, a pair of tights," she said to Henry now.

"Wow," he said. "You must have huge pockets." He checked out her jacket.

She made a face. "Not big enough, obviously. The nuts fell out when I was running from the store security guard."

Even worse, the jar had rolled off the sidewalk and into the parking lot, where a car drove over the plastic container and popped it. "It sounded like an explosion," she said. "Those nuts sprayed out like bullets. The security guard got hit in the leg. He said he got a bruise."

Henry was almost doubled over in his chair, laughing. "They must have been big nuts," he said.

"Uh-huh. Cashews," she answered.

Suddenly, the door opened and Officer Martinez appeared. "Your people are here, young lady," she said, and held the door wide.

Catherine came in first, looking as scared as she'd been that time they'd gone skiing at Killington, when Willow had plowed into a tree and gotten a concussion. Catherine had ridden in the ambulance with her to the hospital, had sponged puke out of her hair and stayed with her all night, sleeping in a brown plastic chair that squeaked like sneakers every time Catherine moved, making Willow laugh despite her pounding headache.

Willow was never so glad to see anybody. She opened her mouth to say this, then shut it again when her real mom came into the room, too. Zoe must have been crying, or maybe she was just pissed off. Her eyes were red and she kept her arms crossed. Nana was next; she smiled at Willow, and said, "Hi, honey," but her eyes didn't smile with her mouth and she grabbed on to the doorframe like she was standing in a windstorm.

Behind Nana was Mom's friend Grey. Even here, in this cramped yellow room, the guy looked like a movie star, the sort that would fight aliens in a long leather coat, his hair a shiny ink black.

And then, like this was one of those clown cars at the Big Apple Circus, another woman stepped into the room, too, some old lady she'd never seen before, dressed in bag-lady clothes. The old woman had black eyes and was staring at her like she could X-ray the inside of Willow's brain.

Willow didn't know where to look, so she turned to Officer Martinez. "You didn't have to call my whole damn family," she said.

"Don't swear, please," Catherine said.

"I didn't. I only called her," Officer Martinez said, pointing at Catherine. "These other people showed up on their own."

"Why?" Willow said, daring now to look at Nana, the safest place to look: Nana would always love her. That much she knew for sure. And now, thinking of that, she was very sorry to be here, and even sorrier that Nana knew what she'd done and had come all this way.

"Because we all love you," Nana said.

"We do, you know," her mom said, though Zoe said this like her teeth hurt and wouldn't look at her. "You can't do things like this, kiddo, or you might turn out like me."

"You scared us to death," Catherine said. "What was going through your mind, Willow? Why did you take off last night without telling anyone you'd be at Mike's? And why were you *stealing*?" She started crying then. Not quiet, pretty actressy tears, either, but howling sobs like that kid on the Cambridge playground did, the one whose nanny never knew what to do.

Willow didn't know what to do, either. This was so humiliating. She wanted to sink under the metal table. Or maybe pass out. With so many people in the room, there wasn't enough air.

Henry stood up and said he'd wait outside to make room, even though he was the only one she wanted with her now. Then the chairs were scraping against the hard floor until everybody was sitting except Grey, who leaned in the corner with one foot propped against the yellow wall, and Officer Martinez, who looked pissed off, like this was her kitchen and she'd have to clean up after everybody when they left.

Which, in a way, she did, Willow supposed, as the policewoman droned on about how Willow was being officially cautioned, and that she was lucky she was only fifteen, because after seventeen you could get arrested and serve time even for shoplifting a lipstick, especially if you "resisted arrest."

Willow opened her mouth to say she wasn't resisting any arrest, just running from the store security guard. But Catherine was staring her down, so she clamped her lips shut and crossed her arms. Maybe she was done talking forever.

In her tired voice, Officer Martinez told them that the store had confiscated the things Willow had stolen and was filing a "no trespass" order, which apparently meant Willow couldn't go into that same drugstore again for sixty days.

Then Willow thought of something. "The nuts!" she cried, tucking her hands into her sleeves. "I can't give those back. They got crushed by that car that ran over them."

Everybody was staring at her like she had two heads. "The security detail didn't mention any nuts," Officer Martinez said, consulting her paper. "So never mind those. You're free to go after signing these papers here. And I expect you to stay out of my sight, young lady. I hope you've learned your lesson."

"She has," Catherine said quickly, her hands fluttering.

"I wasn't talking to you." Officer Martinez's eyes bored into Willow's skull.

"I have," Willow said. "I promise."

She signed her name on one of the papers, and then there was a lot of discussion when the police officer asked who was taking Willow home. Finally, Officer Martinez sighed. "Which one of you is this girl's parent?"

"I'm her mom," Zoe said, uncrossing her arms and sitting straighter in the chair.

"I'm her legal guardian," Catherine said. "I think she should come home with me."

"But I'm her biological parent," Zoe argued.

"Where is this child's home?" Officer Martinez said. "Where does she go to school?"

Catherine actually raised her hand. No wonder she was an A student, Willow thought, then ducked her head to avoid looking at anybody, especially that old lady with the X-ray eyes.

Officer Martinez raised an eyebrow. "I guess you better take her with you, then," she said to Catherine without asking Willow what she wanted.

That was fine. Willow wouldn't have known what to say, because any answer she gave would be wrong.

Outside, the shock of the cold air made Willow's nose and eyes immediately start running. She zipped her jacket and searched for Henry until she saw him in the parking lot, leaning against his dad's black Audi. She ran over to him, ignoring Catherine, who was calling for her.

"I don't want to ride with any of them," she said, tipping her face up to Henry's and touching his sleeve. "Everything is too weird! I want to go with you. Please!"

He smiled down at her, his hair glowing red in the sun. "I'd drive you—I really would—but I can't. I've only had my license for a month, remember? Go on. Man up. I'll see you tomorrow."

"What if I'm grounded?" Willow said.

"I'll see you anyway." Henry bent down suddenly and kissed her. Then, his cheeks as red as his hair, he ducked into the car and started the ignition.

CHAPTER TWENTY-TWO

Catherine drove her mother, Willow, and Grey back to Newburyport, while Zoe drove Madame Justine in the Porsche. Willow fell asleep in the backseat with her head on Eve's shoulder; Catherine glanced at her now and then in the rearview mirror, reassuring herself that the girl was actually there.

Willow woke up when they pulled into Eve's driveway half an hour later and, blessed by being a child, despite her new woman's body, she smiled at Catherine in the mirror, appearing to forget everything that had happened as she stretched and yawned. When she remembered to be angry, Willow quickly wrapped her arms tightly around her body and looked out the window, muttering a good-bye to Eve as she got out of the car with Grey.

"Want to sit up front?" Catherine asked before pulling out of the driveway again.

Willow shook her head.

Another forty minutes south to Cambridge. Willow slept. Catherine put on the radio, glad she didn't have to say anything yet. She needed time to think.

At home, Mike was beside himself at the sight of Willow, launching himself in the air as if his legs were springs. She sank to her knees and rubbed the little dog's body, laughing and letting him lick her face. She took him outside while Catherine made grilled cheese and soup, numb from the effort of not yelling at Willow in the car.

"You can go ahead and ground me," Willow said as she laid spoons and napkins out on the kitchen table without Catherine having to ask her.

"I'm not going to do that," Catherine said. "This is bigger than that. Like I said at the police station, you really scared me. All of us."

They sat across from each other, the bowls steaming between them, the yellow cheese oozing out of the thick slabs of toasted bread. "What can I do to show you I'm sorry?" Willow asked. She looked miserable.

Catherine picked up her napkin, put it on her lap, and said, "Eat something, please."

Willow obeyed, tearing the sandwich into bite-sized pieces with her hands. A habit only a parent could love about a child. Seeing it made Catherine want to weep.

"I'm sorry you felt like you had to find Mike without telling me," Catherine began. "I would have helped you, you know."

"Really?" Willow chewed, her face a mask. "You never did before. Whenever I asked who my dad was, you always said it didn't matter, because I had you and Russell."

"You never actually asked me to help search for him."

Willow rolled her eyes. "You should have known what I wanted. Nola was the only one who'd help me. Don't be mad at her," she added quickly. "I pretty much made her drive me to Framingham."

Nola. Catherine sighed. She'd already burned her mouth on the soup; now she set down the spoon and said, "I've made a mess of things in a lot of ways. But the one thing I've learned, honey, is that life is a lot easier if you come out and ask for what you want."

"So, if I asked you right now if I could live with Mom again, you'd say yes?" Willow challenged.

Catherine wanted to close her eyes. To make all of this a dream she could then wake from. "It's not that simple."

"Because you don't trust her to take care of me?"

"Look, right now this is all theoretical—"

"Why? Because she doesn't want me?"

Catherine knew by the desperate note that had crept into Willow's voice that she was afraid both things might be true: that Zoe didn't want her, and couldn't take care of her anyway. Even worse, Catherine couldn't completely deny those possibilities. Yet, now, after Willow's reckless act and hearing the pleading in Willow's voice, Catherine knew she also had to start thinking seriously about what Willow wanted for her own life. If she didn't work with her, if she didn't really start learning to listen to her daughter, Willow was going to view her as an enemy instead of an ally.

"If your mom goes to court and proves she's clean and responsible," she answered slowly, "then I wouldn't have any legal leg to stand on. She's your biological parent. But I would always be in your life."

"So you'd just let her *have* me?" Willow's voice was shrill now.

"That's not what I'm saying."

"It is, too! And that's why I wanted to find my real dad, you know, in case none of you guys want me. Okay? *Now* do you get it?" Willow shouted. Then she left the table, scooping Mike into her arms on her way out of the kitchen.

"I get it," Catherine whispered as she heard Willow's footsteps on the stairs. "Oh, honey. I get it."

She poured herself a glass of wine and threw the remaining food into the compost. She sat with the wine as she called Dr. Patel and stumbled through a message, saying she needed to take some days off to clear up some personal matters. "Maybe through Thanksgiving," she said, thinking that with the office closed for two days anyway, she could manage a week to herself. "I hope this won't put you in a bind."

Whether it did or not, she needed to spend time with Willow. Forget work, forget Zoe, forget everything else: Willow needed her now, and then maybe Eve would take Willow to Chance Harbor, since she planned to spend one last Thanksgiving there. That would give Catherine time to be on her own and think. Besides, if Zoe went to Canada for Thanksgiving with them, it would be a chance for Willow to spend some supervised time with her. They could see how things went.

She called Russell next. "We're home," she said.

"Thanks for texting me earlier. How did it go? Was she charged with anything?"

"No. Since this was her first offense shoplifting, the officer gave her a diversion. If she does a three-month program, the charges will be wiped clean."

"Good. I wish I could have gone to Salem with you."

"It's all right," Catherine said. "I had lots of company. Mom and Zoe. And one of Zoe's friends."

"Oh." Russell's voice was strained; he was clearly put out not to have been part of the rescue party, and she didn't blame him. No matter how flawed he was as a husband, Russell loved Willow, too. "That's good, I guess. Listen. Can I put Nola on for a minute? She wants to say something to you."

Catherine opened the refrigerator and poured another glass of wine. "If she must."

Nola was blunt, as always. "Look, I know I totally messed up. I'm sorry," she said. "I never should have taken Willow to that guy Mike's house."

Catherine closed her eyes and counted to ten, reminding herself that Nola was still a teenager. A confused, pregnant teenager. "I understand you were trying to help Willow. You were being a friend to her."

Nola sounded startled. "Yeah? Yes. That's exactly what I was doing!" she said. "I really like that kid. She's a good girl. And I'm sorry, you know, for everything else, too."

"Apology accepted," Catherine said, though it wasn't easy. "Good luck with your baby. Just, if you do take Willow somewhere again, please tell us, all right? She's still only fifteen."

"Boy, I know! I thought I was all grown-up at fifteen, like Willow. But I was wrong."

"Yes, you were," Catherine said before she could stop herself. "And you've still got some growing to do." She hung up.

How could she possibly sleep, with her brain on fire like this? Catherine put on a movie and watched it blindly, then watched another, trying to fill her mind with sounds and images other than her own. When the doorbell rang, she glanced at the clock. It was nearly eleven o'clock. Surprisingly, Willow had already been asleep when Catherine had gone upstairs half an hour ago, the dog curled on the pillow next to her. She must be exhausted from her day. She'd looked impossibly young, her hair still damp from a shower and fanned out on the pillow. Catherine hoped the bell didn't wake her now. It must be Russell at the door—who else? She only hoped Nola hadn't come, too. Catherine's patience was shredded by the day's events.

She went to the door, peered through the keyhole, and felt her stomach drop at the sight of Grey. Was Zoe with him? Had they come here, teamed up to convince her that Willow belonged with Zoe? Catherine remembered the awful scene she'd made in her mother's living room. Grey must think she was unhinged. Well, what did it matter what he thought? They had no future together.

Not that her body was being that rational. The sight of Grey, even as tiny as it was through the peephole, immediately aroused desire she'd hoped to satisfy and then set aside for good.

She wanted him. No denying that.

Catherine opened the door a crack, leaving the chain on until she saw that Grey was alone, standing in his customary boots and leather jacket, his hair loose and framing his sharp features beneath the porch light.

She closed the door again to release the chain, then stepped back to let him in.

Grey took off his boots in the hall and bent to kiss her cheek. Catherine didn't say anything beyond the barest of greetings, only folded her arms and waited, keeping her eyes on the floor so that none of her tricky emotions would be revealed on her betraying face. Let him scold her, berate her, whatever. Then he could leave and their business would be finished.

"I came by to make sure you're okay," he said.

Startled, she looked up at him and saw that Grey's expression was not angry, or even irritated. He looked, if anything, worried. Kind. Tender. Sweet.

Catherine's cheeks burned. "I'm fine. I'm just glad we found her."

"Zoe's a mess."

Ah. So that's why he'd come. To plead Zoe's cause. "She should be," Catherine said, and turned her back on him to walk away.

Not that she could put much distance between them in her modest house. Her only choice was to walk to the kitchen at the end of the hall, where she picked up her wineglass and gestured to the cupboard. "Want a glass?"

He shook his head and watched her silently drain her glass. She badly wanted a third.

No. Bad idea.

"Why do you say that Zoe should be a mess?" Grey asked, sitting down at the table.

Catherine took the chair across from his. "It's her own fault that Willow went to Mike's looking for information."

Grey's voice was calm, but she noticed a glint in his eyes. "I don't understand. How is that her fault? Zoe had no idea what Willow was up to, since she hadn't seen her."

"Because she has never told Willow about her real dad. Willow is fifteen. Old enough to know the truth."

He sighed. "Zoe doesn't know who the father is."

"I'd figured as much. Zoe had a lot of fun at the university. I think she spent, like, ten minutes a day studying."

"She didn't have all that much fun. Not after she and Mike broke up." Grey's voice was low; Catherine almost had to lean forward to hear it.

"So that's why she dropped out? Not enough parties for her?"

She heard her own bitchy tone and inwardly winced, uncomfortably aware that the anger flickering in Grey's eyes was growing brighter.

"Why are you looking at me like that?" she said. "You know what Zoe's like."

"Because I want to tell you the truth, but I'm conflicted because I know Zoe wouldn't want me to say anything."

"We're all conflicted," Catherine said. "Believe me, if you know something that will help me understand my crazy sister, then by all means, share it. Though I can't guarantee that I'll listen with an open mind. Too much water under the bridge, you know?"

He nodded. "I got to that point with Sadie. I know what you're feeling. You've been hurt and betrayed so many times that you're almost ready to give up on your sister."

"No. That's where you're wrong." What the hell. Against her best instincts, Catherine stood up and poured herself a third glass of wine. Then she turned around again to face him, the glass in her hand. "I am not 'almost ready' to give up on Zoe. That happened a long time ago. Now my only goal is to keep Willow safe, even if we go to court and I lose custody to Zoe."

"I'm sorry to hear that." He arched an eyebrow. "A custody battle would be tough on Willow, don't you think? What if Zoe continues to play by the rules and Willow wants to live with her some of the time. Would you ever allow that?"

"Look, I don't want to make problems for Willow," she said. "There might come a time in the future when I'd say yes to that, sure. As Willow gets older, I know I'll need to honor her as a person by letting her make her own choices, provided I don't perceive any risk."

"Very noble rhetoric."

Catherine shrugged. "I mean it. I know this may come as a shock to you, but I'm actually a good person most of the time." She took a gulp of wine. The wine was sour and unpleasant; she nearly spit it out.

"You'd better sit down," Grey said.

She dropped into a chair and set the glass down carefully on the table in front of her. She was seated in Willow's place; there were crumbs everywhere. She nearly smiled. A child, still, Willow. Thank God for small mercies.

Grey folded his big hands on the table. His hands were calloused from his boatbuilding, but he wore an expensive-looking watch, a Bvlgari.

"Why are you here?" Catherine asked. "I mean, really? You should be propping Zoe up. You're her friend. And, as you can see, I'm perfectly fine."

"You are not fine," Grey said. "And I wanted to see you, to tell you some things about your sister that you obviously don't know. I think that's the only way you'll forgive her."

"I will never forgive her."

"Maybe not," Grey said. "But I can help you understand, at least. And that might help you both take better care of Willow. Isn't that what you want?"

"Yes. Absolutely." Catherine picked up her glass and took another dainty sip despite the cloud descending on her brain. Why shouldn't she get drunk?

"Do you know the real reason Zoe left school?"

"Sure. Because Mike broke up with her and she was upset. I was worried about her back then because I was about to graduate and wouldn't be around anymore to look out for her. I told Zoe to put on her big-girl underpants and start studying, to actually *do* something with her life after Mike gave her the boot. Instead, she partied hard and came home from school, told us she was pregnant. After that, she was impossible. Mom said it was hormones, but I always thought it was a bad case of regret."

Grey was staring at her now. It wasn't a pleasant look. "It wasn't either of those things, Catherine," he said softly. "It was trauma."

"Yeah? The trauma of a broken heart?" She giggled a little, the wine making her dizzy.

"No. Zoe was gang-raped."

He said it so bluntly that Catherine felt as if he'd slapped her. She put the glass down. "What?"

"She was raped, Catherine. By a group of guys at a house party. Zoe wasn't drinking or doing drugs. She went to a frat party with a friend and somebody spiked her drink."

"And you believe her?" Catherine wanted, so badly, not to believe it.

He nodded. "I do. Zoe is a lot of things, but she has never been a liar about her own poor choices. And that's why Zoe doesn't know who Willow's dad is. It happened that night."

"No! She would have told us." Even as she said this, though, the pieces were clicking into place: Zoe's bruises, faded to yellow by the time their mother convinced Catherine to come home and try talking her into going back to school. Her near-comatose behavior. Her disinterest, at first, in the baby.

Grey was still talking, explaining to Catherine now that Zoe hadn't wanted to report the rape because she didn't know who the boys were. It had happened in a dark room at a party where she knew nobody except the girl who'd brought her. "And she was ashamed," Grey added. "She didn't want anyone to find out. Especially not Mike. She didn't think any of you would believe her anyway."

She was right, Catherine thought, but she couldn't bring herself to say this, not while she was sitting beneath the too-bright overhead light of her own kitchen, her stomach churning from the cheap wine and the day's events and now this, yet more evidence that she had failed Zoe as a sister. Why had she just assumed that whatever happened to her sister was Zoe's own fault?

"You can understand why Zoe would find it difficult to tell Willow about this," Grey said. "She didn't ever want Willow to feel she wasn't wanted."

"Yes." More pieces were tumbling into place: Zoe had told her that she ran away and made herself disappear after a man abused Willow. Given what she'd been through, Zoe would have been understandably terrified and determined to get Willow out of harm's way. Which was exactly what she'd accomplished by having Catherine take over parenting Willow. She might not approve of Zoe's reasoning, but her sister's motives were clear: she wanted Willow to be safe, just as she'd been claiming all along.

Catherine suddenly felt sick and went to the sink. She held her face under the faucet, not caring that Grey was watching her.

He came up to touch her shoulder, but she remained staring blindly at the black square of the kitchen window. "You must hate me," she said, finally mopping her face with a paper towel before turning to him. "The way I've been toward Zoe. How I was today."

He shook his head. "I don't. How could I? You've been fighting for Willow every step of the way. You've been a good mother to her, Catherine. And I know Zoe isn't easy to love."

"But you love her."

He hesitated an instant, then nodded. "But not," he said, "the way I could love you. Maybe already do."

"You can't possibly."

"Why not?"

"You don't even know me."

"Oh, I think I do." Grey gestured at her freshly scrubbed face, at her hair clinging now to her cheeks, at the dampness on her T-shirt. "Is this you? The real you? Angry and sad? Sorrowful, forgiving, scared? Loving? Is all of this you, Catherine? Who you are?"

When she took a step away from him, panicked by the intensity of his eyes, Grey put a hand around her waist, making contact with her bare skin just above her jeans. He held her in place, cupping her waist and studying her face, no longer smiling.

She didn't move. If only she could stand here long enough, with the palm of this man's generous hand warming her entire body, the world would right itself.

"Yes. This is me," she said, and leaned her head on his shoulder.

Had anyone asked her a few weeks ago what she would be most thankful for this year, Eve would never have imagined this possibility even in her most wildly optimistic fantasies: Thanksgiving at Chance Harbor with Zoe, the daughter she had feared dead, and with Willow, the granddaughter she loved beyond words because Willow was so clearly the product of both mothers who had raised her: wild and loving, sweet and mercurial, brave and vulnerable.

The only thing that could have made this holiday more perfect would have been having Catherine with them, too. But Catherine had insisted that they go without her. "It's clear that Willow's trying to figure some things out, and she needs time alone with Zoe," she'd said. "I'd just be in the way."

"What changed your mind about letting Willow come with us?" Eve had asked, truly astounded by this generous gesture. She had been certain that Catherine would fight her sister on everything where Willow was concerned.

"Grey explained some things to me," she said vaguely, "and, anyway, I know you'll be up there to supervise things."

Eve could guess what those things were, and shuddered. "I will," she had promised. "But won't you change your mind and come? It would be so nice for all of us to be together. And I don't want you spending the holiday alone."

Catherine still said no. She had thought about it, she added, but Bethany had invited her for the holiday. "Plus, I need some space to think about my next steps," she said.

They arrived at Chance Harbor as it was getting dark and unloaded the car, stomping through a light crust of snow to carry things into the house. Cousin Jane, bless her, had come by to crank up the thermostat and fill the fridge. The house was warm and smelled of Jane's biscuits and something else, too. Cheese?

Yes, there it was, a block of homemade sheep's cheese on the counter from their neighbor down the road, to go with the biscuits and beef stew Jane had left to welcome them.

Zoe hiked up and down the stairs, making up beds and exclaiming over the new paint in the kitchen, the wallpaper Eve had chosen for her room. She was wearing one of Eve's quilted down jackets; the jacket made Zoe look twice her size, but her eyes were bright and her skin looked healthy.

Willow, though, was unexpectedly quiet, almost sullen. Eve didn't know what that was about, but at least they were here now, the long drive behind them. Zoe and Willow had promised to help around the house, to finish stripping old wallpaper out of the two remaining bedrooms and put up new.

They all went to bed early, exhausted from the drive. When morning came, bringing unexpectedly warm weather for the third week of November, Eve suggested breakfast on the beach, egg and bacon sandwiches washed down by a thermos of hot tea. They ate on the circle of rocks near the base of the wooden stairs leading down the rocky red cliff, watching the gulls circle for crusts.

The wind had died down and the sun was slowly emerging from the clouds, casting a pale yellow light on the Northumberland Strait. The beach was clear of snow and Eve could just make out Cape Breton in the distance. She thought, not of Malcolm or that terrible day she'd traveled there, leaving Andrew on the dock, but of Darcy, of their time together hiking in the headlands, and smiled.

Willow and Zoe were racing up and down the dunes, shrieking and making Mike bark. Eve pushed her hands into her pockets and began walking toward the inlet with Bear. She glanced at the girls over her shoulder once and realized that Willow was so tall now, it was difficult to tell from a distance who was the mother and who was the daughter.

The water was calm, a flat nail-head gray. A pair of seals rode the waves, their sleek doggy heads pointed in her direction. Eve had a sudden memory of being on this beach one chilly autumn morning with Andrew, shortly after Zoe learned to walk. Catherine was probably four years old then and fascinated by seaweed; she ignored the cold and draped sandy strands of it around her neck and around Zoe's too, calling them "princess necklaces." Zoe made comical faces at the feel of the clammy plants on her skin, but put up with it because she would do anything for Catherine.

As Eve and Andrew walked with the girls, the tide was out and they had come across a shipwreck. It had been there awhile, Andrew had told her, though she'd never seen it before. The tidal conditions had to be just right to uncover it.

The ribs of the ship poked out of the sand along with some rusty metal bits. Eve had winced when she saw it, thinking of Malcolm. She'd thought then—as she would think many times in the coming years—about how similar death was to birth. Humans marked both of these events in similar ways, with food and flowers and hushed voices and even prayers. When a baby was born or you lost a loved one, you paced at night, sleepless with grief or joy, overtaken by the absurdity of the human condition. Giving birth and mourning the dead were life's reminders that none of us can control fate.

"You miss him," Andrew had said that day, watching Eve's face as she turned away from the wreck, stricken, despite knowing it couldn't possibly be Malcolm's boat. His vessel had gone down on the north side of the island.

She didn't pretend not to know what Andrew meant. Since her affair, Eve had decided that dishonesty was pointless in a marriage. She'd thought

Andrew had also come to that conclusion, but apparently he hadn't. He'd had a child with Marta, had gone on seeing her. Had even *lost a son*, all without telling Eve. Her husband had his secrets, and yet he'd stayed with her. When she wasn't angry about this—which was more often now—Eve almost pitied Andrew for his lies: how much more difficult it must have been, all of that deep subterfuge, than to just come out and tell the truth.

"Yes," she'd said, when Andrew asked about Malcolm that day on the beach. "But I don't know if I miss him, or the idea of him still being here," she'd admitted. "I loved Malcolm, but not the same way I love you. It just feels, I don't know. Odd. Empty."

"I understand," he'd said, and held her close. "I'm sorry."

Eve had been amazed—and still was—that Andrew could find the strength and generosity within himself to comfort her. She wished that she had known the depth of Andrew's losses. Marta. His son. He had kept that all to himself. No wonder she'd felt that she could never reach him.

She had reached the inlet now. The tide was coming in; she'd have to turn around. Find the girls and go up to the house. Start stripping wallpaper. That thought—not the actual work, but the idea that the house would then be ready to sell—made her legs and arms feel heavy, as leaden as the color of the sky. She didn't want to leave Chance Harbor and the memories it contained of herself as a young lover and new bride, as a wife and mother, and now as an older woman with so much life to be thankful for having lived. This house, this island, was where she'd grown into womanhood. Selling it would be losing herself.

She couldn't do it. She wouldn't. She'd find a way to keep the house.

As Eve walked into the wind with her head down, she heard someone calling and looked up. Darcy! She had told him she would be here for Thanksgiving, had joked about him joining them, but she hadn't taken him seriously when he'd said he'd consider it. Surely he'd want to spend Thanksgiving with his children. Here he was, though, Bear bounding ahead of her to greet him.

"You came!" She laughed, as Bear pushed against Darcy's legs ecstatically and nuzzled his hands. Darcy's face creased in a smile. He was hatless, his hair a tuft of silver feathers rising in the sun, as if he were some exotic seabird.

"Yes. I didn't feel like flying to California to see my son, and my daughter's in Mexico for her anniversary. I'll see the kids at Christmas," he said. "I saw your car in the driveway and came down to the beach. The girls told me where you were." He stopped a respectable distance away. Beyond him, Zoe and Willow were waiting by the staircase leading up to the house and watching them curiously. "How was the trip?"

Eve wanted to push herself against him, to nuzzle his hands as the dog had done. She wanted—and her own desire stunned her—to feel caressed by Darcy. Yet knowing the girls could see them held her back.

"The trip was uneventful," she said, "unlike the days leading up to it."

She hadn't told him much during their phone conversations, only saying there had been "some drama" with Catherine, Zoe, and Willow. Now she felt suddenly shy. This man was a stranger. They'd known each other hardly any time at all.

Darcy reached for her hand. "Can't wait to hear all," he said. "Did you buy your turkey yet?"

She shook her head. "It seemed easier to pretend we'd missed Thanksgiving; after all, we're in Canada and they celebrated weeks ago. Lower expectations during this particular holiday might be a good thing."

"Ah. Well, let's not celebrate Thanksgiving, then. But how about if I cook my turkey at your house, maybe the day after tomorrow?"

"Now, that's an offer I definitely can't refuse," she said, and kissed him.

CHAPTER TWENTY-THREE

This was how Zoe was like Nola: she could sleep forever. Willow would go into her mom's room to wake her, only to be swatted away. Then she sat on the hard wooden chair beside the single bed in the room with its slanted ceiling, watching Mom sleep until Nana called her downstairs for breakfast.

She sat there not because it was so interesting, watching Mom sleep—she slept like a dead person, with one arm tossed over her face like it weighed fifty pounds—but because Willow always hoped she could watch her mom's face and tell what she was dreaming about. Or maybe she would hear her talk in her sleep.

It bothered her that she didn't know what Mom was thinking. In this way, Zoe was very different from Nola, who was always on some kind of panty rant. And from Catherine, who was always TMI-ing. Though, right now, Willow was surprised to find herself missing Catherine. A lot. In the last five years, she had spent every holiday and birthday and summer vacation with Catherine. Catherine always knew how to make a holiday special. Any day, really.

If Catherine were here, they'd make something the Pilgrims made, like brown bread in a can or squash muffins, or she'd ask Willow to help her draw and cut out paper Pilgrim hats or at least some turkey decorations.

One year they'd made turkeys out of pine cones and leftover candy corn from Halloween.

Maybe Nana would help her at least make place mats for the table now that Darcy said he was going to roast a turkey. Willow had plenty of white paper and she'd brought her markers and watercolors.

"Why do you sleep so much?" she finally asked Zoe on their second morning at the house in Chance Harbor, when Zoe came slouching downstairs in an old sweatshirt and flannel pajama pants, then shuffled along the kitchen counter as if she had to feel her way to the coffee.

Zoe peered at her through half-lidded eyes. "Why do you get up so damn early and make such an insane racket?" she said, pouring herself a cup of coffee.

"I'm a kid."

"You're not a kid. You're fourteen!"

"Fifteen," Willow corrected.

She could tell by the way Zoe jerked her head up that she really had forgotten.

"You're not, like, using anything, are you?" Willow asked, watching Zoe continue her slow zombie walk over to the fridge to get milk for her coffee.

Her mom snorted. "What would I be using? There's nothing up here and I don't have a car. I'd have to be smoking potato skins."

This made Willow laugh, but barely.

She and Zoe had spent the previous day stripping the smallest bedroom of old wallpaper and putting up fresh. Willow loved everything about this process: soaking the paper and peeling it off in strips, discovering the layers underneath, scraping and sanding the walls smooth. If this were her house, she'd leave those patches of ancient patterns and colors on the white walls. But Nana had brought rolls of new paper, so she and Zoe helped with this, too, measuring and cutting strips and helping Nana sponge and glue them into place.

Darcy worked with them sometimes, too. He was fun to have around, telling dumb jokes she hadn't heard since third grade: "Why did the little red house call the doctor?"

"Because it had window panes!"

The thought of how she'd gone to Mike's house, assuming he was her dad, still made Willow question her own sanity. She should have known that it was too good to be true. Her real dad was probably a drug addict. Or dead! Sometimes she woke up at night and felt the bones of her face, squinching her eyes shut to picture herself better. Did she look like Zoe? Her grandparents? What part of her didn't belong to this family? Her dad could have been anybody and anything: Egyptian. Mexican. Irish. A cop. A homeless guy. A drunk. A hero.

It wasn't until Darcy and Nana went off to buy more groceries that she and Zoe were finally left alone in the house. They were finishing up in the last bedroom when Willow decided to keep asking questions until she got the answers she needed.

"If my dad isn't Mike, then who is he?" Willow said.

"I told you, all right? I don't know," Zoe said, but she wouldn't look at Willow, so she was probably lying.

"What about this?" Willow said. "Just count back nine months from when I was born and list all the guys you hooked up with during that time, okay? There can't be that many, unless you were a prostitute."

"Jesus, Willow. I should smack you upside the head for saying that." Zoe was staring at her now, with a strip of wallpaper in her hand. The wallpaper was green and white striped; earlier Zoe had said the wallpaper made her feel like they were inside a Christmas candy. "How could you think I'd have sex for *money*?"

Because you bought a lot of drugs and we were always broke, Willow thought, but that wasn't an argument she wanted to have. "You have to tell me who my dad was, Mom," she said. "What if my dad died of cancer or a heart attack? Or had Parkinson's or ALS? They can do things for diseases now if you catch them early. Don't you want to help me stay healthy?"

"Christ. You really have spent too much time with Catherine," Zoe muttered, holding up the strip of paper for Willow to press into place.

"It's not fair to blame her for everything."

"Sure I can. Somebody has to! Perfect Miss Catherine can do no wrong. I've been hearing that since I was born."

Willow bit her bottom lip, focusing for a minute on lining up the stripes. This wasn't easy, since the old floor slanted and so did the ceiling, but she did the best she could. "Let's not talk about her, okay?"

"So that's how it is," Zoe said. "You're on her side. Like everybody else."

"Mom!" Willow said sharply. "Stop! This has nothing to do with her, okay? I need to know who my father was. Why can't you just tell me?"

"Because I don't know who he was!" Zoe shouted back, then fell to her knees, face in her hands, tipping over the bucket of warm water they'd been using to sponge the wallpaper into place.

Willow ran into the bathroom for a towel. By the time she returned to the room, her mother had disappeared. She mopped up the mess, then went in search of her, stomach churning. Zoe was sitting on the floor of her old bedroom, her arms wrapped around her knees. Willow was scared at first—she'd found her mother rocking on the floor in that position a few times, usually during bad trips when she was hallucinating—but when Zoe looked up, her eyes were focused and a very sharp blue, like bits of bright sky showing through clouds.

"I'm sorry I upset you." Willow dropped to the floor and rested her hand on her mother's damp leg.

"You shouldn't have to comfort me," her mother said. "You're the kid! I'm the mother!"

Willow shook her head, remembering what Catherine had said once when Willow had come home upset about something at school, listing all the reasons she was dumb and worthless.

"Don't worry," she said, repeating Catherine's words. "I've got your back, and we'll get through this together."

Zoe snorted and lifted her eyes to the ceiling. "We won't, though. Not if I tell you the truth."

"Why not? Mom, please."

"If you know something, you can't ever unknow it."

"Obviously! Come on. Just say it." Willow patted her mother's leg, feeling awkward, then swiveled to face her. "It's just you and me here. Nobody else is listening."

"How you came into the world?" Her mom's expression turned dreamy. "You always tried to make things easy for me, even on that day. You gave me plenty of warning and my body did the work. I just went along for the ride. No drugs. Done in a few hours. You didn't even cry when you were born, not like those horrible babies you see in movies. You were chubby and red and very pleased with yourself for finding your way into the world. You were completely yourself from the start."

Willow smiled. Her mother had told her this story many times, but now she could picture it better, maybe because she had seen Nola's belly grow. She let her eyes drop to her own mother's slender waist. How was it possible that she'd once been part of her mother's body?

"So he wasn't there when I was born," she said, double-checking. "My dad."

Her mother's face closed again. "No. Your father was not there. He doesn't know you exist."

Willow had figured as much, but hearing this still made her feel lost. Forgotten. "Why not? Why didn't you call him?"

"Because we weren't involved." Zoe looked sad, and that made her look older, the lines around her eyes and mouth sketched in deeply, as if some invisible hand were working on her with a sharp black pencil. "Look, here's the truth. I hardly knew the guy. The pregnancy was an accident. Mike and I had broken up and I was sad, so I went to a party and hooked up. That's all there is to the story, baby. I'm sorry. I don't know your dad's name or what happened to him after that."

"Nothing?"

Mom shook her head. "All I remember is that he seemed smart and sweet." She reached out to Willow, touched her knee. "And cute, too. It didn't matter to me that I didn't have a husband. Or a boyfriend. I was happy to have you on my own. Gave me a great excuse to drop out of school. I always hated school."

Willow knew her mom was lying again. But why? And about what? "So you're saying I'm the product of you fucking some hot guy at a party, and you never tried to see him again?"

Zoe lowered her eyes. "Yes."

"Nice." Willow stood up suddenly, her chest aching. So this was it. The beginning and the end of her story: she didn't have a dad, only an irresponsible party mom. "You meant to have sex that night, to forget about Mike. But not to get pregnant. I was a total accident."

"Yes, but a welcome one."

"So welcome that you couldn't even stop doing drugs!" Willow hurled the words at her, as if the words were bones she had to spit out of her mouth. "You loved having a baby so much that you gave me to your sister! Well, you know what? You did the right thing. Catherine deserves to have a daughter, not you!"

Mutely, Zoe nodded, keeping her eyes fixed on the floor between her knees.

"Okay. We cleared that up, I guess," Willow said. "You're off the hook."

Zoe looked up finally. "I'm trying to be good," she said. "I came back for you, didn't I?"

"*Trying* to be good isn't the same thing as *being* good," Willow said. "I love you, but I'm not taking care of you. I'm done with that. You have to learn how to take care of yourself, and so do I."

Willow left her mother on the floor like a forgotten doll and ran downstairs, feeling a little bit bad, but good, too. She was free.

Bethany woke her out of a sound sleep, using her key to get into the house and coming right upstairs into the bedroom to shake Catherine's shoulder. "Okay, get up," she said. "You can't be like this."

"I don't know how else to be." Catherine pulled the pillow over her head.

She'd taken Thanksgiving week off from work, ostensibly to sort out her finances and decide what strategy to follow if Zoe came back from Chance Harbor saying she wanted custody of Willow. She'd thought she might see Grey, too, and figure things out with him.

What she hadn't counted on was the sudden avalanche of emotions that had rolled over her the minute Willow left with Zoe and her mother, as suddenly as if she were standing at the bottom of a mountain during an explosion. She was drowning in these petty, irrational, juvenile feelings and didn't know how to stay above any of them. There was jealousy, first and foremost: every time she imagined her sister walking the beach below the Chance Harbor house with Willow, or cooking in the kitchen with their mother—roles only Catherine had played for the past five years—she was suffused with a hot, choking jealous rage that she knew was beneath her, and useless besides.

Then, on the heels of her jealousy, there was loneliness. She felt more intensely alone than she could remember feeling at any other time in her life, even that first terrifying week at the university. Part of it was physical: Catherine hadn't been alone in this house for more than one or two nights at a time since kicking Russell out. Now the rooms loomed large around her, and her steps echoed on the bare wooden floors as if she were walking through a castle. She had to take the batteries out of the ticking clock on the kitchen wall because each *ticktock* was like a dart shot into her skin. Part of the problem was her imagination: Catherine could see a time when she would have to grant Willow's wish to live with Zoe, and if she did, this was what it would feel like to live alone. She felt purposeless, abandoned, forgotten.

It was tempting to see Grey. But Catherine had decided against spending time with him after all. That would be a crutch, and she didn't want to give herself any false expectations. There could be no relationship there, period. Grey was Zoe's friend. And if Willow ended up living with Zoe, Catherine would feel better if Zoe could lean on Grey when she needed support.

Still, even recognizing all of these emotions, Catherine was shocked by her own weakness. She told herself, almost hourly, that she was not this sort of person. She had never been prone to depression, flu, cramps, or any other thing that might keep her pinned between the sheets. Each morning, she made herself get up, shower, comb her hair, dress, and eat breakfast. But then she took her clothes off again and went right back to bed, where she fell as if shot and went into a near coma.

Everything that Catherine had once considered bedrock in her life had crumbled. Not slowly, and not bit by bit, but with the sudden, deafening finality of dynamite felling a condemned building in a noisy pile of rubble and dust.

So she slept. When Russell called to ask if he could see her, she told him no, she had the flu. When Grey called, she felt suffused with guilt all over again about what he'd told her, about how Zoe had been through such a horrible thing without her support. Grey asked if he could see her, too.

"Oh, what's the point?" she'd responded. "Everything is such a mess."

"What is?"

"Me! I'm a mess."

"Maybe I could help you," he said.

"No. I'm sorry. I like you. I do. But I need to sort things out on my own," she said, and hung up.

She was convinced that her desire for Grey—as powerful as it was—amounted to nothing more than that: physical sensations. Around Grey, she felt wanton, hedonistic, and giddily irresponsible. That couldn't possibly be real.

Her mother had phoned last night to ask again if she could join them for Thanksgiving. She had even offered to pay for a plane ticket so Catherine wouldn't have to drive to Prince Edward Island alone. She had politely declined this as well, then asked to speak with Willow a few minutes.

The girl sounded fine. Happy. She didn't seem to need Catherine anymore. What a terrible, sad relief that was.

But Bethany was different. They'd known each other too long for Bethany to be fooled by anything Catherine did or said. No matter how hard Catherine ever tried to hide from the world, she was certain Bethany would find her. Whether she was in bed or meditating in a mountain cave, Bethany would drag her kicking and screaming into the light.

Which was what she did now. Three days after Willow left for Chance Harbor, Bethany arrived and literally tugged Catherine out of bed by the hand and made her get dressed in a way that reminded Catherine of how efficient and practical her friend had been in college and nursing school, using index cards and colored markers. These days Bethany was a take-no-prisoners sort of geriatric nurse practitioner, and that, too, was obvious as Bethany literally forced Catherine's arms and legs into the holes of clothing she barely recognized.

Then, properly buttoned and combed and zipped, Catherine found herself sitting at the kitchen table with a pot of coffee between herself and her best friend. As Bethany chattered idly about her new workout routine at the gym—this was an evergreen topic with her—Catherine felt suddenly alert. She was awake, focused, and terrified.

Bethany must have sensed the change, because she began asking questions instead of talking about herself. Catherine told her everything, then sighed. "This is why I can't go anywhere or see anyone," she said. "I feel like my skin's on inside out."

"What does that even mean?"

"That I feel raw. Exposed." Catherine struggled to explain. "Everything's hard. Everything hurts. Bottom line: my life isn't the way I thought it would be."

Bethany laughed. "Welcome to my world. Do you think I expected to have twins so soon after my first kid? Or that I thought I'd get a promotion at work the same month my day care provider got arrested for embezzlement? Honey, having the world be different from our expectations is pretty much the definition of life."

Catherine made a face at her. "Which fortune cookie did you get that out of?"

"Come on. You know what I mean. You've never been naive. You're the most grounded person I know!"

"And where has that gotten me? I'm about to be divorced, Willow's going to want to live with Zoe, and I can't even be mad at my sister because now I feel too sorry for her. Plus, I've been having sex with a gypsy, for God's sake. A guy who's Zoe's roommate and totally wrong for me."

"You can still be mad," Bethany said. "Zoe had a terrible experience.

Horrible, really. But if that had happened to you or me, I doubt we would have done drugs and given up our children." She caught Catherine's shocked look, but didn't back down. "Just saying."

"That's my point, though. It *didn't* happen to me. But that was just lucky. Grey says Zoe wasn't high or drunk when she got raped. Just with the wrong friend at the wrong party. You and I both got into situations like that. If things had turned ugly, who knows what we would have done? Or been like after?"

"Well, we'll never have to know that, thankfully," Bethany said, "but you can't sit around in the house. This isn't helping you decide anything."

"Decide what, though? Everything is out of my control. Zoe and Willow and Russell will do whatever they want. All I can do is react."

"Not necessarily. By wallowing here, don't you think you're being a little bit like Zoe?" Bethany reached across the table to pat her hand.

"What do you mean?"

"You've pretty much abandoned Willow, Catherine! She acted out. Ran away. Shoplifted. You know why? She wanted your attention. But you've completely shut her out in the cold by acting like you don't care if you spend Thanksgiving with her or not."

"I thought it was the right thing to do! To give her time with Zoe," Catherine said, confused. "Free of my interference."

"Has it ever occurred to you that maybe Willow *wants* your interference? You're the one who's always telling me that my teenagers feel free to say they hate me because they know I'll always be there. Maybe that's what this is about. Maybe Willow isn't really trying to find her father as much as she's testing people to see who really cares about her."

"I think I've made it clear to Willow that I'll do everything in my power to keep her safe."

"That's not quite the same thing as telling her that you want her to live with you, but you'll always love her no matter what happens."

Catherine pulled her hand away from Bethany's. Her chest felt tight, imagining Willow in Chance Harbor without her. Without knowing what was going to happen. "God. How can you be so right?"

"Because we're not talking about my life here," Bethany said. "We're talking about yours. I suck at giving myself advice. And I'm even worse at taking it."

Bethany stayed with Catherine while she made the phone call to Eve. Her mother didn't pick up; Catherine left a message saying she'd decided to come for Thanksgiving after all, then hung up, feeling shaky.

"Are you sure this is the right thing?" she asked.

Bethany put her arms around her, rested her chin on Catherine's shoulder. Her body felt round and solid against Catherine's. "I am," she said. "Remember. You don't have to do anything or say anything to Zoe. All you have to do is be there with Willow. You've been her mother for five years. Don't quit now."

"But I'm not her mother."

"You have been her mother in every way that matters," Bethany insisted, giving her a little squeeze before she released her. "Especially in the worry department. Now, get packing. And I want you to promise me you'll stop and see Grey on your way north."

"What would be the point of that?"

Bethany shrugged. "Do you like this gypsy man?"

"Yes."

"Does he treat you right?"

"Yes."

"Do you love getting naked with him?" Bethany gave her a wicked grin.

Catherine grinned back.

"So, what's the problem?" Bethany gave her another little shove. "Go tell him how you feel! Catherine, honey, you have spent way too many years being responsible. For once, follow your heart instead of your head. Let yourself enjoy the moment instead of worrying about what might come next."

An hour later, Catherine's heart was thudding in her throat as she stopped at the trailer park on her way north. She was equally relieved and despondent to discover that Grey wasn't there.

As she was trying to find paper in her car to leave a note, a small blue sedan pulled up in front of the mobile home. Madame Justine stepped out of it wearing a full-length, tan quilted down coat. She looked like a bratwurst with feet.

"You want my son," she said.

Catherine hoped Grey's mother didn't know how literally true this was. "Yes," she said. "I stopped by to tell him happy Thanksgiving. I'm driving north to spend it with my mom and Zoe and Willow."

The other woman nodded. "You will get in my car," she said. "I will take you to him."

"Oh, no. I couldn't bother you."

"You must," Madame Justine insisted. "You are the one," she added ominously. "The healer. I have seen you in my son's cards. The High Priestess."

Whatever that meant. Reluctantly, Catherine slid into the seat next to Madame Justine, whose scent—something spicy, with a hint of coconut and lime—filled the car. Catherine's sinuses, clogged from being in bed for three days straight, cleared instantly.

"I really should be getting on the road," she said, "if I'm going to make it to Prince Edward Island in time for Thanksgiving."

"You will make it." Madame Justine drove like a pro, her hands fluid on the wheel, her foot heavy on the gas, passing other cars smoothly and at a speed that made Catherine grip her seat beneath her thighs.

Catherine wondered whether the woman was well-known in town. She'd have to be, if she told fortunes on the boardwalk. Sure enough, a minute later they passed a state police car, and the two cops inside it waved, grinning. Madame Justine lifted one hand off the wheel just long enough to grace them with a queenly flutter of her plump fingers.

"Where are we going?" Catherine said.

"I will take you to my son's house."

"But I thought he lived in the trailer park. With my sister."

Madame Justine's smile was bountiful. "Not anymore. He is in his own house now. Since last week."

They had backtracked south from Salisbury Beach and were now turning onto Ring's Island. The island overlooked Newburyport's brick and church-steepled skyline on the other side of the Merrimack River. Catherine had been here only twice before, when she was little and her parents took her and Zoe to watch the fireworks.

Once a Colonial fishing village, Ring's Island was now a tiny enclave of restored antique houses set close to the curb along narrow streets. Grey's house was on the water, a classic Colonial painted deep red with silvery teal trim. It was surrounded by a picket fence stained a warm gold and capped in copper. The copper weather vane on the barn roof was shaped like a dinghy.

Catherine could hear an electric power tool buzzing in the barn when Madame Justine shut off the car engine. "You will find Grey inside there," she said, gesturing with her chin. "He is waiting for you."

"But he didn't know I was coming."

Madame Justine smiled. "I told him you would be here."

To Catherine's shock, the minute she was out of the car, Madame Justine began pulling out of the driveway. Great. Now she'd have to ask Grey to give her a ride back to her car.

Catherine studied the building's classic lines and new roof, the expensive landscaping, the new asphalt driveway, and couldn't believe it was Grey's house. It had to have at least four bedrooms, given the number of windows, and the view of the river and the city was spectacular.

She made her way up a brick walk laid in a herringbone pattern—this also looked new—and called Grey's name when she opened the barn door.

He was inside, dressed in jeans and a thick blue sweater dotted with wood shavings. He wore a mask over his face, but lifted it when he saw her, grinning over the boat hull he'd been sanding. "So my mother was right. She said you'd come."

"I don't know whether it would be creepy or useful, having a fortune-teller for a mother." Catherine couldn't help grinning back.

"It's good when my fortune is favorable." He set down the sander and came over to her.

"I came to say good-bye." Catherine felt suddenly nervous.

Grey stopped smiling. "Why? Where are you going?"

"I'm on my way to Chance Harbor to spend Thanksgiving."

Grey's face relaxed. "Good. I'm glad. You and Zoe need to work this out."

"I can't promise that will happen."

He stepped forward and embraced her, resting his chin on top of her head, holding her in place so effectively that she felt rooted to the spot, breathing in sawdust. "You'll try, though," he said.

"Yes."

"Good. Want a coffee before you go?"

"All right."

As the coffee brewed, Grey showed her the new kitchen cupboards he was building out of refurbished barn boards. "There were two barns on the property originally," he said, "but one was in such bad shape, I didn't have any choice but to tear it down."

"I can't believe you're doing all this yourself," she said. "And I'm still having trouble believing that you're a gypsy, living in a house like this."

He looked amused. "Why?"

"I don't know. This house seems so grand and permanent."

"Not a place for gypsies, tramps, and thieves, huh?"

"A rolling stone," she amended. "That's what I thought all gypsies were."

He pulled her close and kissed her. "I'm a rolling stone that favors a particular riverbank. And one particular woman." He kissed her again.

This time, when Grey pulled away Catherine moved closer. Bethany was right: life was made up of moments, and maybe this one could be hers. She wouldn't worry about after.

She was the one to lead them upstairs. They made love in Grey's bedroom, with its windows letting in the milky autumn light, in a cherry sleigh bed piled high with quilts. Afterward, they curled up together on the window seat overlooking the river, which was rapidly darkening beneath the afternoon sky, a black ribbon now edged in silver.

"It's too late for you to go now," Grey murmured. "You'll have to spend the night."

She shook her head. "I can still make it to Bangor."

"I could drive you to Chance Harbor in my Porsche. Fast."

This was tempting. But something inside her resisted. This had to be *her* journey. "I'll see you when I get back," she promised, and knew she would.

Grey drove her back to Newburyport. From there it took her three hours to get to Bangor, where she stayed in a hotel room that smelled of chlorine. She didn't care; she sank into a deep sleep and woke before the alarm she'd set for six o'clock.

The drive to Prince Edward Island was hellishly long without company. She sang with the radio or argued with talk-show hosts to keep herself awake. For lunch she stopped for fish and chips at a small New Brunswick restaurant overlooking the Bay of Fundy.

Every meal, every scene along the road, reminded her of family trips to Chance Harbor. Of her parents talking in the front seat while she and Zoe rode in back and argued or played word games or, sometimes, took turns tracing letters on each other's narrow backs, trying to guess the words they were writing.

Catherine remembered, as she continued along the Bay of Fundy's dramatic shoreline, how they had always stopped for smoked salmon at a tiny family-run smokehouse down one of the side roads leading to a cove. The smokehouse was built of cinder blocks and painted yellow, like some kind of Lego house. The giant rosebush in front of it attracted hummingbirds by the dozen.

They would pack the salmon into a cooler and then drive to the end of that road, to a remote rocky cove with a series of small humpbacked islands rising out of the water like turtles surfacing. It was always foggy there, making the colored fishing boats look even brighter.

Despite the icy water, she and Zoe would take off their shoes, not minding the rocks because they were smooth and slippery. Their bare feet and ankles were soon numbed by the water. Water so cold that the pain roared up their skinny legs and into their spines, a sudden shock of sensation that made them laugh.

Their mother waded with them while their father made sandwiches of salmon and onion and butter on thick crusty bread. Then they'd eat, their family alone in that forgotten misty cove. Their own world. Happy.

And then, one day, they were not happy. Zoe was a teenager and acting out. Her parents were bitter and scared, alienated from each other. Their marriage—now that Catherine had more perspective on it, she could see this—had gone sour. They had stayed together out of sheer stubbornness and loyalty. But maybe that was a form of love. She could see that now, too.

Marriage was such a tricky thing. A creature all its own, separate in many ways from the two people who created it. Like a child, a marriage had to be nurtured and fed, and even then it could have unexpected traits, inherited or brought on by environment.

A marriage could be happy and calm, or petty and jealous, or angry and removed. A separate being that grew bigger and stronger on its own, apart from the couple who made it. Or, alternatively, the marriage became malnourished and eventually withered and died. You could try to mold a marriage into what you wanted and expected. But, sometimes, all the willpower in the world wasn't enough to save it. Triage came too late. That's how it was with Russell. She could never go back to him now.

By the time Catherine reached Chance Harbor, she had exhausted herself not only by driving steadily forward with so few breaks, but also from performing these mental gymnastics. Her reveries about love and marriage and family had led her exactly nowhere.

Or maybe they had, she thought, as she slammed the car door behind her and stood in front of the yellow house, where Willow, spotting her from the window, came bounding outside like a colt, all skinny legs and hopeful face.

Maybe her life, her marriage, had led her exactly here, to a place where she could open her arms wide and welcome this girl who was like a daughter to her, to say, "I'm so glad to see you. I missed you like crazy. I hope you know how much I love you."

CHAPTER TWENTY-FOUR

"Why are you making me see these people?"

Zoe sounded about twelve years old, Eve thought. They were in the car, just the two of them, driving toward North Lake. It was a clear morning, and the potato fields sparkled with snow. Snow swirls rose in front of them as the wind whipped up miniature tornadoes of red dirt mixed with white. "They're family. You know Cousin Jane."

Zoe frowned and buried her chin deeper into the purple quilted down jacket Eve had loaned her. "You mean Dad's cousin? That woman with the bubble butt and the big hair who never stops talking? *That's* who we're going to see? But why?"

"I wanted to bring her a pumpkin pie for Thanksgiving. And I wanted her to see you."

"But it's not even their Thanksgiving. That's already over." Zoe was looking panicked. Trapped. "I don't see what the point is."

"The point is that Jane is Malcolm's older sister," Eve said.

Now Zoe looked like she wanted to open the car door and jump out. But there was no place for her to go: just snow and wind and pine trees and frozen potato fields and bright blue water everywhere she looked. "I don't want to see her."

"I know. But she wants to see you."

"Jesus, Mommy. This is torture."

Eve kept her hands steady on the wheel. "It's a small island, honey. You can't hide from family here."

When they pulled up in front of Jane's small brown house, three other cars and a pickup truck were parked in the driveway. "Who else is here?" Zoe nearly yelled.

"I have no idea. More family, I imagine."

"Do they all know?" Zoe glanced at Eve, eyes wide.

"I don't think so," Eve said, but her own knees were unsteady as she climbed out of the car and got the pie from the backseat. "Ten minutes," she promised. "That's all. Then we'll say we have to go home and help Darcy cook."

They did not visit for ten minutes, of course. More like an hour. Jane had gathered all of her children—four of them, three with spouses—as well as her grandchildren, and Malcolm's two children as well. Malcolm's children, both sons, looked and sounded so much like him, and like Andrew, too, with their fair hair and ruddy complexions, and their talk of fishing and farming, that Eve had to sit down quickly in the kitchen with the women. Jane pressed her to eat a cheese biscuit with her tea, served on what was clearly her best flowered china.

Zoe was embraced by one relative after another, most of whom remembered her as a child and a teenager. They regaled her with questions about life in the United States, especially sports, and Eve was relieved to see Zoe open up, as if it hadn't been more than fifteen years since her last visit. At one point, one of her half brothers said, "Jesus and Mary, if this girl isn't the spittin' image of himself, our uncle Andrew, eh?" at which point Jane met Eve's eyes over the table and smiled.

"Thank you for bringing her," Jane said, pressing Eve's hands between her own as they were leaving. Jane's hands felt warm and solid as two new loaves of bread. "I just wanted to see his children gathered together again, now that they're all grown-up."

"I wish it could have happened sooner, but after Zoe dropped out of college, she was living a bit rough," Eve said. "I'm sorry. We couldn't get her to do anything with the family, and then she disappeared for years."

To her surprise, Jane nodded. "Aye, I know you've been through a rough time with this girl of yours. But so many of the young ones go through a rough patch, and we're always glad to see them return. I'm very glad to see your girl here now. I know Malcolm is watching and feeling very pleased, too."

Zoe was carrying on with her cousins outside, tossing snowballs as if she really were twelve years old again. "I bet she'll come back," Eve said. "Should we tell anyone else?"

"I don't know about that," Jane said. "Let's just leave things as they are, eh? We'll let Zoe do it, if she's a mind to, when she feels ready."

"All right." Eve kissed Jane on the cheek. "I love you. And your family. I hope you know how much."

"You're one of us—don't forget that," Jane said. "So don't you go selling that house. You need to keep one foot on the island. For your girls, if nothing else."

"I've decided to keep the house," Eve said.

Jane, in her customary no-nonsense way, did nothing more than nod, but her eyes were bright. "Well, there. That's all settled, then."

On the drive back, Eve glanced at Zoe, whose profile was serene against the deepening blue sky. "So what do you think of the island, now that you're back?"

"That it's nice to be in a place where most of my memories are happy." Zoe turned in her seat to look at Eve. "Was it very awful, thinking I was dead?"

The question stunned Eve. "I mostly didn't believe you were really dead," she said when she could trust her voice. "I thought I'd know if you were. But, yes, the few times I let my mind go there, it was awful."

"Still, it must have been easier in a lot of ways, not having to worry about me."

Eve was so angry that she jerked the car over to the side of the road, flinging Zoe against the window, and slammed it into park. She unclasped her seat belt and turned to look at her daughter. "Do not ever dare say that again," she said. "Do not ever think that I would wish you dead. You are my *child*!" she yelled, and burst into tears.

"Oh, Mommy," Zoe said, and slid across the seat to hold her.

They'd been kicked out of the house. "Go, go, go!" Eve cried, actually shooing them out of the kitchen door with a dish towel.

Catherine suspected her mother had contrived this as a way to push her into talking alone with Zoe. So far, she and her sister had been circling like territorial cats, polite but for the occasional hiss, with Willow nervously bouncing between them and giggling like a hyper eight-year-old or clinging to Catherine.

"Let us at least help peel potatoes or something," Catherine said. There was no part of her that felt ready to be alone with Zoe.

"This kitchen isn't big enough for both of you," Eve snapped. "You can help with cleanup later. Go down to the beach and get some air while it's still light out. You've been moping around underfoot, and I can't stand it anymore."

"We're not moping," Zoe said. "I was doing a puzzle."

"I don't care what you were doing. You girls need some fresh air to work up an appetite," Eve said. Then, when Willow began putting her jacket on to follow them, she hauled her back. "Not you, Willow. You stay here and set the table."

Catherine stepped outside and hesitated as Zoe bounded toward the cliff, declaring her intention to walk the beach as far as Basin Head. "You can come or not," she tossed over her shoulder, and disappeared down the steep wooden staircase leading to the water.

In this late-afternoon light, the sun slanted orange over the snowy fields. Catherine could make out bird and mouse tracks on top of the slight crust of snow, proving that even in the dead of winter, even on this remote corner of a remote island, life went on, no matter what silly business the humans were conducting.

She took the staircase gingerly because some of the boards were icy, hating herself for being so cautious. Zoe, whom she could see striding along the beach, had probably descended the steps at a run, or maybe even jumped from the halfway point.

The beach was mostly free of snow. If they'd been at home, it would be getting dark by now. But on Prince Edward Island, the light lingered in the sky and turned all shades of color, as if someone up there were constantly tie-dyeing the horizon, refusing to create the same crazy color combinations twice. Just now the clouds were shadowed in purple and laced in green and yellow.

Catherine picked her way through the enormous red rocks, staying close to the cliff to keep out of the wind. Zoe had stopped to examine something in the sand—deliberately?—and Catherine caught up with her by the first trio of tall dunes.

"Sea glass," Zoe said, holding out her palm. A triangular piece of glass lay there, a delicate turquoise color.

"Pretty."

"Probably one of the same pieces we picked up as kids. I always thought Mom tossed them back on the beach at night after we found them."

"Me, too."

They walked into the wind toward Basin Head. Catherine's forehead was numb with cold. She couldn't think of how to begin to tell Zoe what she'd found out from Grey, and that one confession seemed to have lodged in her throat, preventing any other conversation.

"What do you think of Darcy?" Zoe asked. "Pretty hunky for sixty."

Catherine laughed, glad to have a distraction. "He's probably pushing seventy."

"Whatever. It's still weird, right, how he and Mom can hardly keep their eyes off each other? I even saw them holding hands. It's like chaperoning a pair of lovesick teenagers."

"They do seem pretty smitten."

"Guess that's better than her being alone. And he's kind of sweet. Nicer than Dad in a lot of ways. I still can't believe the guy's cooking us a turkey."

"Mom could do worse," Catherine agreed. She'd forgotten this: how much time she and Zoe used to spend watching their parents, dissecting their moods. She supposed all children must do that, and then shuddered to think of what Willow must have observed between her and Russell. "Observing the animals in their natural habitat," Zoe had called it in middle school when she'd spy on their parents and report something back to Catherine like, "The male of the species is now circling the watering hole, in search of whiskey, while the female flicks her tail feathers and issues indignant squawks. This is their weekly mating ritual."

Nobody could make her laugh as hard as her sister. Now, as they continued walking in silence, Zoe's silhouette beside her seemed so familiar that Catherine felt almost as if they were walking back through time, to the childhood and adolescence they'd spent on this beach with innumerable MacLeish cousins.

Just then Zoe glanced at her, eyebrows raised beneath the old blue watch cap of their father's she'd shoved onto her head, her yellow bangs pressed flat beneath it. "How weird is this?" she said, echoing Catherine's thoughts. "I feel like I'm ten again."

"I know. I was just thinking the same thing."

"I'm glad you came for Thanksgiving," Zoe said. "It's good you're here. You made Mom's holiday happier. Willow's, too. They were missing you."

Was Zoe, too? Catherine wished she knew. She searched the patterned sand at their feet, looking for the right words written there in the scrolls of the sea. "Listen. I know what happened to you at school. How you got pregnant. And I'm sorry."

Zoe stopped walking and shoved her hands deep into her pockets. "Who told you? Mom?"

So their mother knew, too. This surprised Catherine, but she wasn't about to tell Zoe it was Grey. He was Zoe's best friend; it might be worse if it had come from him.

"When did you tell her the truth?" Catherine asked to avoid answering her question.

"Not long ago."

"I'm so sorry," Catherine said again. "I wish I'd known."

"I didn't *want* you to know." Zoe started walking again, faster. "I still wish nobody did."

Catherine had to step up her pace and felt suddenly breathless, remembering this, too, from their childhood at Chance Harbor: Zoe, after about age eight, was always faster, stronger, and more impulsive than she was. So mercurial that Catherine had often felt like she was a faint light trailing after her sister's own bright flare.

"Does Willow know?"

Zoe shook her head, hard. "I would never tell her, and don't you do it, either," she said fiercely, stopping again to grab Catherine's arm. "Please."

"But she has to know. Otherwise she'll keep asking questions."

"No. I don't think so. Yesterday I told her a partial truth, okay? Enough. I just said I'd met this guy at a party and hooked up with him. That he was a nice guy, but it was a onetime thing and I never looked for him. That's all she knows."

"Why don't you want to tell her?"

"I don't want Willow to ever think the rape had anything to do with her. I don't want her tainted by it," Zoe said. "I know that's a medieval word, and I know I'm supposed to be a feminist and all that, but Willow doesn't have to know everything, okay? Promise me that."

"I promise," Catherine said, touched by her sister's determined generosity. "For what it's worth, I think you're probably right not to tell her."

Zoe turned away, but not before Catherine could see that she was crying, one cheek shinier than the other. "Thanks."

"You're welcome. But I still don't understand why you didn't tell me. I was right there, Zoe!"

"You were busy getting ready to graduate."

"You're my sister. I would have dropped everything for you!"

Zoe shrugged, the purple jacket hunching up around her ears as if it had been pulled upward by strings. "You did that enough. You'd already made it clear you were done with me, after I came crying to you about Mike so many times."

This was true. Catherine thought back to how Zoe had wept, her eyes red-rimmed for weeks after Mike broke up with her. How she'd refused to eat and couldn't sleep without dope or antihistamines. By then Catherine had met Russell, was busy planning not only her graduation party, but their wedding. Then would come nursing school. Her future was set. Zoe, she had thought, was wallowing. Again.

"My sister's a histrionic attention-seeker," was how she'd described Zoe to Russell one night when they'd come home to find Zoe sitting on the doorstep of her apartment in the rain, begging to spend the night.

Now, thinking of what Zoe had gone through during the rape and its aftermath, of how alone she must have felt, Catherine's stomach turned. "I was an awful sister to you," she said, hurrying to catch up because Zoe was ahead of her again. She linked arms with Zoe this time, using such a strong grip that Zoe made a little noise of surprise.

"It doesn't matter. That was a long time ago. Anyway, you were never awful," Zoe said. "I was always the awful one."

"Oh, I see how it is. It's still the Sister Olympics around here. You have to be a faster walker *and* more awful, too?"

To her relief, Zoe laughed. "Look, I know I never made things easy for us. For Mom and Dad, either. But I understand myself better now."

"Good. Me, too."

Zoe shook her head. "No. I mean, I understand who I am and where I came from. There's something I need to tell you."

Catherine felt a sharp stone of dread in her throat and couldn't swallow. "What?"

"Dad? He's not my real father."

"What?" Catherine stopped and pulled Zoe around by the arm to face her. Zoe's cheeks were bright red from the wind, her freckles almost invisible. "You can't be serious."

"I am. Mom told me. She had an affair with Malcolm. You know, Dad's cousin?"

Catherine frowned. She'd heard that name. "Cousin Jane's brother? The one who drowned?"

"Yes. I guess Dad fooled around, and Mom felt lonely, so . . ." She shrugged. "And I was the result."

"My God," Catherine said. "Does anybody else know?"

"Only Cousin Jane, apparently."

"Of course. Nothing gets past her. Funny she kept it a secret."

Zoe nodded. "I know. Maybe she didn't want Dad to be embarrassed. Or maybe it was out of respect for Malcolm after he died, you know, because he had kids." She smiled, her teeth very white in the late-afternoon light, which was burnishing the gold grass at the tops of the dunes a fiery orange, making the dunes look like they'd caught fire. "I saw Malcolm's kids yesterday. So freaky."

"When?"

"When you took Willow to the store." Zoe made a face. "Mom made me go with her when she brought them a pie. She must have arranged it ahead of time with Cousin Jane somehow, because there were, like, a hundred people there. Including my two half brothers, who I hadn't seen since the summer after my senior year of high school. They're much older than I am, but it was weird, seeing how much I actually look like them now that we're all adults."

"Jesus. I always thought you and I looked alike." Catherine was having trouble keeping up with all this; she imagined the same red sunset glow over her head as her brain overheated.

"We do. But Malcolm was Dad's cousin, so I guess that makes sense," Zoe said. She laughed. "It's like we're all one big MacLeish herd. Doesn't really matter who our dads were in some ways because that bloodline is so strong."

"Seriously, Zoe. How did you feel, seeing them, now that you know?"

Zoe shrugged. "Surprisingly okay. I've always felt so alone, you know? It's good to be in a place where people just accept me as family. And now I understand why Dad felt responsible for me but couldn't completely claim me as his. He must have looked at me and seen Malcolm, but I always reminded him of Mom cheating on him, too."

"He cheated on her first," Catherine said, thinking of the trip to Cape

Breton, of her mother being pregnant with Zoe as their father wept down on the dock, waving good-bye. Now that final puzzle piece fell into place, too, and she told Zoe.

"Wow," Zoe said.

"Right. Wow."

"So we're only half sisters." Zoe said this matter-of-factly, but Catherine heard the pain in her voice.

"Are you kidding?" Catherine said. "I held you in my arms the day you were born. You've been the kind of pain in the ass only a real sister could be."

Zoe laughed. Her nose was running, Catherine saw, and her eyes, too. Maybe it was the wind, but she didn't think so.

"We'd better get back," Zoe said. "My face is freezing off."

"Mine, too."

They had made it halfway to the stairs leading up to the house when Zoe said, "We need to talk about Willow."

The tide was coming in, so they had to walk on higher ground, where there were rocks and dried clumps of seaweed. Catherine stumbled a little in the sand, the dread she'd been carrying suddenly boulder-sized. "What about her?" she asked, then made herself say it. "You want custody, I guess."

Zoe shook her head. "No. I think Willow should keep living with you."

Catherine was stunned. "Are you sure? You're her mother, Zoe."

Zoe put a hand to her face and didn't speak for a moment. When she brought her hand down, her voice was shaky and difficult to hear over the surf. "The thing is, every time you look at Willow, you see the baby you always wanted, the girl you love. A beautiful child," she said slowly. "But when I look at her, I only see that sometimes. Other times Willow reminds me, you know, of everything that happened. Of every mistake I ever made."

"But that's crazy. What happened wasn't your fault."

"I know the rape wasn't my fault. But how many times did I make the wrong choices, Cat? How many times did I choose the easy way out, instead of doing all the hard things, like going to school and working and taking care of my damn kid?" Zoe's voice had risen, as if she were shouting at herself. "You were right. I've screwed her up, and I need to stop doing that."

Catherine's entire being had gone very still. She focused only on her sister now. She said, "Willow is her own person, Zoe, with her own life ahead of her. That's what you and I have to keep remembering: we are only two people in her life. Two important people, but only two. Willow has Mom and Russell, teachers and friends. Someday she might even have a family of her own. You have tried your hardest to do the right things for her. I see that now. If you want custody, I won't fight you. I'll try to help you any way I can. You and Willow."

"Wow. Quite the speech." Zoe was smiling. "Thanks. But I'm not able to be a parent the way you are, Cat. I want her to live with you. It'll be better for her. I think Willow knows that, too. She loves you. And, more importantly, she trusts you."

"And you? What will you do?" Catherine was standing very close to her sister now, close enough that they were sheltering each other from the wind. "You're not leaving, are you?" She felt unexpectedly panicked by the idea.

Zoe shook her head. "I'll stick around. I don't want to bail on Willow again. Grey says I can live in the trailer as long as I need a place, and Mom's willing to help me with tuition if I go back to school. Or maybe I'll move up here in the spring, help Mom out with the house. Tuition's even cheaper at the university here. I'll see Willow wherever I go. That's the only sure thing. Otherwise, one day at a time, right? And today is Thanksgiving. We'd better go up and eat some of that turkey."

The darkness had fallen completely as they began their ascent up the cliff. Now the moon was out, just a sliver of white.

As she reached the top of the ladder, Catherine saw that the lights in the Chance Harbor house were on, the windows gleaming yellow squares. Through one of them, she could see Willow in the kitchen, waiting for them to return, her face turned toward the window.

Right after they'd eaten and washed the china, wiped the counters and fallen into living room chairs with books and another endless puzzle,

Darcy announced he had a surprise for them. "Time for us to go outside," he said. "Bundle up!"

"You're out of your mind," Eve said, but she forced herself off the sofa, groaning a little from the turkey and potatoes. She got her coat and scarf from the pegs outside the kitchen and told Willow to help Catherine and Zoe carry the wool blankets they'd stacked on the porch.

"Wait. Turn off all the lights," Darcy said as they were shoving their feet into boots and hands into mittens.

"This is crazy," Zoe said, but she went upstairs and did as he asked, while Willow and Catherine turned off the lights downstairs.

They felt their way through the dark onto the back lawn, where Darcy had somehow managed to pull the Adirondack chairs out of the barn and line them up on the cliff without Eve noticing. It must have been while she and Willow were cutting out decorations, as she was fretting about her daughters alone on the beach. Whatever had happened between them must have settled something, she decided, after watching them laugh and tell stories at the table.

Darcy instructed them to sit in the chairs. The surf rushed in and out below, the Northumberland Strait breathing like a dragon at their feet.

"Not you, though," Darcy said to Willow. "I need you as my assistant."

Willow went over to him. Once Eve's eyes adjusted to the darkness—nearly complete, with the lights turned off in the house and no ambient light other than that thumbnail of moon—she saw that Darcy had set up a tripod with a camera on it. He turned around for a moment to smile at her, a glimmer of white in the inky blue. His Cheshire-cat grin, she thought fondly. The grin that announced life was good. And perhaps it was, the way Darcy always chose to see it. She hoped to learn that trick from him.

"What we're witnessing tonight," Darcy announced, gesturing grandly at the sky above them, "are the Leonids, the annual meteor shower associated with Earth crossing paths with a comet called Tempel-Tuttle."

"Why isn't it called the Tempel-Tuttle meteor shower, then?" Zoe called from her chair.

"Ah, so glad you asked," Darcy said. "It's because the radiant of this particular meteor shower—the place where it's brightest—is the constellation Leo. Now, no more questions. I'll answer those later. Right now I want you all to keep your eyes on the sky. Except you," he added, touching Willow's shoulder. "I need you to help me record the event. Okay, if I told you the wider the lens, the more sky we'd see, what lens would you choose? Here's what I have."

Darcy and Willow squatted over a case holding his camera lenses, conferring quietly. Eve tipped her head up, pulling the woolen blanket to her chin. On this clear, cold night, the stars were so abundant that she wondered if she'd see any meteors at all. Then, quite suddenly, there was a streak of light across the sky, making her gasp, and then more of them, as if the sky were raining light.

Zoe and Catherine were huddled on the Adirondack love seat beneath a blanket. One of them pointed to the sky and said something Eve couldn't hear. She couldn't tell one voice from the other, and with their heads bent so close together, her daughters appeared to be a single creature. Later, she would take Catherine aside and try to say all of the things she should have said long ago: about Andrew and Marta and their son, to start with, and then a longer conversation about how sorry Eve was about seeming to always favor Zoe over Catherine, when Catherine had needed her just as much as a child. And about how proud she was of Catherine's accomplishments and of how generous and loving a mother she had become.

Eve hoped it wasn't too late for those conversations with her older daughter. What else could a mother do, but keep trying? Meanwhile, for now she was happy to know that her daughters were together. Looking out for each other.

Willow and Darcy had put the lens on the camera and were watching the sky now, too, standing side by side, tipping their heads so comically far back that they looked related, especially with strands of Willow's hair escaping from the hood of her black jacket and floating, almost silver in the moonlight, just like Darcy's.

Watching them, and feeling her daughters beside her, something in Eve let go, that small sad creature inside of her that had been clinging with its monkey paws to the idea that loneliness was her permanent state, because she had been married to a man for whom she was not enough and had lost a daughter, because she had been widowed and worried that she might lose her daughter a second time once every secret was out.

That creature inside her morphed now into something else for Eve, into the sparkling feathered realization that she had family gathered around her, noisy and flawed and generous. She wasn't lonely after all, but a woman who loved and was loved. A woman who would ask for forgiveness and receive it, for all of the mistakes she'd made, and would continue to make, as long as she lived beneath a sky that rained light.

ACKNOWLEDGMENTS

Where, oh where, would I be without my family? I wouldn't be a writer—that's for sure. Whether I need somebody to do the grocery shopping or leave me alone for a weekend while I hammer out pages, my husband, my mom, and my children are infinitely supportive, even bringing me food and tea at the dining room table when I'm tearing my hair out over a manuscript. Thank you, my peeps. I love you all.

My brother Donald and his family—Jean, Emily, and Jill—continue to urge me on from afar, and one of these days I will definitely set a book in England so I can hang out in their glorious riverside brick farmhouse. I might have to set a few scenes in Ithaca, too, where my brother Phil plays any instrument with strings.

My wonderful extended family—all of you Cooksons, Boyles, Schneiders and Robinsons—gives me the confidence to believe in myself by believing in me. I'm proud to be one of you!

My agent, Richard Parks, has become family as well, after two decades of helping me usher books into the world. Thank you, dear man. I hope you know how much I adore you.

At New American Library, I'm blessed to have a fantastic team supporting the production of my books. Special thanks to my savvy whirlwind editor, Tracy Bernstein, whose knowledge of all things literary, academic, and Broadway knows no bounds and whose love of story is equal to mine. I am also blessed to have NAL publisher, Kara Welsh, in my corner, along with the best design, marketing, and publicity people in this crazy business. Thank you, all.

In addition to my in-house publishing team, I want to thank Rachel Tarlow Gul of Over the River Public Relations for her energetic efforts to find the best readers for my books. And there are many people I treasure in my writing community:

First among my writer-mom friends, I want to thank Susan Straight, Emily Ferrara, and Toby Neal, who all know and love Prince Edward Island as much as I do. I couldn't have written this book without you keeping me company on my various writing retreats there. I also had the support of my caring neighbors on Prince Edward Island, who are always ready to share their stories: Bruce and Pat Craig, Wendell and Barbara Baker, David and Mary Mahar, the Jarvis family, and of course, Rusty and Linda at Elliot's store—thank you for making my family feel so welcome on the island.

Other writers and editors have also been instrumental in helping me talk and think about my writing. A special shout-out especially to Kristin Bair O'Keeffe, Maddie Dawson, Elisabeth Elo, Ann Garvin, Rachael Herron, Terri Giuliano Long, Amy Sue Nathan, Jay Neugeboren, Carla Panciera, Sandi Kahn Shelton, Virginia Smith, Lorrie Thomson, and Sonja Yoerg for being in my corner. I see you waving those pom-poms! I also must thank Melanie Wold, who always seems to have an extra house on hand at the very moment when I need a writing sanctuary most and is so generous about sharing her spaces. And, last but not least, thank you to Brian Simpson, who is not only a fine hairstylist but also a great storyteller—one of his anecdotes made it into this book.

Finally, I wish to extend my sincerest gratitude to all of the bookstore owners and readers who continue to make this novelist's dreams come true. Your support means everything to me.

CONVERSATION GUIDE

CHANCE HARBOR

HOLLY ROBINSON

This Conversation Guide is intended to enrich the individual reading experience, as well as encourage us to explore these topics together—because books, and life, are meant for sharing.

A CONVERSATION WITH HOLLY ROBINSON

Q. Where did the inspiration come from for Chance Harbor?

A. Writing is a bit like cooking: sometimes ingredients come together in ways that surprise you. I love looking back at a book I've written and realizing how many different ingredients went into making it. The original kernel for *Chance Harbor* was a story my mom told me about one of her friends, whose mother abandoned her at a bus station when she was a child. Another important piece was my memory of a beautiful high school classmate who had an affair with one of my teachers—she was already the mother of a toddler, and seemed worlds older than I was. Both of those incidents served as key plot ingredients for this book. Then, as the novel came to a simmer, and then to a slow boil, these original components blended with other ideas and took on complex flavors of their own.

Q. Much of this novel is set in Nova Scotia and on Prince Edward Island. Why there?

A. In all of my books, settings are more than places. For instance, in one of my previous novels, *Beach Plum Island*, the setting was a barrier island that is constantly shape-shifting due to storms and erosion. That island served as a metaphor for how the characters' lives were changing shape as family secrets were revealed and the drama unfolded. I chose to set some of *Chance Harbor* on Prince Edward Island because I divide my time between my homes there and in Massachusetts. I always feel freer to be myself on that island because it's so remote. Likewise, Cape Breton Island—part of Nova Scotia, and a short ferry ride across the Northumberland Strait from my part of PEI—is so wild and mysterious that you feel inspired to open your mind to new ideas as you hike the mountains and view the changing sea from the forested hills and windy headlands.

Q. By now you've published several novels. Do you have a favorite? And has your approach to writing fiction changed since that first attempt?

A. Whatever book I have finished most recently is always my favorite, and I usually hate the manuscript I'm currently working on until the very end. That's because, somewhere in the middle third of every book, I become convinced I will fail. I start each novel with a synopsis, so I go into the actual writing with a pretty firm idea of the plot and the outcome I'm trying to achieve. However, in some mysterious, inexplicable way, the characters begin to demand that I leave the story to *them*, for heaven's sake, and quit trying to boss them around. I then have no choice but to watch the chaos unfold. I had no idea, for instance, that in *Chance Harbor* Eve would be an unfaithful wife and that her adultery would have such an impact on her family's life. With every book I have to consciously make the decision to let go of having absolute control and let the magic happen on the page. That means trusting my subconscious process to take over—which is easier to do, since I have my brilliant editor, Tracy Bernstein, to help me revise whatever doesn't work!

Q. Previously, you've written about women who are painters, potters, farmers, psychologists, and even a DJ. Here, Eve is a retired public relations executive and Catherine is a nurse practitioner. Why do all of your women work?

A. Because most women work, and one of the recurring themes in the lives of all women is that there isn't enough of us to go around. We all feel fractured as we try (and often fail) to balance the demands of home, family, work, and our own physical and mental health. However, I feel, as most of the women in my novels do, that work is also a source of pride and passion and can keep us grounded during times of great stress or grief.

Q. In this novel, Catherine longs for a child, but her unreliable sister, Zoe, abandons hers, and the teen mothers Catherine sees in her practice are often too young to be prepared for parenthood. It hardly seems fair that Catherine can't have children of her own.

A. I know. I thought about creating a plot where Catherine gets pregnant, or ends up adopting one of the infants in her pediatric practice. Then I thought, no, that wouldn't be true to life, would it? So often, being a "good" person doesn't necessarily mean you will be rewarded by good things happening to you. We must all learn to accept, and even embrace, our lives as they unfold. In addition, I believe that family isn't about DNA. Your family is made up of the people who care about you, or whom you care for, whether those people are relatives, neighbors, or friends. We all have the potential to build happy families no matter how dysfunctional our families of origin might be.

QUESTIONS FOR DISCUSSION

1. Why do you think Catherine and Zoe turned out to be so different as sisters? Was it a matter of biology, the way they were raised, or other factors?

2. Eve and her husband, Andrew, are both unfaithful during the course of their marriage. Do you think they truly loved each other? Whose betrayal was greater?

3. When Russell became physically involved with his student, do you think he should have been charged with a crime? Why or why not?

4. Sexual abuse affects many of the women in this novel. How do you think her sexual history impacted Zoe? What about Willow and Nola, who both experienced abuse as children?

5. It's never easy for the family of a substance abuser to know what steps to take to support a loved one who's struggling with addiction. In your opinion, who do you think parented Zoe more effectively? Eve, who loved her unconditionally and continued giving her money? Or Andrew, who thought they needed to take a tough-love approach and let Zoe sink or swim? What would you have done, if Zoe were your daughter?

6. At two different points in the novel, Russell suggests that he and Catherine should live together again, if only as roommates. Would you have let Russell move back if you were in Catherine's situation?

7. Did the novel end up the way you thought it should, or were you predicting a different resolution?

8. Do you consider this a "happy" ending?

Photo by Meg Manion

Holly Robinson is a ghostwriter and journalist whose work appears regularly in national venues such as *Better Homes and Gardens*, Huffington Post, *More*, Open Salon, and *Parents*. She is the author of *The Gerbil Farmer's Daughter: A Memoir* and three other NAL Accent novels, *Haven Lake*, *The Wishing Hill*, and *Beach Plum Island*. She holds a BA in biology from Clark University and an MFA in creative writing from the University of Massachusetts, Amherst.

CONNECT ONLINE

authorhollyrobinson.com